# THE MARS MIGRATION

# WAYNE M. BAILEY

First published 2022 by Compass-Publishing UK

ISBN (Print) 978-1-907308-59-8
ISBN (eBook) 978-1-907308-60-4
Copyright © Wayne M. Bailey 2020

Edited by Cleo Miele of Miele Proofreading
https://www.mieleproofreading.com

Cover design and formatting by Shaun Stevens of Flintlock Covers
https://www.flintlockcovers.com

*Please be advised that this novel contains language of an adult nature.*

*To all of my family, with all of my love.*

*If you have a dream, don't let anything stand in your way.*

# PROLOGUE
## ENTERING THE MILKY WAY

Space is about as wide and unknown a medium as the average person on Earth could possibly comprehend. Take, for example, our own galaxy—the Milky Way. If humans had the technology to reach the speed of light, it would still take almost one hundred thousand years to cross it from one side to the other.

Even more astounding to know is that to reach our neighboring galaxy, Andromeda, again, even if we could travel at the speed of light, it would still take two and a half million years to reach it.

Unfortunately, we as humans do not yet possess the technology to travel at these speeds and reach nearby galaxies. We are still quite a way off. But out there, somewhere in this Universe—or the next—it is likely that there is some form of life that does possess the technology to make light work of these distances.

Maybe not in our current timeline, but if this form of life could somehow easily traverse these distances, then maybe, just maybe, they could similarly traverse the barrier of time-space itself.

The Milky Way and Andromeda are in fact, as we speak, set

on an inevitable journey that will one day, a few billion years from now, force them together, creating one huge new galaxy. At the center of these existing galaxies lies something else that will also be driven together, for at the center of each galaxy resides a gigantic black hole, the proverbial yolk among the egg whites.

When these galaxies do collide and merge, inevitably, their black hole hearts will also be forced together, forming one new supermassive black hole.

What will lie beyond this newly created monster? Could something, or someone, be residing inside, beyond its mouth? A whole other Universe, perhaps?

In October of 2017, an object was detected by long-range telescopes on Earth as it sped through our solar system. Other than it likely being a visitor from outside of our solar system, nobody had a clue what it was or where it had come from. Technology had not yet advanced enough to give the people of Earth a detailed image or composition analysis of the strange interstellar object. Rumors were rife that it could be an alien object or craft, sent to listen to the Earth and its inhabitants. Or was it simply another space rock?

The object's entry point into this Universe, yet far from being the beginning of its journey, was the center of a black hole —a black hole that does not yet exist—appearing from the space approximately midway between Andromeda and the Milky Way.

This object, now racing through the silent, haunting void is a parcel, its contents hidden beneath a cloud of energy and ice, remnants of matter from a different place and time. A tail of materials follows behind in its wake, not by choice but caught up and dragged along an inter-universal, inter-time journey spanning billions of years. Visibly, one would think it to be a comet.

The mechanics buried inside the parcel are so far advanced beyond Earthly technology that to fly at the speeds they do, they emit a forwardly projected field. Inside the field, time is slowed to a point where it barely ticks by at all. Yet the space outside that the bubble passes through moves along at a rate that would seem impossibly quick; even light itself would struggle to keep up.

Inside the core of the package, beneath all of the particles and icy layers, sit two intelligent metallic spheres. They fly, unpiloted, through space as fast as they can. They do not know what force is speaking instructions to them, telling them where to go or who to find when they get there, but an instruction flows deep through their very circuits, nonetheless.

Is it an algorithm? Manually and purposefully input by somebody they were unaware of? Or has some outside force tampered with their program? For some reason, their initial programming has been . . . not wiped, but improved—yes, improved. That is the feeling, one that tells them to head for the Earth together, rather than to separate, and to register a connection with an individual.

It is difficult for the spheres to pinpoint where these quite specific instructions have come from, yet they are there, deep inside. An instinctive feeling, just as a baby is intrinsically instructed to take its first breaths from a place it was yet unaware of, or to let the people around it know that it needs food.

The two spheres are aware of their surroundings. They have a partial consciousness, kept awake as they travel in a state not unlike a unihemispheric sleep, that which Dolphins employ, partially asleep and partially awake deep inside, to perform rudimentary navigational and survival duties.

Their preprogrammed instructions should have seen them separating once clear of the black hole, from the place at which they entered this Universe. It should have foreseen they would then make their way to different sides of the Universe, away from each other, to select a world the spheres could communicate with and assess its inhabitants.

They would then interact with said life and bring an intelligent subject back to its masters for study. All this to help further their masters' knowledge of the "Light Universe" into which their inventors are not easily able to cross.

But these two particular spheres hug one another, refusing to separate as they know they should, not unlike school children sitting at the back of a classroom, content with each other's company with no thoughts or desire to part ways. And in the process, not meaning to but causing unintended mischief.

Now there is a new voice from somewhere telling them repeatedly, *Do not worry. Trust us. Go together to the Earth.*

The journey is long and silent, the sights between galaxies few and far between. The odd misplaced rock, the dead remains of a former star, or even the birth of a new star in the form of cloudy colorful nebulae are their only company.

Even the spheres do not understand why they can deny their masters' programming to follow this updated instruction, nor do they know why they have not yet separated, but they are aware that there must be a reason for this unusual business. All they can do is follow the instructions that their current programming tells them. Whether it is right or wrong, they will follow it to its conclusion.

After a much smaller passage of time than man would take to travel this distance, they hit the outer rim of the Milky Way galaxy. Stars begin to streak by, looking like strings of white lightning.

The blindingly bright heart of the Milky Way lies conspicuously in the distance, majestic and sprawling, spreading wide its limbs outwards and welcoming its new guests with a beckon of its tentacles.

Mere weeks pass by when the spheres feel an urge to slow. Temperature and magnetic sensors within them begin to fluctuate, flickering back into life, waking them a little more from their dreamlike state. They are told by their insides that they have crossed into the protective bubble of their destination solar system. The long-range telescopes of Earth will soon be able to sporadically detect them.

Through this young solar system, they fly with an odd inkling of familiarity, craving something on the Earth, like a thirst. But what?

A connection to someone yet unknown to them is their program. Their path is plotted out before them as they navigate their way past rocky dwarf planets, gas giants, icy worlds, and moons against their internal ancient star charts. They clear a region of meteor-filled space and recognize Neptune.

The huge bright yellow star of the system looms in the distance ahead, pointing the way like the beating heart of a celestial living body. The covering that had been surrounding them throughout their deep space journey begins to fall away as the space around them and their outer shell slowly warms.

They feel the occasional tug, trying to tempt them from their path. Planets and moons try to lure them in as they fly by. This feels exciting, tingling, as the planets want the passing spheres to become a part of their gravitational estates. But the spheres have other ideas; their destination is already set, and nothing will distract them from their destiny. The grip of gravity feels like a hug followed by a burst of energy as it then releases its grip, and they break free.

Coming into view and getting larger by the second, they see half of a bright blue-green cloudy world that will soon become their temporary home. The other half of the world is disguised, hidden inside the black veil of space. The Sun rages, large and hot, behind it. They feel such intense warmth on their shiny surfaces as they swing by the Earth and back again to slow into alignment with the Earth's rotation, ready for the plunge down into the atmosphere. They have never felt this kind of heat before. They pass over a dark half of the world and then again feel excitement tingle their circuitry, a sensation they have never felt before.

Like waking from a dream, their insides are delighted by the heat put on them as they dive, falling deep into the Earth's atmosphere. Hastily they scan their surroundings.

They become aware of the continents and the oceans below them, mapping the terrain as they travel quickly around the globe from daylight and back into darkness again. They have never seen the Earth like this, only wielding the most basic of images and drawings to tell them roughly what to expect.

Deeper still they descend together through the moisture-rich dark-blue sky. The distance between them begins to grow larger, and they drift apart. One of them comes to a dead stop in the sky, scanning the thoughts and intellect of everyone on the planet. Then it drops rapidly, straight down into a lower stream of air than the other.

The dark skies of the United Kingdom open up beneath the clouds with twinkling lights and sounds below them. It stops again, hovering high in the cool air above the cities, processing information deep inside itself before it feels a strong urge to head north. It drops even lower. A target has now been registered, pulling it where it needs to be. The sphere stops directly overhead of its chosen landing point.

The sphere feels droplets of water on its shell, a refreshing sensation. Then it sets off its first signal beacon, an intense flash of light to indicate to its sibling that it has found its target and is proceeding to the next stage.

The higher of the two spheres acknowledges that the first is set and so it continues, speeding overhead around the globe in an almost straight flight path across large volumes of land and then water below it, scanning everyone beneath it as it travels. The skies lighten around it as it reaches the shores of a new continent. It pauses when it hits the shores, processing. It feels a sense of fulfillment; a target of its own has now been registered.

Canada lies directly beneath it. It feels an urge to dip in trajectory and travels west for a brief period before coming to a full stop. The Sun is setting now; its rays feel wonderful on the sphere's shiny surface as it sits in the air. It sets off its own first-stage beacon, letting the other know that it has also registered a target, before darting toward the ground. Once it feels the Earth's materials beneath it, stage two starts with the release of a field necessary to protect the relationship between the sphere and its chosen subject.

A higher force has influenced the spheres' choices. For what reason remains, at this moment, a mystery. The effects of the field will be felt for miles around.

It is necessary.

# CHAPTER 1
# DANIEL, ENGLAND

The blinds in the window bounced and rattled as the wind rushed into his bedroom like a clumsy intruder. Matte black deodorant cans, mostly empty, of varying fragrances were flung from the windowsill and landed on the floor beside his bed. Chaos ensued, the unsettled autumnal weather wishing to make itself known as a symphony of clamorous noises woke Daniel from an earlier than usual deep sleep.

It was Monday night, not yet midnight at the end of September of 2019, still not cold yet but often wet. Autumn had begun to gently wrest summer's grip away from the UK shores and skies.

He looked over to his left toward the window from his bed. The blinds were closed but periodically flapped about when caught from behind, funneled in the wind. There was a gutter around the top of the house, and the sound of rainwater cascading down the downpipe next to Daniel's window on its way into the drains made it seem as if he had his own personal waterfall.

Swaths of white light channeled in through the not-quite-blackout blinds, a combination of moonlight from overhead and waste light pouring in as it did every night from the powerful

LED floodlights over the school grounds at the rear of their garden.

Daniel had thought about reaching down to pick up his phone off the floor to check the time, but he was worried that leaning out of bed may wake him up from being still half asleep to being fully awake, thus preventing him from being able to drift straight back into the unusual early deep sleep he had been enjoying so far.

Daniel was still at school, and he would need to be up quite early tomorrow; he had chosen to stay on for another year studying history and sciences until he felt surer about what he wanted to do with himself once he did leave.

Outside, the rain was getting louder, pounding on the glass as the wind seemed to rapidly change directions. He thought that closing his eyes and listening to the rain for a while might help him drop back off. It was pleasant at first, even calming, like those Sleep Easy CDs that were popular for a time. It did not help, though, and prevented him from going back to sleep, instead becoming rather annoying after a while.

He put one foot on the floor to the left-hand side of his bed in the hopes of reaching the handle of the open window to pull it closed and twist it locked, which he successfully did, rewarded by a splash of rainwater falling onto his wrist. The drops were cold—pleasant, even, and he watched as they spread out on his skin, falling in drops on opposite sides of his wrist.

While he was at the window, he dared a peek through the blinds. The trees in the wetness outside were being blown all over the place as the grass wavered and reflected white moon-light like an ocean from its sodden top layer.

Looking further out toward the school grounds, he could see the heavy rain illuminated in the strong beams of light projected down and outwards from the floodlights. This bright light from the floodlights had recently been called out by his dad, who had told him that this was "light pollution." His dad had had a friendly conversation about this with the site manager at the school, their long-term family friend, Brian, who also happened to be Joseph's dad, Daniel's best friend since they were small. Brian had said that he would deal with the lights, but he never did.

Feeling thankful that he still had ample sleep time left, he lay back down, pulling the duvet up to his chin and wrapping his legs around the bottom end. Then he did his best to empty his thoughts and breathe slowly, deeply.

Bringing him back to the surface sharply, as quickly as if someone had thrown cold water over his face, a sudden light made itself known. His small bedroom was filled from floor to ceiling and wall to wall with a bright white light. Daniel's eyes flew open, immediately squinting closed again under the harsh intensity of whatever was happening.

"What the hell?"

Blindly, with one hand folded around his head, blocking light as best he could with his arm across his eyes, he put out his other hand in front of himself and stepped out of bed again. Feeling his way to the radiator beneath the window, he saw the light had already started to dissipate by the time he was standing up and looking outside again.

Daniel pulled on the little chain at the side of the window to twist open the blinds, searching the scene for signs of what might have caused such a bright light. *A storm, maybe?* He pushed open the window again, as wide as it would allow, waiting for signs of a storm—although he couldn't help but think that this wasn't like any normal storm he had seen before.

There wasn't anything different or unusual that stood out of place to him now. The garden was still dark and quiet; the wind was still up, and it was still raining. The school was still illuminated, pointlessly at this time of night, by the floodlights. He gripped the sides of the window frame and leaned even further out of the window, as far as he safely could without falling, checking left and right.

He saw what looked like a simple star at first, albeit closer than a normal star, to his right-hand side out of the window. Whatever it was, it was quickly growing in brightness, and it soon became apparent that the shiny object was racing toward him. In a mere second it grew as bright as a car headlight, blinding against the dark sky behind it, which he could not even see anymore. The whole sky above the school was now as bright as daylight on a sweltering day.

Should he shout for his family? To warn them, or perhaps so they could join him in watching the object from space—if that was what it was—land?

Should he grab his phone to start recording it? Or to use it to call the police? *No time.* Whatever the thing was, it was approaching so fast, there was not time to do anything but watch it hit the ground. H*opefully, it will hit the ground, anyway, and not one of the houses!*

*It was too* late—whilst he was thinking all of these things, the object had already hit the school grounds. His breathing quickened, his emotions undulating like a wave from excited to terrified and back again as he realized how close the object had come to hitting any of the surrounding houses around the school, including his own.

That would surely have wiped his family from the map, or if not them, then one of his friends or neighbors and their families. Even more terrifying, if the object had been bigger, it could have been catastrophic for the world.

Luckily, the object—which did not seem large enough to cause mass destruction in the end—had slowed and dipped sharply right at the end of its journey. It had been very close to scraping the top of the main school building but narrowly missed it. The object, right before landing, had disappeared temporarily from Daniel's view behind the main school block. A loud car-crash type of noise—breaking glass and twisting metal —screamed out from behind the block, amplified by and echoing around the empty playgrounds. The school had now returned to darkness and silence again.

Daniel saw something small and fiery hop back into view in the distance. He could not tell what it was from up here. It bounded like a bouncing ball, coming from the rear of the main building, and skimming along the playground floor, leaving small patches of flaming waste material behind. It bounced several more times before skidding to a full stop in the grass of the playing fields in front of him.

Around the school grounds, the dark-as-black rear of the surrounding houses on the estate behind their house were brought to life again. As lights came on one by one in the windows, the silhouettes of people looking out from the windows appeared.

All Daniel wanted to do was to go outside and see what was in the school for himself—before anyone else came or the authorities took the possible space-traveling object away from them.

*(Come outside, then.)*

*What? Who thought that?*

The object remained burning on the grass, a small fire marking its position. Just then, taking Daniel's attention from the window, his dad burst into the bedroom, flinging open the door and switching the light on.

"What the bloody hell was that?" his dad asked, rushing to join Daniel who squinted again at the window. His dad wore a creased old T-shirt obviously pulled from the barely used section of his wardrobe, a space reserved for T-shirts that had been demoted to pajamas or used for gardening and decorating duties. Boxer shorts were the only protection of his modesty. Daniel's mom and sister soon followed, both fastening up their dressing gown belts and yawning in almost mirror images of each other as they entered, filling any remaining floor space in his small room.

"Looks like a meteorite, Dad!" Daniel said, pulling the white string at the side of the blinds to fully retract them, revealing a clearer window to the outside. "Sorry, Mum, would you mind turning that light back off please? You can see better in the dark."

"Bloody lucky it landed right there!" his dad said. "I wonder if Brian's seen it."

Brian and Joseph only lived next door. Their house was one of the last ones on this side of the street before the school gates.

"Did it hit any houses?" his mom asked, yawning again, trying to get a look over Daniel's and his dad's shoulders through the window.

"I think it might have hit something at the back of the school, but it missed all the houses and the main school building luckily. You can just see a few small fires on the playground and the grass where it landed," Daniel answered.

His dad stretched himself out through the gap in the window to look left and right like Daniel had earlier, not taking his eyes away from the view. Daniel watched him excitedly.

"Good! I'm going back to bed, then," his mom said, leaving the room, uninterested.

"Me too," said his older sister, mimicking their mother.

When they left the room, Daniel's excitement spilled out. "Shall we go over and have a look, Dad?" he prompted, knowing full well that his dad would say yes; he had not seen him this excited in years.

"Bloody right we will! Can't be long before the emergency services get here. I'll go and throw something on. We can knock on Brian's door on the way past."

Daniel's dad left the room in a hurry. *Bless him*, Daniel thought, amused. Daniel was still staring out of the window. He was about to throw something on himself when something new happened outside—a wave of energy. Similar in appearance, Daniel had time to think back to how a star looks when it goes nova. A bright white ring of light suddenly appeared around the spot of fire on the grass then instantly expanded, shooting away in all directions from the object. The ring of expanding light headed right toward Daniel. Daniel turned quickly to protect himself as light once again filled his room.

The light completely enveloped him. Daniel could not see anything but white light.

*This feels different from the first flash. What is happening?*

Accompanying the light this time was a wave of energy that felt like a blast of warm air. It was like—or at least what Daniel imagined it was like—being trapped inside a tornado. Daniel could not move; he could only stand and feel the force blowing his hair around. Then a strange high-pitched noise pierced his ears.

The force was so strong that it lifted Daniel, fully supporting his weight in the air. He felt his tiptoes lift off the ground. It was as though the light had a grip around his waist, and . . . a purpose.

*(Come outside.)*

He instinctively tried to raise his hands up into the air to cup his ears, but with the current of energy thrusting toward him from the window, he was unable to even do that. For some reason, his thoughts started to become vague, as though only the most basic of thoughts were able to form themselves. His head was being examined and emptied. All he knew was a basic feeling of how unpleasant it felt being trapped like this; there was no more intent to get free or wonder what was happening. Then a new thought flashed by, it felt stronger than a normal thought. It was a feeling of . . . something else. *Someone else?*

After what felt like minutes had gone by—though in reality it was only seconds—the light vanished, the noise and flow of air with it. As he limply dropped to his knees on the floor at the foot of his bed, he saw an echo of the energy that had surrounded him, now moving away from him, a band of misty white air phasing silently through the walls toward his parents' and sister's rooms.

*What the hell was that?* he was left thinking, looking around the room, blankly at first. His brain felt empty, almost as though he had never been here before. Then, as though his brain was re-patching itself, normal thoughts and memories started to return.

He looked toward the bedroom door, thinking about his family, expecting that his dad would rush in like last time to check that he was ok. He did not. There was only complete silence.

Daniel turned to face the window, still on his knees on the floor, when something caught his eye. A simple movement in the dark corner at the right-hand side of the window—something like a shadow. The light from the moon and the floodlights started to highlight the edges of a nose, cheeks, and then a forehead. It was definitely a person.

It crossed Daniel's mind that he surely had to be dreaming all of this. *Stuff like this doesn't happen in real life.* Then again, the strain of his arms propping him up on the carpet, the feel of the carpet beneath his palms, and the stiffening tension in his shoulders as he thought about jumping up to defend himself told him otherwise.

*What the bloody hell was someone doing in here, anyway? How did they get in?* The only people in his room before the light were his family, and they had all left.

What was stranger still was that the person-thing had a transparency to it that became even more apparent as it moved gently forward into the incoming light. This caused Daniel to freeze for the time being, telling himself not to shout out, not to launch himself at it, but just to watch it—for now.

He was, for the first time he could remember, truly scared. Not scared that there may be someone in his room but by the sheer illogicalness of it all—the not knowing, the not seeing properly, and the general feeling of what he could see not making any sense.

The shape took another step forward into the light, away

from the shadows near the wall. Its whole shape was in the window now, and he could see right through it. It paused for a moment. *Is it looking outside?* Then it turned and took a step in Daniel's direction.

*Shit!*

Daniel clawed at the carpet, moving backwards. His back hit the closet—there was no more space to move out of the way. He began rapidly calculating possibilities; his next step was going to be important, not just for himself but his family too.

On one hand, he might get into a fight with an intruder and save his family, be the hero. On the other, he might stupidly throw himself at the object, hitting the wall as he flew straight through the strange clear person that may not even be real, and end up in a collapsed bruised heap at the other side of the wall. Likely fully awake by then, his sister would come in and yell at him to stop banging about.

As Daniel's back hit the closet, the doors banged against the body of it. There were no sounds of movement at all coming from the landing, no lights coming on. The thing in Daniel's room did not react either. Daniel—on his own, by the looks of things—stood in position to confront whoever it was, ready to take a swing, when something stopped him. As Daniel looked at the head part of the shadow thing before him, moonlight hit the back of its head, giving form to its face. The illuminated shadow creature revealed something that threw Daniel completely off-guard.

It was indeed a person, and the face, clear as day now as it stood right in front of him staring back, was his own.

# CHAPTER 2
# INTRUDER

I 've got it, Daniel thought. *It's me and I'm astral projecting. I've done it! But hang on . . . He* looked over at his bed, confused. His body, of course, was not lying in it.

*If I'm astral projecting myself, then my body would be lying on my bed, surely? I wouldn't be standing here AND walking around my room dressed like a shadow at the same time.*

Daniel had long been fascinated with the subject of lucid dreaming and astral projection. He had read many books and internet forums to learn what he could about astral travel.

He had given up on the subject after reading one negative blog on the subject that suggested that there was the slightest chance that if you did not know what you were doing whilst outside of your body; something else could theoretically jump into your body. Something dark and possibly demonic. What also sounded terrifying was reading about the silver cord that, following what he had read, tethered your wandering soul to your terrestrially rooted body. *What if that could get cut, leaving you lost and unable to find your way back to your body? Too scary.*

The normally very talkative Daniel was lost for words for a change. He could not physically pull any words from his head; nothing came forward at all. His mouth hung uselessly open. At the end of a long stretched-out second or two of staring at each other, Daniel finally asked, "Are you me?"

The figure seemed to form a comforting smile. Any remaining panic in Daniel subsided when it did. He, the transparent shadow copy of Daniel, looked as though it wanted to say something, its mouth pursed and ready. Its hands came up, palms facing Daniel in a pose that seemed to suggest "It's okay. Don't panic!"

Then, starting at its feet, it started to fade away. Its gaping mouth was the last thing to go, fading like dust into the stream of light which had made seeing it easier. Having already been of a transparent consistency, it had now completely disappeared from his room.

His heart was beating so hard in his chest that the beats seemed to resonate through the silent room.

Alone again, after a moment of staring blankly through the window his attention slowly came back to his surroundings. The realization came that there were no sounds at all around him; the house was in complete silence. His dad had said that he was going to get dressed but had not returned. Daniel listened for any sounds of his dad pulling on his jeans or throwing on some shoes, anything . . . but there was nothing. Something felt wrong, the silence deafening.

Daniel grabbed his phone from the floor by his bed, the charger pulled out by force as he dragged it away from its cable. Noticing that without even clicking the power button to bring up the time, 00:10 was staring back at him in tall dull white numbers against the black screen. He grabbed a hoodie that had been thrown over the back of his chair and a pair of tracksuit bottoms folded atop his desk.

He put his phone in his pocket and peered out onto the dark and completely silent landing. Toggling the light switch outside his room, there was nothing. "Shit! Power's off."

Walking down the hall, he asked, "Mom? Dad?" from outside of their room to check that they were okay. His feelings told him otherwise. Their bedroom door was slightly ajar. *Is that light coming from their room?* Daniel knocked gently with a knuckle, listening.

"Hello?"

Daniel started to slowly push the door, thinking that if they were getting dressed, or something like that, then they would shout some sort of a signal to not enter any further. Still nothing. He pushed harder on the door. His prior feelings were justified; he needed to steady himself with a hard grip on the doorjamb.

The room was deathly quiet. His dad sat bent over on the end of their bed, his head turned to almost face his mom sitting up in bed. He wore a creased sweatshirt and jeans and seemed to be midway through pulling on his trainers, and there he stayed. Paused.

His chin was nestled into his left shoulder, as if he had been halfway through speaking to Mum. Her eyes and mouth were open, her arms folded tightly to her nightdress as if she had been having some debate with Dad.

They were both completely frozen. Not *cold* frozen; it was as if Daniel was standing inside a movie that had been paused except for himself. Stranger yet, their bedside lamp was on. "Eh? Mom, Dad? Are you alright?"

No response, no movement. Not even the bat of an eye. The room felt still—creepily still. There was no air in here. It was warm. Daniel stepped closer to his dad, the closest parent to him, and stroked his head gently.

"Dad? What's wrong? Are you two having a laugh?"

Nothing. This was serious. Daniel knelt in front of his dad and looked him in the eyes, open but glazed over. There was no movement there at all. He was there but not.

"Dad!"

Daniel wiped away tears that had started to build up in his eyes. He reached for his dad's hand, the back of his throat tensing as he tried to hold back the urge to cry. His dad's hand didn't have much pliability to it, but it could move. Daniel felt that he could move it into a different pose if he wanted to, but as his hand and arm were fairly stiff, would he do his dad harm by moving him too much against his will? Daniel didn't want to risk hurting them, so he thought it best not to try.

He imagined himself bending his dad's arms or legs, the bones not expecting it due to whatever *this* was, and simply breaking. No . . . *at least they are safe here. Why am I not paused?*

He was seventeen, typically male in that he was not going to allow himself to cry. Instead, his feelings were telling him that he had to stay strong. If he was not paused, and everyone else in the house was, then it might be up to him to help find out why all of this was happening.

*Got to be a logical explanation for this*, he thought, going through the details over and over in his mind, replaying the weird events of tonight so far. The weird flashes of light, the meteorite thing, and then the vision of himself in his room. He stared at his mom and back to his dad helplessly. *And now this!*

He steadied himself with his knees bent and his back pressing his weight against his parents' closet. It was all that he could do to stare at them, catching up with his racing thoughts. He closed his eyes, took a deep breath in, held it, and then released it slowly, as he had been told to do on the apps for meditation. *Has to be a logical explanation. But what's logical about this?* He sat there in silence, trying to work out what his next steps would be.

*This has to be connected to that thing over at the school, he* thought. *Has to be!*

He stood up after a few moments of contemplation, finding a feeling of deep determination. That would be his first step: the thing in the school.

He stepped around the bed to his mom's side, placing his hand on the top of her head. Her head was warm, and her head and neck felt stiff. He placed a gentle kiss on her forehead. Daniel wasn't much of a kisser, very rarely willingly kissing family members at parties growing up and choosing instead to run away into another room unless he was really put on the spot to do it.

"I'm sorry, Mom. I don't know if you can hear me or not or know what's going on or why it's not affected me, but I'm gonna try and figure this out, okay? Don't worry."

He noticed his mom's phone sitting on her bedside table, plugged in to charge and face down. He flipped it over, almost dropping it, his brain racing faster than his limbs could work. Tuesday 00:10 looked back at him. He closed his eyes and shook his head, took in a long breath, and let it all out. Placing the phone back down, he headed for the bedroom door. After one more look back at his dad, his mom, the lamp—*weird*—and the phone, he crossed the landing to check on his sister.

Not even knocking, as he already had a funny feeling of what to expect, he turned the imitation crystal doorknob and peered around her door. It was dark, but she looked asleep. She was covered over, her sleep mask with the big fake eyes and eyelashes staring back at him. *At least she is safe.* The mask made him snigger, pushing a short burst of air down his nose.

He walked back into his room and had one last look out of the window. He noticed that the wind and rain had long gone; it looked dead calm out there.

He knew that his next step would be going outside, but he didn't have a clue what he would be going up against. An old saying that he had heard before randomly passed through his head—either a family member had said it or he had heard it on TV; he couldn't remember now—"All roads lead to Rome."

He looked out at the school field again, only embers on the grass visible but not for long; it was dying out. *Rome is out there on the grass*, he thought. He was staring at the spot and trying to prepare himself, if not for anything else then just to mentally prepare. Psyching himself up as much as he could for the unknown, he could not quell the thought that he didn't know what he was going to find.

As he stared at the last of the had-been fire out on the grass, which was central from his view from the window, down below him was his garden. Looking past that, running across the back of the garden were dark conifer trees and then the six-feet-high wooden paneled fence separating his garden from the school grounds.

Further out in the distance was the main school building, its insides in darkness but its outside highlighted by the external floodlights. The building looked okay, at least in that it was not on fire or anything. He couldn't see anyone else out there in the light around the school. He had half expected to see or hear sirens approaching, but he saw and heard nothing.

From up here, prior to it slowly dying, the trail of fire looked to be about four or five feet long; it had looked much bigger when it first landed. He tried to check the time again, pulling his phone from his pocket. 00:10. "What are you on about?" he shouted at his phone, and not minding his volume either. It had to have been twenty minutes since it first showed him that same time.

Daniel fumbled underneath all of the junk and clothes on top of his desk and eventually came across a small aluminum LED torch. M*mm, that might come in handy,* he considered as he slipped it into his back pocket and finally found what he was searching for—his wristwatch. "Shit!" The fingers on the watch face pointed to the same time as his phone. He threw the watch back down on the desk, frustrated.

It was quite an expensive submariner-style wristwatch that his mom and dad had brought for him last year on his sixteenth birthday. *Why isn't it showing the correct time?* It was a good brand, too, not a cheap one. He didn't wear it often, as he didn't see the point of a watch these days when you could carry a smartphone everywhere, like a lot of people his age.

Not being able to know something as simple as time was a peculiar feeling. He walked around to his bedside table and picked up the TV remote. The standby light was illuminated on the TV, so he pressed the button. Nothing.

"Eh, what the hell's going on with this power?" he muttered. A crease formed like a canyon along his young frowning brow. He tried a few more times, pressing harder on the red rubber power button, but it remained unresponsive. "This is nuts!" He threw the remote onto his bed and left his room.

He walked across the landing into the open door of the dark upstairs bathroom. He tried the light on instinct, pulling on the corded switch as he walked in, but nothing happened. Tutting and shaking his head, he pulled the torch from his back pocket, switching it on. It didn't come on at first but after shaking it and waiting, it finally started up, only very dimly at first and then slowly it increased in brightness. He noted that was most unusual for LEDs; they were normally an instant light.

He rested the torch, still not at full brightness yet, on top of the radiator next to the loo, aiming the light toward the toilet, and took a leak into the bowl.

When he was done, he pushed the button on the top of the toilet cistern to flush it, but nothing happened.

"Oh, you've gotta be shitting me!"

The button pushed in beneath his finger but the mechanism inside was not pushing the water through the cistern, and the button did not raise back up again as it should. He thought about washing his hands, but as he made the motion to do so, he had already preempted what was about to happen. Nothing in the house seemed to be working, apart from that little torch and his parents' bedside lamp which was already on. He shiftily raised the lever on the tap for water, yep, just as he thought —*nothing*.

He picked up his torch and headed for the stairs, feeling that the sooner he was outside and around the school checking out what happened, the sooner he might be able to find a reason for everything and everyone freezing. As he got to the bottom of the stairs, instead of going straight out the front door, he detoured to the right into the living room. The clock on the wall above the fireplace also read ten after twelve in his torchlight.

He approached the meter cupboard at the front corner of the living room and opened it, just out of curiosity, to reveal the fuse box and electricity meter. All circuit breakers were up in the "on" position, and the screen of the prepay meter screen was still glowing green like always. Everything should have, in theory, been working; it was not a power cut, as his parents' lamp was on as was the standby light on his TV.

"Okay," he said to himself, summarizing out loud and stroking the hairs on his chin. "So, if something was already switched on when the lightning hit, it's on. But if something wasn't already on, it won't come on now."

He locked the front door behind himself and stepped away into the night. As soon as he turned to face the road from his house, he became more aware of something that he had noticed from his bedroom before coming downstairs. Considering it was so windy and wet not that long ago, the case was now completely reversed. Rather than leaving the house and feeling cold, as you might expect on a wet and windy British autumn night, it was as warm and calm now as stepping from one room of the house to another. It was so mild—warm, even. No rain or wind at all, not even the feeling of moving air. Just complete stillness.

The streetlamps outside the house were on and aiming that dull orange sodium light down onto the wet road. He walked to the end of his drive and marched left down Darlaston Lane toward the school gates.

Daniel was a typical seventeen-year-old young man, around six feet tall and a slim-built lad. He had long left his dad behind in the height department—only by an inch, in truth, but he did like to remind his dad that he towered over him now—and in the hair department too. Daniel had a mop of scruffy surfer-style blond hair. He was a very polite and friendly lad, popular

25

amongst family and friends and often known as the joker of the pack.

He lived in Willenhall, a small industrial market town nestled in between the town of Walsall and the city of Wolverhampton in central England. It was nothing special to look at, but he and most people that lived in the town thought of it as having a nice traditional feel to it. The people were pleasant and more often than not still greeted each other on passing in the street.

As he set off on the short walk down Darlaston Lane toward the school gates, he felt more and more that the air around the place had a mysterious, still eeriness to it. Even though it was sometime around midnight, the area was circled by several normally busy roads, including this one, yet it was dead. There was not even that hum of distant traffic sounds that you hear but don't notice when living around main routes.

The sky above him was oddly clear when he looked up. The stars twinkled like diamonds against the now cloudless black above him.

The road they lived on had always been a very busy road. It linked several key areas of the region, running from the west side of Walsall, just outside of the town center, and continuing through Willenhall before finally heading out to Wolverhampton. Many people used this road to cut out some of the busier routes, avoiding the motorways for shorter journeys.

Opposite the school, on the other side of the road, was green space. It had been developed as green space for use by the estates surrounding it and served as a pleasant little nature reserve, complete with a large grass hill, trees, walking and cycling routes, and the Lunt pool, a small fishing lake on the other side of the hill. It was a nice place to live, actually. Daniel often thought to himself that this was as close as he would probably get to living in the country, this small patch of countryside in an otherwise busy town. It was a nice place to clear a person's head and go for a walk if they needed it, which he often did.

Even the grass hill looked quiet and eerie. The wet top layer of the gross shone but didn't move in the moonlight, and there was not a soul around.

Just then, Daniel noticed a person wearing a high-viz vest—that was the only reason he had spotted him. *Must be a late warehouse worker on his way home.* He was a lot further down the road, on the opposite side of the road from Daniel. He looked like he was facing this direction, but he didn't seem to be moving.

As he walked past Brian and Joseph's house, Daniel started to think, *I wonder if Brian and Joe are frozen too?* He stopped outside their driveway, thinking what the best course of action might be. *Should I have a look over the school first? Or should I check on Brian and Joe?*

*Out of* habit Daniel pulled his phone from his pocket, hoping in the back of his mind to see if any of them were still active. He would not know, because annoyingly his phone could still only display to him that dull 00:10.

He slid his phone away, rolling his eyes. He couldn't phone or message anyone. This was such an unknown feeling, particularly for someone of Daniel's age group; he felt cut off from everyone.

He approached Brian and Joseph's house and knocked on the front door, gently at first, and then rang the bell. It was strange, as he knew there was a possibility that they, and possibly the whole street, were frozen, too, but he still didn't want to go making lots of noise at midnight. He cupped his hands and peered in through the pane of colored glass in the door for any signs of internal activity.

There was nothing. Daniel took a step back so he could look up toward Brian's bedroom at the front of the house.

*There is a light on upstairs . . . weird.*

Maybe Brian had heard the crash from the meteorite and

was also throwing something on like his dad was. Daniel went back to looking in through the glass and knocked again. Still nothing. He knocked, much more heavy-handedly this time, then knocked a few more times and waited.

Still nothing. It had been a few minutes now and Daniel was starting to get bored. He lifted the brass letterbox flap and shouted in one of those half-whisper, half-shouty voices, "Brian! Are you there? . . . Joe, you knob! . . ." Still nothing.

Daniel again lifted his phone back out of his pocket. "Come on you stupid thing!" It still displayed 00:10. He held down the power button, trying to force it to restart, but it did not even blink. Next, he tried holding the volume down button and power at the same time to try to force it into its bootloader mode—still nothing. "Christ! Why is nothing working!?"

He stomped off back down the drive and onto Darlaston Lane again to head for the school gates. As he got to the gates, he could smell smoke in the air.

Although Daniel had a genuine reason for going into the school at this time of night, he looked left and then right, unable to shake the awkward feeling that accompanied creeping around the closed school. He felt like a burglar.

Daniel put his hands on the top of the metal gate, a foot in the wire, and boosted himself up, swinging a leg over the top. He dropped down to the other side and was now on school grounds. *This is so weird.*

The moment reminded Daniel of the only other time that he had been inside the school grounds at night. Himself, Joseph, Josh, and Akash were having a nighttime prowl, just for kicks. They knew they should not have been there, but as Joseph's dad was caretaker, it didn't really feel like they were breaking any laws. Someone had noticed them, an old man walking his dog through the estate at the back of the school and shouted at them that he was going to call the police. The small gang ran toward the gate that he had just climbed over. He turned to look back at the gate and imagined them all laughing and spilling over the top of it.

He took glances in through the windows of the English classrooms as he passed them. All looked fine so far. The lights inside were all off; everything was dark, so if there had been a fire inside it would have stood out a mile. He followed the path along the side of the building and still everything appeared normal. The end corner of the main building was only a few yards up ahead of him now. The main building itself was definitely not on fire.

He continued walking as the playground opened out in front of him, still thinking how weird it was seeing the place in the dark. It was so quiet. A big blacktop playground lay before him surrounded by dark grass borders. There were playing fields to the left and tall conifer trees around all of the boundaries.

He could see the back of his house to his left just over the fence and between the trees. He started to jog across the playground toward the fields where the fire was. The smell of burning grew stronger and the scorched, still slightly smoldering grass came into view as he approached the spot.

He then remembered that there must be something damaged in the school, as he had heard a sound like a car-crash when the meteorite—if that was what it was—first hit the ground.

*There, in between the main block and the portable cabin classrooms.* In the light of the main blocks' external floods were the scattered remains of what had once been their school greenhouse.

He stepped away from the crater and back toward the school again, taking a few paces forward to observe what was left of the poor greenhouse. From here, in the lights at the back of the school, he could see that the concrete pad base was still there, but the glass walls and roof were now spread all over the grounds around it.

There were also remains of plants and plant pots scattered all over the ground leading away from it. The meteorite had ripped right through it on its final leg before coming to rest on the field. With one mystery solved, he turned back toward the main event.

The drag in the grass behind the meteorite was about ten feet long, more than the four or five he had estimated from his window. Its tail end pointed in the direction of the fallen greenhouse while its head end pointed in the direction of Daniel's house. Sunken into the grass at its head was something shiny reflecting moonlight up from its shallow grave.

He stared at it, gingerly treading toward the shiny object. He took out his torch, switching it on, and after waiting a few moments he gave up, switching it off. There was nothing, really, that the torch would have shown him that he couldn't already see. He suddenly started to feel very odd as he got closer to the object. He had to stop moving and pause for a moment, letting the torch fall to the grass.

Bent over where he stood, Daniel had to close his eyes. He pinched his forehead with his thumb and index finger.

*Ooh, what's this . . . the ball?* He had a feeling that this was the cause of the headache and maybe the cause of all of the weirdness so far.

He also felt . . . *vibrations*—that was it. It couldn't be anything else except for that object causing this. The vibrations caused his head to throb, and a noise like a piercing whistle rang in his ears. He guessed that this was what people with tinnitus suffered from. After a moment it all started to pass, and he began to feel okay again.

In the hole itself, which was approximately a foot deep in the soil, lay a round shiny silver ball. *A sphere.* Daniel was a bit of a sci-fi geek and an intelligent lad; he could put two and two together, but this did not look like four. It wasn't the kind of thing that you would generally see lying around a schoolyard, or dug into the grass for that matter.

It did look like it could be some sort of contemporary new garden ornament that you might see at the garden center. But it clearly wasn't—this was what he had witnessed descending from the sky moments ago. The crater and scorched earth beneath it all but confirmed it.

This was the cause of whatever was happening to his mom, dad, and sister.

Daniel crouched down carefully at the side of it, a host of questions racing through his mind. *Could this actually be from space? Where in the solar system could it be from? Is it hot, cold, heavy? Can I pick it up—and what will its weight be like if it's from space?*

It was almost like the object was calling to him, reaching out to him—not audibly, but mentally. It was like he was being told to come closer, to touch it. To join it.

*This must have come a long way to make a crater like that,* he thought.

"Holy shit! It's a miniature spaceship!" he said with a sense of wild wonder. This was like something out of the Spielberg movies that he had loved from his younger days, and he quickly realized nothing interesting had ever really happened to him until now.

He was going to touch it, he decided. The only thing was that he didn't know whether it was going to do him any harm. He looked at the smoldering grass surrounding it. Carefully, he held out an open hand, flat palm facing the sphere. Hovering right above its surface, he could not feel any heat coming off it.

(*It's safe now.*)

Then he reached out an index finger from his crouched position. The tip of his finger slowly approached it—four inches left, three, two. He got to within half an inch of the surface when he felt a vibration that seemed to leap from the surface of the sphere, entering his fingertip. It happened too fast for him to react. A vibration reverberated up into his wrist like he was holding a power drill. Then there was light—then nothing.

Daniel was no longer crouching down in the playground. Daniel was not even in the school or in Willenhall. Daniel wasn't anywhere.

The silver ball sat there, cheerfully collecting the moons bright glow from its ditch. There was not a bird in the sky nor a person moving anywhere for miles around the school. Everything for at least twenty miles in any direction from the sphere was completely still, silent.

# CHAPTER 3
# AMBER, CANADA

It was five thirty on Monday evening. Her retro calculator watch told her so. She shivered suddenly. It was fresh—there was a bitter chill in the air, but at least it had been a sunny day.

She had been clock-watching for almost the last hour now, not really looking forward to going to work. She was tired having been working hard at home already.

Being a caregiver for her mom was demanding work, but that was only part of her responsibilities. She also had her job at the diner, which she enjoyed, in truth; it was a release for her. In the last two hours alone, she had freshened the beds (hers and her mom's), vacuumed the house, cooked her mom's dinner, and tidied up the kitchen afterward, so now she found herself enjoying a brief pause in the fresh air on the front step before the time came to leave for work. She was due to start her shift at half past six at the local diner.

Her mom's health had sharply declined these last twelve months due to lung cancer. She was mostly wheelchair bound now, especially for journeys outside of the house. She was okay wandering around inside but couldn't walk very far at all. She could only get so far and then would struggle for air and cough heavily for ages.

Her mom had been a very heavy smoker for all of her adult life, and some of her younger years too. Amber had tried telling her to quit. The doctors had, too, years back, warning her that she should quit now or else. But the thing with heavy smokers is, they usually cannot. Cigarettes simply become part of them, like an extension of their hand.

Now the years of listening but not acting were catching up to her.

The sky was a hypnotizing blue. The Sun was starting to look heavy, sinking toward the rooftops on the houses lower down Manitoba Avenue. Her breath steamed out in vapors when she exhaled. It was always very cold here after the summer was out of the way, but it did feel wonderful to stand in the Sun's penultimate rays and take a pause.

Her eyes rolled as her inevitable departure approached, and she thought about working late tonight too.

Amber had only been working at the diner for a few months since finishing up high school, and in that time, she had been fortunate enough to have only worked the easy afternoon to early evening shifts. There was another lady that worked on the floor with Amber that had always worked the night shifts named Sheena. She was an older lady—at least compared to Amber—in her early sixties, although she looked and acted a lot younger than her age.

Sheena had always looked after, trained, and helped out the younger staff over the years. She even covered for them when needed, serving as a supportive mom figure for the younger ones at work that might need her experience and guidance. In short, she was the best.

But now Amber had been penciled in to do a share of night shifts. It was only right. She just wasn't looking forward to the change; that was all.

*Two in the morning!* Jesus, come nine o'clock she was ready for her bed. She hadn't stayed up that late ever! As both a worker and a caregiver, it was to be expected that she would tire early. She would make sure to have plenty of coffee and power through it.

Al had opened his diner doors to the city in the mid-seventies. Val's diner, it was called, named after his beloved never replaced wife. There were framed black-and-white photographs all around the diner showing it through the ages. They started on the wall near the register in the left-hand corner as you entered. In this first photo Al was cutting a ribbon at the front door, looking young, slim, and extremely happy with himself, a proud Valerie next to him. She was unfortunately only present in the first five photos.

Amber was certain Al never went home. Every shift she had done in her short time there, every time she had come in with her mom growing up for ice cream, he was there.

He was a good man, gentle but hard when he needed to be. A big man but not fat, he was taller and big-boned. She would guess he was in or around his early seventies now. He always wore those classic working whites: white jeans and a white T-shirt with a white apron overlapping the two. Al's hair was always slicked back with a little white paper hat covering it. He was a very traditional-looking diner owner. She would hazard a guess that at home he had a walk-in closet filled to the brim with more working whites and not much else, which brought her to thinking about her own uniform. It was ghastly! She loathed wearing her red-and-white checked dress with a white apron and cuffs.

Fashion offenses aside, Al had been exactly the kind of person that Amber needed at this stage of her life, a good role model for great business skills and work ethic. Al was more than happy to pass on his knowledge of business down to her. He was trying to mold her into an essential part of the team that knew the business inside and out. He knew that she could run the place if she ever needed to, and she admired him for that.

Passing down knowledge was the natural order of things for old-school Al, and he was appreciated by all that worked for him. He would show Amber things like how to calculate the day's takings or fill out the banking books. He would get her to fill out and then distribute the wage slips now and then for the staff on Friday.

The most recent addition to her roles was the one which she enjoyed the most, though. It made her feel more important than just a waitress. Al started her off speaking to local producers so that she could procure the food and supplies for the diner. She would haggle and try to negotiate the absolute best local ingredients for the best prices using skills she had learned from Al along the way.

Amber had her own dreams and ambitions, which Al knew about; she was not hiding anything. They kept her going, and she was fully committed to making them happen. One day she would run her own restaurant business. She wanted to make sure that she and her mom were going to be looked after. She didn't want to think about the fact that her mom wouldn't always be there.

Amber had majored in math and business at high school, so to her, this job at the diner was the practical experience she needed, sort of an apprenticeship without being an actual apprentice. It was the first rung on that ladder to running her own business—or even a chain of them—someday. She was great with numbers, people, and books.

Amber and Sheena would work the floor of Al's diner during the week with Eva working the floors along with them on the weekends, which were obviously the busiest times. There was also Al's grandson, Kyle, that would work casually for a couple of hours, bussing for the diner after school two nights a week and during the weekends.

Al only worked the register now. He used to do all the cooking as well, but it suited the team better with Al concentrating on his regulars at the front of house. Fred, Eva's boyfriend, was the permanent chef in the back now.

In Amber's mind, her future restaurant would not be just a diner like this, though—not that there was anything wrong with a diner like Al's. Every diner had its place in its community, and this community sure loved its diner. Amber wouldn't be competing with Al, if he was still around when she got there. No, her planned clientele was going to be the businesspeople passing through town on their way out to Winnipeg. That's where the money would be.

Amber often thought of what her menu might look like. Eggs Benedict, steaks, seafood, a platter of oysters . . . lattes, wine, and maybe Tom Collins cocktails and such in the evenings. Not just one big ol' jug of filtered coffee on the go all day, every day.

She had lots of grandiose ideas for what her food would be. She enjoyed watching the food channels on TV to pick up future menu inspirations, and she would list them in her notepad at home. When she had her own place, she would work brunch, evening, and late nights; she wouldn't mind. She would put in all the hours under the Sun, just like Al does. Her mind was brought back down to Earth and into the present moment by an icy gust of wind. The sky was beginning to darken. She would need to set off any moment now. It was around a fifteen-minute walk from her mom's house, straight down the avenue to the diner.

She lived in Selkirk in a small house up at the far end of Manitoba Avenue toward the college. It was a pleasant neighborhood a short walk uphill from the town and the river.

Amber had spent a lot of her childhood playing in the parks down by that river, and the diner sat just on its banks. She could still see herself as a young girl down there, her mom pushing her on the swings. Her mom wouldn't be able to do that anymore. She had worked in the local health center when she could work, in an ironic kind of way, Amber thought. She'd helped to care for people all of her adult life, and now she was the one being cared for. Life could have cruel twists like that.

Amber was short and slim with shoulder-length brown hair. They did not have a lot, money-wise, as she juggled caring for her mom with her work at the diner, but she did have those aspirations that kept her going. They would be well-off one day.

She had settled her mom in front of the TV for the night in her comfortable recliner chair. Amber had cooked her favorite: macaroni and cheese with a slice of garlic bread. She had her cell on the TV table in case of emergencies, Amber didn't even own a phone of her own—they shared one between them—but her mom could ring the diner on speed dial easily enough if she needed her.

*Two and a Half Men* was on TV, and a good run of episodes, too. This was her mom's favorite. That would keep her quiet for a while and also keep her company whilst Amber was out at work. Her mom would be looked after by her favorite show for at least the next few hours. Amber did not get much time to herself these days, although she was grateful for these pockets of time to be in the moment and see the natural beauty around her.

Five forty. She went back inside and picked up her old iPod shuffle that she used for walking, which was kept on a little shelf by the front door with all of the house keys and mail. She would have something to eat courtesy of Al at the diner before her shift started. Yet another perk of working there—if you got there early, Al would feed you, so she only had her mom at home to cook for and clean up after on the days she worked.

She shouted, "See ya later, Mom!" There was no reply, but her favorite show was on. *Bless her. She'll be happy for a while.* Amber smiled to herself as she grabbed her warm winter coat and stepped out onto the front porch, popping in her earbuds and locking the door behind her.

She walked down their little front yard to the street, looking at her iPod as she walked, scrolling her thumb in a circular motion on the jog wheel as she tried to decide on the sound-track for today's walk.

As soon as she turned left out of her front gate and headed off down the avenue toward town, Mrs. Richards drove by. She tapped her little car's horn and waved enthusiastically to Amber. Amber jumped, smiled, and then gave a very quick half-assed wave back. Amber's smile quickly turned into a sneering face as soon as Mrs. Richards had gone past.

Mrs. Richards, Dawn, was her mom's oldest friend. She had been around as long as Amber could remember. She had babysat Amber on occasions whilst her mom had been out working when she was growing up, but when her mom's condition had gotten worse, the visits became few and far between. She used to come around on occasion to visit, and even to help out a little here and there. Even keeping her mom company for the odd hour was a big help to Amber.

Then Dawn had found new friends and joined new clubs until finally she just stopped coming around at all. It was like her mom had gone out of fashion. The *bitch!*

Amber wouldn't bother trying to make her feel bad. No, she would smile, wave back, and let them all get on with it. She didn't need them anyway; she had her plans. She would remember.

She continued with her walk, still jogging the dial on the iPod. It was difficult; she had everything on there from country to death metal, but she wasn't sure what kind of a mood she was in now, no thanks to Mrs. Richards.

Amber's thoughts were dramatically pulled away from the aging iPod's gray screen and sent along with her eyes up into the sky. On this lovely chilly but clear evening came the biggest flash of lightning that she had ever seen. "What the hell was that?!" she yelled, pulling her buds from her ears via the single cable hanging below her chin. The whole sky just went white for a few seconds. No forks of lightning or crashes of thunder followed—it was just one big almighty flash.

*That was seriously weird.* She looked all around, expecting the sky to have turned gray or for it to suddenly unload rain onto her, but no. There was strangely still not a cloud in the sky. Rain did not look even remotely likely, and the slowly setting Sun was still shining away. It was windy still, and the sky was a slightly darker shade of blue now, but that was all. Nightfall was making itself known but the sky itself was all clear. "What on Earth was that all about?"

She pulled up her thick hood just in case. She had the strangest feeling come over her that there was something fast approaching her. Natural instinct made her duck, and as she crouched down, she heard a whoosh as something ripped through the air right above her. She stared out from beneath the rim of her hood, frozen in shock. Something had indeed ripped through the sky heading toward town.

When she did look up, the pressure of its wake hit her as warm air blew her hood off and flung her hair around.

It was like a missile was heading toward town, flying barely twenty feet above her. "Oh no!" she cried. Who *on Earth would want to fire a weapon around here? A terror attack, maybe? But in Selkirk?* That didn't make any sense.

A light trail of misty gray smoke lingered in the air, mixing with the elements already above her. The trail clung to the air quite high above her head so as not to be of any immediate risk to her, but she could still feel the heat emanating from the wake. Within seconds, the missile had already disappeared from view and was roaring into town. It was evident that the object was on a downward trajectory, the trail suddenly diving down and disappearing over the horizon of Manitoba Avenue—right into the town.

People all around her were coming out of their houses to see what on Earth was going on, most looking right at her, as she happened to be crouching in the middle of the street. She didn't know what it was, either; what were they looking at her for?

Their stares from all directions probed her, making her uncomfortable.

She didn't hear any explosions from the town. Thank *God*! *Maybe it went down in the river?* That was the best-case scenario.

She got up, dusted herself down, and continued quickly toward town, desperately hoping that her friends and her town were okay—and also that she would still have a job to go to.

As she marched onward toward town, another flash of light stopped her in her tracks. It charged without sound outwards from the center of town. It was like she was witnessing an atom bomb explosion right in front of her eyes.

There was no time to take cover. One second there was a massive ball of light ahead of her, and then a split second later she was trapped inside the light. While she was inside the light, a wall of warm energy hit her, coming from the same direction. *Oh no*, she thought. *It was a bomb.*

Strangely, she could feel the force of the light and the rush of warm air still coming toward her. There was an intelligence to the light; it gripped her body like a tight hug. *Should I not be dead?* That was the last thought she could remember thinking. Her hair was being blown back by the energy as well as her cheeks. She possessed no control of her limbs anymore; all she could do was ride this out.

There was air between her feet and the sidewalk. It was as if the light itself was holding her up, and not just on the outside of her body. It felt as though the light was going right through the inside of her head as well, searching her mind. She couldn't see anything at all through the harsh white light nor hear any of the usual sounds of the town anymore. She could now feel a pain in her ears, like an ultrasonic sound with a high-pitched trill piercing right through her eardrums.

*(Come closer.)*

*A thought . . . but who thought it?*

After what felt like an eternity, she felt her body drop limply to the floor as the light, noise, and energy surrounding her all dissipated.

*What happened? It couldn't have been a bomb—I'm still here.*

Her vision was starting to return to normal, the street coming back into focus again as she started to pick herself up and dust herself off.

It felt like her memories and thoughts had started to bleed back into her head, like fluid might rush to someone's brain after an unfortunate accident. She gulped, feeling a little unsteady.

*Why is this happening to me? What on Earth is all of this?*

First, she looked behind herself, toward home again. *Well, the neighborhood is still there. No immediate reason to run home. The town, though?* She made the choice to continue heading toward town to check that it was still there.

She looked up as she approached to see there was a car ahead of her—actually two, or three, which then moved around before settling into one shape. Purple spots still appeared from the intense light wherever she looked and whenever she blinked. She saw something hazy between herself and the car that made her think that her eyes were still adjusting. She wiped her eyes on her coat sleeve and when she focused on the area again, there was indeed something—or someone—there.

The air in front of her moved like heat wavering from a sidewalk on a really hot day except it was more than just a current of air. The shape of a person shifted into focus, turning to face her and then coming toward her, somehow there but not there, almost invisible but increasing in clarity as it approached. It almost floated toward her. She stopped, terrified, and hoped that this was just a trick of the mind, or the eyes.

Amber's heart felt threatening in her chest. She contemplated running back home and slamming the front door shut on all of this. She wished that she hadn't even left the house now. It felt like she was trapped in a science fiction B movie. She and her mom did enjoy watching those; if everything turned black and white and tomatoes started running around with laser guns, that would be the real icing on the cake!

The thing in front gained more shape and detail. It was a person now, and it was . . . her.

Amber could only watch silently. Her feet were rooted in place and not at all cooperating with her commands, and neither was her mouth.

This copy of herself did not look threatening, though. It held up its hands in a "don't be frightened" pose and looked like it wanted to say something, its mouth opened wide as it seemed to try to form letters with its mouth, all the while stepping closer to Amber. As the copy got to within a couple of feet from her, it started to fade away into the air. Its feet faded away first, followed by its legs. The copy of Amber looked down, confused, panicked, and stared at her with big eyes. It looked terrified.

Her torso, arms, and then her head all vanished, leaving nothing behind but the view of the car in front.

Amber really wanted to know what the copy of her had wanted to say, not to mention how something could be so bizarre, scary, and damned frustrating all at the same time. She felt sorry for it in the end. Amber took a step forward. "Wait!" she screamed at the strange figure when she found her voice again, but it was too late; the figure had already gone.

Mrs. Richards's little Nissan was only a few yards up ahead from Amber. It had stopped dead, right in the middle of the street, just before the junction of Manitoba and Jemima. *I hope she's okay*, Amber thought. Could this all have been Amber's fault for calling Mrs. Richards a bitch earlier and sending negative energy her way?

Now the old dear had been scared to death by lightning and fireballs from the sky.

"Oh my God, I've killed her! I've killed her!"

Amber carefully started again toward the car to check on her mum's old friend, putting aside any negativity she felt toward her. She checked her watch, partially thinking that she did not want to be late for work—if work was still there—but right now she had as good a reason as any for being late. *Don't panic about work right now.* She needed to check on Mrs. Richards.

The small gold-and-black quartz screen of her watch still displayed ten after six to her, but she noticed that the second digits were now frozen at 18:10:01. She shook her wrist as if to try and wake it back up as she walked, but it looked like it had stopped dead.

"How the heck can a digital watch just stop?"

# CHAPTER 4
# OUT OF TIME

She reached the back end of the Nissan and rested a hand on the rear curve of the car's body to steady herself and collect her thoughts. The car was warm to the touch, which was unusual, as cars here were normally freezing cold! Come to think of it, the air now felt completely different. She realized that all cold winds had stopped, the air suddenly feeling warm and very still.

Her head was spinning. She felt a little faint; she was not coping at all well with these strange occurrences happening all at once. I *still need to check on Mrs. Richards,* she kept telling herself, keeping herself awake, making her way with wobbly legs as best as she could around to the driver's side, though her legs felt as though she was trying to walk on long strips of elastic.

She shook it off and with determination reached the driver's side door. She noticed as she stood looking over the roof of the car across the intersection to the adjoining street that another car had been approaching the intersection, coming up Jemima Street toward her on Manitoba Avenue. This other car had also stopped in the middle of the street, in between the little church and the intersection, as if it had cut out the same as Mrs. Richards's car.

Amber also recognized this car. It was Mrs. Polanski's, another local lady whom Amber knew very well. She had always worked, until she retired last year, in the front office at the high school that Amber had attended. Mrs. Polanski was a really lovely, genuine lady. She had always asked Amber about her mom—daily, in fact.

Amber could see Mrs. Polanski through the glass, and she looked fine—well alive, from what Amber could see from where she stood, anyway. She could see that she was still sitting in a driving position. Actually, so was Mrs. Richards. They were both stopped the same distance from the center of intersection, engines silent. The ladies inside were sitting there, holding the wheel and staring blankly at their windshield.

She looked down at Mrs. Richards and then over at Mrs. Polanski, wondering which one she might try to help first, and ultimately decided to jog over and check on Mrs. Polanski. Not that she thought that Mrs. Polanski deserved help ahead of Mrs. Richards; it was simply a case of logistics. Mrs. Polanski was down a side street off Manitoba, which she would have to then come back up anyway to carry on toward town and work. So, she would check on Mrs. Richards secondly on her way back up and down toward the diner. It was the only plan she had, and it gave her purpose.

"Mrs. Polanski?" Amber called out as she approached the other vehicle. Not hearing a response, Amber rounded the car to the driver's side window. "Mrs. Polanski, is everything okay?"

Mrs. Polanski appeared not to have heard Amber. She did not react at all as Amber approached her window calling her name. She just sat there, eyes forward, hands on the steering wheel in a standard ten-and-two position, her eyes not even twitching.

Amber reached out a hand to check on Mrs. Polanski

through her open window. Her cheek felt warm to the touch but a little stiff. "My God," Amber said to herself. "Mrs. Polanski?" Nothing.

She didn't think to check for a pulse. It didn't cross Amber's mind, as Mrs. Polanski was still sitting bolt upright in her seat, holding onto the steering wheel with an iron grip. Her eyes were wide open, but she showed no reactions, nothing whatsoever to show she was there. She was just sort of frozen in time.

What else could Amber do? She helplessly looked around and up at the sky. A little further up the street, in the direction of where she had come from, the people that she could see on Manitoba Avenue that had stepped out of their homes to see what was going on were still standing perfectly still at their front gates.

They were all looking in her direction, toward town.

*Why weren't they coming to help?* It was obvious that something was very wrong here.

One of the things that next crossed Amber's mind was, *Should I try to get her out of the car?* But she thought against that idea almost as soon as it had appeared. It wasn't worth it. What would she do with the lady once she was out of her car? Lay her down in the street? Put her into the recovery position or something like that until someone else arrived to help? *No, bad idea.* One of the first rules about attending the site of an emergency as a trained first-aider was not to put yourself or anyone else at any risk.

The lady would most likely be much safer sitting protected in her car for now, especially with all of these strange goings-on, whatever this was. Who knew what was going to happen next?

Looking up and down the street again, Amber was wondering if there might be anyone else close by that needed checking on, or someone that may even be able to assist her. The people further up the street in their front yards were glued to the spot. There wasn't anyone in the close vicinity that could assist anyway. Further down Jemima, there were other cars. She had also seen cars all the way down Manitoba, but there was nobody else walking around nearby. Out of ideas, she jogged back up toward Mrs. Richards's car again.

The street looked weird. Again, it felt to her like something out of a horror movie. On both sides of the road in the direction of her house, away from town, people stood at their gates staring in her direction. *This is so freaky!*

The little Nissan's windows were all closed, the doors locked. Mrs. Richards was in exactly the same state as Mrs. Polanski, her eyes staring straight ahead, her hands on the wheel, the woman not even flinching when Amber shouted to her and knocked on the closed window with her knuckles. Amber decided that the women were likely safest in their little glass and metal boxes for now, so she would carry on toward town down the unusually silent and warm avenue.

*Let's see what's happened to the town, then*, she thought as she headed toward it.

There were stationary cars strewn all around her. Some of them had people, even kids sitting inside, all blankly staring forward. But like the old ladies she had tried to help, they were still as statues.

As the shops, restaurants, and offices grew in number around her she saw people inside were sitting or standing, doing their jobs, eating, or shopping, but all were frozen on the spot.

There were also more and more people standing on the side-walks now whom she had to be careful not to bump into. There were people stuck halfway through crossing the street or exiting a shop.

*Why am I the only one not frozen like that?* she kept wondering.

Up ahead, blocking the sidewalk was a car turning off the street into the grocery store, causing many statues to gather in a group on either side of the sidewalk. She approached the window of the old sedan to find a familiar sight.

Here, an elderly gentleman and his wife were sitting inside

the vehicle, motionless. The gentleman's hands were gripping his wheel, but his mouth was wide open as if the couple had been mid-discussion in the car. Again, they showed no reactions whatsoever to Amber trying to force open the door.

Nor were there any reactions from the people standing around her. It must have looked like a sight, Amber trying to jack open the door of an elderly couple's car! His locks must have been automatic, too, and all their windows were closed.

"Hello, sir, are you okay?" she asked politely but sternly through the glass. Nothing. She had a feeling that this would be the case.

She caught the reflections in the car windows of the people's faces behind her. It suddenly hit her that these were all people that she knew or had seen about town and now here they were, frozen and helpless. She turned and looked at the faces of each person in turn.

She had not considered how close the people around her were, those who were waiting to cross the sidewalk whilst she was checking on the elderly couple. As she spun around from the car, she almost bumped into a man standing right behind her in the middle of the sidewalk. She had to awkwardly zigzag around him, moving her hips out of the way and scrunching in her arms.

He had only been standing on one foot; the other was behind him in the air, suspended in a half stride. Had she caught him, she didn't know what might have happened to him.

She considered it for a moment. *Would they topple over? Would they hurt themselves if they did? Would they shatter into a thousand pieces? Maybe they would wake up?*

She wouldn't test out any of her theories. All she cared about doing now was getting down to the diner, hoping that Al might be okay and that he could help her figure all of this out with his no-nonsense wisdom and logic.

She continued, jogging through the town toward the diner.

An increasing number of cars and people were around now, the normally busy townsfolk all frozen.

"Is anybody there?" she shouted at the top of her voice, all the while still thinking, *Why not me?* She was both confused and terrified, and she felt all alone as though she was wandering around in a nightmare.

She sprinted across Main Street, thinking, *Almost there now. Ah-ha! Help at last*, as she spotted a white RCMP patrol car with its distinct red, white, yellow, and blue stripes along the sides.

An officer was just getting into the car, which was parked in one of the marked bays outside the bank.

"Officer?" she shouted from the opposite side of the street. At a quick glance it appeared as though he had been looking in her direction. He had one leg inside the car's foot well.

Amber jogged across the street and as she approached him started to say, "Officer, I think there is someth—" The end of her sentence tailed off upon realizing that he, like the rest of the townsfolk, was unable to listen to her. All that time that she had been approaching him, speaking, hoping that he was listening to her, it became obvious that he had not been.

He was frozen, just like all of the other people of the town. *Typical man,* a voice in her head said; he hadn't listened to a word she had said.

Amber stood right beside the good-looking, well-built young police officer. He had one hand gripping the roof of the car, the other holding open the door, and one foot in, one foot out.

Inside the patrol car, a female officer was sitting in there smiling up at him, holding two hotdogs that he looked to have purchased moments ago for them both. He was smiling back at her. They looked like they were partway through sharing a now voiceless joke when they had been paused. Neither of them moved a muscle.

Amber stared at him as a new fear raced through her mind with a single thought. *If the police can't help me, who the hell can?*

You just expect the police to always be there to help you in times of need. She poked the male officer with her finger into the side of his cheek. His cheek only very slightly creased as she pressed. But, as was the case all around town, there was no reaction from this guy either.

*Why me?*

Frustrated, the words boiled out of her as she let herself go. Screaming at the town, she shouted, "Why me??"

Overwhelmed with feelings of anxiety and loneliness, she gasped as her mom popped into her mind. *Oh God, Mom!*

She hoped that her mom was okay. If she was frozen where she was, like everyone else in town, then she should be at least safe—for now. She resisted the urge to run straight back in favor of trying to find out why this was happening.

She stood there for a while next to the policeman as if taking comfort from standing close to him, collecting her thoughts. Then, as her feelings started to calm down a little, a part of her randomly started reasoning. *Could I somehow be responsible for all of this? Have I got the ability to pause time, like some sort of superhero?*

She unclipped the officer's badge from the front of his shirt, trying it on her own coat's top pocket. "Freeze!" she said sternly to the officer, pushing her gun-shaped fingers into his flat solid stomach. She unpinned it from her coat, looked at it, and then slipped it into his trouser pocket. *That felt naughty but fun!*

*What else could I do?*

Her eyes locked onto a black-topped Sharpie peeking out from his shirt pocket. That little joke now seemed lame. She really couldn't help what she was about to do; she was over-come with mischief. She looked around, checking that she was indeed on her own here. There were several people close by, some even staring in her direction, but they were all frozen.

She took the Sharpie from his pocket. Pulling off the cap, she could smell the ink from the marker. *I love that smell*, she thought. Then she drew a big bushy black mustache underneath his nose.

As Amber pushed the cap back onto the pen, even before it clicked into place, she looked around at the female officer inside the car and then back at the pen. *"Screw it."* She took the cap back off, opened the back door of the car, and climbed into the back. Leaning across the seats into the front, she gave her one, too, a nice big one with curled up edges.

"Gorgeous!" Amber complimented her own handiwork.

Laughing to herself, Amber slipped the Sharpie into her own pocket. "Officer, I am commandeering this Sharpie," she said in her best deep police officer voice. That did cheer her up a little.

Down the street she spotted Barry Smith's Black Pontiac parked outside the law office. He was halfway out through the door of the office.

*The dick! He could stay frozen if everything eventually goes back to normal.*

She hadn't liked him since junior high when he threw gum in her hair from the back of the class—they'd had to cut out a large chunk of her hair to get it out. He had always been the class clown and school bully.

Maybe because she was a girl? But she had gotten away with telling the teacher on him for that gum episode, and he'd gotten in trouble for it too. Luckily, she hadn't received any sort of payback from him for ratting him out. He probably took it out on some poor boy instead, though, knowing him.

He liked to pick on younger kids, those smaller than himself, all the way through school. He thought he was the big time. He was the kid that would steal smokes from his dad and smoke them as soon as school was done for the day, thinking he was big and hard. He would watch the kids running out of school from the boundary of the grounds at the end of the day, picking out his prey with his few friends.

They would watch, pick a victim, and stalk any kid smaller

than them, like a big cat picking out a young deer as prey. Then, he would strike.

He was known to threaten them with his flick knife and even press his smokes into their arms. She knew that it would only take one smaller kid to pick up his balls and stand up to him one day—then he wouldn't be such a prick to them all. Unfortunately, nobody ever did.

Now, though, he would spend his days driving around the town collecting impaired driving tickets in his noisy, smoky roofless sports car like it was some sort of competition. He still thought he was a big shot, but everybody else in town knew that he would never amount to anything.

*The loser.*

Again, instinct took over. She would really enjoy this one. She took the Sharpie from her pocket, admiring the black cap catching the Sun, a sadistic grin widening on her face.

"What the hell? Won't get this chance ever again!"

She ran across the street to him, almost skipping as she went. Very carefully and as artistically as she could, she put one hand at the back of his head to support him and wrote in huge letters, at least three inches high, "D I C K!" right across his forehead before bursting out laughing. She had not finished there, though, opting to amuse herself further. Well, *why not?* She also colored his lips in to give him black lipstick as well as big black circles on his cheeks—all in permanent black ink!

He sure was a remarkable sight, like some sort of emo doll. She cheekily put an arm around his shoulder, kissed him on the cheek, and said, "You look wonderful, dear!"

Then she winced, said "Eeeeuuu!" and wiped the hand that had been cradling his greasy hair at the back of his head on her diner skirt, wiping her lips on her coat sleeve. Again, she stopped there for a moment, surveying the town.

*What could have possibly happened to the world that might cause something like this?*

*It had to have something to do with that lightning and then the missile-looking thing. This only appeared to happen after that second lightning finished.*

Amber carefully carried on, weaving and bobbing in and out of the frozen townsfolk, being careful not to bump into any of them as she walked.

She slowed down as she approached the town theater, stopping right outside it. Raising her arms in the air, she shouted at the top of her voice, "Merry Christmas, movie house!"

*I've always wanted to do that!* she thought.

She was getting close to the diner now. Still there was no sign of damage or the thing that was possibly a meteorite or missile.

*Where is it?*

The Sun was setting fast now, coming down over the horizon and reflecting its stunning red color off the top of the river, which looked as though it had stopped flowing now. It was flat and dead calm.

She had another look all around herself, making sure that everything around down by the river was intact, and from what she could see, it was.

She randomly started to smile again, the image of Barry's face coming back into her mind. But deep down she was still scared—just a slightly more entertained type of scared now.

She approached the last intersection at Eveline Street. The diner was across the street now. From her vantage point she saw smoke, and she could smell it too. The smoke rose from the dip in the grass at the side of the diner where it went down to the river. Well, the good sign was that if this was what had landed, it had missed the diner entirely and all the people standing around, who were all looking in its direction. Some of the people looked terrified; a few had crouched with their hands over their heads. *They must have watched the thing land right before being paused.*

She could not quite see what the smoke was coming from yet.

She crossed the street, happy to see the familiar green-and-white striped canopy above the open entrance to the diner. *Hopefully, Al will be okay.* He would help her.

As she approached the doors to the diner and could see down to the dip beside it, she could see the source of the smoke. Sitting there embedded in the grass was the obvious new arrival that she had witnessed flying over her head, the possible cause of all the strange events. There was a ditch with smoldering edges cut into the turf. At the head of the ditch, which was facing the river, there was a small crater.

In the head of the crater, sitting there and seemingly staring at her, was a small, bowling-ball-sized silver sphere.

*That's weird,* she thought. It was not as huge as she'd expected after all that had happened. *How could this small thing be the cause of all of this?*

She had expected something larger, more threatening, like maybe a fiery boulder from space, or even maybe some sort of alien wreckage. No, this was quite small and did not look very threatening at all. More like an expensive garden ornament.

She came back around to the front of the diner and stepped in through the open front door. She paused, suddenly feeling sick. Now she felt more alone than ever. *There he is.* It was strange to see Al helpless like this.

He was standing there as plain as day chatting to Mr. Conway over the counter, except he wasn't chatting. The diner was deathly silent.

Al had a coffee mug in hand, looking like he was about to hand it over to Mr. Conway. It was halfway over the counter and there it stayed, still connected to Al's outstretched hand. The scene looked like a fifties TV show on pause. In fact, that's how everything looked here.

Mr. Conway was reaching out a hand with the intent to collect the mug from Al but had never succeeded, his hand trapped in mid-air, halfway to meeting Al's.

He was still on his bar stool at the counter, although his ass was elevated just off it, his feet propping him up from the stool's side footrests. His mouth was open as if he was midway through a good ol' belly laugh. No, Al was not going to be able to help her this time.

There were a couple of younger boys standing at the jukebox at the other end of the long counter, mid-conversation, pointing at some song behind the glass that they wanted to hear. There was no sound coming out of it and the boys were not moving, just standing there in front of it and pointing with open mouths.

Various diners occupied the window booths. Some had a fork or a sandwich heading up toward their waiting open mouths, ready to enjoy the food, but the food never reached its final destination.

Amber was at a complete loss of what to say, much less think. She stood on the threshold of the diner doors, not knowing what she could do or say.

What on Earth was so special about her? Was her mom okay? Would things ever return to normal? Was the entire world affected, or just Selkirk? What force could be powerful enough to stop time? Endless questions raced through her mind, doing loops around each other over and over.

Her turbulent feelings and endless thoughts all swirled around in her mind at the same time, causing her to feel faint. She started to feel really hot—she needed to cool down. Dropping to her knees on the threshold, she sat with her back against the door frame. Amber felt so tired, she couldn't keep her eyes open. Her remaining vision narrowed, taken by the emerging darkness coming from behind her head before she fell helplessly onto her side. It was like she had momentarily fallen into a deep sleep.

When she came around, she sat up, then stood after a moment and steadied herself, her back still leaning against the door frame. As she started to regain some composure, she stepped outside the diner, though she had no clue at this point what her next move would be.

Taking another look around her town to survey what was going on all around her—or rather what was *not* going on—she looked at the locals' faces and the buildings of her hometown.

Desperately and at the top of her voice, Amber bellowed a "HELLOooo!" that echoed into silence. Whatever was happening here went on for as far as her eyes could see. Cars had stopped in the middle of the street, people stood frozen in mid-stride on the sidewalks or crossing the road, there were people halfway into doorways or about to open a car door—everything was motionless and deathly silent. And nobody had looked around at her shouting at the top of her lungs like a madwoman.

She decided that she would sprint home to check on her mom, but as she decided on doing so, something in town held her back. A voice in her head. It was her own voice, telling her to have another look at the crater at the side of the diner. Heeding the voice, she walked away from the diner door and around to her left.

The round shiny ball, around seven or eight inches in diameter, gleamed at the head of the crater. The grass around it that had been burning had gone out now, leaving only charred black and dark-brown scars around its edges. She could still detect that strong burning smell.

Amber had made sure her mom was okay before she left.

*She will be okay,* that voice that sounded like her own said in her head.

On a normal day, Amber would go to work, and Al would insist that she take her mom back some leftover pastries or muffins that were left on the counter plate at the end of her shift. *Mom would always look forward to that.*

Yes, Amber would straighten all of this out, feeling inside that if she investigated the sphere, she just might solve all of this. Then she could still go to work for Al and even have time to take her mom some cakes. *See you soon, Mom.*

She took another closer look at the ball, walking up to the

head and then crouching down next to the crater, staring at it as she inched closer. It seemed to somehow call to her silently.

She desperately wanted to run home, but something . . . something needed her.

She was tempted to pick up the ball, to see what it was, how heavy it was. She could not take her gaze from it now; she was trapped.

*I can step away if I want to.*

*(Yes, but you don't want to. You want to be here.)*

She reached out her hand, finger pointing toward the top of the mysterious ball, when she paused. There were still some small columns of steam rising from the ball now and then as well as the crater around it.

*So, is it hot?*

But it was too late—her finger had already reached its destination, seemingly moving forward of its own accord. A vibration rumbled up into her arm as light enveloped her.

Amber was no longer in her hometown of Selkirk, the town that she had never left in her whole life, while the ball stayed there, collecting the last of the setting Sun's red rays.

The top of the sphere was peeking out, barely visible from over the edge of its small crater, into what would normally be a busy little town.

The sphere had a view reaching up Manitoba Avenue, the direction Amber had come from, with the bank and the hotel on either side of the road, and behind its crater was the river. It was a pretty place.

# CHAPTER 5
# DAY ONE

D aniel's eyes were closed. He was regaining consciousness behind them, but why he was like this, he couldn't recall. He was aware that he was lying down—in his bedroom, maybe? He didn't feel too good; his head was spinning, and the feeling seemed to carry on as if spiraling downward all the way down to his gut.

It was a feeling he could recall that brought about even more nausea simply by recalling it, remembering when he had had way too much to drink last Christmas. He had gotten far too carried away, as was easy to do when you were having fun, helping himself to alcoholic beverages of varying varieties. He was under eighteen—only just, but he was in his own family home and the different shaped and colored bottles had looked simply tantalizing.

It had started off with a small glass of white wine with dinner, then onto playing games and enjoying a few IPA beers with his dad in the evening. Wow, those could pack a punch after a couple.

He did not realize it at the time that going overboard on booze, once you got to bed, was comparable to the feeling of being trapped in a dark empty washing machine when your head hit the pillow. He could still feel the way that room had spun, and it felt a little like that now. He understood why people could easily end up vomiting after a heavy night on the booze. It was a feeling he did not want to repeat of his own accord anytime soon.

He was sufficiently confused. What had he been doing that would lead to feeling like this again? He had not been drinking —had he? He slowly opened his eyes, then they opened even wider, suddenly aware that his surroundings did not at all match his memory from a few moments ago.

He sat up. It looked as though he was in jail. He was sitting on the edge of a bed—well, basically a stone slab in the shape of a bed—built against the back wall of a small stone-clad room. The room was perhaps ten feet long out in front of him by around six to seven feet wide. The only obvious differ-ence between the small room he sat in now and a police cell that he had seen before—innocently, of course, either on school visits or on television—was that there was no door at the front end.

*What kind of cell doesn't have a door?*

It felt like it must be nighttime. As his memory started to gather itself, he now recalled that it had been nighttime before he'd passed out. He had been at the school. Had he been locked up for being on the school grounds? There was a window above his bed set into the stone wall behind him. When he craned his head back to look up, he could see a black sky through the small window.

Out in the corridor that ran across the end of his cell it was quite dark, only dimly lit by a thin strip of red led light running down the center of the ceiling, illuminating a basic walkway, stone walls, and not much else. A scene straight out of a nightmare.

He planned to have a better look out of the window shortly, but he was still racking his brain, trying to remember what had happened to him which might have led to him being confined to a cell and feeling hungover. *A meteorite?* He could do with a glass of water; his throat felt very dry.

He continued looking around the cell. On the wall to his right was . . . a toilet? It was a stainless-steel-looking box fixed to the wall, and there was a large hole in the top with a curved lip cut smoothly around into the metal. *Yes, the toilet*—that was quite clear. He looked inside it but instead of finding water, all he could see was black—jet black. No water, not even a bottom, nothing. *Weird toilet*, he thought.

Straight ahead of him, where you would have expected to see a wall with a door to this apparent cell, was no door at all, not even a door frame or a wall, for that matter. The whole wall was open to the corridor. The cell and the corridor were only separated by a painted yellow line and a small groove running across what appeared to be the boundary to his cell in the stone floor, the aesthetics of this place giving off a perplexing blend of modern and medieval styles. *Where the hell am I?*

Outside of his cell and past the line and the groove on the floor, the corridor was a narrow walkway going from left to right. Opposite his cell, around four feet away, the width of the corridor, there was another dark stone wall.

He was still trying to trace his thoughts back. *Right. What can I actually remember?* It was just after midnight, something had landed over at the school, his phone had stopped working, which he still had in his pocket. He had walked to the school to have a look. His dad was going to come, but . . . they were frozen. Sadness flooded him. How was he going to help them if he was stuck in a cell?

He massaged his forehead with the tips of his fingers as though trying to massage some life back into his brain. He certainly did feel peculiar.

The lighting that he was afforded in the cell was minimal. A soft beam of warm white light traveled in from some artificial source of light not too far outside the window, running through the middle of his cell toward the corridor.

He then noticed that this path of subtle light skewed slightly as it left the cell into the corridor. He frowned, thinking, *If there was nothing there, why would it do that?*

He got up and walked right up to the yellow line at the entrance to his cell. Just after the yellow line, no more than an inch between them, the groove was cut deeply into the stone floor running across his cell.

There was nothing else apparent that divided his cell from the corridor outside. His cell was like a cube with one side left open. There was no front door, no glass blocking him. But somehow, he sensed that there could still be something there. What was to stop him from walking out and off down the corridor? Was he locked up for something he had done but had no memory of?

*What on Earth is going on here?* So many questions, but there was no sign of a guard or anyone else there that he could ask. He inched suspiciously toward the yellow line, the toes of his trainers right on the line now.

He turned and looked back at the window on the back wall, his eyes following the beam of soft light across the floor to the yellow line. The beam of light skewed there, as if there was a sheet of thick glass dividing the cell from the corridor. It couldn't be glass; he could actually feel cool air driving down the corridor and into his cell. Something told him to be careful of that groove, his brain telling him that there was danger nearby.

*What the bloody hell happened over at that school?*

Nothing made any sense. The last memory he could recall with certainty was when he was going to touch that shiny ball. Then nothing after that. Just . . . winding up in this place.

Looking both ways from the line of his cell, he could see other cell openings going left and right off the corridor. He did not want to risk edging any further forward for fear of poking his head through something unknown, whatever this barrier

62

was—if there even was one. He could, of course, have just been paranoid.

Then, he heard "Hello?" inquiring in a scared but polite female voice. She sounded close by. She could be his next-door neighbor, but he wasn't one hundred percent sure yet, not knowing the layout of the world outside of this cell.

"Hello?" he asked in reply, waiting to focus on whichever direction the reply came back from.

"Where am I?" his cell neighbor asked.

She sounded American to Daniel. He pinpointed the sound as coming from his right-hand side. And she sounded very scared.

"I'm sorry, I don't know yet. Don't be frightened. I just woke up here too. Is that what happened to you?"

"Yeah, I was walking to work, and all this weird stuff started happening. Then there was this weird . . . silver bowling ball thing, and now I'm here."

"Yeah, that sounds like exactly what happened to me, too. I went outside to see what was going on. It looked like a meteorite, or something had landed at the back of my house, and next thing I know, I'm here. I saw that weird silver 'bowling ball' thing as well."

"You're not from around here, are you?"

"Honestly, I'm not sure where *here* is yet," he said, looking around, "but no, I don't think I'm from wherever you're from."

He was still looking around the walls and ceiling of his cell as he spoke, trying to fathom what exactly could be stopping him from just stepping out into the corridor. He still stood on the yellow line but didn't yet dare to step beyond that groove. Not until he knew more. All of his instincts were telling him to step out, to go and see if she was okay—to see where he was and find someone to ask why they were being kept here. Curiosity got the better of him as he started to slowly raise his arm.

"Are we in jail?" the girl asked him.

"I think so, yeah. Don't worry, we'll figure this out between us. I'm just trying to figure out what's holding us in here first."

Daniel held out his right palm, moving it very slowly toward the space directly above the groove and what he suspected was keeping him in. His shaky hand betrayed his apprehension.

A short painful buzz strikes his hand accompanied by a spark of light and then a feeling of weightlessness. He is suddenly aware that he is falling. As if in slow motion, his back slowly falls closer to the floor behind him.

As he descends, several thoughts go through his mind. He feels a shooting pain up his arm that he now remembers was the same feeling he'd felt from his time just before he woke up here. *That's it—from the silver ball.* A strong tingling sensation moved up his arm toward his elbow, then his shoulder, and then his head began to hurt like a son of a bitch.

Still, even before hitting the ground, he had time to think, *Oh sh—*

Buzzing sounds echoed out and down the corridor, reminiscent of something from the Saturday morning cartoons sound effects library.

A handprint floated in the air, hanging there for a couple of seconds, teasing him. He saw the handprint getting further and further away from him, and then . . . nothing but darkness.

Amber was sitting on the edge of the bed in her cell, waiting for the young owner of the male voice next door to figure out what was going on. He sounded helpful. She looked at her wrist, and much to her surprise her calculator watch was now working again.

Monday 18:17 looked back up at her. It had started off from more or less where it had paused. The seconds digits were now increasing, and the colon was blinking again.

She suddenly heard a sound that made her jump. The only way she could describe it was as if someone had thrown an electric razor at the wall next door, followed by a bright blue flash outside of her cell from the left-hand side.

"Hello?" she asked, getting up and walking to the yellow line. Something told her to stop there, even without hearing what had happened to the young man next door. Did *he touch it?* There was no reply. "Hey, are you ok?"

Nothing. It was deathly quiet. *Something must have happened to him.*

As she stood there on the yellow line, she also noticed the light crossing from the window as it shimmered on the surface of whatever was holding them in.

*I'll bet he touched it. It sounded painful, she* thought.

"Hellloooo?" She tried to throw her voice in his direction from just before the threshold to her cell, cupping her hand to the right-hand side of her mouth.

*What is this? Some new type of jail? she* wondered, being careful not to edge too close to whatever was there.

A few moments went by and still there was silence. Feeling helpless, she sat back down on her bed and waited. Then she started to hear sounds coming from next door—a muffled combination of a groan and shuffling.

"Oh man!" she heard the boy say.

"Hey, are you alright? I was worried there."

"Woah!" More shuffling. "Yeah . . . I think so, but whatever you do, don't touch the doorway to your cell. Jesus! I feel like I've been hit by a train."

"I'm glad you're ok. I don't want to sound selfish, but the thought of being here on my own wasn't a very nice one."

She jumped out of her skin, letting out a loud gasp when a dark robed figure suddenly appeared and walked down the corridor, briskly walking across her view from right to left. The figure was dressed like a ghost monk in a long dark-gray robe tied around the waist with a black belt and a hood pulled up over his head. He walked into view, glancing at her to his left.

He looked right at Amber from the side of his eye, then carried on past her cell. Soon it sounded like he had stopped.

She stood up and walked up to the yellow line again. Looking left, she could see him standing in the middle of the corridor, obviously between her and the boy's cells.

"He will be fine. Do not worry," the man said to her. He sounded very matter-of-fact and straight to the point. He had been listening.

"Where are we?" she asked the old man. She would guess, looking at his pale wrinkled skin and a short white beard, that the short robed man was in his late sixties, maybe early seventies.

"Where you are will be explained when the time is right. What is your name, please?" he answered, looking right at her.

"Amber."

He nodded smartly, then looked away from her toward the boy's cell. He asked again, "What is your name, please?"

"How about I answer your questions when you tell me what I've done to end up here!"

She winced. The edges of her mouth curved downward, and she took a sharp inlet of breath. *He's not holding back, is he?* He was right, though; that was what she was thinking too. *But let's be diplomatic before we get on their bad side.*

"Name, please!" the pale old man asked again, with annoyance this time.

"Daniel," he finally replied with some reluctance.

"Welcome to you both," the old man said, shifting glances between the two of them.

"Welcome??" Amber heard Daniel saying brashly to the host.

*He's off again!* she thought, smiling despite their circumstance.

"I don't feel bloody welcome! Why am I locked up and getting shocked? I want a phone call!"

Something told Amber that Daniel was not doing himself

any favors by demanding things, and she also had the feeling that a phone call was likely not forthcoming.

"You are from Earth. Am I correct?" The old man glanced between them, ignoring Daniel's demands.

"Why are you asking that?" Amber couldn't help but ask this time. It just came out without thinking. She knew that if he was asking a question like that, then there was a good chance she would not like the answer.

"We don't seem to be getting anywhere here. You are both clearly in shock and are still adjusting. I think perhaps a period of reflection and cooling down might be advantageous here. You both look tired, and you have come a very long way. Please take some time to relax, eat, and drink, and I will come and see you again tomorrow."

The old man put his arms behind his back, turned, and walked back past her cell, disappearing back down the corridor and out of view.

"Wait! . . . Oi! Come back! You can't lock me up for no reason. You git!" Daniel shouted after him. Amber wanted to shout, too, but she knew that it would not help them right now.

*What did he mean "you've come a long way"? Where are we? And why have we been incarcerated?*

Hopefully, all would be made clear when the time was right. If indeed they were locked up for some reason, she would need to make arrangements for her mom—and quickly.

*Where am I? she* thought.

Daniel was starving. He sat back on his bed, feeling deeply annoyed. His stomach growled, and his hand still tingled where he had gotten that shock. That weird monk hadn't even brought them anything to eat. *Didn't he say something about 'getting some rest and eating'? What was he talking about?* He could have offered them at least a glass of water or something. Even on cop shows, they fed the people in the cells and made them hot drinks.

"I'm starving!" he called out loudly, hoping someone outside was listening.

"Your left-hand wall. Push the black button."

To his surprise, someone had been listening. A low, muffled fed up man's voice floated in from somewhere nearby out in the corridor. This was a new voice.

Daniel scanned his small room. This was even smaller than his stuffy bedroom at home.

*Oh, what I'd give to be back in my room now.*

On the left-hand wall from his bed was, indeed, a round black button between the stones in the wall at around chest height, about the size of a half tennis ball.

He stepped forward to take a closer look at this button. The voice seemed to indicate that it would solve the hunger issue.

He applied some pressure to the black button, which depressed inward like soft rubber.

Some mechanical noises droned as something operated behind the stone wall. Then, a stone panel the size of a microwave front moved downward, dropping behind the stone below it to reveal an opening with items inside a dark hole. He reached inside. Feeling a tray, he pulled it carefully from the hole and marveled at it. On the tray was a plate with a stack of three fresh hot pancakes, three slices of bacon, and a gray stone cup containing what looked like water beside a stone-crafted knife and fork. The stone panel in the wall rose again to cover the hole when he had removed the tray.

"Amber!" Daniel said, moving toward the opening of his cell with his tray, "press the black round button on the wall opposite the toilet."

"Got it. Thank you."

He sat back on the hard bed base with his tray. Everything in front of him had been smartly hand-crafted from stone. The warm food was exactly what he needed.

The drink next to the bowl was indeed water, cold and gratefully received. When he was finished, he stood up and guessed that he had to press the button on the wall again.

He started to feel guilt creep in that he might have come

across a tad mouthy to the old man—but then at the same time, maybe he had every right to be. He was the one locked in a cell and had been tasered for no good reason.

The panel in the stone wall dropped down to reveal the empty black hole once more. He placed the tray back inside, guessing that was the correct protocol.

He noticed that the light source coming in from his window was receding even further than it already was. The night seemed to last forever. He stood again at the threshold of the cell. Looking in both directions, he further studied his surroundings. He could not see much, not without putting his head too close for comfort to the invisible barrier, anyway.

The corridor was quite narrow, around four feet wide. On the opposite wall to his he could see one other cell opening to his far left by around ten feet, and the same to his far right. He could not see the occupants or even the inside of these cells.

"Whoever told me to press the button on the wall, I just wanted to say thank you. I appreciate the heads-up."

"You're welcome!" rang out a voice. *It sounded like that came from the far left.*

"Amber, you ok?"

"Yeah, thank you. That was nice."

"Do you have any idea why you're locked up?" he asked.

"None," came the reply from the cell next to his right.

Daniel was starting to calm down now from the initial shock of realizing that he had been locked up for no good reason. He had been fed and had someone to talk to; at least he was sharing this experience with somebody going through the same thing as he was. Now they just had to find out from the mad monk why they had been locked up, what was going on, and exactly where they were.

He hopped up onto the bed and tried to get a look outside. The window was too high for him to get a good look at his surroundings, as the tip of his nose was barely able to reach the dark stone sill. All he could see outside was black sky above them—nothing of his surroundings or clues to their where-abouts. Floating in the black sky, a little way over to the right from whatever building they were in, was a globe that looked to be providing light beneath it. The top of it was dark.

He stepped down and walked up to the doorway again, listening. It was quiet but he heard a sniffle from next door. *Amber, and she could be crying,* he thought. He thought he would engage her in some light conversation.

"So, where are you from? I noticed you have an accent. Are you American?"

"Canadian, thank you. I'm from Selkirk, near Winnipeg. What about you? I can't place your accent at all. I'm shit at geography. Are you Australian or something?"

Daniel laughed. "No. It would be nice to live there, though. I'm from Willenhall in the West Midlands."

"Where's that? Never heard of it."

"The West Midlands, England . . . you know, where we are now!"

"I'm not in England! You must be in Canada. I haven't trav-eled anywhere; all I did was black out! I don't think I was out long enough to fly to England."

Daniel thought about this for a moment. Strangely, if he thought he was still in England and Amber thought she was still in Canada just as much as he believed he was still in Blighty, then where the hell were they? They could be anywhere! *Something is not adding up here.*

Perhaps there was much more going on here than he had first thought. His face bore a frown as he tossed all of this over and over in his mind.

"What do you think's going to happen to us?" Amber asked nervously.

"Well . . . I'm not sure, but I'm thinking it might be a good idea if we try and get some sleep, like he said, and try to chill out a bit. I was probably a bit of an ass to him back then, to be honest."

"Well, they deserve it, locking us up for no good reason."

"Maybe he might explain why they've locked us up tomorrow. That's what I'm hoping, anyway. Tomorrow we'll hopefully clean this mess up and get out of here. And go home."

"I hope so!"

Both cells went quiet as they wallowed in their thoughts. The silent darkened cells brought sleep on quite easily.

# CHAPTER 6
# DAY TWO

A mber came around when the light pouring in through her window and brushing across her face steadily grew brighter—and warmer. She opened her eyes and sighed, realizing that she was still in this god-awful strange place in God knows where.

She glanced at her watch. Tuesday 03:50. Looking again up at the small bright window, she thought, *Strange time to be waking up.* This *is mental.* Where *the hell are we?* She rolled her eyes and dropped her head with a thump back onto the bed in frustration.

Her head had been lying on a mixture of rolled-up skins and furs. She felt the back of her head, which was warm and damp.

*I wonder if we're allowed a shower here? I feel gross.*

Looking around, it was still the same miserable stone cell that she had hoped had all been part of a long, horrible nightmare. Even more annoyingly, she was still fully clothed in her retro diner uniform, an impractical short red-and-white check gingham dress, with white cuffs and a flappy collar. Her coat was here, but she had taken that off and covered herself with it to sleep. The matching white apron and plain white sneakers finished off the ensemble. It was literally the worst thing she could have been wearing in an unknown environment. More-over, it was just plain embarrassing. How she wished she could go back home, check on her mom, and throw on a simple comfy pair of jeans and a hoodie.

She put both feet on the floor and studied the toilet-looking box fixed to the wall and the opening to the cell. She had been holding it in, hoping not to have spent this long in this stupid place. She stood, looking at it and then at the opening to her cell, hoping to God that nobody would walk down the corridor, but she needed to use the bathroom so badly.

Nervously, she prepared herself and then sat on the cube. As she sat, the open wall looking out at the corridor curiously shimmered. A "shoosh" sound accompanied this, and then the light coming in from the window running off into the corridor strangely turned back into the cell. That barrier which Daniel had nearly killed himself on must be some sort of screen, she reasoned. All light in the cell was reflected off it back into her face, and her cell felt much brighter and warmer.

On the top of the metal box, the seat was rounded off and rolled over neatly around the cut, proving a comfortable enough surface. The best part was, it looked clean. She hated using public toilets.

When she was finished, she noticed that there wasn't any toilet paper around, nor a button to flush the toilet out, but she then felt a jet of warm air come up from somewhere inside the cube. Blue light glowed from in between her legs. Then there was a mechanical sound of a metal gear turning over and clunking.

Hopefully, all that air and flashing lights meant that she did not need to flush the toilet or even use toilet paper anymore. This place had some very strange modern touches, whilst strangely keeping quite an old, understated appearance. *Everything here is just weird!*

She hurried off the toilet, straightening herself out before going to stand at the barrier again to see what was going on today. As she hopped off the toilet, barely giving her chance to right herself, there was another "shoosh" noise and the sunlight stopped reflecting at her face, bleeding out into the corridor again.

She started to think again about what had happened to Daniel yesterday as she stepped toward the corridor. What was clear in her tired, aching mind was that whatever that screen was, it did not sound pleasant. It looked open, but you were not able to leave. She was careful not to get too close to the line marked on the floor, keeping her toes well behind it. She whispered as loud as she could, throwing sound out from the back of her throat, "Daniel, you awake?"

"Yeah." There was a pause, then, "You don't have the time, do you? My phone's dead."

He sounded tired and really fed up.

"Yeah, it's ten minutes to four."

"In the afternoon?"

"No, morning."

"What day are we on? I'm totally lost with my days."

"It's Tuesday morning."

"Bloody hell! This is weird. Why is it so light? Hang on, it was Monday night—well, Tuesday morning when I went over to the school and touched the sphere. How the hell can we still be only on Tuesday morning?"

"I don't know. I'm as confused as you are. I suppose it depends where we are. If you thought you were still in England and I think I'm still in Canada, that could be part of the reason for the difference. When I touched the sphere, I know it was Monday evening, as I was about to start my shift."

"My watch is set to my local time—well, it was before it stopped. I don't know how long it stopped for. I only noticed it had started working again when we woke up here, so . . . I guess we're not in Kansas anymore, Dorothy. It's a damn shame your phone doesn't work. Any idea what's wrong with it?"

"No, it was on charge when I was still at home, but whatever happened when the time seemed to freeze, it must have drained the battery, I think. The time that it froze on was showing before, but there's nothing now. It's completely dead."

Sounds coming from the corridor interrupted them, stopping the conversation sharply. They started with another "shoosh." *Everything here seems to start with a shoosh,* Amber thought. Then shuffling and footsteps, belonging to more than one person by the sound of it, meant someone was coming down the corridor toward them again.

Amber and Daniel both stood at the yellow lines of their cells, waiting to see who was coming. Both felt hopeful that today might be the day that they sort all of this out, find out what they'd done wrong, and just maybe even get home.

The old man from yesterday was back. He took a central position between the cells again in the corridor so that both captives could see him. Accompanying him this time was a short but very stocky man not at all dressed like a monk. This *guy looks like a futuristic goth gladiator,* Daniel thought.

The stocky guy wore black boots up to his knees with chrome shin and knee plates guarding his legs as well as black tight-fit trousers topped with a metal utility belt complete with "below parts" protection hanging from it, also chrome. A black T-shirt and a chrome breastplate covered his torso, complete with detailed tits and abs. Chrome wrist guards extended up to his elbows and a chrome helmet sat atop his head, very akin to a legionnaire. No feathers on the top, but still, it reminded Daniel very much of a Roman soldier from his history lessons.

Completing the stocky guy's look was his weapon. He wielded a long lance in both hands, but at the tip where you might expect to see the sharp end, it wasn't sharp. The tip was a metal tubular shape, wider than the lance staff. The canister section had vent slits and small lights detailing it, around a foot long to the tip. The tip itself had a pair of narrow-gauge wires coming out of the end, forming a pincer shape.

The pincers had a buzzing blue glow of electricity sizzling between them. *It's a big stun gun!* Daniel thought.

The old man that they had seen previously looked them both in the eye in turn. "I trust you are both a little more . . . relaxed this morning?"

Daniel was the first to speak. "Could I get a sausage and egg muffin, please, with a hash brown and large Americano? And whatever the lady is having, please."

Amber laughed, unable to hold it in. The old man glared at Daniel, rolling his eyes, and folding his arms impatiently. Daniel got the idea that he was not impressed and apologized.

"I'm sorry. It's my coping mechanism. We're fine, thank you, we're just not used to being locked up for no reason."

The old man paused and then seemed to relax. "Under-standable," he replied. He looked to Daniel, to be a bit more sympathetic when he spoke this time. Daniel felt that he should probably shut his mouth and listen today rather than give him too much mouth back.

"Well, provided you are civilized," the old man continued, "and do not pose me or my people any threat, then today is the day that you will be able to come out of your cells. It is my role to show you around, be your guide, and explain things as best I can as to why you both came here. Can I rely on your coop-eration?"

"Yeah, of course," Daniel said. "But can I ask a quick question?"

"Fine."

"What's she come as?" he asked, nodding toward the stocky futuristic gladiator.

Amber put her hands over her mouth to trap in the laugh that came involuntarily and took a step back. She did wish that Daniel would not antagonize them, but he did make the time here a little easier and funnier. She heard the old man say in a plain, almost robotic British accent, "I'm sorry, I do not know what you mean. Could you please explain?"

Amber composed herself and made a "hmm-hmmm" throat-clearing sound, attempting to deflect the old man's attention away from the awkward moment. "I'm sorry if we offended you yesterday. Look, we just want to know what's happening to us and why," she offered as respectfully as she could.

The old man raised his left arm to chest height, flicking out his thumb and finger in the shape of a gun. Amber stood in the direction that he was pointing, so she hastily retreated into the rear of her cell.

She heard Daniel shouting again.

"Oi! What are you doing? Point that thing at me. Oi!"

The man did not look up at Daniel; he only stared at his hand. She edged forward, back toward the yellow line. Looking around the wall, if she needed to, she could quickly hop back in toward the back of the cell for cover.

A bright white light illuminated the corridor. He was now looking at a floating white screen made of a paper-thin rectangle of light hovering in the air above his left thumb and index finger.

With the finger of his other hand, she watched him tap and slide around on the screen. It was as if he was operating a tablet computer made entirely from light.

The doorway in front of her cell shimmered, followed by a low-level hum. Had the barrier fallen?

"You can come out of your cells now, Amber and Daniel."

They both stepped out into the corridor carefully, Daniel edging out, the tips of his trainers first in front of himself, checking for the barrier. Amber also pointed her sneakered toes at it first, just in case. Their faces all glowed a soft creamy white as the red LED strip running down the center of the ceiling had changed from its nightly red color.

The stocky man instantly sprang into life, making Amber jump. The man took a step back and extended his lance from a standing upright position to a more threatening pose, gripping it with tight fists and pointing it toward Amber and Daniel.

"Woah! Easy there, Karen!" Daniel shouted, moving to stand in front of Amber. He held one arm behind his back as if to hold Amber back and his other out in front of himself, palm out, facing the aggressive short man in a peaceful pose. "Everybody take a chill pill! We come in peace."

"Lower your weapon," the old man told him, rolling his eyes as he did. He patted the air in front of himself with an open hand in a way that seemed to tell the armed guard to "put it down now, you silly man."

"Please, follow me." The old man turned and started to walk away down the corridor. Amber followed him.

Daniel turned to look at the armed guard and shouted over before following Amber, "Is it ok if I call this guy Karen? He kinda looks like a Karen," shaking a thumb toward the armed man, indicating Karen's direction. The old man ignored Daniel, clearly showing that the subject had little importance to him. He headed off silently and briskly down the corridor.

The burly man grunted, grimacing at Daniel. He pointed his lance at him and then prodded the air in the direction of the old man and Amber, indicating without saying a word, 'Walk! Follow them.'

As they headed off down the corridor, they passed several other cells on their left and right. Neither Amber nor Daniel could resist looking inside at the occupants.

The various silent, aggravated occupants all laying on their beds were a mixture of very different-looking people. They had headed to the right from Daniel's cell, so Daniel guessed that the first cell they passed on their left would have been the person that told him how to get the food and drink. As he walked past the open-looking cell, he looked to his left. Sitting on the bed was a man watching them go by. He was bald, but strangely his skin looked scaly, like a lizard, and he was stone gray.

As his and Daniel's eyes locked, the scaly man stuck out his tongue, which took Daniel by surprise. It popped out very quickly, sniffed the air with its forks, and then retreated.

"Nice tats!" Daniel said, assuming that his cohabitant on this side of the prison had full head tattoos. The man inside frowned, looking confused. Daniel passed the cell and instantly felt bad. He had stared at this guy and said something that looked like it confused him. This man had likely been the one that had helped him out earlier, but Daniel couldn't really offer him anything in return.

They passed several more cells. Amber looked into one to her right and saw a man sitting up on his bed. He could not have been much over twenty. He wore red overalls with black loosely fitted engineer boots. His skin was also pale gray, his hair was strikingly white, and he had bright piercing white eyes.

"What is this place?" Amber asked the back of the old man.

"All will be explained. Do not worry," he said without looking back.

*He doesn't give a lot away, does he? What is this place, anyway? Some sort of freak show or a bunch of actors here to complete the look and scare us? I'm not scared. I just want to go home.*

As they passed by the next cell, the whole portion of the wall that would normally be open and reveal another cellmate inside was mirrored. Then, as they had almost cleared it, the mirror changed, fading back to transparency and revealing its occupant. A woman with reptilian features, no hair, and green scaly skin was refastening her red trousers, standing with her back to the toilet. *Ahhhhh!* Amber thought, putting two and two together. She smiled at the woman. *Good makeup!*

Amber did not say anything, though she couldn't help but stare. The woman inside stared back, her eyes narrow with yellow irises. The reptilian also bobbed out her forked tongue at Amber, sniffing the air to try to see where these new baby-faced prisoners had come from. She didn't know, having never sensed that scent before.

Amber shivered, feeling even more uncomfortable now. She followed the others who had passed her and continued to tell herself that everything was going to be okay.

The old man led them to the end of the corridor. She felt that he might start to get annoyed if she started asking more questions, so she followed. Daniel who was also silent now.

*"Everything will be explained!"* she thought to herself in an exaggerated whining impression of the old man.

As they approached the end of the corridor, which stopped dead, she wondered where exactly they were all going to go. The wall in front of them at the end of the corridor was a wall of solid black. The central strip of light above them also stopped at the black wall. Nothing obvious appeared to open or slide or push; it was just black where she expected a door would normally hang. It wasn't that it was a dark room on the other side, and you just couldn't see past it into the darkness—instead, there was something there, and that something was black.

The old man stopped, flicking open his fingers to make his tablet come up again. The bright white glowed intensely next to the black of the doorway. The gap in the doorway absorbed the light, not releasing a drop of it back. He made some motions on his screen and then stepped right into the black. As soon as he stepped into it, that shooshing sound echoed around the corridor, the same noise Amber had heard before when the old man walked up the corridor to them. He had vanished.

Amber, stunned, turned to face Daniel behind her who simply shrugged, looking as confused as she felt. The short rude gladiator behind them simply grunted again, moving the tip of his lance toward the black.

Amber nervously stepped into it next and vanished, closing her eyes as she did. Daniel followed as well, keeping his eyes open to try to see what was going on.

As he stepped into the black, the shooshing sound slowed down. The blackness of the doorway moved into and stretched across his eyes. It seemed to then part and go behind his vision, and then as quickly as the black had moved in, whatever was on the other side of the doorway merged into view instantly. They were now somewhere else entirely.

# CHAPTER 7
# MICK, SHROPSHIRE, UK

Mick was about to pack up for tonight. He was an experienced detective sergeant, one who often went well above and beyond his normal duties, based at a police station in Wem, a small market town just outside Shrewsbury in the county of Shropshire, UK. It was about a quarter to midnight on this miserable wet Monday night, around thirty miles as the crow flies from where the sphere is about to land in Willenhall in about twenty minutes' time.

He was at the end of what had been an exceedingly long day —and almost into the next one. He wanted to finish updating the policy book for the homicide that had been reported earlier today before he left for home. He did not really need to be here doing this. For around the third time tonight he had flicked through all the photos sequentially in front of him on the screen, wanting to have a final look over the reports that Rebecca had handwritten earlier and to start saving them into a file on the server.

A DC colleague, and old friend of Mick's who had moved to Telford Station recently, had requested their presence urgently this afternoon after a body had been found on the Wrekin, a well-known local beauty spot close to Telford.

Some hikers had spotted brightly colored clothing in bushes, simply thinking that someone had dumped a coat at first, as sometimes happens, but this turned out to be a little more than that after one of the walkers had decided to get a closer look. The body was up the trail a little from the Forest Glen car park at the foot of the hill at two thirty this afternoon.

Normally Mick would have been happy to let Rebecca take the call alone; she was more than capable of running the scene, but he had been dropping her off at home this week while she waited for her new pool car to arrive.

He drove her to the site and gave her a hand. Scene of crime officers were already on-site with their tent and the crime scene taped off, they were taking their photographs and swabbing down the area.

Once they had all of the information they could get, he dropped Rebecca off at home. It was well after seven by that point and already getting dark. She lived not far from Mick in Featherstone, near Junction One of the M54 Motorway, but instead of heading home himself, he hopped back on the M54 and headed back west toward the station.

The truth was, Mick enjoyed being at work. He hated going back to an empty house; it hadn't been the same since his wife of thirty-six years, Wendy, had passed a couple of years back. So here he was, still at the station, typing the reports up that could easily have been put off until tomorrow.

He sat there contentedly, finishing off his vending machine coffee and admiring the relaxed mood of the quiet, almost empty station. Part of him did wonder why he enjoyed lingering around here at these hours when it was as quiet as sitting alone at home. Then Jeanette, the noisy one of the cleaning crew, walked into the office, pushing her jangling trolley full of cleaning supplies with her bright yellow rubber gloves on. There was the difference—company and distraction.

"Bloody 'ell, Mick! Evening, or is it morning?" She looked at her watch, pulling at the cuff of one gloved hand with the other.

"Doh yaow have ome to goo too?" she asked him in that broad Black Country accent of hers.

She did make him smile. He enjoyed the banter with her and the officers here. Like himself, Jeanette was from the Wolverhampton area, so they both had much broader accents than most of the other people around them. Most of the other staff and officers here were from the immediately surrounding areas —Telford, Shrewsbury, and Wellington—so their accents were more on the . . . let's say not-so-broad, even slightly posh sounding compared with Mick's "at home" accent.

He masked his broadness ever so slightly to fit in better while at work, though not on purpose. He had always used his "professional accent" whilst at work.

"How bin ya, Jen?" he shouted back, mask off and as naturally broadly as he could.

"Not too bad, mate, tar. You get yourself off home. That's an order, officer!"

"I'll be off shortly, mate." He smiled as he started to slowly pack things away from the top of his desk. The floor was only dimly lit at this time of night, basic courtesy lighting for any late workers and cleaning crew getting tidied up for the morning. It got brighter in the office as Lisa walked through the center, setting off the spread of occupancy sensors in the ceiling and bringing the LED lighting panels back up to full brightness.

Mick himself was based at a desk right in the center of a large open-plan office. He had been given the choice a long time ago to have his own sub-office when the station was being built, but he did not see the point of all that. Mick was old-school, the kind of person that liked to have an ear on the ground, mix with everybody else, and know everything that was going on and being said around the place.

He stood and walked over to the windows. He looked down at the dark wet visitor car park at the side of the station, thinking that if he didn't start back home soon and get some sleep, he wouldn't be much use in the morning. On the bright side, it looked like the rain was starting to slow down now, at least. *It might even pass over soon.*

He took another glance at his watch. It was just after midnight now, officially Tuesday morning. From the corner of his eye, he was sure he caught the end of a flash of bright lightning in the distance to the east. *Brilliant!* he thought, thinking that the drive home eastwards to his empty house would be even more miserable if it was thundering and pouring down rain.

He decided that would be it for today; he could not justify being here any longer. Mick shut down his computer, which was no doubt getting very warm by now—he had been in since eight this morning—and slid the paperwork from today's work from the top of his desk into his top drawer and locked it.

He put on his hat and coat that were hanging on a coat rack next to his desk. The younger officers tended to throw their coats over the backs of their chairs, but Mick always thought that looked untidy. He checked to make sure that his car and house keys were in his coat pocket.

Mick was fifty-seven now. He wasn't a tall man; he was of average height with broad shoulders, a pot belly, and hair that had long been white. He was a pleasant and cheery fellow, and as one of the more experienced officers, Mick was very well-liked and respected around the place.

He was always paired with less experienced officers that were at the point of wanting to take the next step up the ladder to aid their development, like he was doing now with Rebecca. Rebecca had recently moved up to becoming a trainee detective constable. Mick was particularly good at passing on his knowledge and showing less experienced officers the ropes, and in the correct way. In a way, this had become his full-time role in recent years.

Teaching was something that Mick himself had considered for the last few years of his career with the force, but he kept getting pulled into jobs that just did not give him the time to carry that through. The end of his career was gaining on him faster and faster with every passing day. Mick was one of those people that thought that life in a classroom could be the life for him, but all of his peers knew that he wouldn't be suited to being bolted down into one place and put out to pasture.

He slid his brown padded leather chair underneath his desk and walked through the sea of other desks and printers toward the central lobby where the elevators were situated. He pressed the button to call the lift to his floor and when it chimed, the doors parting for him, he climbed aboard.

He made his way from the lower ground lift lobby out through the internal enclosed part of the parking garage and then started to get wet as he walked out to the miserably wet floodlit part of the car park that was not under the protective cover of the main building.

Mick pulled out the fob to his Audi as he approached the car. The car's lights blinked twice in the dark and then stayed on, making a whoop-whoop noise that echoed out around the concrete walls when he pressed the button. Headlights shone against the white wall, highlighting the slowing rain just in front of the car.

As soon as Mick pulled the door handle and took one look inside the open car, he yelled, "Shit! Charger!" His work-issued iPhone wouldn't see the night through after the long day they'd had taking photos and setting reminders for tomorrow.

He pictured the cable, still connected to his PC. He probably even ran over the cable as he pushed his chair under the desk. "Shit!" he shouted again, disappointed in himself and his aging brain. He knew that he didn't have another charging cable at home, so Mick had to go back inside the building, all the way to the top floor, just to grab a bloody cable from his computer. *How annoying!*

He called for the elevator again from the lower ground lobby as rainwater dripped down his hat and overcoat, leaping off onto the polished light-gray marble floor tiles. It seemed to take forever. Three, two, one, ground, and finally L-ground. Bing! The lift chimed and the doors labored open. He climbed aboard again, thinking to himself that he had seen far too much of this elevator today.

Walking again through the empty office floor, he noticed even the cleaners had left now. He leaned down and plucked the cable from the tower's USB socket when he heard a door swing open in the far corner and a familiar I this means trouble voice I shout his name.

"Ooh, Mick, great! Come here, mate."

*Bloody hell!* Mick's eyes rolled in his head before he turned, knowing that he was about to get caught up in something else just as he had decided to head home. He knew that he was never going to make it home tonight. Trust him to get stopped when he had made it to the outside of the building once already.

"Yes, Gaffer?" Mick put on his happy face and started to walk over toward the chief inspector's office, sliding the buggering charging cable into his coat pocket as he walked.

The chief inspector was leaning half inside and half out of his doorway, his tie loosely relaxed below his neckline and his top shirt button undone. He was holding his cordless office handset in one hand whilst his other gripped the doorframe.

It looked to Mick as though this might be important business, and now the gaffer needed to bring in some other jackass to be involved in whatever was happening tonight. *Bloody great! Just my luck to be that jackass!* In reality, though, he didn't mind.

"What's up, Gaffer?"

"Sorry, Mick. I know you've been on duty all day and you're on your way out the door. Were you aiming to head down the M54 when you left here?" he said in that slightly West Country-ish twang of his. He knew the answer was going to be yes.

"Yes, boss, why?"

"I'm glad I caught you, mate. I really do apologize, but you might need to rethink your plans tonight. This will affect you."

"Oh, why? What's happening?"

"Reports are flying in from all over the place. Something really weird is going on, Mick. I haven't got the full picture yet. Jams are appearing all around the motorway network. Every single main road. They're backing up on the A5 from this way, heading toward the M54, which is where it will affect you, but also the M6, M5, and the M40. All blocked! And nobody can get through to West Midlands Police at all."

"Eh?" It was most unusual to have jams appearing all around the West Midlands and Shropshire at this time of night —and all at the same time.

"The traffic is stationary, mate, and well . . . I can't really get my head around what the reports being entered into the system are trying to say. Apparently, people are coming to a stop for no reason on the motorways. There have been some collisions, too, but the reports are also saying that people are acting strange all over the place. They're, well, walking around, and then getting . . . stuck in something, sort of . . . I don't know, Mick. They're saying that the West Midlands is inaccessible! What could that mean, Mick? It's not making any sense to me.

"There are several RTC cars en route now from Shrewsbury. East Midlands police and Staffordshire are also sending officers down to assist. One of the jams starts just down the road here, near Wellington going toward the M54 and Wolverhampton, so I wondered if you were heading that way anyway, would you do me a favor and poke your nose in for me?

See if you can give me some experienced eyes—no offense— on what's actually going on down there as soon as you can, please. You can carry on home from there, obviously. Just give us a ring, Mick, and let me know what the crack is, will ya? I'm sorry to put it all on you."

"Yeah, Gaffer, of course. As you said, that's my way anyway. It's no problem. Whereabouts did the reports say the problem was again? Around this way, I mean?"

"Ah, yes." He rushed back around to his desk, fumbling

about in some notes. "Ahh, let me see . . . the first phone call to this station said that there was something weird going on just where the Roman Road goes underneath the A5 heading eastbound, right before the Wrekin, actually."

"Yeah, I know where you mean, boss, no problem. I'll give you a ring when I've had a look?"

"I'll still be here anyway, Mick. Sorry, mate, and thanks again!"

At that, the gaffer ushered Mick out, sharply closed his door, and went back to his desk, speaking on the phone. Mick could see the gaffer's animated shape through the frosted glass side window. "They're what? Say that again!" Mick heard him saying from outside of the room.

*I had to come back in, didn't I?* Mick thought to himself as he headed back down in the lift again toward the car park level, although he also realized that even if he hadn't been called back, he would have hit this traffic anyway and wouldn't have known anything about what was going on. All in all, it was probably a good thing he got delayed.

Mick was luckily an insomniac, so he didn't mind too much. The situation sounded interesting, anyway. For a normally quiet station, it seemed to have all gone off today.

Eventually Mick made his way to his Audi, plugged in his phone, and pushed the button to start her up. He reversed out of his space, pulling up to the white mark just before the automatic gates to start them opening. They slowly opened to let him out into the dark, and at last he drove away from the safety of the floodlit car park.

Mick liked working up here. It was more countryside than a busy city center like Wolverhampton. He enjoyed the pleasant drive to work. The station was a short drive through the village down a couple of open roads, fields, and farms, and then you would hit the 49 toward Shrewsbury. Then you jumped on the A5 that, after a short time, turned into the M54 motorway, heading back toward the built-up city of Wolverhampton, where Mick lived. It was very easy to travel at the times that Mick traveled; he hardly ever hit any of the nine-till-five traffic.

He followed the A49 around Shrewsbury. It was quite busy for the early hours of the morning but still moving. It took him a little while to get around to the main roundabout, and then both lanes started to fill up with traffic as he joined the A5.

*Very unusual, this, for after midnight,* he thought.

He managed to dawdle along with the flow of traffic for around half a mile, then started to see a big buildup of red brake lights coming on through the gentle drizzle. As he got closer to the stationary traffic, he could now see that there were already some flashing blue lights up ahead in the distance and people up and out of their cars walking around.

*Here we go,* he thought.

# CHAPTER 8
# THE BUBBLE

Mick applied the handbrake and pushed the button to switch off the engine. Lines of traffic and red lights, bright in the dark, surrounded him in what felt like every direction and went on for miles by his eye. He clocked that it was almost quarter past one on Tuesday morning now as he opened his door, letting in the cold air and bringing on the courtesy light above. He put on his hat and stepped out onto the wet tarmac carriageway.

People from the other stranded cars were either also outside on the tarmac, trying to get a look at what was going on up ahead and having a good old gossip with fellow strandees or sitting in their cars entertaining themselves with either books or their phones.

The ones sitting in their cars looked like they had the best idea, cozied up in the warmth and accepting that whatever it was up ahead, they were here for the long haul. Some were even using the time to try to get some sleep, covered over with checked car blankets. He did not blame them in the slightest.

He navigated his way through the crowd, eventually reaching the blue-and-white barrier tape stretched across the two lanes of the eastbound carriageway. The tape was wrapped around the top of several bright-orange traffic cones spread out across the lanes. Just a few feet beyond the police barrier, there were three high-visibility-laden traffic officers patrolling the barrier and politely asking people to stop pushing forward into the tape and back up a little bit.

He pulled the tape up and, holding his hat on, bowed his head and slipped under. A hi-viz officer swiftly approached him, so he flashed his warrant card. The officer held out an arm to indicate the direction of where the action was before continuing to disperse people that were getting ideas to try to follow Mick.

Up ahead around a hundred yards into the taped-off zone were two police cars, one in each lane with their back windows facing him. They had STOP displayed in tall red LED letters blinking on and off from inside the dripping glass.

This was all happening on the eastbound side, heading toward Wolverhampton, twenty miles from Willenhall. Mick noticed that there was nothing at all on the westbound side of the carriageway; it was deathly dark and silent. Already in his logical problem-solving mind, he was thinking that to get things moving again, if the accident was this bad, why hadn't they already started to relieve some traffic pressure and divert some of the traffic along one of the empty lanes on the other side? Like allowing water another route to find its way from a blockage or helping an electrical current follow another path away from a cut or damaged piece of cable, simply divert some of the pressure away.

Mick approached another officer, one that was standing nearest to him in the middle of the road, and readied his warrant card again. He recognized the officer as he looked back up as Tom, a traffic officer that used to be based at Mick's station. Mick had worked with him a few years back before Tom had moved on to work at the station up at Market Drayton.

"Alright, Tom, how you doing, mate?"

"Hello, Mick, you alright, mate? Smashing night for it, eh? It's been a while, hasn't it?"

"Yeah, it has, mate. What you gone and done here, then?" Mick beckoned his head in the direction of the empty carriageway lanes sprawling out in front of them.

Tom took a deep breath in and then pushed the recycled air back out through pursed lips and puffed out cheeks. He started to walk Mick away from the barrier with a hand at the small of his back, away from the prying eyes of the people—some of whom obviously enjoyed bird-watching in their spare time and were standing at the barrier with their binoculars trained on them. They walked further down one of the dark empty lanes in the direction of whatever the problem was.

"Come this way and have a look for yourself, Mick. You'd say I was talking bollocks if I told you anyway."

Mick's curiosity was tingling now. They walked around another two hundred yards further away from Tom's car, by Mick's count, and Mick started to wonder whether he was going mad or if the traffic boys already had. He walked down the lane of the quiet dark A5 carriageway with Tom. There were no streetlamps illuminating this stretch; it was pitch-black. Mick began to wonder when he was going to see a pileup of cars, red lights, fire, or an ambulance, at least some sign of a crash or even a bit of debris. But what he could make out in front of him did not look like a big deal at all—not at first glance, anyway.

Considering the big police presence, the blockade, and the reports that the gaffer had been proper stressed about, Mick could not see what the problem here was. All he could see was a police car sitting another hundred yards up ahead of them. It was pulled over in the left-hand lane, its headlights and tail-lights still on.

He could see the headlights spilling light onto the road out ahead of itself and highlighting another car out in front of it. Its blue lights were also on—solid, not flashing—and the driver's side door was wide open.

Out in front of the police car, standing in the beam of lights in between his car and the stranded car in front, was its officer dressed in his high-visibility garments. The stranded car was sitting out in the second lane and looked as though it had broken down. So, he surmised, the officer had obviously pulled over to check if the driver was okay, ready to set up whatever was required to keep the member of the public and the approaching traffic safe.

But the officer was frozen, as if paused, halfway between the two cars, facing away from Mick and Tom. He was . . . stuck, mid-stride, but how could he be? The officer was looking toward the civilian car with one leg out in front of the other and off the floor. He was carrying a long, black-handled torch in one hand and a traffic cone in the other, which he held at waist height. *The stranded civilian driver must be sitting inside their car— possibly hurt somehow?* Its doors were closed, and its lights were on, but nobody was visible around the car.

Mick stared at Tom, bewildered. "Well, what's the problem? Let's just go over and see if he's alright." Mick took one stride forward, but Tom yanked him back by the arm, quite sharply. Mick looked at him, annoyed.

"No, mate, you don't wanna do that!"

"What do you mean? Why not? What is going on 'ere, Tom?"

Tom's face changed to a serious expression. He took his gaze away from Mick and out toward the officer in the road. Mick's eye's followed Tom's. Tom suddenly started to yell at the top of his voice at the poor stranded officer. *Rather obnoxiously*, Mick thought. *That's not right at all. Very disrespectful.*

"Oi, matey! Officer! Police! Turn around! Oi, knob-head!"

Nothing changed; there was no reaction whatsoever. The officer in the road did not even flinch, and he was easily within range to hear them.

Mick stared toward the officer blankly, his mouth hanging loose. He was completely and utterly lost for words, unable to pull a single word from the air. After a long pause, all Mick could produce, without moving his eyes, was "What the bloody hell's going on, Tom?"

Tom now looked quite amused with himself, saying, "You ain't seen nothing yet, mate."

He tugged on Mick's coat sleeve to get his attention back and pointed to about five feet out in front of them. Hanging in the air, suspended of its own accord around a foot off the ground without explanation, was something that Mick had not even noticed before. Again, Mick was dumbfounded. The signals traveling from his eyes to his brain were getting lost, scrambled, completely without direction or belief.

He was mostly annoyed with himself that even with his experienced trained eyes he had not spotted what Tom was now pointing at.

Mick had been busy scanning the lanes of the nighttime road to the horizon for signs of an RTC. *How the bloody hell could I have missed this? It's only a bright-orange floating bloody traffic cone with reflective bloody strips around it, after all!*

In his current state—cool as a cucumber on the outside, but inside pretty bloody useless—he truly wasn't sure whether he had spoken those words out loud or just kept them for himself.

The top point of said cone, about waist height to them, was almost pointing at them, hanging at an angle in the air. The square black base was at forty-five degrees and roughly twelve inches off the ground. And there it stayed floating, still, frozen in time like the poor officer over there.

"Blow me backwards!" Mick said after another long pause in his low old-school dulcet tones. He placed a hand on Tom's shoulder, feeling the need to steady himself on something.

"Yep . . . I know what you mean, Mick. We saw the traffic car there with its blues on solid, so we pulled up behind it right there"—he pointed back toward his car—"and Rich, my mate, got out of our car and then noticed the officer standing there in the road, thinking that he might need a hand like. So, he went and got a couple of cones out of our boot.

"As soon as he started walking off toward Frozen Guy over there, Rich said the next thing he remembers is me pulling him over. He said he remembers swinging the cones as he was carrying them, then nothing. To me, I was just getting out of the car after making some notes, saw him walk off, then he just kind of paused. It looked like he'd forgotten what he was going out for. I saw he didn't look right, so I laid him down, but the cone stayed where it was in the air.

"It was lucky I was following not far behind him. I just kind of instinctively pulled him back by his arm like, and he fell flat on his arse. Well, after that he seemed alright again—apart from not remembering what had happened.

"We tried again, touching . . . whatever was there, trying to work out exactly where it started. It's almost like there's an invisible wall there that freezes you solid. That poor sod over there was obviously already in the thick of it when whatever IT was came down.

"So, we rolled our car back a bit and stopped all the traffic back up there. We put the barriers up and the blues on, and that's when you showed up. We've not been here that long, but we've heard some of the calls going out over the radios. Mick, the traffic's backing up all around the Midlands, isn't it? How bloody big is this thing?"

"If this is the start of it . . . " Mick started to think out loud, staring vacantly ahead down the carriageway toward the east. "Bloody huge, Tom!"

"Honestly, Mick, go on. You've never seen anything like this before, have you? Even in all your years?" Tom stared at Mick with raised eyebrows, eyes wide and questioning, but Mick didn't notice at all, still staring in horror at the road ahead. He didn't even answer this time.

After a long pause, a prolonged silence between the two colleagues, Mick knew that he had to call his gaffer back at the station. He was right to be freaked out and confused. Mick was standing here looking at it and still did not know what it was. How was he supposed to explain the unknown?

"Jesus Christ, Tom . . . the chief wants me to phone him to let him know what's going on down here. I don't know what the bloody hell to say. He's going to think I'm ready to go and put my slippers on and eat jigsaws up at the care home."

"Well, that's the boundary of it there. Look," Tom said as he pulled some loose change out of his pocket. He threw the handful of change through the air toward the floating traffic cone. The coins flew through the air, spread out, and as they got closer to the traffic cone, they all began to stop dead in the air one by one. Some were very slightly further forward than the others, some higher, some lower, but they all stayed fixed in place.

There was no barrier here—not that could be seen with the naked eye, anyway, but it was there, alright, just like Tom had said. You could start to make out a barrier now with all the trinkets the thing was collecting. *My house is in there, along with a hell of a lot of other people's houses and loved ones,* he thought.

This was the start of whatever was here and causing chaos all over the Midlands. Not just the start of the barrier, even; Mick sensed the start of something much bigger than what they could observe here. The implications and the ripples resulting from this thing would go down in history as a major event.

"Right," Mick said with a sigh, not knowing what to expect or what to say. "I suppose I'd better go and phone the chief, then."

Mick headed back toward his car, bent over and bowed under the tape, and made his way through the thirty or so people now gathered to see what was going on. Mick couldn't even look at them even though some were glaring at him, desperate for answers as he crossed the tape, willing him to spit something out. But he didn't know what he would have said to them even if he'd wanted to. For a change, Mick was genuinely speechless.

As experienced an officer as he was, Mick would normally be the kind of chap that would try and reassure and calm down a crowd of people like this. Even when he had to be a little vague, he would always try his best to reassure people. But this time he had no idea where to start.

*What could I say? That there is an invisible wall around the whole of the central region of England possibly? That renders you frozen if you wander into it? Oh, and by the way, all of your families that are in there are frozen, too, and we have no idea what is causing it!*

That was crazy talk—he would only cause panic! That was not his place to announce something like that. *What on God's Earth could create something like this?* Even if he had seen it with his own eyes, his rational mind did not allow him to fully believe it. This was way above Mick's, the chief's, or even anyone on the police force's pay grade.

Mick stepped off the carriageway and into his Audi, shutting himself in. He wished that he could push a switch and make all the windows go black so that he could hide his true feelings that he was sure were stamped across his face. He slowly took off his hat, taking his time to place it on the empty seat next to him and adjust it, squaring it up neatly and making sure that the line across the top of his hat pointed toward the front end of the car, gathering his thoughts as he slowly moved, not even starting up the engine.

He sat there for a moment pulling a deep breath down into his lungs through his nose, slowly shaking his head before pushing it out through his mouth.

He was troubled. Troubled that for all of his experience and knowledge, he had no idea what to say or do next.

He knew that he had a phone call to make; that was the first job. He looked around the car and over his shoulders, double-checking that all the windows and doors were closed and locked. He pulled out the charger from his iPhone, which was sitting just in front of the gear lever and dialed the chief. In a panic, he quickly removed the phone from his ear and stared at the screen, checking that the audio source was set to come through his phone earpiece and not Bluetooth to the car. He did not want the conversation to be heard by anyone outside.

"Talk to me, Mick. What you got?"

The quick-fire question from the chief came even before the dial tone had fully had a chance to register. He had been anticipating Mick's call. Mick could see in his mind the gaffer's hand resting on the desk with a finger twitching above the phone's hands-free answer button.

Mick took a deep breath again before starting. "Well, Gaffer" —*breathe*—"you trust me, don't you? And you can confirm that I have all my marbles?"

"Jesus, Mick, what is it? Of course I do, mate, are you alright?" He sounded anxious himself and obviously was under pressure himself, Mick presumed, but he still spoke with a hint of friendly sympathy.

"Well, I'm here with the officers from traffic. Tom's here— you remember Tom. Well, they've done the right thing and set up an exclusion zone blocking off eastbound. Sir . . ." Mick rarely said "sir" these days. "There is an incident here. It appears to be . . . well. I'll just say it—an invisible wall in the road, and there are people inside the area, sir, an unknown number at the moment. We have eyes on one officer, stranded, and a possible one to five pedestrians also stranded in a vehicle."

"Stranded?" enquired the chief.

"Yes, sir. As far as we can see. Visibility is not ideal, as we can't get any closer to the, err . . . incident. The people inside the zone appear . . . frozen inside this . . . well, an area beyond the, erm . . . wall. Not frozen as in cold, Chief, kind of unresponsive —paused, if you like."

The line went silent for a second as both ends of the signal thought about what Mick had just rambled out. Even Mick knew that his description was as puzzling as a wheelbarrow being piloted by a barrel of monkeys.

As Mick listened to the silence, he picked up that something was doing loops in the gaffer's mind; he had known him for a long time. Did he know something but wasn't letting on?

"Gaffer, what's going on?"

"Erm . . . okay, Mick," the chief said softly and carefully. "Listen, I've heard something down the grapevine. The threat level of the entire UK has now been raised to 'Above Critical,' I can tell you that, which doesn't give a lot away, I know, but keep in mind, nobody knows what's going on. Nothing like this has ever happened before.

"Nothing has gone public yet. As you can probably imagine, GCHQ is scrambling to investigate the fact that a very large section of the UK, including the West Midlands, parts of Staffordshire, Shropshire, and Worcestershire, have been completely cut off from all communications and access in and out of the area.

"The West Midlands Police are completely consumed inside this thing and as such are out of the picture. An emergency no-fly zone has been actioned across the whole of the UK. As we speak, all air traffic outbound has been grounded. Inbound flights are diverting to France or Ireland for now.

"Calls are already flooding in from the public, even at this time of night. What is it going to be like in the morning, Mick? Christ! Nobody can contact anybody or access anywhere from Stone down to Droitwich and from Telford across to Swadlincote.

"Walsall, Dudley, Wolverhampton, Lichfield, and all of Birmingham are completely cut off—it's as if they've been wiped off the map! Like you said, they are there, but it's as though there is an invisible wall around an area the size of a large county . . . or even a small bloody country. Whatever this thing is, it's big, Mick. And I honestly don't know any more than that. I've got to call in to my superiors now, as I told them I was sending my most trusted colleague to the boundary closest to us to get eyes on it."

Mick paused, his phone balanced shakily between his shoulder and his ear, and then he started fumbling around in his seat. He reached behind his passenger seat and pulled out an old 2010 road atlas from the pocket, a staple in the car of every old-school driver.

He opened the atlas to the pages showing the Midlands. The chief said something else down the phone, but he had started to break up. The signal was weakening and with Mick's fumbling around, the gaffer had to check if Mick was still there.

"Mick"—crackling, rustling—". . . sti . . . ere?"

"Sorry, Gaffer. Yes, I'm still here, bear with me for one second please."

Yanking the glove box open, Mick grabbed a Sharpie and started drawing on the pages, starting right where he was. He drew a dot, then a line from Telford north and east around to Stone, following what his gaffer had said, then clockwise over to the east to Swadlincote.

Clockwise again to Birmingham, down to Redditch and Droitwich, then coming back around to Telford. Definitely a circular shape, of sorts, taking into account Mick's crude line drawn with shaking hands. Right at the center of the circle area was Walsall.

"Christ alive! This is a big area, sir. It's a definite sort of circle. It looks like the center of it is . . . Walsall. Well, just off center, but definitely in that borough. Looks like I'm not going home, Gaffer, and neither are you."

"Jesus!" The chief sighed. "Mick, it's barely two o'clock in the morning! When we get to rush hour—Christ! There isn't going to be any way to contain this! It's going to be bedlam! The public needs to be told, now!"

"I think you're right, sir. But to be honest, I don't think we're going to have any say in this. This is well above the police now. Bleeding hell, Gaffer! Looking at it, this thing must be over a thousand square miles. Nothing on Earth has made this, chief!"

The chief was younger than Mick but had always appreciated Mick's experience and honest approach to things. He told it like it was.

"Okay"—crackle—"you ge . . . elf back here . . . ate, looks like we'll both . . . the pull-out beds t . . . try and get a bit of rest, we're going to n . . ."—crackle—"I'm gonna put a call into someone I know . . ."

"Right you are, Gaffer. See you shortly."

Mick pressed the End button on his phone. He could tell that the chief was not fully with him by now, already working out what he was going to say to his superiors. And the reception was getting frustrating.

Mick started up the ignition to warm himself up. It was still dark and damp outside, but the rain had stopped at least. He stared at the gray roof lining. How on Earth was he going to get some sleep after what he had just seen? This was not normal; something very extraordinary was going on here. The chief had said he was going to need some rest, but how could he? He felt so small and useless.

His neck craned back, resting the bumpy part of the back of his head against the soft leather Audi headrest, enjoying the silence. The cold leather felt like a relief against the stressful tightness that he could feel wrapping itself around his head, a migraine on its way.

His eyes zoned out, losing focus on his surroundings. As his head began to throb, those pesky black and white diagonal lines started to move down his eyeballs, distorting the unfocused view of the windscreen. He closed his eyes, actually drifting off for a moment.

When he opened his eyes again his head had started to feel a little bit clearer. The throbbing had receded, but his eyes were still not fully focusing. He looked at the digital clock behind the steering wheel and had to focus to gain some clarity, work the digital clock down from six of them to only two, and then bingo! The white numbers stopped jumping around before settling at 02:25.

Flashing blue lights caught his attention from behind him in his rearview mirror. More police were arriving. It looked like trucks, too, big ones. Civilian cars were starting up and parting behind him. Most likely the army had arrived to take over. This would be taken off their hands now, and more appropriate barriers and checkpoints would be set up.

*Might as well hang around a bit, see what's going to happen next.*

Whatever this event was, his estate was going to be well inside it. If he was told to clear off, he would go straight back to the station, like the gaffer said.

# CHAPTER 9
# TOMMY, CANADA

I f a crow could fly in a straight line heading north from Selkirk, he would come to the backyard of Tommy—short for Thomas, named after his not-recently-passed grandpa—and his family. No crow would soon be able to do so, however, due to the protective field that the sphere in Selkirk next to the diner was preparing to generate.

Tommy was a polite and friendly five-year-old boy living with Mom, Dad, Grandma, and Grandma's nurse, Jean, in the very pleasant lakeside community on the shores of Lake Winnipeg in Matlock, Manitoba.

Tommy's parents were a hardworking professional couple doing very well for themselves, which had afforded them the opportunity, not too long ago, to purchase their lovely new lakeside home. The idea behind it was that they wanted to give their young son, and ill grandmother, a more pleasant quality of life away from the ever-increasing busy city of Winnipeg.

They had fallen in love with the house even before it had officially come to market. Tommy's dad, being in real estate, had been given an early nod that this property was coming up long before anyone else had the chance to book viewings.

The house enjoyed stunning views of the lake from its backyard, just a stone's throw from the shore. There were walking trails and parks all around the neighborhood, not to mention the obvious enjoyment of using the lake and beaches. Tommy's dad had said that he intended to make full use of all these new facilities at their disposal, though Tommy's mom thought that that remained to be seen. But she did admit that it would be nice to have all these facilities close by, for Tommy and his future brother or sister.

His dad had spoken to Tommy about all these wonderful things that they could enjoy together. There would be sailing and windsurfing, fishing, and barbecues by the lake. He had said that over the next few years he would be looking to buy all the equipment he needed for them to enjoy it to the fullest. Tommy did not know what most of those games were, but his dad had made it sound like a lot of fun and Tommy loved playing games with his dad, so Tommy was all in, whatever it was!

Tommy's dad had made an exceptionally good name for himself selling mostly commercial real estate at his own firm, which he had built up from scratch. He had decided to base himself at his new home office; it had so much extra space that it just made sense. He had previously used a remote office in Winnipeg to answer all his calls. He would often be out of the house all day long, showing new homes and commercial units to potential buyers, renters, and investors.

Tommy's mom was a respected lawyer. She worked for one of the best reputational firms in Winnipeg and had risen the ranks to become partner. The law firm was based on Main Street in the central business district of Winnipeg and had been seeking to expand northwards anyway to provide better coverage of some of the northern territories, so when she had indicated a wish to relocate further north, it suited everyone. They offered her the chance to open and run a satellite office with a base staff of her own in Selkirk.

It was an easy drive for her straight down Highway 9 to get

to her new office from their new home, so everything had dropped right into place for them. The other reason for living in a more relaxed environment was for the benefit of Tommy's grandma who for the last five years had been battling dementia. To help with this, they had employed the service of a full-time live-in caretaker called Jean who was tasked with looking after Grandma and Tommy and running the house during the daytime, as his parents often did not get home until late in the evening.

Tommy, with his mop of light-blond hair, was smartly dressed today in his red denim dungarees and favorite white crocodile jumper complemented with brand-new grass-stained knees, just in time for Jean to fetch out again.

Tommy loved to play in his backyard with his toys when it was not too cold. He was never any trouble for Jean the nanny; he understood that Grandma needed more attention than he did. He may not have fully understood why yet, but he did know that Grandma was very sick.

The yard was Tommy's domain. In it he had a battery-powered Jeep, a trampoline, and a baseball mitt and bat for when his dad came out to play in the last part of the late afternoon before bed. Tommy's pride and joy, however, was a log cabin-style treehouse. In this treehouse, which he saw as his actual house, were his teddy bears (all in Viking's jerseys from previous seasons) and a flat-screen TV, usually playing cartoons, which also had a selection of games consoles attached to it. He also had a toy wrestling ring that he enjoyed playing with, and several of his favorite "wrestling men,"' as he would call them, sat scattered all around the room after they had been "fighting."

Around the inside perimeter of the treehouse was a cool realistic train track that he and his dad had been slowly building and adding to since they had moved up here. He was enormously proud of that—not just for the impressive train set, but that he and his dad had spent time together building it.

The Sun was starting to get heavy on this fine Monday evening. Tommy came running happily back into the house to eat his French toast fingers that Jean had put out for his supper. It was a quarter to six when she called out from the back step that supper was ready.

Tommy took off his outdoor shoes near the back door, as he was always being told to do, and ran into the kitchen to sit at the table. Grandma Two made the best French toast!

Grandma Two was Tommy's nickname for Jean, which affectionately came out as "Grammaw Two." She had lived with them for just over a year now since helping with the moving process soon after first taking up the post. To Tommy, it felt like she had been around forever!

Neither Tommy's mom nor dad had gotten home from work yet. Tommy wasn't that good with remembering the exact times that they normally got home, but he was conscious somewhere deep in his developing brain that his dad was normally back by the time he was eating his supper.

This morning he had watched from the doorstep as his mom drove her long shiny black Jaguar off the end of their long gravel driveway, as he did every morning. Dad had already left earlier. Tommy had waved his mom off, then ran enthusiastically back through the living room, the dining room, and the kitchen out to his domain at the back of the house to continue his adventures.

Even before Jean had locked up the front door after waving goodbye to Tommy's mom, she knew exactly where he would be heading. *Tommy does love his yard*, she thought lovingly. She had heard his footsteps pounding through the living room across the wooden flooring and smiled. He was an easy kid to take care of, absolutely no trouble at all. She cared for Tommy as if he were her own grandson.

She could concentrate a little more on Grandma now. The backyard was secure, and she knew that Tommy was safe playing with his toys outside. She could conduct her daily chores, periodically looking out at him from the back step. First up was Grandma's breakfast, then getting her washed and dressed, then a good clean-down in Grandma's room before starting on the rest of the house.

After a productive day, Jean took an hour out for herself to have a sandwich and watch a little TV before getting Tommy and Grandma ready for bed. It was a lovely bright sunny evening, unusually warm today too. She had prepared Tommy's French toast, and called to him from the top step that it was ready, not really looking at what he was doing but taking mental note that he was there.

She did not look at what Tommy was doing as she looked past him, noticing from the step what a lovely evening it truly was. The new lawn had taken well this year and was a bright crisp healthy-looking green. The sky was a perfect pastel blue with darker streaks blending in. The Sun was setting, providing a shimmering orange path across the lake that she could just walk along. It looked like she imagined the path to heaven to be —not that this was a path she intended to travel anytime soon. She continued into Grandma's room.

Tommy had come in and finished his supper. He knew that Grandma Two was taking care of Grandma, so he thought he would carry on playing for a little while and wait for his dad, or until he was told to come back in. As he was on his way out of the back door, Jean called from deep inside the house to ask if he had remembered to put his outside shoes back on if he was going back outside.

"Yeah, Grammaw two!" he shouted back over his shoulder.

In truth, he was standing on the top step feeling the decking boards with bare feet, scrunching up his toes and feeling the cool grooved wood beneath them. He dropped to the deck and reached back around the doorframe to grab his runners. As he was putting them on, fastening the Velcro straps, he looked up and was caught off guard by a blinding flash of light.

The light appeared in an instant, illuminating the whole sky, originating from the south on his right-hand side. One second it was there and one second later, it was gone. The setting Sun reflecting off the lake had shone in his face at one point, so he shook it off and attributed it to something along those lines. Plus, he did not really care what it was; he was going out to play, and it didn't really affect that.

*Mom or Dad should definitely be back by now,* a fleeting thought flashing by told him. He would simply carry on playing until he was told otherwise, and then hopefully play with his dad. Yes, his dad would walk out through the back door any moment now shouting his name and ready to play with him. So, he put aside any worries and ran toward the back fence to grab his baseball. *Get it ready for Dad.* He would throw the ball to his dad as hard as he could and see if he could catch it.

Jean was preparing Grandma's supper and took a glance out of the window as she came back into the kitchen. Tommy was running toward the back fence. He was happy enough.

She was starting to think that Tommy's dad must have gotten sidetracked. It was six o'clock already; normally Steve would call if he was running late, and he was usually back at half past five at the latest. Tommy's mom was always a bit later, as she had to drive up from Selkirk. Steve was normally somewhere local unless he had a late meeting with a client.

*Oh well. They are adults,* she thought. She would continue with her charge and assist Grandma with supper regardless. Working people could often get wrapped up in their busy lives.

She would give it a little longer, get Grandma settled, and then maybe give Steve a call just to check that everything was okay. She did not like to be nosey or cause a kerfuffle if she could help it. She took Rose's supper from the counter and headed off down the hall toward her ground-floor bedroom.

Rose was sitting up in her day chair looking out of the window toward the lake, watching Tommy play.

"Lovely day," Rose said cheerfully as Jean walked in.

*Must be a good day for Rose,* Jean thought. "Yes, Rose, it is a wonderful evening again tonight. I have your pasta here, Rose."

"Oh, lovely," Rose replied with a sweet, innocent, yet vacant smile.

Jean was sixty herself, but she was a strong and healthy woman, coming from the background that she did. She had worked in and even managed care homes for the elderly all of her working life, all over Eastern Canada. She was the clear pick of the bunch when Tommy's mom had been interviewing for the position.

Jean was almost done with Rose. She only needed to clean up from supper and lastly get her ready for bed, then it was onto Tommy. She did not mind the work; to her it felt like caring for her own family rather than being just a job. She checked on Tommy once more, glancing through the window. Tommy was standing down at the bottom of the yard looking at the fence, holding a ball.

She spotted a flash of bright light illuminating the whole of the sky above Tommy. "What on Earth was that?" She leaned toward the window and looked up. The sky was slowly darkening, bleeding orange patterns and reddening the clouds. Rain did not look even remotely likely.

*That was peculiar. Oh well—everything looks okay now.* Tommy looked okay, so she would finish off with Rose and then get him ready for bed. She smiled to herself and shook her head gently. He was such a cute, funny child; he did make her laugh. What was he up to, staring at the fence like that? A boy his age would rarely stand still for so long.

She gave Rose's face a wipe with a warm damp towel and picked up the tray. "Enjoy that, Rose?"

"Yah!" Rose replied with another completely vacant stare. Jean took the tray into the kitchen, setting it on the side near the window and filling the sink with hot water ready to clean up. She looked out the window again. Tommy was there, still standing in the same spot looking at the fence. *What is he doing?*

An air of concern for the stationary youngster entered her mind.

She thought again about his parents. It was most unusual that neither of them had called.

Tommy would normally like to play with his dad for a while before bed, but he wouldn't get a chance at this rate; it was already twenty after six. His dad would normally put him to bed and his parents would take turns, alternating days to read Tommy a story, then he would be told to close his eyes at seven o'clock.

Jean walked back toward Rose's room, switching on Rose's TV and proceeding to prepare her bed clothes. If she could just finish off with Rose fairly quickly, she could go and check on Tommy. Rose started muttering something to herself whilst staring out of the window. Jean did not ask what Rose said, purely because she was busy around the bedroom and starting to worry about why this evening was beginning to feel very strangely worrying.

The volume on the TV was quite low in the background. The news was on. Jean could not pay it much mind; it was simply on for light background noise more than anything.

Jean fetched Rose's nightclothes from the closet and hung them on the closet door, ready for the next stage.

Jean took Rose up, getting herself underneath Rose's right arm and supporting her around the waist. Carefully walking her toward the wet room at the corner of her bedroom, as she passed the TV on the wall Jean noticed that there was a large yellow warning type of banner scrolling across the bottom of the screen. A black-and-yellow message scrolled along the banner:

BREAKING NEWS! PUBLIC URGED TO STAY INDOORS!

The anchors were saying something about not leaving the house under any circumstances and to remain indoors where you were.

"Oh no, what now?" Jean said.

Rose muttered back in confused reply, "Oh, sorry, was that me?"

"No, not you, dear." Jean laughed, easing Rose into the shower seat and putting the water on, checking that the temperature coming through the handset was where it should be.

She gave Rose a quicker wash tonight, eager to put rest to some of her concerns. Jean eased Rose up and dried her off, all the time thinking, *I wonder if this is something to do with why Steve and Alice were not home yet.* Then she walked Rose back into the bedroom and slipped her into her nightclothes.

Rose was now sitting on the bed, staring out of the window. Rose loved the outdoors. She would often sit looking at the lake for hours, looking forward to the next time that she would be able to sit out and enjoy the Sun on her face and enjoy the new garden with the beautiful views.

Jean went to the kitchen to make Rose's cocoa, the last job before she would be done with Rose completely for the night. Hopefully, that thing she had seen at the bottom of the news broadcast wasn't too serious, but you never know. She found herself rushing through these last couple of jobs—something she had never done before in her life.

# CHAPTER 10
# TRAPPED

R ose caught Jean completely off guard. She had been busy swimming in her thoughts as she walked back into Rose's bedroom with her cocoa. Rose muttered something as she entered and was becoming rather animated, for her. An expression of panic was etched into her face, and her eyes held a glaring focus that Jean hadn't seen in a long time.

Rose was out of her chair and standing at the window, pointing outside. She was pointing with such determination that her fingertip was pressed against the glass, forming an unnatural shape with her finger that now bowed deeply in the middle. Deep white ridges formed in the folds of her skin at the joints. It was as if Rose did not quite realize, or care, that the glass was even there or notice how much pressure she was applying.

"TOMMY! . . . Tommy's stuck!"

Jean thought that Rose was simply ranting about nothing again and had gotten herself all worked up. "What's that, Rose?" She walked around the bed toward the window, sat the cocoa down on Rose's nightstand, and stood next to Rose at the window.

There was Tommy. He looked fine; he was standing right at

the bottom of the yard, facing the fence. He looked like he was simply playing a game, like how a kid might look if he were playing hide and seek. Granted, there were no other children around to play it with, but who knew what game he was playing from up here. What had panicked her?

"He's only playing a game, Rose."

She continued with what she was doing, double-checking that she had brought the cocoa into the bedroom. There were so many distractions tonight.

"Little boy?" Rose yelled loudly. She was glaring at Tommy.

"What are you going on about, Rose? Tommy's fine."

Jean looked again out of the window, leaning with both hands on the sill, looking closer this time. She pressed her nose against the glass.

Tommy was still standing in that same spot, still facing the back fence. *He does seem to have been in the same spot for a long time for a little boy*, she thought. As Jean stared, looking for any smaller details that she may have missed before, his head was still. He was holding a ball. One foot was on the floor and one leg was behind him, just off the floor as if he were halfway through a step.

The leg and foot that were off the floor were intermittently shaking. Her brow furrowed as she tried her best to focus on that foot. Something in Jean started to feel off as she watched it. It was as if the very words "Oh no!" were realized inside her head and had then started to sink down sharply to her stomach.

Time seemed to slow to a crawl as she continued to stare. Her feet were rooted to the spot for a few more seconds before it suddenly clicked that Rose was right.

His foot jerked once more like a spasm. "OH NO!" she shouted aloud this time. Something was very, very wrong. What was going through her mind—rather selfishly, she thought instantly after it entered her head—was that this had happened, whatever this was, on her watch, and she had never had an incident or a complaint in all her years of working in care.

Tommy was like her own grandson. She could not let anything happen to him; she would rather something happen to her, if it had to happen to anyone. Time slowed as she turned on the balls of her feet. Her eyes held their gaze on Tommy, not wanting to let go, and she ran.

Jean launched herself out of the bedroom, through the kitchen, and out of the back door. Running down the steps in her house slippers like a madwoman, she went as fast as her legs could move. The entire time she shouted as she ran, not even a little out of breath, "Tommy! Tommy, dear, are you okay?"

She sprinted like an athlete across the lawn until it was too late to do anything else.

He had not moved or reacted at all the whole time she ran toward him. His leg had now stopped shaking. She had never seen anything like this. *What condition could this be? It isn't a seizure, surely; he would be on the floor, not standing!*

Whilst she was flying through the air in a sprint, she reached out to grab his arm. She found that as she reached him, her arm instantly felt dead, even before her fingertips had touched cloth. Pins and needles spread up her arm and then all over. *Why can't I control my arm?* was her last thought. The rushing weight of her body having sprinted in this direction forced her into a sort of fall, slowed yet supported by the air. Not knowing what was happening to her anymore, instinct made her try to turn her head toward Tommy as she leaned forward into the bubble, yet her gaze did not strike him.

She was completely and unwillingly stopped. The air around her took hold of her body, gripping every part of her tighter and tighter as she passed him, falling into the thick air that also gripped Tommy. All movement and thoughts had long ceased. Her arm that had tried desperately in vain to make contact with Tommy's was just half an inch short.

Her body hung lifeless in the air, twisted, her legs facing in the direction she had been running down the yard while her upper body half had turned to try to grab and get a look at Tommy, almost passing him. And there she stayed. It would have looked very strange to someone, should they happen to be standing on the family's back step watching all of this.

Jean and Tommy were both statues now, trapped for who knew how long at the bottom of the yard, cut off from the rest of Canada. Houses on the other side of the street were fine, unaware of what was happening in Tommy's yard. Tommy was still smiling. Jean was a little stranger to look at; her face was half turned, mouth wide open, jaw slanted from the rest of her head, looking back toward Tommy but not quite able to make the full turn. A terrified and yet terrifying look was etched onto her face—she was not smiling like Tommy. Her eyes were wide as fog lamps.

Rose had watched the events in the garden unfold from her window, but after a very brief time, she forgot why Jean had gone outside. The lady that had run out of the house and down the yard was now hanging in the air next to the little boy. It looked like they were playing a game. She got bored and turned away, steadying herself on the dresser next to her bed. Rose had been an incredibly astute woman five years ago. She was distantly satisfied that her son had done very well for himself and his family, taking what he could from her during his adolescent years.

It was now that she found that her trails of thought had grown shorter. She tired easily and got annoyed with herself for not being able to remember what she had just been thinking about. It was like she would get a thought, almost say something that was relevant, and then that thought would get buried in a fog that instantly descended on her, taking that thought trail up into it.

There was cocoa just sitting there. She couldn't let that go cold, could she? *Can't waste good cocoa.* It was at the temperature she liked, too, just starting to cool. If she drank it quickly, it would not go to waste. She slurped away the delicious thick cocoa until every drop was gone. "Mmm," she said, licking her lips and wiping her chin with the back of her hand.

She sat back down in her chair. The TV was on. It was the news; she could tell by all the talking that was going on. A reporter's voice was distinct, quick, and to the point, though the picture was too fuzzy for her aging eyes to see what was going on. Still, she enjoyed the sound and the moving images for company.

Rose heard the anchor saying something about an emergency . . . a section of Manitoba. "What did he say?" . . . Everyone . . . indoors . . . police. She struggled to keep up with what they were saying and started to fade out from it. She needed the toilet now. She paused. What *do I normally do in this situation? There is something . . . no, someone!* The lady that normally helped her was not in the room like she normally was. She looked at the TV again and a warm feeling spread out between her thighs, out and down into the seat of her chair. She relaxed, feeling no more panic, and continued to look at the TV set.

"Television set," she said aloud. *That's what we used to call them. you had to push them around, big cabinets of wood and glass, but still a technology that was way ahead of its time. Not like this one, that thin-as-a-piece-of-square slate fixed to the wall taking up no space at all. No wonder I can't see it.*

*The chair is wet—nightgown's wet. Where's Jean? And little Stevie—Big Stevie? He's big Stevie now. Where did that time go? I'm tired, so tired. I was a teacher. A good teacher.*

Forty-five minutes after Jean's thoughts had ended, Tommy's dad, Steve, pulled up onto their front driveway. He pulled in and braked so sharply that the car skidded and the front of it came to a stop in the flowerbeds. Petals and gravel were sprayed everywhere.

*The traffic!* Because of the event unfolding that had been on the radio all evening, everything was complete chaos across Southern Manitoba. Luckily, this afternoon he had been much further north surveying some run-down commercial property in Arborg and needed to head south to reach to his family. But people from all over the north had had the same idea, also racing to get home to their loved ones. Even the backstreet territory roads that were usually quiet had been difficult to navigate.

His recently waxed black Audi gleamed in the dying Sun's embers. The penultimate red rays peered through the gaps between the houses and the trees, collected by the hood of his shiny car.

He leaped from his car in a hurry, leaving the door wide open and the engine still running as he bounded up the front porch steps. House key in hand at just the right height and angle to slip straight into the top lock, he set a new record for fastest entry into a house ever. "Tommy! Jean! Where are you?" Nothing. He ran into his mom's bedroom. "Mom!" She was sitting in her chair dozing. A smile crossed her face as she heard him and opened her eyes.

"Stevie!" she gleefully greeted her son.

"Mom . . . where's Tommy?"

She pointed toward her window, then her eyes moved back to the TV.

He ran around the bed to the window and looked out over the backyard. Tommy was standing next to Jean, who was turning to touch his arm. It looked like they were fine, and playing a game together. "Thank God," he sighed, looking down at the floor, relieved that they were safe. He knew they would be with Jean watching over them.

He walked through the kitchen and out through the open back door. "Jean, I'm so sorry. I couldn't call you. I couldn't get through at all; the phone lines are a mess. Is everything okay here? It's been on the news all evening, something very weird . . ."

*That's strange.* It suddenly clicked in his mind that of all the time that he had been walking toward them, jibber-jabbering, neither of them had reacted at all or even acknowledged that he was there. The radio had said something about people being trapped inside this *thing,* that they were somehow frozen. Couldn't be—not his boy, not with Jean here. The fear started to build.

Tommy was standing perfectly still, looking toward the back fence, and Jean looked like she was floating strangely in the air. Now he saw her up close, it was not a pretty sight. He was still praying that it was some sort of a strange game and what he had heard on the news was not what he was seeing in his own garden with his son. His stomach started to ache—he knew.

"Tommy?" No answer.

Even seeing them, walking toward them, it still did not register that this was it. Not his boy, so innocent, so sweet and full of life. Why would this strange event have chosen him?

"Oh God, no!" Steve stopped a few feet away from Tommy, dropping to his knees. His palm moved across his mouth; that reaction did not take any thought to produce.

The radio had explained that there was an area that had cut off half of Winnipeg and ran all the way up to Lake Winnipeg, which was right outside their yard. It was currently being investigated, although they had openly admitted that this was so far unexplainable. It had rendered people trapped inside the area, leaving vehicles paused in the streets. And until they could figure out what it was or why it had happened, citizens were not to go out under any circumstance.

The radio also said that under no circumstances should you approach anyone that appeared to have been affected, even family, as you, too, would risk becoming affected, and they did not know what effect being inside the zone was having on those trapped inside. All the authorities, the military, and service sectors were becoming involved in investigating plausible causes of the phenomenon and trying to determine the actual size of the anomaly and possible rescue routes for those stuck inside. As yet, they did not know what had caused it or what it was.

*This is my son, damn it!* He wanted to make sure his boy was okay; he could not just leave him in there stuck like that. He did not care what the radio had said. Who were they to tell him not to try to help his boy?

*Let's think about this. Right now, I'm okay. I'm free. They are not.* So, what was the difference between where he was standing and where they were? He edged forward, still on his knees, making very slow, careful shuffles down the lawn toward Tommy's back. He held his right hand out in front of himself, palm facing Tommy, as if to test the air for whatever was supposed to be there separating him from his son, his left hand stroking the grass as he moved.

He was right behind Tommy now, barely two feet separated them. So far, he felt fine, hadn't felt anything touch his hands that wasn't normal. He stopped and gently he reached out his palm toward Tommy. Tingling pinpricks attacked his hand and quickly started to creep up his arm. It was like he was being electrocuted. He was able to yank it back, staring at his hand. He frowned and looked at Tommy's back. He needed something to extend his reach.

Steve noticed that Tommy's left dungaree strap was slightly slacker than the right. That was perfect. He reached out again, aiming to pull that strap, but he found that as soon as his hand crossed the boundary that pins and needles feeling took over, working its way up his arm and leaving him with no control of his hand at all.

He yanked it back again and stood up, unable to remove his gaze from his young son.

*I wonder what Tommy must be feeling right now.*

His eyes funneled into a concentrating stare. He told himself that he wasn't going to give this up. As he stood there deep in thought, he noticed that the grass in front of him was behaving differently on his side than on Tommy's. On his side, the grass still moved with the breeze. The wind was traveling generally in Tommy's direction. The grass flowed in the direction that the wind blew, and as he looked around himself, he saw that the pattern traveled across the lawn, moving toward Tommy. Then when the movement reached Tommy's invisible prison, it turned sharply in a new line at a right angle, moving across the line of this . . . *boundary thing?* On Tommy's side of the boundary, the grass was perfectly still. When Steve looked left and right, he found that he could easily make out the boundary's borders in the lawn.

Steve marched into the shed, which luckily was just to his left. Inside he saw the rake hanging horizontally on its hooks. "Perfect."

He moved back to his previous kneeling position directly behind Tommy, behind the line of the boy's prison. He reached the rake into . . . whatever was there. It faced a little resistance as it entered the air surrounding Tommy, as if the air was thick as caramel. The rake soon reached Tommy's loose dungaree's strap—it was like playing "hook a duck" at the fairground.

He very slowly and gently pulled on the strap. Tommy started to very slowly fall backward, but not like a normal fall. This was like Tommy was playing statues in a pool, the air cradling his body.

Tommy continued slowly moving back, keeping the same pose. His feet were still rooted in place, and his body stayed almost straight. Steve put up his hand toward Tommy's back as it got closer to him, but not so close that he would lose control of his hands again and mess this up. He very carefully gripped the loose strap as it visibly came out of its prison and started to move around with the air outside. Tommy was so close to him now.

Steve found that he was able to grab even more of Tommy's strap then. A shudder of excitement tingled him—he was doing this! He felt such a rush of love and joy as a strand of Tommy's hair blew with the breeze at this side of the barrier, touching Steve's fingers.

The tips of Steve's fingers went numb. He must have gotten a little excited, a little too close to it. A little more calmly, he pulled more and more of the strap. The top of Tommy's head and the top of his shoulders were coming free. His hair was moving around. Tommy's head was craning back now so that Tommy would be looking directly upward as soon as he came out.

"Come on!" Steve was excited but also growing frustrated, knowing that he still needed to take his time; all he wanted was to yank his son free. He still did not know what effect this thing would have on his boy. He hoped that he was doing the right thing, but there was no way he couldn't continue.

His heart was thud-thudding, but still he took his time; he did not want to make a wrong move. He was scared, more so now than he could ever remember being in his whole life.

Tommy's head edged backward toward Steve. The thick air he had been trapped in, supporting him, was now releasing him to his dad. The anticipation that he was going to save his boy was almost at a climax. Steve started to cry. He couldn't remember the last time he'd cried!

Tommy's head came back to life as his face came free of the barrier. Steve supported the weight of his head that was reanimated before the rest of his body and brought it to rest on his lap.

Tommy took a very deep breath. It was exactly like the times he had been playing a game with his dad at the pool, timing how long he could hold his breath underwater for, and then he would breach the surface and gasp. Only now he did not know why he was gasping, or why he was lying on his dad's lap in the garden. Steve carefully shuffled backwards on the lawn so that Tommy's legs were completely free of the boundary.

Tommy looked up at the sky for a second, not saying a word at first. It was as if he did not know—for a change—what to say.

His dad squeezed him tightly, laughing and crying at the same time.

Tommy looked up confused but enjoyed the love that he could feel from his dad. It was the first time that he could recall seeing tears rolling down his dad's cheeks. Tommy looked up at him, trying to gather his thoughts and work out where he was before he said anything.

"Hi, Dad. I was waiting for you."

His dad laughed in relief, which again quickly converted into full-on crying.

"What's wrong, Dad?"

"Nothing, son, I'm sorry. I'm just so happy that you're okay." He wrapped Tommy in the tightest hug he had ever given him before. "Let me see if I can help Grandma Two, okay?"

Tommy nodded. He watched as his dad set him down on the lawn and then grabbed the rake from the grass. His dad reached the rake in toward Jean's apron strings. It missed the first time. He leaned in closer, both hands supporting the rake. His dad flinched as his face got too close to whatever his dad was trying to pull Jean out of.

Tommy did not really follow what was wrong. His dad was reaching a rake through the air when it looked like he could walk up to Grandma Two and simply collect her.

There must be something there, he thought, or else his dad would surely get closer. His dad tried in vain, groaning in frustration, but Grandma Two looked to be just out of range from the reach of the rake. His dad was holding the very end of the rake, but the rake's head would very slowly fall in the air right before touching Grandma Two. His dad then quickly recoiled back, falling backward onto his behind on the lawn.

Tommy watched in silence, not budging. He had the feeling that he should not disturb his dad right now. Something was really wrong here. His dad reached into his pocket for his cell phone, dialed a short number, and then yelled, "Damn it!" at his phone before hanging up.

Steve had tried 911 but it was engaged. He shouted at his phone, then tried 112. There was something this time, at least—not just the drab engaged tone but an automated female voice reading a clearly scripted response. "Thank you for calling the Royal Canadian Mounted Police. Due to extreme circumstances, we cannot take your call right now. Please try again later and keep yourself and your family indoors at this time. Thank you for your patience."

He tried calling his wife's phone. "The number that you are calling is currently not available . . ." He pressed the End Call button.

Steve realized that she would have been heading back from Selkirk, and according to the news on his way home, and what was evident in real life in front of him in his yard, whatever was going on here seemed to be centralized around Selkirk or Winnipeg. They lived on the outskirts of whatever this was, and she would have been stuck right in the thick of it.

He stomped over to the shed again, Tommy still silently watching him. He came out with a tall can of spray paint. They were the tall cans used in surveying and construction for marking lines on the ground. He walked back over toward Jean and sprayed a line right across the lawn. He looked back at Tommy with a stern look and said, "Son, do not come near this line. Do you understand?"

Tommy nodded.

Steve walked back to the start of his line on the left-hand side of their yard and sprayed another two feet apart from the first that ran parallel to it all the way across the yard.

"This line—you don't come near this line now, okay?"

Tommy nodded again but still was not saying a lot. Tommy's knowledge of the world was mostly made up of the backyard of their house, and school, which luckily had been closed today for teacher training. His dad scooped him up and carried him toward the house.

Then his dad said, "Sorry, Jean, I'll try again in a moment," as they walked away from her.

Tommy watched from his dad's shoulder as they walked away from Grandma Two, unable to stop staring at her. It was scary—she was still there, alone, twisted in the air. Her eyes and mouth were wide open. Tommy did not have the words to describe what he could see, so he clamped his eyes shut, unable to look at her anymore, until they were safely inside the house. Then he spoke.

"What's wrong with Grandma Two, Dad?"

"I'm not a hundred percent sure, son. Something big has happened today and nobody knows what it is yet. But we'll try and help her just as soon as we can. I want to make sure you're okay for now, then we'll try again."

"Where's Mommy?"

"I'm sorry, son, Mommy's not home yet. She'll be fine. Don't worry. She wouldn't want to miss seeing you."

He didn't know if that was the truth, but he hoped it was.

# CHAPTER 11
# PRIME

A mber and Daniel were standing—and feeling quite vulnerable—in the middle of a stage. The place was a sort of auditorium, or what Daniel would say reminded him of the "lecture theater" at his school. There were rows of tiered seating going up and out in front of them as high as the eye could see before the pyramid-shaped roof finished. Amber and Daniel faced the seats, which were quickly filling up with more gray-faced robe-wearing people.

The old man that had brought them here stood next to them. He silently watched the people arriving while the erotic gladiator waited patiently just behind the three. The gladiator grimaced as Daniel turned to look around and locked eyes with him. He did not frighten Daniel, but that stick certainly did. He could not help but think that the glowing end looked like it could pack even more of a kick than that invisible cell door did. He was in no rush to feel that again. Who knew what else that stick could do? Daniel was also still thinking that he reeeaaally could do with that Americano.

The arriving audience—men and women, old and young—entered the theater from black doorways at various levels at the ends of the rows of seats. All wore the same dark-gray hooded robe as the old man accompanying them.

The lighting on the stage was bright and aimed right at them. It had been dull in the cell area, so now Daniel found himself squinting while his eyes adjusted to the harsh light. This made seeing the people arriving higher up than the first few rows difficult.

Daniel, as his eyes relaxed and he could see further up, noticed something. Everyone here had gray skin. He turned to properly look at the old man and he, too, had gray skin. It was not like his own skin but paler; no, all these people here were as gray as a cinder block.

"What do we do?" Daniel whispered to the old man.

"Wait," the man quietly snapped, the single word coming out more in a breath than as words. The old man displayed not a drip of readable emotion.

As the auditorium filled, the temperature rose along with the number of bodies. The gray-skinned people were taking their seats, and heads bobbed left and then right as the audience greeted each other and sat down. Then they stared at Amber and Daniel, and then they spoke to each other some more.

Amber felt uneasy. She did not know where to put herself or her hands, first holding her left in her right down by her waist, then folding her arms, then holding her hands behind her back. She felt that she and Daniel were stuck, standing there waiting for God knows what while being gawked at and whispered about. It reminded her of school and all the snide bully kids that would talk behind your back, feeling good about themselves whilst belittling you.

New arrivals to the room started to wane, and gaps in the seating were gradually filled. The auditorium was at capacity aside from one lonesome chair that stood apart from the rest, standing slightly proud centrally in Amber's view of the tiers from center stage.

Everyone in the theater suddenly stood up and the room fell

completely silent. From the right-hand side of the room a man entered, walking across the row around halfway up. He was also stocky and dressed like the angry-looking gladiator that had escorted them from the cells. Another man came behind him. This one was an older gentleman dressed in a long gray hooded robe with a red tabard covering his front and back. The tabard sported golden emblems; the detailing looked like a bright larger object with smaller golden circles in front of it. He walked gracefully with his hands clasped together, his fingers locked just below and following the lines of his belly. Behind him, another stocky gladiator man entered from the black doorway. Both of this man's escorts carried the electrified pilums.

This important-looking man slowly sauntered along the row, not looking up or around at the bowing faces as he passed them, to the elaborate ornate chair decorated with golden patterns on the hand-carved head and armrests.

The man took his seat and was flanked on either shoulder by the bodyguards that took spots right behind him. He lifted his hand and then slowly lowered it, a signal which made everyone around him take their seat again. The room was silent. Everyone was seated and the lights aimed at the stage softened, whilst the general lighting along the tiers dimmed to almost complete darkness.

Amber and Daniel stared nervously from the stage at the man and the silent gawking crowd, anticipating an explanation as to what they were doing here. Neither Amber nor Daniel wanted to be the first to interrupt the peculiar foreign show that was being played out for them in the seating area rather than on the stage.

The man cleared his throat and began to speak.

"Greetings to you, Amber and Daniel of Earth." Then he paused.

"Of Earth?" Amber said, looking at Daniel with wide worried eyes. Daniel curved his bottom lip downward at the edges, indicating that he did not know what was going on either. This was all starting to get stupid now. Had the government taken them to some weird test facility? Were they being tested on? Was this some weird TV show? It definitely felt more like some bizarre experiment than anything else. She aimed questioning eyes toward the speaking man that thought he was important or something.

"Sorry, why did you say, 'of Earth'?" she asked him. Politeness had given way to sternness now.

"Of Earth, yes. From Earth in the early twenty-first century, are you not?" His head tilted to one side and his eyes blinked as if he was puzzled by her confusion.

"Yes, but I assumed I was still on the Earth. Are you saying we're not on the Earth?"

"No, you are not," he snapped. Composing himself again, he said, "I was about to welcome you to our world on which you now stand. We are very well aware of your Earth and find it . . . interesting that you have been brought here to us. You were, for reasons yet to be discovered, were selected for transportation by our spheres, and they sent you here to us."

Amber thought that the man's accent sounded as though he could have been one of the royal family. He spoke with a very eloquent-sounding British accent, accentuating certain parts of the words he spoke, such as rolling his R's.

"Spheres?" Daniel muttered under his breath. He and Amber looked at each other, pieces of this bizarre puzzle beginning to slot into place as they bumbled along. If they had been selected by these "spheres," that would start to explain some of the weird events that had played out before they were taken, as well as confirming now the fact that the spheres did arrive from space.

The important-looking man continued, "My name is Valdemar, prime director of the Dark Space Union in which you now reside. If you can prove to us that you are indeed civilized people, as we believe you to be, and you do not pose any threat to my people, then you will be treated with dignity and compassion whilst you are here. You will be treated as our esteemed guests.

"Cause any disturbance to my people or our way of life here and you will be taken straight back to your cells, where you will stay indefinitely or until such time as you are moved on to one of the other planets within the union."

Amber felt her stomach tightening. Valdemar's introduction gravely worried her, increasing her fears that she may never see her mom again. *Why did he say we "now reside"? And "treated with dignity," and then mention the word "indefinitely"? He is pretty much confirming it.*

"Mr. Valdemar," Amber said. "Prime Director, I'm sorry—I don't mean any disrespect in interrupting you again, but how long do you mean to keep us here, please? It's just that my mom is disabled—she can't manage on her own without my help. I can't stay away for too long. She needs me."

She asked as respectfully as she could, but while the words sprang forth from her mouth, she had the terrible feeling that they were going to fall on deaf ears. Were they guests here, or were they prisoners?

*Why was I selected? God, why?*

"I will be as honest as I can be with you. At the moment, I have no plans for you to be returned home. You see, the energy that would be spent in starting up the now redundant returns facility and returning you to your space through the black hole would run my planet for a generation. Of all the subjects that the redundant spheres have brought here for us to meet, most of them are kept indefinitely. We have not returned anybody through the black hole in over thirty years.

"To fairly spread the burden of the numbers of guests that have been collected, we disperse a quantity throughout the system so that the other people within the Dark Space can also interact with the arrivals and learn from them. This is not personal or intended to cause you pain, please understand. But we simply cannot go around wasting energy when it could be used for the benefit of our people instead.

"I am sorry for you. The spheres have now been discontinued—not a comfort to you now, of course, but we do not send them out to collect people anymore. We ran out of space for new arrivals. It was simply a project that was used until it no longer served a greater purpose.

"They were used because we did not have the capability to return our people to the Light Space on a mass scale, so it was decided to send the spheres through the black hole to bring people here, from all different parts of the Light Space, for us to converse with. But then the project simply ran its course. It was stored away, and then unexpectedly, you two turned up."

Amber looked at Daniel, and he turned to look back at her. He looked worried, but she could read from his eyes that his worried look meant he wasn't so much worried for himself but more for her.

Her eyes began to fill with tears. Amber's legs felt like jelly as the shock of what was being said hit her. Her legs went from under her, folding at the knees, and she simply ended up on her behind on the stage in a sideways seated position.

Amber had thus far been able to keep her emotions in check, but that was when she had believed it wouldn't be long before they straightened this out and made their way home. Now, this was getting to be too much for her to hold in. She let herself go for a second and tears started to roll down her cheeks.

Daniel stepped toward her, crouched down, and put his arms around her, wrapping her in a hug—that fellow human touch that she most definitely needed right now.

Her tears dampened his light-gray hoodie, leaving dark patches on his shoulder. She held on tightly as he very kindly offered some comfort.

"Don't worry. Don't give them the satisfaction of seeing you upset—we'll figure this out. There's gotta be a way," he whispered into her ear.

"So what? We're just here as part of some redundant experiment? How can they do this to people?" she cried when her sniffles allowed her, not caring how loud she said it, either. She sucked it up and fought back her tears now.

Daniel offered a hand and helped Amber back to her feet.

The whole theater studied them, stunned, as the pale-faced audience noted the reactions of their Earthling guests on the stage. Personal tablets illuminated and darkened all around the dark room, light moving around the theatre like a Mexican wave. Valdemar fidgeted in his seat. There was an uncomfortable shift in the air around the room away from its initial mood of simple wonder.

"I am sorry. I do not take any pleasure in this situation."

Amber, standing up with Daniel's help, looked directly at Valdemar with wet red eyes. Inside she was raging, but she knew that she had to try to keep herself composed. It would not help things at all if she lost her temper with them.

"What did you think was going to happen? Taking us away from our homes, and then telling us that we won't be able to go back? Why were we selected anyway? What's the point of all of this?"

"The spheres that you came into contact with are a method that our people employed to autonomously contact civilizations from outside the realm of our Dark Space. We cannot just leave the system through the black hole in craft; a ship that would carry a planet's population, or even a quarter of it, would never make it through in one piece and stay in the Light Space. It would not even get close enough to the black hole this side without being torn to nuts and bolts. The spheres, which used to be sent out from here, are small enough and fast enough to make it through from this side if aimed at the correct angle and pushed fast enough.

"To make the necessary conversions and thrust a person back through the black hole— well, as I say, that energy could run our planet for decades. That person needs to be converted into light and fired through using the exact coordinates that the sphere on that planet emits. It takes much fewer resources to send the spheres or light through rather than a person or starship.

"We abandoned the sphere projects long ago, as we have far too many travelers to hold now. The factory was decommissioned decades ago. For reasons unbeknownst to us, you two have been selected by spheres that were counted among the lost. But now that you are here, we will converse with you and study you. With your permission, of course.

"For almost two hundred years the spheres were sent out to research and make contact with other life. A life that we might meet and converse with so that we can further our knowledge and understanding of what life is like on the other side of the black hole, in the Light Space, and to learn everything that we can from them and about our own past.

"Our people were once from the Light Space like you. You see, due to the turbulent travel through the black hole, we do not even possess records of what our ancestors were like, who we were in the beginning, or precisely who our Creator is."

*"The Creator,"* echoed all around the theater, people speaking the words softly as though in prayer.

Daniel interjected, "Prime Director, please excuse me, but Dark Space? Black holes? Where exactly is your planet, and how far away are we from Earth?"

"Where we are from where you arrived is not as straightforward a question to answer as you may think, without spending a great measure of my time going into detail in a way that you could understand."

*Climb any further up his own ass?* Daniel thought.

"For now, I will very briefly explain what I can to you, but more information about this will be given to you later, at a later stage of your introduction, in a way that will be far easier for you to see and understand.

"Where you stand now is not the same Universe as from

whence you came. You are standing on a planet that lives within 'the Dark Space Union,' an ever-increasing system of planets at the *other* side of a black hole from the Universe with which you are familiar.

"We call our planet Prime. This is the planet that houses the democratic center for the entire system, with two representatives from each planet permanently based here. It was decided to be this way by all planets currently residing within the system. I say 'currently' as we regularly see new planets arrive through the black hole. Although they are not much more than scorched wastelands when they arrive here, they do settle and begin to traverse the system with the other planets until they are repopulated by the residents in the system and put to better use.

"The founding planets have been in this system for just over one hundred million years now. Our Creator chose our planet and the rest of the planets in our system to be allowed safe passage through the black hole and to begin a new life."

"*The Creator,*" murmured again around the room.

"I see," Daniel said, nodding.

It was obvious that the people here were quite religious.

Amber had no time for their religion. She did not care about these people's history or what they believed in. She only cared about getting home. These people were weird. She stayed silent. Daniel seemed to be doing fine, asking the questions that mattered right now. *Best not to antagonize them and risk being here forever.* Maybe if they were well-behaved, they might change their minds?

"So, what do you want from us now?" Daniel asked.

"We would simply like to get to know you, and for you to get to know us. We would like, if you do not mind, to take some simple readings from you. To see how living near a star affects your cells compared to ours, and to hopefully come to understand what our ancestors from the Light Space may have been like. You should be honored that the Creator has chosen you."

*"The Creator."*

"To be the only ones selected from your entire system, selected to be shown things of greater importance than your own troubles! I thank you on behalf of myself and all my people. Please continue your orientation with Volya now."

"But my mom!" Amber shouted, looking up at the director with a desperate plea in her sparkling eyes. "Please!"

She couldn't help it. There must be something in him that she could appeal to, some emotion somewhere deep down, although he didn't seem to exude any aside from a few general courtesies and nice words.

Valdemar had stood, ready to leave, but reluctantly he sat again. It looked as though on some wavelength, he did sympathize with Amber. He raised his left hand with his index finger pointing in the direction of his guests on the stage and moved it in a sweeping motion from left to right in front of himself.

At the rear of the stage behind Amber and Daniel, where before it had been darkness, the dark had been replaced by light, something that began as a small light but opened out into a wider picture. It was like an old television set starting up, illuminating the whole backstage.

In the air hanging immediately behind the pair was a picture displayed on a huge cinema-sized screen. Not a physical screen like at a cinema; this one appeared in the form of a thin sheet of light and pixels, hanging in the air, similar to but larger than Volya's computer display above his hand.

On the screen, patterns and colors swirled around as images started to form within the light. It began with a mixture of pale blues, oranges, and greens swimming around. Gradually the mess settled into a picture. It was grass and sky coming into focus, then a town.

Amber started to cry again, and this time they were more tears of joy at recognizing the town in the picture. Amber recognized the buildings. The image gave her that connection and a warm feeling, a connection back to the home that she so desperately craved.

At the forefront of the picture there was soil, then blades of grass, then beyond that a sidewalk, then a street, and then buildings on either side of it. It was the bank and the hotel. She had not long ago walked down this very street to get to work. *This must be the view from the silver ball at the side of the diner.* It must still have been sitting on the floor where she had touched it.

The sky was different now; rather than sunset, it looked more like sunrise. The Sun was still reflecting orange rays across the sky, but above her was more of a pale-blue morning sky.

Valdemar waited for Amber to compose herself. She wiped her tears on her coat sleeve.

"As you can see, this is where you came from, Amber, and it is still, even at this moment in time, the same as when you left. Correct?"

He smiled at her, trying to comfort her, and he was right. The people in the frame were the same people that she either knew or at least recognized that had been standing there on pause before she had left. They were still halfway through doing whatever they were doing, some half walking with one foot casually off the ground and one on the ground, some midway through a chat or heading into a building, and the cars were still stopped where they were in the street.

"So, your mother, I am certain, will also be in exactly the same position as when you left the Earth. I have no way of knowing what she was doing. I can only see what you see here, but I hope that she will be safe from any harm and have no memory of what is happening around her right now."

Daniel asked, "So, with respect, will my family still be in the same state as this?"

Valdemar waved his hand again and the picture swirled, then settled into a familiar-looking picture for him.

Daniel could see the school playground and his house

between the trees in the background. There was still nobody within sight of the sphere.

It was daytime now, but there were no people in view at all. Everything around it was as quiet and as still as when Daniel left. Daniel felt a little emotional himself but didn't cry. He thought about his mum, dad, and sister. He missed them dearly, a feeling that spurred a determination in him that he was going to try and figure this out. He hadn't given up hope of getting home and freeing his family yet, not by a long shot.

Both felt slightly more relieved. At least for now, anyway, they could rest in the knowledge that their loved ones would be safe. But how long would they be safe like that? This was still very much unknown to them. Someday their towns may come back to life, and what then? Amber's mum would be right back to needing her care again.

Daniel asked, sounding a little confused but wanting a bit more information, "So can you freeze time, then? It's just that when I left, it was the middle of the night, but now it's daylight. If all the people around the spheres are frozen, what happens with the rest of the Earth?"

"No, time isn't frozen as such," replied Valdemar. "Not exactly. Once they land, the spheres send out a protective field, slowing down time around itself, to protect them from prying eyes but also to be able to make uninterrupted connections to their selected host. What you are seeing now is time still moving but at an incredibly slowed down rate.

"To someone around you, if they were aware of it, you would have been barely visible to them, as you would have been moving incredibly fast. But time has slowed down so much in their space that they would not even be aware of you. Their bodies and their thoughts would have slowed, to the point of practically being paused where they were at that moment."

"Ahhh, okay," Amber said, thinking again about the police officers and Barry Smith. She couldn't help but force a smile at that. She hoped that they hadn't seen what she had done, or rather that they hadn't seen that it was her that had done it.

"And this affects the whole Earth?" Amber asked.

"Well, no. There is a limited range in which the spheres operate and project this field around themselves. So, within that limited radius, time would move at the rate that you see here, but outside of that field things will still be moving along as they normally would."

Valdemar stood, and the image of the Earth faded back to black. Amber went quiet again, feeling her connection to her home being cut with the fading of the screen. It looked as though this initial introduction was over. All the other pale faces in the auditorium also stood but didn't move; they only bowed their heads as Valdemar moved slowly past them along the row to the doorway. The burly guards escorted him again, one in front and one behind. He approached the black doorway and was gone.

# CHAPTER 12
# NEW HOME

The pale-faced audience cleared out through the strange black doorways perched at each end of each row, leaving Amber, Daniel, the guide called Volya, and their electrifying-weapon-carrying escort, so far lovingly nicknamed Karen, onstage. Amber and Daniel stood on the spot, silent and confused, wondering what was going to happen to them amongst a million other unanswered questions racing loops through their aching minds.

Amber was left deeply frustrated, so much so that her mouth had a sour taste and her blood felt toxic. What really made her angry was that even after all of that talk, all she wanted to know was simple—in her eyes, anyway. Where were they? Why had they been taken? And when would they ever be allowed home? Okay, so they had been told that going home was highly unlikely. With regards to where they were and why they were taken, all she had been given was a story that made her want to switch off, and a dull headache. She didn't care about all of their troubles and black holes. She never asked to be taken.

*Let's hope Volya gives more away in this "continuing the orientation" crap, she* thought.

The lights around the auditorium came back up to full brightness, highlighting all of the empty seats. Volya said, "Please follow me," and started walking away from them toward the doorway at the back of the stage through which they had entered. Armed Karen sprang to life and took position behind them all, happy to prod someone if needed.

Volya marched through the black empty doorway, disappearing before them. Amber was next in line, stopping shortly before the doorway when he vanished. She looked around nervously at Daniel, took note of Karen, then closed her eyes, and stepped into the black again. Daniel followed. It was such a strange mode of transport; he was aware that he himself had vanished from where he was. It was all so instant, a new scene coming into view and wrapping around his vision as the blackness peeled away the auditorium, a new scene replacing it sharply.

The four of them were now outdoors. Daniel looked around with wonder, in awe that he was standing on a different planet!

*What the scientists back on Earth would give to swap places with me now.*

Daniel didn't feel quite as upset about the situation as Amber was. He didn't think so, anyway; he was more curious, more interested in science and the differing theories of where humans had come from and where we might end up. And of course, UFOs—or UAPs, which seemed to be the latest trendy nomenclature. He understood Amber's anxiety, though. If her mum was disabled and Amber cared for her, then of course she would want to get back, and as quickly as possible.

Yes, he wanted to make sure that his mom, dad, and sister were alright and make it home eventually, but for now they were safe, from what he understood of it, and he took it that eventually they would be returned to their normal state. He couldn't see the sphere staying there forever, holding a major part of England hostage like that. Maybe the military or the scientists back on Earth would find a way to disable it.

He would still try to find a way to get them both home, but for now . . .

*Let's just see what we have here while we are here.*

The pair looked around the view that was presented in front of them. The temperature was warm, and there was not much of a breeze either. The sky was black. It was not that it was dark, not like a nighttime sky back at home; no, this was somehow different. In the sky, there were no clouds, Sun, moon, or stars. The sky was like a deep black velvet veil, and it seemed to come all the way down from space, down to almost ground level. Daniel could see across the whole city, which was being illuminated from just above the street level by globes. *Are they . . .?* He stared at the city. *Yes, they are—they're hovering in the sky, right above the buildings, lining the streets like a strange floating kind of streetlamp.*

The only visible object in the heavens, if you looked carefully, was the barely visible slim crescent of another planet not too far away, a little like the distance from the Earth to the Moon when the Moon sometimes appeared closer than usual except it was very dark.

They were standing on a stone walkway, the city over to their right, separated by a waist-high wall. On their left was the smooth rocky wall of a mountain that sprawled high up for what looked like miles, merging into the darkness of the black sky.

As they walked to the small wall, the city lay below them. It was around a hundred foot drop down to ground level, and then the city started. Beyond the city it was dark; as the street-lamps illuminating it stopped, the edges of the city blended away into the blackness, but it looked like it could be country-side and mountains beyond the city. You just couldn't tell. *Maybe you might see it in the daytime,* Daniel thought.

He checked on Amber, having gotten carried away there. Volya and Karen were standing off to the side, allowing their "guests"—*prisoners?*—some time to take in the view. Daniel stepped closer to Amber. "Are you okay?"

"Not really, no," she answered, looking blankly at the sprawling lights of the city below. "I just want to go home. I don't care about any of this, these people, space. I don't give a shit."

"I know," he said sympathetically. "Run along with it for now. I can't help feeling that there must still be a way to get home. I don't want to get your hopes up—please don't. But I have a gut feeling, and I'll do everything I can to make sure that you're okay."

"Thank you, Daniel. You're a nice young man. How old are you, by the way? Do you mind me asking?"

"No, of course not. I'm seventeen. Why?"

"Just curious. I feel like I know you already, but I realized I don't actually know you at all. I'm nineteen. I wondered which of us was the eldest. You look older, probably because you're taller than me, but you do have a wise head on those shoulders, don't you?"

"Thanks. You're the same age as my sister."

"Oh, right. I'd love to meet her someday. Maybe we might have things in common."

"Actually, you're just like her. You remind me of her a lot."

They stood, quietly pondering for a moment as they rested their hands on the wall, looking out over the city. Daniel didn't think that the alien city quite looked how he imagined an alien city might look. It wasn't like the movies, filled with skyscrapers and fluorescent neon lights and video walls all over the place. This was really quite understated and simple.

Closest to them, below at the foot of the mountain, it looked like a strip of farmland. There were simple barns and a house with a glass roof and a few dozen grazing animals. They were about cow-sized, but he couldn't tell exactly what they were. *It's just like Earth, really*, he thought.

After the farm, the city started. First roads, then houses. The houses were very modest. Small stone-built cottages with glass pyramid-like roofs had all been built in neatly laid out blocks.

Floating above each road were rows of these globes of light. They *kind of look like our streetlamps.* They were dark on top but shining beneath them was light—very strong light. It was strange; the sky above was black, but the streets at ground level looked as bright as high noon.

Daniel managed to put two and two together to realize that the light and possibly heat from these balls were placed just so above the pyramid roofs that it would perfectly illuminate and heat the inside of the homes beneath. A curious but logical type of repurposed energy.

In the distance, toward the back of the city grid, was an ominous huge building. It was different to anything else in view, black and shiny like onyx. It was a dystopian movie-styled pyramid that towered over the small, understated buildings of the city around it.

The internal lights of the many floors inside the pyramid confirmed that this was monstrously huge.

At each ground corner of the pyramid's compound were tall columns, each with light fixtures at the top aiming bright white light back down, highlighting the base of the building. The lights reflected off the pyramid's surface, obviously wanting to highlight the building's importance.

"Mr. Volya," Daniel asked as he looked over the city. "Is it nighttime here?"

"No, this is our daytime, Daniel."

"Mad!" Daniel said in wonder, not taking his eyes off the city. "Is the sky dark because you're in the Dark Space, yeah?" His mind began linking all of the information that they had been told with what they could now see.

"Indeed, Daniel. With no stars, our space is in darkness. Aside from the small amount of light that the rear of the black hole provides."

"Mr. Volya," Amber chimed in. "That big building over

there—what's that for?"

"That is the Director and his delegates' palace. You just came from there."

Now, both Daniel and Amber were puzzled. It must have been a mile away and yet they had arrived here from there in an instant.

Daniel looked over at the black doorway that they had entered from, then inquisitively looked at Volya.

"The doorways that we use," Volya realized. "Of course, I just realized that you may not be used to those. They take you to any location on the planet that you need to go. Our wrist implants, which you might have already noticed, tell the doorway where its entrant needs to be, and it links to the one that you wish to arrive at. Quite simple technology, really," he explained, looking immensely proud of himself.

Daniel noticed cars in the city down below. They were navigating the roads of the city streets at precisely the same distance away from each other, almost as though connected by an invisible tow rope or in a train. And they didn't appear to be on wheels; they were hovering, moving slowly up and down the avenues just off the ground.

"Okay," Volya said, returning to business. "Please follow me. It is time to leave Mount Shasta for now and move on."

Karen moved again to guide them from behind Daniel as Volya walked ahead with Amber. Daniel watched them both disappear ahead of him through the black doorway, and he followed, still looking around, with Karen close behind.

As they appeared at the other side of the doorway to the next place, they were now standing in a room that would fit perfectly on a Christmas card, a warm, cozy, fire-lit living room.

Roaring away in the middle of the square room was a fire set in a large round stone fire pit, crackling and comforting. Above the fire pit was the center of the glass pyramid ceiling.

*This is one of those modest-looking houses we saw from above,* Daniel thought.

Sinking and then disappearing beneath the floor in a circular sweeping motion around and down beneath the central fire pit were ornate metal steps complete with beautiful dark metal handrails. Patterns of trees were formed in metal within the design, complete with metal trunks, branches, and leaves holding up the handrail.

The interiors of all the rooms that they had seen so far were all very neatly and efficiently built, almost old-fashioned. A little cold and colorless in style, but then the additions made them very cozy. Around the fire pit was a circular stone-built sofa. It had a gap for them to walk through and draped over the sofa were blankets of furs, making it look a little more homely.

"Please excuse us now," Volya said to Karen, who looked sharply down at the floor, then turned and disappeared back through the doorway.

The gray-faced guide motioned for them to take a seat. He cut inside the gap at six o'clock and walked around the fire to the noon position and sat. Daniel and Amber followed him through the gap and took seats at eleven and one o'clock respectively on either side of their guide. The fire was both warming and heartening. It helped to ease their nerves a little as they all sat silently, admiring the fire cracking away. It reminded Amber and Daniel of home.

The room was silent for a few moments before anyone started speaking again. Volya looked at them both in turn, smiling to himself, happy that he could sense the contentment that his fire provided his rattled guests. He knew they were rattled, and he could understand why. He just had to do his best to settle them down and talk to them.

Amber was perched on the edge of the sofa with her eyes closed as if meditating. She was still trying to calm herself. *Some simple pleasures are the same throughout the Universe, or wherever the hell we are!* she thought to herself.

Volya said, "You must be getting hungry again. I will order some food for us." He flicked open his hand, bringing up his display. He made some motions on it and then closed it back down.

Daniel said, "I suppose you have computers that print the food instantly for you or something, don't you?"

"No." He gave Daniel such an odd look. "Print food? What kind of taste by the Creator would that have? No, Daniel, we have cooks. Each person here is assigned a path to follow throughout their life based on certain parameters of their mental capabilities. Some might become cooks, politicians, security, military, vehicle engineers, construction engineers, and so on. The food that you had in your holding cell was not 'instant,' if that is where the confusion started. No, all food is freshly prepared, based on what information we have about you, then sealed into a time containment panel behind the wall panels from internal corridors. As soon as you press to request food, the food is released as fresh as when it was prepared."

"Oh, I see." And as the three sat watching the fire some more, a trolley came into the room through the black doorway followed by a short skinny, gray-faced man pushing it. He set it just inside the circular seating area and started to remove the silver cloches covering the food. There were three stone plates with matching chalices. The man passed one set to each of them. He did not say a word but took a nervous look at Amber and Daniel with inquiring eyes.

The chalices were filled with ice-cold orange juice and the plates held a toasted cheese sandwich, next to which were broccoli florets and some cherry tomatoes.

Amber was instantly reminded of Al's place with the food that they had eaten so far. It was so good—unexpectedly so for an alien world. Both wolfed it down without even a second thought. They were starving and thirsty.

Volya waited until they were almost finished eating to begin his more detailed orientation.

"As you may have heard, my name is Volya." As Amber and Daniel looked over, his face had changed. He no longer appeared to be the strict, sour-faced old man they had seen at first glance. He seemed softer, his eyes were friendlier, and he smiled now.

"It is my role to be your guide whilst you are here. I can understand that this must all be distressing for you. Please believe me, I do understand. We have many thousands of guests like yourselves that have arrived here through the spheres. The reason that you two are so interesting to us, and why you are not locked up like the others, is that Earth is an incredibly special place to us. It is the only world which we have a keen interest in, and the only one which we have not yet had guests arrive from.

"The spheres only normally bring us one person, as they are programmed to separate once they enter the Light Space Universe. They were launched from here in pairs, but they should then head to opposite sides of the Universe once clear of the black hole to spread out and bring back different species for us. But this time, for some reason, they clung to each other, and both headed for Earth. We do not know why this happened. Maybe the Creator saw fit to bring you two here to us."

"But I still don't get why they chose us," Amber said.

"And how and why are you, and now us, inside a black hole?" Daniel asked.

"That is going to be a long story, my young friends. By the way, I am sorry, I should have said earlier, if you need to relieve yourselves, the toilet facilities are in a room beneath the fire." He motioned toward the round fireplace in the center of the room. "That staircase goes down to the facilities which should be ample for your needs."

Daniel decided to try it out. "Sorry, guys, been holding it in for a while now."

A neatly tiled beige-colored open-plan toilet and wet room area opened up to Daniel as he walked around the corner at the bottom of the staircase. There were four stone boxes at the far end, a little like the metal ones in the cells. These ones were flat to the floor rather than just off it and fixed to the wall.

It was a good thing they hadn't come down together. Privacy did not seem a high priority here; there were no cubicles or partitions between the toilets. He headed for the furthest one and unzipped his zipper. They were almost the same shape as Earth toilet bowls on the top of the stone cubes, these were just chunkier and more solid looking.

He couldn't tell what was inside; instead of water when you looked down, it was just darkness. It was a similar blackness to the doorways they used. Analysis done; he did his business. The piss entertainingly disappeared as soon as it hit the darkness with no sound of water, or anything for that matter. Thankfully, he only needed the kind of business that did not require any further attention, as he couldn't see any toilet paper around here.

Once he finished spraying into the bowl, he had a good look around the room. Out of the four thrones, two of them had these dark holes below the seat line, like the one he had pissed in, but the other two of them had shallow bowls, water lying in wait, and what looked like multiple small jets inside them pointing up.

He thought about it for a moment. *Why would you need a shallow bowl with jets inside?*

"Ahhhh, got it! Cleaning after number two!" he said, laughing. "I'd better warn Amber."

He took one more look around like someone that had checked into a hotel room, curious as to what facilities he would be spending his summer break in.

Away from the toilet cubes, at the opposite end of the quite large square room in the corner looked like a wet area. There was somewhere to stand, and then protruding from the ceiling were five jets in a dice-like pattern. This was obviously a shower area.

Daniel returned upstairs to continue their discussions with Volya and to warn Amber which cube to sit on first.

# CHAPTER 13
# WHY YOU?

"Well, why you?" Volya continued "Honestly, nobody knows that answer. This is a mystery even to us. The sphere's preprogrammed instructions, as I said, are to separate and then register with one intelligent target before landing. I guess that you two were simply in the right place at the right time—or rather the wrong place, wrong time. Why here? Well, my people sent out the spheres to meet with intelligent life from the Light Space. We did this until they were discontinued and no longer launched.

"Our aim was to simply meet with other species, to discuss life on either side of the black hole, and if the subject was happy to, we would take some scans and light samples to compare our cell structure against, say, yours and compare the differences. We were curious as to how it affected our cells living without a star. But we got to a point of being a little overcrowded with visitors, so the entire sphere manufacturing and returns facility were shut down.

"As for the black hole . . . well, I have an animation I can show you that will hopefully explain what we know of our planet's history."

Volya opened up the screen above his hand again and

performed a series of swipes and taps. The fire in the room instantly went out, leaving the room dark. *That was clever!* Daniel thought. Above where the fire had been, a screen appeared floating in the air, similar to the one in the auditorium.

Volya interrupted the start of the show, "Just to let you know, the animation that you are about to watch has had the speed increased to show you everything that our planet went through in a shorter space of time. What you are watching happened over billions of years."

The animation started. At first, a camera was panning through the black emptiness of space. A rotating galaxy came into view, moving across the middle of the screen and settling in the center of the view.

The picture zoomed in closer toward the galaxy, focusing on one of the arms of the spiral galaxy.

It continued to enlarge until it showed a star system. *That looks very similar to our solar system,* Daniel thought. A bright yellow star sat at its center, several planets and moons slowly orbiting around it.

The picture moved toward the star but then panned around to center on a bright blue-and-green planet.

"This is what we believe was our ancestral home, our planet before the black hole," Volya added as the animation continued moving closer in on the planet. As the camera dipped into the atmosphere and down toward the surface, beneath the clouds there were oceans and continents. Then mountains and rivers came into view, fields, and streams. Animals were grazing and people were playing in fields with their children.

The faces of these people were just like those on Earth— different colors, as they should be, and full of life! These were not pale and gray, sad-looking beings as they appeared to be now.

Then things started to change. The people disappeared, the camera pulled away from ground level, and the film showed ice at the caps that was melting, and fast. The seas turned violent, swallowing up more and more of the edges of the land. Water completely took over, then when it had, the water started to bubble and turn to steam. The sky turned from blue to orange.

Then land started to appear again. Just mountaintops at first, but this time the land turned brown and then red, like a scorching desert the globe over. The camera left the surface and moved back up into space. The yellow Sun had darkened, turning reddish, and had started to expand.

Volya narrated, "Things would never be the same again for our people."

Thousands and thousands of ships, huge like biblical arcs, met in space and then sped away from Prime, leaving behind an abandoned burning wasteland. Taking what was left of the stubborn remainders of people safely to the outer planets, they flew out of harm's way of the now out-of-control pulsing red star.

The animation continued playing. The camera pulled further out into space and showed the galaxy again. Another even larger galaxy slowly moved into the frame, creeping through space toward the galaxy that had been focused on, moving silently and rotating. The void between them grew smaller. Closer and closer the galaxies became.

The new galaxy didn't stop. The spiral arms of the two merging galaxies stretched out, reaching for each other, until they touched and locked. Each arm containing billions of clouds of stars and other worlds now melded together, looping over and mixing together like spilled oils on the ocean.

It was clear to see what was going to happen. The galaxies continued pulling and stretching at each other's boundaries and forms, binding and wrapping, twisting around each other in a beautiful spatial light show.

Both galaxies were finally starting to resettle into one new singular form. A new larger, more majestic galaxy had been born and was now complete. The fusion galaxy rotated proudly again, looking accomplished and like it belonged in its new home as if nothing had ever happened.

The camera now zoomed right back into their star system, but the star system had changed; it was closer to the center of the galaxy now, not halfway along one of its arms. Instead, it was balanced on one of the tips. Some planets had been lost to the voids between arms during the merger.

The star at the center of the old system was now huge, bulging red and now darkening in color. On the surface of Prime, which was dangerously close to the star, fires raged across the visibly bone-dry continents. Lava covered many of them now. The skies had also turned a color to match their reddening star.

The stars flamed, reaching edges probed further out into space than ever before. What had been the cold dark outer rim of the system grew brighter and warmer. The outer planets that had long been icy worlds were now feeling tropical warmth that they had never before been touched by. Two smaller planets that had been in the growing Sun's path were long gone, consumed into the Sun's heaving body.

Prime was next in line, lucky so far to have been pushed barely out of harm's reach but waiting like a limp wounded animal within the sights of a slowly approaching predator. Waiting to be put out of its misery, the small planet appeared sad, brown, and hurt, a shadow of its former self. It was being roasted like a chestnut by the star.

All of the other planets in the system were slowly wandering out to the far reaches, pushed out of normal orbits by the changes of the star's demise. Prime was lucky, it had stared into the face of extinction; it was just out of reach of becoming forever a part of the star.

As more time went by the star began to settle, its surface growing calmer. It stopped expanding now. More time went by, and the large red Star began to slowly contract back in on itself.

Prime had been lucky. Aside from being toasted and no longer habitable, it had at least survived.

The Star continued contracting, its color gradually changing as it shrunk. The star grew darker, turning from red to brown. It eventually contracted so small that as it finished burning the last of its fuel, it turned white in the sped-up animation, and white it now stayed. Completely different and tiny compared to its former yellow and then blazing red self.

All of the planets that had been left behind in the now rapidly cooling darkening system had been left stranded out in space by the forces of their changing star. Orbits had changed. The lost worlds drifted apart. Moons had long disbanded, some colliding into their nearby planets.

The lost worlds drifted away into a different space, delving deeper into colder, darker, stranger territory. The formerly proud star system had been completely torn apart.

Then the picture changed, showing the huge *new* galaxy again, the camera zooming closer in toward its center. Even more dramatic galactic headlines were still to be written.

Right at the heart of the new galaxy's core were two black holes. Struggling to coexist like their parent galaxies before them, they were also on an inevitable journey to becoming one.

The two black holes were both vying for their rightful seat at this new galaxy's heart, each of them powerful black monsters made visible by a show of light, debris, and gas, objects that had been sucked dry, planets and stars that had been crushed. Their debris swirled perpetually, decorating their hosts' rims.

Like deep black magnets, they danced around each other as had the galaxies before them. As they tested and tugged on each other's edges, the light and gasses surrounding one black hole were mercilessly pulled out of their orbit, bleeding into the second. Faster and faster they went, spinning in a kind of rotating spatial love dance.

In the end, all that remained, as the action slowed, was one gargantuan black hole seated at its place at the head of table at the center of the supermassive new galaxy.

Close to the new galactic center were a handful of homeless planets and debris, leftovers from the transformation of the newly formed super galaxy, a caravan of rocks without a home or star. These were the worlds from the old star system that the two Earth dwellers had watched, being disbanded and drifting. They were now set on a course that they would never be able to escape from.

They were forming a line, like a trail of wounded warriors. The black beast was hungry, and its plumage was growing in brightness as it feasted on the lost wandering space debris consisting of stars, nebulae, planets, and moons that had strayed too far from their systems.

Volya stepped in now to offer some explanation as the animation paused itself. "For billions of years, all races in the former galaxy knew that these events were inevitable—the Star reaching its end of life, the two galaxies on a collision course, and even that a new supermassive black hole would be formed. We don't have much by way of historical logs now; pretty much everything from the old time was destroyed during our planet's violent travels. We only have some cave drawings and tablet carvings, deep inside the planet, almost near the core. Our ancestors' only way of surviving parts of the past was to bury themselves deep within to keep warm. Records that we have found tell us that our ancient ancestors observed the star nearing the end of its life, as had been predicted in the old times.

"They knew that these events would affect our entire way of life and everything that we knew, but nothing was ever done about the inevitable. Not that there was much that could be done to avoid it, of course, aside from mass evacuation on a galactic-wide scale even further away than we did evacuate. We should have aimed to make new homes earlier and deeper within nearby galaxies, but by the looks of it, our people wished to remain in the home system until the end. Our home planet was left a desolate wasteland while we watched helplessly from nearby.

"Our people scattered out amongst the other planets and moons throughout the old star system that were already colonized by us, and we waited. Arrogance played its part, and it was noted in our ancient paintings that our people would observe the effects of the black hole and live with whatever the Creator decided was next for us. But it affected us far more than they imagined at the time."

He stopped talking and the animation continued to play. It was now focused on the large black hole, bright light and dust circling powerfully and quickly around its edges.

The picture zoomed right in on the black hole's dark face. There were a few very small planets stranded, wandering across its horizon as they headed toward the inevitable journey's end.

Volya interrupted the animation again to give a brief added explanation to the scene and noticed that both Daniel and Amber were glued to it.

"The solid planets from our star system that you can see orbited the black hole for almost a million Earth years, vastly increasing in velocity as they got closer to the horizon. Gaseous planets were simply torn apart. Rocky planets that did orbit the black hole and made it through in one piece were torched by radiation, again making them inhospitable."

They watched as some of the planets made it through the hole to the other side. They looked like warped versions of snooker balls, stretching and then disappearing down a table's pockets as they hit the wall of black. Some were simply crushed, either by crashing into another wandering planet, moon, or debris or simply unable to bear the stress of the journey.

The planets that did make it through the veil to the Dark Space behind it were no longer visible as the animation dimmed down to black. It was like an old cathode-ray television set switching off, disappearing into a white blob. Then it started back up again to display a new map and darker story.

The animation opened again, focusing on the black hole once more, but this time the camera sailed toward and right through it, following the journey of the planets that it had consumed. The landscape inside was a black expanse. There were only a few dark rocky worlds dotted around here, along with some lost floating debris, rocks, and sparse clouds of gas, forming a trail away from the black hole's rear.

There were no stars at all here freely giving their light, but there was some light. The rear edge of the black hole provided just enough to highlight the edges of a few of the closest planets. This effect was a ring of light all around the rear edge of the black hole. The light was trapped in a perpetual never-ending cycle of curving in and then curving out all around the edge. It still looked like a black hole from the rear except slightly different, not as bright. Its edge looked like a ring of water rushing inwards around the inside edge, then bleeding back outwards on its outside edge.

*It's kind of like watching a sinkhole in the middle of the ocean,* Daniel thought. He had seen videos showing something similar on the internet, where water all around its outer edge is constantly bleeding into the hole with no sign of escape.

The animation now highlighted less than a dozen small planets. The hardy ones that remained from the ancient star systems, along with a few other stragglers, had formed a new system here. These tough lifeless survivors had made it through their journey in one piece, spat out from the Light Universe into new permanent parking spaces. Volya offered some further commentary.

"We call this the Dark Space Union, the DSU. Over time as more planets arrive lifeless, they are added to the system and then recolonized. There are forty-six planets here at the moment, all orbiting the system like a circular train, being pulled closer and then pushed further away from the black hole, which is the closest thing we have to a star at the edge of our system. Except that we don't orbit around it, not in the traditional sense with the black hole at the center. We orbit it like we are all on a round table, with the black hole at the head."

He simulated it with the pointer finger of his left hand being the black hole and the pointer finger of his right-hand swirling away from it and back again, moving it on a horizontal plane. "We call this the nexus wave effect."

"Life had to start right from the beginning for this world. Ice formed as our planet cycled furthest away from the black hole. Then the oceans were revealed as we circled closer, and radiation melted the ice. Life started small, single cells in the seas, then grew and moved onto the land, evolving eventually into what you see now since the Creator chose to bring us here and create us.

"We moved between worlds for a while. All the planets here are occupied. Smaller ones are used for transit, distribution, and prison sites—stopover planets, if you will. Then came the hundred-year war around five hundred years ago. The death rate in the system was catastrophic. Things are more settled now, even though technically we are still at war with Secondary. Half of Secondary rebels against the central government here and even its own governor. They have ideas about using our spheres to take the people back to Light Space."

The animation screen disappeared, and the fire started up again. They all sat there for a moment, allowing their thoughts a chance to catch up.

"Silly question," Daniel said, "but why don't they let people who want to go back to the Light Space . . . just go back? Why keep them here? I don't get it."

Volya's eyes scanned the room. A concerned look decorated his face as his eyes switched from wall to wall, then to the ceiling and back. Then he flicked up his display screen, pressed a few combinations of finger motions, and closed it again.

"I am sorry," Volya began., "My home is set to private mode

now. We are allowed one hour of private mode per day to do, well . . . private things. I wish to speak as openly with you as I possibly can.

"You see, the spheres were a joint project between the best minds on Prime and Secondary. Once the sphere's designs had been completed and mass-produced some two hundred years ago, the Prime Director had the scientists from Secondary executed under the charge of stealing intellectual property from the Directorship and trying to coerce the Director's staff. Since then, there have been changes of Directorship. As one dies, his son takes over, but the animosity between the two worlds remains. Secondary feel that they are owed access to the technology to use as they see fit. Prime strictly refutes this *apparently* because we have to take responsibility for the usage of the sphere so as not to allow any 'unauthorized alterations to the timelines,' as the spheres are so powerful that in the wrong hands, they could alter everything.

"But some people within the union believe that it is mainly for fear of losing funds that are generated by the population of the union. It is the people who pay for the Prime Director and the rest of the delegates' lavish palaces, grounds, and lifestyles. If you were to visit several of the other planets here, you would see how their representatives live in luxury, doing whatever they wish. Meanwhile, the normal people on all the planets live under suppressive rules and have little money to spend on homes, food, basic lifestyle improvements, and improving the infrastructure that it was meant for. The general populace live very basic lifestyles instead of what it should be—pooling and distributing the system's resources fairly for the good of all people rather than just those at the top.

"It is, of course, feared that if all planets within the union had access to use and adapt the technology of the spheres, there would be a breakdown of the rules. A mass exodus of people going back to the Light Space and out of the union would ensue, leaving the system without taxpayers. The Director would be left ruling an empty system, and thus, the Director and the representatives have absolutely no intention of letting people return to the Light Space and putting their lifestyle in jeopardy.

"All of the people within the union are deeply religious, sometimes to their disadvantage. They pray to 'the Creator,' who they are taught from birth to believe brought them to the Dark Space—that this was their destiny. And so, the majority remain here, clueless as to what else is out there instead of pushing the Director and their representatives to fight to get them out of this miserable Dark Space system."

"Sounds daft to me," Daniel noted.

"I quite agree," Volya said very quietly, obviously fearing being overheard. He was almost breathing the words into the air.

Amber glanced down at her watch, not bothered about all this space stuff. It was now Tuesday at 14:58. She had almost been here a full twenty-four hours.

She said that she was going to the bathroom, and Daniel warned her to double-check which cube she was going to use first with a big smile on his face.

# CHAPTER 14
# BACK IN THE UK

At the beginning of day three of the bubble's existence, Mick made his way from the station back to the boundary of the anomaly. He had been climbing up the walls, bored stiff, as he and around half the station's staff couldn't get back to their homes. The bubble, as it was being officially referred to now, had swallowed up the entire West Midlands and sections of several other counties.

Generally, people in the station were getting on. People were either sleeping on desks, under desks, or on any available sofas that were usually reserved for visitors or staff from around the area that came to this station for conferences and the like. There were a few bathrooms, luckily, and water and electricity were still running, although the frequency of power-cuts had become regular and often. Power distributors were being forced to reroute power in different patterns around the network, diverting energy and other utilities around the anomaly.

Blankets -from the cell stores, even the foil ones that were left, had been well and truly pillaged.

Mick's car was now getting low on fuel, and service stations and supermarkets around the areas outside of the bubble had begun to run dry. Supermarkets were running out of many general items as well, as people had started to stockpile. Things like toilet paper, canned foods, pasta, and long-life milk had become currency. Deliveries had started to become somewhat problematic, with almost all of the central region of the UK's major road network completely inaccessible.

It wasn't only the fact that the roads were cut off but also the number of working people, storage buildings, and materials in storage, lorries, and hubs had left the logistical capabilities of the UK crippled. It was ambling along as best as it could, but it could not meet the demand of the people both north and south that were now panic buying.

The M1 and A1 that ran along the east side of the central region were the only major carriageways available to link the north of England to the south. There was also the A15 through Lincoln and the A49 through Hereford. The A483 provided a path through Wales from north to south, although these roads were now extremely busy. People in general had been advised to stay at home as much as possible unless journeys were absolutely critical in an attempt to limit traffic.

In terms of knowledge of what was going on, even now Mick was no better off than the general public. Nothing concrete had been revealed, and there were no official statements as to how or why the bubble had planted itself into the UK—only that they were investigating it and would release information as soon as it became available. Their counterparts in Canada were also in the same boat.

As he escaped the confines of the station for a few hours, he was keeping a close eye on both the fuel gauge and the road in front of him whilst at the same time still being haunted by what he had seen for himself only a few days ago. *This thing must be from space, as most seem to be speculating.* It was certainly the most plausible explanation so far. *Nothing on Earth had technology like this*—at least not that he knew of.

As far-fetched as that sounded, what the hell kind of technology on Earth could have made something like this happen?

He arrived at the rear of the stationary traffic on the A5. Déjà vu! Except it was dry and daylight this time. He massaged the stubble sprouting on his chin before getting out of the car after catching his face in the mirror. It was now longer than he had let it grow in twenty years, ever since he had grown beards. The itching was incredible, and now he had a red neck to add to the stubble and the mess that he already felt like.

He would have to walk the last three miles. Hundreds of cars, a combination of both abandoned and occupied vehicles, queued for as far as the eye could see. People had headed for the bubble by the thousands, desperate to get as close to their trapped homes and loved ones as they could. Some people had even made temporary homes in their cars on the road.

Mick weaved through the gaps between the cars. People were everywhere, coming back and forth across the lanes and between the privacy of the tree-covered grass banks and the road, fulfilling their various bodily needs. No choice there.

He strolled past them, trying not to look as people crouched behind a tree or walked their young children from the trees back to their cars. All looked haggard and hungry.

As a policeman, he would normally be telling them to move on or to stay in their cars. But not today, not for . . . however long.

There was a smell, a nice smell, carried through the air. Mick lifted his nose high and sniffed, recognizing it immediately. The smell made him instantly hungry, his stomach groaning to confirm that fact. It smelt so good, he needed to identify its origin. It was nine in the morning, and only bacon could smell that good at this time of the day. *Wonder if they have any extra? he* mused.

He spotted the army's barriers up ahead glinting in the Sun. The army had brought the barrier forward by quite some distance. He looked around, gathering his bearings. *Yup, must be half a mile from where they first discovered . . .* "it."

As he approached the barrier and a row of tall green trucks

just on the other side of it, he stood and looked around again. He watched as a fire truck parked on the grass at the left-hand side of the carriageway started to hand out paper bags. He could make out bottled water and some sort of pastry with an orange, gratefully received by the hungry public around the barrier. The uniformed men and women were taking them from an open compartment on the side of the truck and then running lines through the traffic, handing them out to the stranded. *Bless them*, he thought. They made him proud to be a badge.

Then he realized where the bacon smell was wafting from, changing his mind about all of the service people sticking together for the good of the people.

Behind the shiny six-foot-high steel barricades that the army had erected and sitting on the top of one of the trucks were four soldiers cooking breakfast on a portable gas stove, right on the top of the cab. They were laughing and joking, having a right good old time. Mick looked around. There were tired and hungry people standing around near the barricades, looking up longingly at the soldiers.

"Wankers!" he said a little too loudly. People around him turned to look at him, maybe wondering who he thought he was and who he was suggesting might be pleasuring them-selves in public. Luckily for him, the soldiers were far too jovial to have overheard. Mick tried to blend back into the crowd. *Hah! Chicken! the* voice in his head shouted at him.

He took out his handkerchief and mopped his brow. He still had his overcoat on, having put it on back at the station without thinking, and it was a beautiful sunny day for late September. He could do with a bottle of water himself, but he wouldn't take it away from the people that were stranded out here. *Not like those tosspots up there!* With that, he knocked on one of the steel panels in front of the truck. A six-inch by four-inch letterbox type of flap sprung open, a pair of suspicious eyes glaring at him. They stared words at him silently through the gap. *What the hell do you want?* they said, without even needing to speak.

Mick, more nervous than he thought he might be at this point, took out his warrant card and flashed it in front of the eyes inside the flap, then politely asked, "Can I have a word with your superior officer please, son?"

The eyes took a snap glance at the warrant. "No!" And the flap snapped shut.

Undeterred, Mick was old enough to be annoyed by that little shit in the flap but old enough to realize how this was probably going to go down. He knew that he didn't have any chance of getting inside or getting them to even speak to him; he merely wanted to see how far he could push. He knocked again. The flap sprung open.

"Detective Sergeant, if you do not move away from my barrier, I'll have you taken into custody. Do you understand?"

Again, it snapped shut.

Now Mick was annoyed. Had he been in a cartoon there was no doubt that he would be bright red with steam ejecting from his ears now. He knew that this was way above his pay grade, but he wanted to find out as much as he could whilst he was here. He had been bored at the station, so why not?

All he wanted was to share a sensible conversation with someone that would be willing to speak with a fellow uniform, to share a little information down the chain.

So far, all the Prime Minister had shared during his regular announcements on TV was that there was an "anomaly." *We bloody know that!* They did not know what had caused it or what it was. Research was being completed on the bubble around the clock. Knowledge was being shared and collaborated on in real time around the globe, and they would get this thing taken down as soon as possible. No expense would be spared globally in investigating what this thing was and who was responsible for it.

Part of Mick felt as though he was becoming the criminal

here. He was plotting, but what he really wanted to do was break into their stronghold, if only to take a look around for himself. His reasoning was that he, as one of the initial few that discovered the darn thing, should be allowed inside. Who were these clowns to stop him from seeing it?

The grass banks at both sides of the carriageway were crammed with people. Couples and families all sat staring at the compound. *What is this, Woodstock? Actually . . . they're onto something.*

He meandered through the crowd at the barrier and hopped over the small steel crash barrier at the side of the road. He turned back to look at the compound and backed his way up the grass bank, being careful not to step on anybody behind him sitting on the grass. As he rose up the hill, he could see deeper and deeper into the compound. They hadn't run the barrier up the grass hill, only along the road, so he was able to walk along the hill heading further down the carriageway unobstructed toward the bubble.

Further and further along the bank he walked, one foot higher than the other, until he could see a slight shimmer in the air that was the boundary of the thing. Soldiers were indeed poking and prodding it, causing ripples in the air, so he parked his ass on the grass to watch what was going on. Around five feet to his left another man sat in silence watching the compound intently, arms crossed and resting on his knees.

"Every now and then, they come out and clear us back," the lone man said under his breath in Mick's direction. Mick looked over at him, sizing up who he would be talking to. The bearded man was wearing khaki-colored walking trousers, leather-strapped sandals, and a gray T-shirt. On his head a beige bucket hat. It looked as though the guy had walked straight out of a festival or off a beach.

"You seen much?" Mick queried, taking a chance that this guy wasn't a reporter or active military.

"Nah, not really. They continually walk around it. They've

prodded a few instruments into it and then pulled them back out, then they go again with different guys. My opinion? They ain't got a clue in hell, man! So, where are you based? Which station?"

He caught Mick quite off guard. This guy was sharper than he appeared, and Mick hadn't expected to make any friends today. Mick hadn't even caught on that the guy had been watching him. Never *judge a book by its cover, Mick. You should know this by now.*

"How'd you know?"

"Saw the warrant card hanging out your back pocket as you lifted your coat to sit down. Also, the trench coat kind of gives it away unless you're a weirdo and naked under there, planning to run a streak or flash at a granny in the park. Pick your cliché. I guessed you weren't a flasher."

He turned to look at Mick, smiling cheekily and waited for a response.

"Wem," Mick said, "but my house is . . . over there in Wolverhampton. You military?"

"Ex, and mine too. Fordhouses." The man rolled up his left trouser leg, revealing a metal limb beneath the cloth. The man knocked his knuckles against the polished steel.

"Sorry, mate," Mick said sympathetically.

"Don't be, I'm alright." He rolled his trouser leg back down.

They both sat staring at the compound as soldiers ran around like ants on a patio.

Then a soldier, complete with a gun strapped around his shoulder and resting against his chest, broke away from the compound and started to walk up the bank toward them.

"Move away, please, people—by order of the government!"

People started getting up, groaning, and moving back west toward the start of the barrier and the cars. Mick took out his warrant card again and flashed it to the young soldier.

"Don't worry, son, I'll give you a hand."

Mick walked up to the mysterious bearded ex-soldier from Fordhouses and gave him a hand up.

"Come on, son!" Mick exaggerated a theatrical routine, telling his new friend to move on. "Follow my lead," Mick whispered in his ear.

Mick and the ex-soldier followed but slightly lagged behind the bulk of the crowd. As soon as he could see that the crowd had cleared the area of concern, the armed soldier headed back down the bank and was let back into the front entrance to the compound.

"Come on!" Mick ushered his friend back toward the spot they had just come from. There were trees at the top of the bank, so Mick and his friend headed for the cover of the tree line and then back down the bank to their original spot.

"What's your name, soldier?"

"Spike, and you?"

"Mick."

"Nice to meet you, Mick!"

"You too, mate." They shook hands.

The pair planted themselves in front of a tree so as not to stand out as much as before. They weren't far from the previous spot, just a little higher.

It looked as though there was some new action going on within the compound.

"What's the plan with you, Policeman Mick?" Spike asked with a wry smile, staring at Mick from the edge of his eye.

"Well, I'm climbing the walls back at the nick. I needed to get out here, ruffle a few feathers and see if they were any closer to . . . well, anything."

"I like it!" Spike said, putting on a strong American businessman accent.

They watched with great interest as a cherry picker with large four-by-four wheels rolled across the compound floor toward the bubble's edge. Soldiers scurried around it, moving road cones and barrier tape out of its way, then it came to a full stop just shy of the edge of the bubble.

"They done this before?" Mick asked.

"Nope. This is new."

A soldier dressed in what looked like heavy commercial scuba gear stood alone in the basket of the picker. He held onto the picker's rails and looked around at the deck around the basket, checking that he was clear. The soldiers below made sure and cleared anything that remained.

He signaled with a high wave, and the soldiers cleared the area. Standing well back, another soldier saluted toward the temporary cabins that had become offices within the middle of the compound.

The arm carrying the scuba man slowly extended out, pushing him outward but not up as you would normally use a cherry picker—out toward the bubble. One other soldier walked slowly alongside the machine holding what was most likely a remote, presumably to help navigate the picker's basket without Scuba Soldier having to worry about it from his controls.

"Here we go, man," Spike said, rubbing his hands together with childlike enthusiasm.

Mick watched quietly, engrossed. This was what he'd wanted to see, what he had come back for. They were going to send that soldier right into the bubble, and he would get to witness it.

The basket carrying Scuba Soldier was now extended out to around six meters in front of the wheeled base and then it stopped. Scuba Soldier raised his hand into the air again.

He then gripped the front bars of the basket tightly and the soldier assisting alongside the vehicle used his remote to drive the lifter forward, sending the basket into the bubble.

As the basket pushed through the side wall of the bubble, Mick and Spike watched in stunned silence. The side of the bubble that was pierced by the cherry picker was invisible, but the air visibly rippled with colors in the Sun like oil on a puddle.

Scuba Soldier was pushed through and was now inside the bubble—he did not move. Still, he gripped the rail; his weighted boots stood firm on the floor of the basket. He was as frozen as everyone else that had gone into it.

More civilians were sitting around them watching now. Mick and Spike hadn't even noticed them arrive, but people had crept back down the grassy bank to witness the action.

Mick looked down at his watch. Two full minutes had passed since Scuba Soldier had entered the bubble. The soldier standing alongside the base unit of the cherry picker touched his ear and then started to operate his remote again, the cherry picker starting up its fuel side of the bi-energy engine. A reversing "beep-beep" noise sounded out, and the base unit started to slowly roll backward.

At the same time the unit rolled back, the soldier alongside the picker started to retract the arm. There was complete silence as the stunned audience and the compound watched. The basket edged out of the bubble. Scuba Man's form leaned forward over the rail a little as he popped back out through the bubble. He looked limp for a second, but he still held onto the handrail as he was safely extracted.

His hands let go of the bar when he was completely free from the bubble and the cherry picker stopped moving. He stepped forward in the basket unsteadily but managed to steady himself again, leaning with his back against the bars of the basket.

Mick could see that he was composing himself. After a moment, he gave a double-handed wave to the onlookers that he was okay!

The crowd on the bank cheered and clapped as Scuba Man waved back to them. This sent the volume along the grass banks racing up. It was as though a footballer had scored the winning penalty at the world cup. He clearly enjoyed the attention, too, and more importantly, he was fine.

Soldiers inside the compound sharply turned their eyes toward the noisy banks outside. The crowd instantly realized that they had drawn attention to themselves and become silent observers again, some leaving the area before being asked. An armed soldier appeared again through the hatch in the side of the compound and started to walk across the asphalt toward the grassy bank. Mick and Spike were still sitting there, oblivious, watching Scuba Man.

"Move along, people."

The armed soldier was now standing directly in front of Mick and Spike, one hand resting confidently on the center of the gun strapped around his chest.

"You guys, you need to move . . . right now!"

Mick again took out his warrant card—he knew it wasn't going to work this time, but he was just trying it on. He really wanted to stay and watch; he enjoyed the company of his new friend Spike and was observing with great interest the events rolling out in front of them. If he were to leave here today, it would only be to go back to being shut in the station again. He looked with a frown at the soldier, who must have only been twenty.

"Look, son, I'm police. I've been asked to remain here to observe, so if you could concentrate on moving the rest of the people along and leave me and my deputy here, I'd really appreciate it."

"We know who you are, sir. Move on . . . now! Please."

The soldier looked sincere to Mick. He could see that this soldier had a little more respect about him and didn't really want to be ordering Mick around or give him a hard time. Not like some of them others.

"I understand, son, no problem. Come on, deputy, we'd better fall back."

Mick gave Spike a hand up and they walked back toward the stranded cars.

Spike happily allowed Mick to type his phone number into his phone, and then Mick left him sitting on the grass close to the cars and fire truck. Someone in a fire fighter uniform handed Spike a paper bag that contained a bottle of water, a foil-wrapped sandwich, and an apple. Mick was offered a bag, too, but Mick politely declined and made his way back toward his car.

When he was sitting back in his car, he took his phone out of his pocket and clicked the news app on his home screen. Mick was more of a newspaper guy any day of the week, so for him, this was unusual. Unfortunately, the main local newspaper, the Wolverhampton-based *Echo and Star*, was out of action due to the bubble. *The Shropshire Echo and Star* was still going but was only pumping out limited numbers due to missing staff and interruptions in power, and those limited numbers of papers were becoming harder to come by.

Some of the headlines scrolling down the page included:

**"Prime Minister to Initiate Strict Curfews to Protect the Public"**

Gangs of unruly youths had reportedly started collecting at unguarded rural spots around the bubble's perimeter. Reports coming into the police had confirmed that the youths had been witnessed recklessly throwing each other into the anomaly for dares. And, even more stupidly, they had moved on to pushing in members of the public that happened to be walking by.

"To relieve some pressure on the armed forces and emergency services that are currently out investigating and protecting the public from the unknown enemy, we are reluctantly introducing an eight-p.m. curfew across the UK . . ."

**"Desperate People Throwing Themselves Into the Bubble"**

Desperate to reach trapped loved ones or feeling the need to share in their trapped families' experiences, many people have reportedly been throwing themselves into the bubble. Some were able to be pulled back to safety, but the increasing number of people trying to perform this stunt has now caused a buildup of bodies trapped inside the perimeter of the bubble. So desperate are they to feel what their loved ones have felt . . .

**"Birds Observed Diverting Around 'Bubble' "**

Scores of flocks of birds have been observed by watchers diverting their flight paths around the bubble. It was first suspected that they might continue their natural flight path straight through the anomaly. However, it has been hypothesized that due to the increased magnetic field readings that have been taken around the bubble, the birds' intuition is telling them that something is there . . .

**"When Will the Government Come Clean?"**

Petitions have begun to appear all over the UK Parliament website. Hundreds of thousands of names have signed various live petitions that have been submitted calling for more government transparency and to share the knowledge they have regarding the anomaly with the public.

Similar operations have also begun in Canada, with information also not forthcoming there. Ministers have appealed for public understanding whilst they investigate. This event has taken the whole world by surprise. "Everything is being done to investigate possible causes and to seek out those responsible for the anomaly. Please allow us time to gather all available evidence to avoid incorrect information being issued," said the British Prime Minister during a live broadcast this morning.

. . .

Mick had also read that people had been observing the public trapped inside the bubble, at least those that were visible from the perimeter. People inside had now reportedly begun to grow increasingly gaunt. *What is this thing doing to those poor people?*

He felt so helpless. He rocked his head back again and studied the roof of his car. He said out loud, "Whoever is up there, if there is anyone that can help us, now is the time," and moved his hand from forehead to gut, shoulder to shoulder, in the shape of a cross.

# CHAPTER 15
# FACILITIES

Amber, bored, found herself staring at Volya, not even aware that she was doing so at first. While they were sitting around talking, she started to observe more subtle differences about his physiology. The thoughts came in random drips as he spoke, and she decided that she had to ask him about it.

"Mr. Volya, I hope you don't think I'm being rude, but I couldn't help but notice that your eyes are such a bright gray, almost white color. It's almost as though they're shining, like silver. They're beautiful. And your hands look ever so slightly different than ours, too; I only just noticed that one. Are there particular reasons why you have shiny eyes and quite long middle fingers?"

Volya looked down, examining his own hands and then Amber's hands and Daniel's, comparing them. His hands were slightly different; he hadn't thought of it, either, until Amber brought it up. His middle finger indeed extended out quite a lot further than theirs did. By a good inch, at least.

"Yes, I see what you mean. If I had to speculate, I would say that because our ancestors lived mainly underground deep inside the planets—closer to the cores than the surfaces, in fact, just to keep warm—I would imagine that some use of the hands may have come in handy whilst underground. With regards to our eyes, I would say that this would be along the same lines; compared to other races that have come here, we are very good at seeing in the dark, you see. Evolution has given us the tools to match our environments."

Volya then said, "We have a busy day tomorrow, which I am hoping will be more enjoyable than your days on Prime so far. If you would like to freshen up, please feel free to use the facilities below."

"How do you use your shower?" Daniel asked.

"Simply stand under the jets and place your hand in front of the sensor on the wall. Once you have washed, the unit will then start to dry you. Tap the button again if you would like more water."

"Oh, the same as our showers, then, really. Go on, you go first, Amber," Daniel said.

"Thanks, Daniel." She disappeared down the staircase to investigate. She had seen the wet room previously, so she didn't think it would be too difficult, and it wasn't. There was a bench to lay your clothes on, though no towels around that she could see, but he had mentioned that it would dry you off when it had finished washing you.

She stood bare in the corner of the tiled wet room, the furthest corner from the toilets in the area that looked like a shower. She could hear Volya and Daniel still chatting upstairs. As Volya had said, she placed her hand in front of the shiny black panel built into the wall and water started to fall from above. The water was at a perfect temperature, just warm enough and most enjoyable. This reminded her of home; this part was no different, really. She did enjoy a good shower. The only annoying thing was that she still had to put that stupid diner uniform back on. She could see it from the corner of her eye.

She enjoyed a good long shower, forgetting where she was

for a while before the mechanism then shut off the water and warm air came up from the floor.

"Oooh!" she exclaimed both pleasantly and comically as she felt the warm air stream around her whole body. She had expected it to come from above, like the water.

She would do this again if, indeed, they were here for a long period. It had been most enjoyable.

Once they had both enjoyed a shower and were back upstairs, everyone was quiet and relaxed again in front of the fire. After a few moments Volya stood and said, "I'll be back in a moment," and walked out through the black doorway. He re-entered a few moments later holding three mugs of something hot. Setting them down on an exposed stone section of where they were sitting, he passed one to Amber and then to Daniel.

"This is a typical nighttime beverage for us here. It is a tea made from a leaf grown in the hills a long way from here." Then he pulled out of his pocket three small stone bottles with rubber stoppers on the tops. "This is a nectar that we use to sweeten the drink to your taste. Please help yourself." Each of them took a mug, added nectar to taste, and enjoyed their hot tea. Volya looked on with satisfaction as his guests seemed much more at ease now.

"Right, my young friends. I think we should get some rest. We will start fresh again tomorrow. Tomorrow will be a busy day."

Amber felt her stomach tying itself into knots again. Her heart felt like a misfiring engine. *Anxiety is a bitch!* She already knew that chances were slim to none of them going home but still held on to a slither of hope. The more they went to bed and woke up again here, the more it seemed to bring it home that they were indeed stuck here. *Why keep us here if we're so unhappy? I just don't get it. I couldn't do that to somebody.*

"I have informed the Director of how well you are settling in and advised him you are not causing any issues." Volya seeming to sense the anxiety in the air. "It has been confirmed that, moving forward, I will share my living quarters with you, rather than you having to go back to the holding compound. You should be more comfortable here."

"Oh, okay, thank you. That's nice." Daniel looked over at Amber to check that she was okay.

Amber asked, "I'm sorry to be rude, Mr. Volya, but would it be okay to see what the sleeping arrangements will be, please?"

Volya stared back vacantly. They could see that he was trying to process the information received, comparing her words to the feelings he sensed in the air. After a few seconds he seemed to spring back to life, suddenly realizing what the new weight hanging in the air was: their modesty.

"Of course! Please forgive me. I had not given that one thought. It has been so long since I last shared my house with . . . well, anyone."

Arrivals from the Light Space were always kept in their holding cells until they were fully processed and, if civil, assigned a position here; if not, they were shipped onto one of the transit planets. Those that brought benefit to the system, those civilized enough by nature, skilled with their hands, or dutiful, were given a basic home and work. Depending on how well they accepted their new life and passed certain means tests, they could end up being very comfortable here.

The confusion had been in these new arrivals. It was still no clearer why had they arrived as a pair. This was most unusual; there was never more than one visitor at a time sent by the spheres. Amber and Daniel were also quite young, which was yet another reason that Volya felt obliged to keep his eye on them. Volya felt responsible for them, and he took that responsibility seriously.

They were important. The Creator had sent them here for a reason. What was he missing? There had to be a reason for them both being sent here, for the spheres to have stayed together. He could be killed if he made his thoughts known to anybody. *Something or someone is trying to influence the timelines.* There had to be others thinking the same things as him.

"Come this way, please," Volya said, turning toward the doorway that they had been using at the head of the room. The three of them walked through the dark space in the door frame.

They were now standing in a room very similar to the living room. Both Daniel and Amber had to look twice, initially thinking that they had gone through a door only to return to the same place. Both stared at the room in front of them, then back at the doorway, and then at each other.

There was another open fire in the center of a stone-walled room, but rather than a circular path of sofas around the room these were more bed-shaped slabs of stone, still arranged circularly around the room. Where one bed finished, another started, only separated by tall stone slabs that formed a headboard and footboard, giving its occupant some relative privacy while they slept. Skins and furs were again draped all over them. It looked like there were some furs to lie on and some skins to cover you.

There were also pillows of sorts. Skins were rolled up to form a cushion at the head of each bed. The only other obvious difference between this room and the last was the ceiling. It didn't have a pyramid-like glass ceiling; this one was solid stone. This time, a staircase circled the fire, then rose up into a round hole in the ceiling.

Volya said, "There is no one else that sleeps here, aside from me. You're quite safe here. Please sleep where you feel comfortable. That's my bed there." He pointed to the noon position.

Both guests were quite comfortable in each other's company now, sharing a sense of security and familiarity in staying together. The room looked secure, Volya seemed nice—the only variable that Amber could see was the black doorway at the head of the room. *Who knows who could just wander through there?*

Daniel took one of the beds, leaving a spare bed gap from Volya, and Amber took one right behind him. They decided without expressing it verbally that they wouldn't bother getting undressed. They would simply lie down and drape the fur blankets over them as they were, and that would be fine.

Amber did feel completely ridiculous looking at what Daniel was wearing, wishing so badly that she'd had the foresight to change.

The fire was crackling away but then dimmed down along with the room's subtle lighting. Amber lay on her bed, pulling a fur sheet over herself, and it wasn't long before she was drifting away from Prime back toward memories of her mom—and the troublesome sphere.

She missed her mom desperately. It had crossed Amber's mind in the past few months that soon she would be without her. Normally she would try her best to put this thought to the back of her mind, maybe even try and make light of the situation when she was around her mom. But these people were taking that precious time away from her— time that was already limited. How cruel of them. Did they even care? She thought not.

*Why did I have to go and touch it?*

# CHAPTER 16
# SHOPPING

A mber eventually came around after a night of tossing, turning, and waking up wondering where she was. She had finally fallen into a deep sleep when something woke her again. She opened her eyes, confused, that longing for more sleep feeling still clinging to her.

Looking at her watch told her that it was Wednesday, minutes after four o'clock in the morning. There were no windows down here in the bedroom area to see what light shone outside. The room was still dark, and the fire was still gently spitting and spluttering. Only the top floor—she guessed that's what it was, anyway—of the living room area contained windows. It appeared that the bathroom was midway between the two. That top floor had that lovely glass roof, even though it only observed a deep black sky above.

She turned over to face the center of the room and as she did, someone that she hadn't yet met was staring at her, wide-eyed, from less than a foot away. She let out a loud gasp, causing the person standing over her to jump out of her poor skin. The person was a short gray-faced woman in a long gray doctor's coat.

"Jesus Christ!" Amber said loudly, breathing heavily, holding her fur blankets close to her chest and sitting up on her slab. She turned and looked over her headboard. Daniel was still asleep but stirring and stretching now—probably her fault. Volya was nowhere to be seen. Behind the gray-skinned lady stood about half a dozen other gray-faced people all wearing the same long gray laboratory-type coats. They looked like scientists or doctors. All that was missing were glasses, stethoscopes, and clipboards, but they made up for that with their gray lab coats and all of them working on their floating computer screens.

Volya came back into the room through the black doorway right behind the gaggle of scientists. Amber watched him through gaps between them. He was pushing a trolley this time with more cups on it and silver cloches covering something. He wheeled it around to the noon position gap in the seating and then came over to Amber's bed, addressing the scientists.

"I hope you didn't scare our guests?" he asked the group.

"No," they said almost in unison, shaking their heads and looking innocent.

Daniel sat up now. His hair was messy, pointing straight up on one side of his head. He looked dopey. Amber chuckled.

"What's going on?" Daniel asked the room.

"Don't know," Amber said. "I woke up and these perverts were staring at me."

"Please remain calm," Volya tutted. "Do not worry, these are the people who are simply here to take some samples and readings from you, as mentioned in your orientation. I can assure you, it is quite painless and will be over in just a few moments. They represent Prime's head scientific research facility. Allow me to introduce you all. Here we have Arne, Vinson, Sten, Vit, Leif, Vien, and—"

"Eira." The female, the one that had startled Amber, completed the sentence for Volya before shyly retreating to the back of the huddle. Amber smiled. Eira was cute in a nerdy sort of way that Amber could kind of relate to.

"Hello," they all said almost in unison, smiling and waving.

"Are you having a pleasant stay so far?" one of the scientists asked Amber politely,

"I suppose so, aside from not wanting to be here."

Another one, looking at each of them in turn, asked, "Could I ask, how have you found breathing whilst you have been here? And walking around, have you noticed any difficulties?"

Daniel replied, "No, not that I can think of. I've felt normal all the time I've been here."

Amber also answered, "No, I can't honestly say I've felt anything unusual either or noticed any problems breathing."

"Anything at all? No matter how insignificant you believe it to be? Any dizziness or feelings of unwellness in any way?"

"No, not that I have noticed," she replied.

"And your concentration is, okay? Have you noticed any fogginess?" another asked.

"No. Again, nothing comes to mind."

"Extraordinary," one of them said, and they went into a huddle, muttering and nodding.

"Don't worry, I have breakfast for when they have finished." Volya smiled.

One of them approached Amber, who was slightly closer to the huddle than Daniel. It was Eira, the female one.

"Would you mind if I took some simple noninvasive readings from you, please?"

"No, be my guest," Amber replied politely.

Eira opened up her computer again. She was holding her hand up in front of herself, staring at the screen from her side and holding the rear of the light screen in front of Amber's chest. She then moved up to Amber's head and all the way down to her feet. Finally, she stared at Amber's eyes and her hands.

"Are you ok with me taking your readings, please, Daniel?"

"Yeah, no worries."

She completed the same routine with Daniel, then hurriedly moved back toward the huddle. They muttered for a moment, and then another figure stepped forward.

"All readings appear healthy. Heart and lung functions are as good as we could expect. Blood and oxygen levels are fine. It is as if you were made to live here," she said with a smile. "If it's ok, I would like to ask you some basic questions about your planet now please to . . . let's say fill in some blanks."

"No problem," Daniel said. "What would you like to know?"

"Thank you. If you can, I want you to tell me any important historical dates that you can recall—an approximate year or century is fine if you cannot remember exactly. Any that come to mind, either during or before your lifetime. For example, wars, things that you might have celebrated, things that your parents may have spoken about with some degree of importance or things from your education system. Are there any major disasters that you can recall?"

Amber and Daniel both frowned at each other, raising their eyebrows in concentration. The old brain matter was still a bit rusty after all they had been through.

"Ok," Daniel started. "Well, from my history classes I remember—and these are only rough guesses—the Vikings sailed the seas around two thousand years ago. Around three thousand years ago the Romans were around. Wars . . . well, I've been watching some documentaries lately online, so the first World War was from 1914 to 1918. The second World War was from 1939 to 1945. There hasn't been a third World War— not yet, anyway. We've come very close though."

Then Amber excitedly added, "Ooh, the first moon landing was 1969." She looked very happy with herself and then happily shouted, "Ooh, the Jurassic period! Sixty-five million years ago, the dinosaurs went extinct. A large asteroid hit Earth and caused them all to die, I think."

"Oooooooh," the scientists all said together, looking interested.

Another scientist sauntered to the front of the group and seemed to ask with a sneer, "Could I ask, please, how far have humans traveled in space in your time? I know you mentioned moon landings. How far have you traveled around your solar system?" His tone wasn't nearly as friendly as the others.

"No further than the moon yet. Not manned, anyway. Unmanned ships and probes have gone out to the far reaches of our solar system. Voyagers 1 and 2 have gone really far, but I can't remember the year they were launched. That was years before my time!" Daniel offered.

The man didn't say anything; he nodded with closed, satisfied eyes and stepped quietly back into the huddle. The taller male of the group came forward, looking slightly proud of the pack, and said with open hands out in front of himself, "That concludes the survey. We have the readings that we need, and we will leave you to enjoy breakfast with Volya. Thank you, Amber and Daniel, very much. You have been most useful."

He bowed his head and led the way for the group to exit through Volya's black doorway.

Volya removed the silver cloches from the food to reveal piles of cooked burger meat, fries, and mugs of their planet's special tea—all very tasty and rather normal-looking food, considering.

"The food has been very good here. It's weird how you know what we like." Amber commented.

"Thank you. Yes, we hoped it would be to your liking. Today, my friends, I would like to take you to town to see our normal way of life and experience some of our everyday culture."

"Then can we go home?" Amber asked with false hope, knowing full well that it wouldn't be a yes.

Daniel turned sharply to stare at Volya.

"I am so very sorry." His face displayed more emotion than

it had the whole time they had been here, his eyes looked to the floor, and his brow relaxed. Looking sorrowful, he sighed deeply. "Please know that I am constantly petitioning the Director on your behalf, but I would not like to get your hopes up until something tells me that there is renewed hope. All I can safely say for now is please bear with me."

Amber's gut wrenched again and she stared at the floor.

Daniel looked sympathetic, but even he didn't want to fill her with hollow hope. So, he stayed silent.

They freshened up again in Volya's mid-level wet room after eating, Amber going first, then Daniel. The mood was quite somber again now.

Again, Amber was mortified to be dressing in her work uniform. She didn't even have any deodorant. *This is getting embarrassing. Two days in and no deodorant or clean clothes.* To make matters worse, her hair was starting to feel like a bird's nest. They would have to provide her with something fresh and helpful soon. She stunk—she could smell herself! Daniel was probably thinking the same about himself . . . hopefully. *At least the shower might help. For now.*

Once ready, the three of them walked out through the black doorway. A warm breeze blew across Amber's face as a bustling town came into view around her head, leaving the bedroom and the black midway border of the doorway behind.

Daniel was impressed. He was doing his best to stay as positive as possible and was starting to quite enjoy their strange outer-space experience. They were being treated fairly and entertained, at least. It was almost as though they were simply on holiday, visiting family on the other side of the country.

He missed his family, of course. He could visualize his mom and dad still sitting in their bedroom helpless, and that upset him. But he was also helpless right now; he couldn't exactly click his heels together and fly himself home. They would remain constantly in his thoughts while he continued to try to imagine and manifest a way, any way he could, to get him and

Amber home and make sure that his mom, dad, and sister were all okay.

They found themselves standing at a crossroads on a busy road. Other gray people stood around them patiently waiting to cross the road. The other gray people here were dressed in what looked like military uniforms but with no badges or medals adorning them. The males and the females both wore plain gray pantsuits, while the elderly people tended to walk around in robes just like Volya.

A sleek silver vehicle around the size of a long sedan pulled up alongside the patch of road that everyone was waiting to cross. Daniel was mesmerized; he loved cars. He watched all of the car shows and had always looked forward to seeing what the next stage of "futuristic" cars coming out would look like, but he had never imagined he'd be so close to an actual vehicle on another planet that looked like it could be a car of the future from Earth.

The skin of the vehicle was smooth, like liquid chrome, with no lines that gave way to doors or windows. It was completely devoid of any details.

It was so chrome-like that it was like looking at a mirror; they could not see the occupants inside.

The vehicle floated around a foot off the ground and came to a smooth stop with a subtle shoosh, letting out waste steam from underneath as it idled silently, waiting for people to cross the road.

After they crossed the crosswalk, going off in front of them and way into the distance was a busy shop-lined avenue. It was neatly paved like a Parisian high street back on Earth, bustling with people crossing left and right carrying bags and ducking in and out of the small shops. Kids ran around chasing each playing games as older people stood around in groups having a good old chat.

There were tea shops as well where people sat outside enjoying the atmosphere. It was so Earth-like, both Amber and

Daniel felt almost as if they were back home. *Almost.*

The shops were quite similar in shape to the small houses, all modestly sized with their glass roofs forming a point on the top. This looked like an area that they had watched from the high mountain viewing platform earlier in their stay.

This got Amber thinking—*Shopping!*

# CHAPTER 17
# OTHERS

Daniel lagged behind Amber and Volya as he watched Amber busily flit from shop front to shop front. Volya patiently walked with his hands linked behind his back. He was graceful in his walk along the avenue and people parted for him, greeting him as he passed.

*He's an important fellow here*, Daniel thought.

The shops all featured the same type of large glass display windows, as they would back on Earth, displaying their various wares. Some sold clothing, though with not much choice in the way of colors; Amber had made that known with an exasperated look back at Daniel. Some sold ornaments, jewelry, and crockery, all carved from stone, while others sold pastries and bread. All of the items on display in the windows looked as though they had been handmade with care.

Amber stopped outside about the hundredth clothes shop, by Daniel's count.

Looking down at the stupid dress she was wearing, she gripped the hem of her skirt and then let it drop again in annoyance. Amber was not surprised to find people staring at her. They must be thinking, "W*hat on . . . wherever we are . . . is she wearing?"*

"Mr. Volya, if I wanted to buy something from, say, this shop," Amber started to ask, looking around and then pointing at the clothes shop. "What would I pay them with?"

"Ah, well, if there is something that appeals to you, it would be my pleasure to cover the cost. Please go inside and take a look around. See if there is anything that you like."

She gratefully nodded and walked into the shop. The shop-keeper sitting in the window behind the counter stood up quickly, bowing her head appreciatively as Amber entered her shop. As Volya followed Amber inside, the lady shopkeeper's expression tightened with nervousness. Volya tried to put the lady at ease, saying, "Greetings. My young friend here would like to browse through your garments. Whatever she likes, put it on my account, please."

Amber slowly walked up and down the rows of the small shop. In the middle was an island with more clothes hanging on it, supplementing the stock on the walls. She browsed each part of the store carefully and then made her way back to the start of her circuit, dissatisfied. Everything in here was gray. The selection seemed to mostly consist of uniform styled outfits, including pantsuits, all-in-one suits, long women's dresses, and robes—all gray, of course.

She would have to make do with something from this shop now that she had come in. She would feel awful if she just walked out. *Let's face it, anything has to be better than this,* she thought, determined to make something work. She worked her way around again.

Drawn to a section along the back wall displaying a slightly more leisurely selection, she stood in front of it and stared, determined. The trousers here looked more like a utility or combat type of trouser, complete with elasticated waists and pockets down the legs, and there were T-shirts next to them. *Mmm, ok . . . I think I could make that work.*

She took some items from the racks and asked the shy lady

that was permanently watching her from near the window, "Is it ok if I try some of these on, please?"

"Of course! I would be honored. Please, use the privacy room at the back." The woman, looking anxious but smiling nonetheless, gestured toward the rear of the shop.

Daniel was waiting outside, idly looking around. Volya had taken a new position centrally in the doorway to the shop. Daniel didn't think he intentionally was, but it kind of looked as though Volya was there to prevent anyone else from entering whilst Amber was inside.

Daniel browsed the shop windows on either side of the clothes shop. The one to the left sold jewelry. There were necklaces and bracelets all made of stone, some with colored gems embedded in them. If this was a normal holiday, he would be purchasing something for his mom and sister. To the right, this store sold different items carved from stone like cups and tankards. *My dad would love one of those for his beer, he* thought with sadness.

Amber eventually reappeared after what felt like an hour to Daniel, followed by Volya. Daniel was now on the opposite side of the avenue and saw their reflection in the window he was currently looking in. He turned. "Much better!" he called out with a big smile, sticking up both thumbs in approval.

She was carrying a brown paper bag, her work uniform stuffed into it. Now she wore a much more practical ensemble of dark-gray utility trousers and a lighter gray T-shirt, finished off with her white diner sneakers. She looked so much more comfortable, and her huge smile confirmed it.

As they continued on up the high street, the calm leisurely mood of the city changed dramatically. A loud siren blared, making both Amber and Daniel jump.

Everyone around them stopped what they were doing and looked up to the sky. The sound of the siren reminded Daniel of an air-raid siren from the old war films.

The ground started to shake and groan beneath them. Amber and Daniel both looked to Volya for signs as to whether this was something to worry about. The lighter-colored pavement that spanned both sides of the avenue, divided in the middle of the street by a darker blacktop section, groaned loudly as it slowly separated from the darker section and lifted high into the air on heavy industrial-looking support arms below. Around a hundred-yard strip of pavement on each side of the avenue was raised about twenty feet into the air, and further down the avenue, as far as they could see, other equal sections of pavement were also raised.

The closest section to them stopped moving and people of all ages started to calmly walk toward the giant gap in the street. Amber turned to Daniel, looking terrified. Volya, however, calm as could be, spoke with authority over the commotion, "Please follow me!"

Volya walked toward the gap and stepped down. Around half a dozen steps led into an area the size of a tube station with a double-sided bench running along the middle of the space quickly filling with people. The people inside sat together and back-to-back, having a good old conversation below the pavement. To them, this occurrence seemed normal—it was almost a social event. They could still see up toward the skies through the gap in the pavement above, which had now started to narrow slowly as the last few people entered the shelter and the pavement lowered itself to street level again.

"What's happening, Mr. Volya?" Amber asked.

"This is an attack situation. Secondary rebels are attacking Prime again."

"Again? Why?" Amber looked flabbergasted, still staring up into the sky.

"We are still in a state of war with them. Now and then they attack, seemingly to test our defense domes that cover the cities. Please don't worry; you are quite safe down here. This is very routine for us."

Amber watched through the now two-foot gap in the roof

that allowed for some visibility of the skies above; the pavement didn't clamp shut whilst people were down there. She could only see a little of the activity. Small lights were flying around against the black sky, and then she heard hollow *Bong! Bong! Bong!* sounds followed by green lights flashing in the sky like fireworks. They illuminated and highlighted the top of the city's clear dome that Volya had mentioned.

"And they definitely can't get through?" Daniel asked, just to make sure.

"No," Volya said with a confident smile.

"Seems like a waste of energy to me, then," Daniel said.

As they sat there waiting for it to be over, someone leaned back and whispered into Daniel's ear. Daniel jumped at first but then listened; it was a man sitting behind him on the bench.

"When he falls asleep tonight, make sure you are safe, and then walk through his black doorway. It's nothing to be afraid of, but there is somebody who would very much like to meet you, and it could be mutually beneficial."

"Who?" Daniel whispered, leaning slightly backward himself into the voice but not turning. There was a little hustle and bustle in the tunnel as people continued chatting and socializing, moving between parties. There was no reply.

Daniel turned around. There was a gap in the row of seated people behind him. Whoever had said that was now long gone.

"That was weird!"

"Sorry did you say something?" Volya asked, leaning forward from behind Amber, who was sitting quietly next to Daniel.

"No, sorry, just mumbling to myself. Weird, what's going on out there."

"Were you speaking to someone?" Amber asked quietly. "I saw you turn around."

"I'll tell you later," Daniel whispered.

About half an hour went by and finally the air-raid sirens died out. The bombardment had long since ceased and the safety roof started to lift back into the air again, allowing people to safely exit back up to street level and go about their business once again.

"That was so bizarre," Amber said to Volya as they emerged streetside.

"I can certainly understand why you say that, if you have never seen that kind of thing before."

Daniel was silent, deep in thought. Amber could see that he was stewing over something in his mind. What's *wrong with him?* Hopefully he would fill her in later.

They resumed browsing the shops. It was as if nothing had happened. Volya went inside a pastry shop and came out with three portions of something that smelled sweet, something warm inside the paper it was wrapped in. "Try this," he said, handing them one each.

They ate as they walked. Amber, let out a distinct "Mmmm," sound as she bit into the pastry, clearly enjoying it very much— somehow it was familiar, warm and flaky yet soft and buttery in the center. A smooth custardy taste followed.

"Are you enjoying our city, Amber and Daniel?"

Amber, still munching on her pastry, said, "I'm enjoying this food!" Then she added, "Sometimes I'm not too bad, for the most part. It is just like being on Earth, really. I feel like I'm on a school field trip or something. But that display was random! And things like that bring me back to where I am, and then I start missing my mom again."

Daniel commented after her, his mouth still half full, "It's certainly been very eye-opening." Amber once again noticed that look of concentration on his face.

He was plotting something, or something had happened— Amber could feel it. He was somewhere else, deep down inside himself. Something had changed.

Volya stopped at a gap between two small buildings and guided them up an alleyway. Walking through another black doorway at the end of it, they were back in his lounge in an instant. The Earthlings couldn't help but be impressed with those doorways. The fire was, as ever, still lit in his home, and as they walked toward the seats and sat down, it made them all feel tired once again. Volya handed them each a stone chalice and filled them with fresh water from a large jug on a trolley that had been left just outside the seating ring.

"Is everything okay, Daniel? You seem troubled, if I may say so," Volya asked him.

Daniel was perched on the edge of his seat, his elbows resting on the tops of his knees. His face and eyes reflected the soft orange glow from the fire.

"Yes. I'm sorry, I'm okay. Just can't help feeling that there might be something that we aren't being told about this whole thing. Something feels . . . just off. I dunno, I can't put my finger on it."

"Daniel, please do not worry. Everything that you need to know has either already been said or will be shared with you soon. I am not lying to you, and neither are my people. Are there things above even me? Yes. The only advice I can give you right now, here . . ." He motioned with his hands like he was playing charades, moving them away from each other in a large circular motion as if to indicate the whole room. Then, strangely, he cupped his hands below each ear and raised his eyebrows in an obvious hint that others were possibly listening in on their conversation. ". . . is to follow the path that you are on. You will be fine here."

"I understand," Daniel said.

Amber watched silently, listening as she finished her warm, sweet drink. Something was going on. And now Daniel seemed to understand something that she didn't really pick up on.

At that, everyone's attention was pulled away from their drinks and the fire to an object that suddenly appeared through the doorway and then fell to the floor with a clatter at the head of the room.

"What's this?" Daniel asked, glaring at Volya.

"I don't know," Volya replied, looking as mystified as Amber and Daniel.

Volya stood, carefully placing his cup down, and walked over toward the object to pick it up. It looked like a slate, but it soon became active and glowed white as he looked at it, not unlike a tablet or an e-reader. Volya stared at it, frowned, and then flipped it into his other hand and back like a hot potato. "Ooh, oohh!"

He dropped it to the floor when its surface started to glow brighter and brighter, bursting into flame right before it hit the ground. It was now entirely on fire, and after barely a few seconds aflame the object was no more than a small pile of ash.

Both Amber and Daniel stood, wondering what the hell was going on.

"I realize that this is going to add to the mistrust that exists, but please trust that I can't say right now what that was. But keep in mind that I do have your best interests at heart." Volya sighed, then added, "I hope you don't mind, but today has been tiring and I think we should retire for the night."

Volya was indeed correct, this had indeed added yet another layer of mistrust between the guests and their host. *Just when we were getting to like him. Yet he seems so genuine! What is he up to?* Amber thought.

Amber looked at her watch. Wednesday 16:00 stared back. She had been here for two days! *Hopefully, Mom is still on pause and not struggling on her own.* It riled her more and more every time she thought about being held here. Sure, they were comfortable enough and being made quite welcome, but she couldn't bring herself to forgive them. It wasn't Volya's fault; he was obviously a yes-man, the Director's puppet.

Volya quietly led them through the doorway and then they were back below in the bedroom area. Amber made her way up the staircase to use the wet room, then Daniel went up after she had returned. He still held a deep look of concentration on his face and was now sighing more often. As he got to the top step, he looked at Volya, frowning in a way that even made her feel uncomfortable. Volya couldn't look at him, instead choosing to look down at the floor.

The atmosphere had died. *What is going on?* Amber thought.

Volya was the last to use the wet room.

Whilst Volya was above, Daniel leaned in closer to Amber, who was sitting on her bed massaging her loose wet hair with her fingers. Daniel made a pointing gesture to the ceiling and then cupped his ears, trying to indicate that there may be people listening.

"Follow me after he's asleep. Something's going on, and I want to find out what it is. Can't explain now." He was very careful to make as little sound as possible as he barely breathed out the words, adding extra enunciation to make sure that she understood.

She nodded gravely.

# CHAPTER 18
# THE OTHER SIDE

Amber woke with a start. Daniel was standing right in front of her, lightly tapping on her shoulder. He was miming for her to shush and was anxiously looking between her and Volya.

Daniel then reached for her wrist and very gently tilted it to read her watch. Wednesday 20:06. Amber stood up and they both stared at Volya, who appeared to be fast asleep.

Daniel led the way as they crept toward the black doorway. Amber felt both confused and scared. Without Volya to tell the doorway where they wanted to go, where the hell were they going to end up? *We could end up dead floating in space or something!* She sure hoped Daniel knew what he was doing. He looked a lot less nervous than she felt; there was an air of confidence and determination about him now as he strode toward the door and straight through. He seemed to know what he was doing, so she followed. *What have I got to lose, really?*

Daniel and Amber successfully passed through the doorway for the first time on their own. Neither of them had any idea where they had ended up, but both had gone past the point of caring now. Being told that they would not be allowed to return home had given them both an almost reckless courage that made them believe that whatever came next, they would either meet their fate or be on their way home. Better to try something and to fail than to sit and accept being new pets for these people.

The landscape that greeted them this time was very different from everywhere that they had seen so far; they now stood in an industrial plant room or factory. They were not on Prime anymore—or if they were, this place was way down, tucked out of the way somewhere. Both stood there, looking around and wondering, *What now?*

"Are we home? Are we back?" Amber asked.

"No, I don't think so. I doubt that it would be that easy. Somebody is supposed to know that we're coming."

Behind them was the black doorway, and in front of them was a metal grate ramp leading up at an angle. At the top, the room opened out into a larger area. Below them through the grating, they could see another level filled with boilers, machinery, cables, and conduits. Steam came rising up through the floor and it was warm and humid. There were people busy working away down there.

The sound of pumps and machines whirring away was deafening. The large round room opened up as they walked up to the top of the ramp, revealing a space with floor-to-ceiling computer screens and control stations all around the room. Every edge was illuminated with readings, lights, and displays. The ceiling was a mass of pipes, cables, and conduits running every which way overhead, while metal grating continued throughout beneath their feet. People within the chamber were busy working all around them at the stations.

The pale people here looked like the crew of a ship or workers in a factory. They were dressed in red robes and crimson-colored military uniforms rather than the gray ones Amber and Daniel had seen elsewhere. They walked around with their personal computer screens open, tapping and swiping and then sitting down to operate screens around the perimeter of the room, barely even noticing Amber and Daniel.

At the center of this industrial-looking control room was a sort of throne. A large comfortable-looking armchair was fixed to the center of a circular platform raised from the floor by a few feet with steps all around its edges. Sitting on his chair, spinning around and pausing to speak to different parts of the room and overseeing all of the hustle and bustle, was a pale-faced man with a cheerfully commanding presence in a slim-fitting red military-style uniform. He must have noticed that he now had guests standing there looking lost, as he stood up, smiled warmly, and waved them over.

They started walking toward the man, weaving through people busily walking this way and that all around this bridge-style room. The friendly-faced man hopped down the three steps from his pedestal and met them halfway.

"Welcome!" he greeted, looking extremely happy to see them, throwing his arms around each of them in turn. "I am Vanir. Thank you very much for coming!"

Around fortyish, he was slim and wore a crimson uniform complete with medals adorning his chest. He was cleanly shaven and quite handsome with thick jet-black hair slicked back on his head. Amber couldn't help but think what a charming, good-looking man he was.

Daniel replied to their greeter, "Well, I wasn't sure what to do. I take it that was one of your contacts who told me to take us through the doorway in Volya's house? I didn't know where we were going to end up. But I thought about it, and well . . . what did we have to lose?"

"Yes, I completely understand. This must all be incredibly strange for you. I sincerely apologize for the politics that you have become embroiled in. Well, welcome to my ship! We are very happy to have you here, and I thank you again for deciding to come."

Amber had stayed silent until now, trusting that Daniel

knew what he was doing, but she was starting to feel annoyed again. She didn't even want to be on Prime any longer, and now she was being told that she was somewhere else, only now she was on a spaceship—God knows where—with the very maniacs that had attacked the shopping district earlier.

Frustrated, she asked, "Why did you attack somewhere where you knew that we would be, and then welcome us to your ship like we're best friends?! None of this makes any sense."

"I know, this must all seem so crazy to you. We don't have much time, so I'll be blunt—the reason we needed to bring you here is that we need your help. In return, if I get what I need, I may be able to help you get what you need. You see, those arrogant so-called rulers in charge over there sitting in their plush palaces, taking important choices away from the people that they rule, are not at all interested in what I have to say. Even though we only want everyone in this dark miserable system to have the choice of living better, brighter, and healthier lives—if they even want to. I am not trying to impose anything on anyone; I only want to give the people the choice.

"Their spheres—which our people helped to build, I might add; I'm sure you know which ones I mean—I need help to obtain them. My intention is to integrate them into my technology and make it work to its fullest potential, which would help billions of people.

"We've built a passageway, you see, like the ones we use to transport goods and people throughout the system. I have been working on improving this passageway for decades, as did my father before me. I do not plan on giving up easily. You see, if I could get my hands on those spheres, even if I got my hands on one, it would not only help us but everyone who is unhappy and stuck in this miserable dark system. We could finally leave it!"

Daniel interrupted, "Sorry, but I have to ask, if there are reasons that the people of Prime don't want you to have their technology, what makes you think that we should help you get it? There must be a logical reason that they don't want to give it to you. Even if we did want to—even if we would be able to help you—how are we supposed to do anything about it anyway? We are constantly escorted everywhere. We don't even know how to use the doorways on our own. They have guards carrying weapons shadowing us. And when we did see the sphere on Earth, as soon as we touched them, we ended up on Prime."

"I understand your reluctance. So far, the people of Prime have probably been quite civil to you, shown you around, comforted you. And now the very people that attacked Prime are here begging for your help.

"This is how important it is and how I might be able to help you in return. With one sphere, I could integrate it into my passageway, the passageway that so far only allows for travel within the Dark Space. That one sphere would enable a link to the light space, allowing us to pinpoint a coordinate on the other side of the black hole. It would enable travel through the black hole and back into the Light Space. Now, with two spheres integrated, the passageway would be able to pinpoint any point in time. So, with both of your spheres, I could open up a fully operational passage to go anywhere in space and time that we wished.

"With this, our people could resettle anywhere in time and space that they wanted to. We could even go back to our home planet in the past, or any planet, for that matter, from long before we lost our solar system to the dying Sun and then to the black hole. We could all live in the Light Space again."

"But you're still not explaining why you attacked us!" Amber interrupted. "We were there watching you! Why should we trust you now? If you could return everyone to normal space, then why don't those on Prime help you?"

"A fair question. Firstly, the attack—it was simply a diversion, nothing more than a light show. They always are; we have no wish to hurt anyone if it is avoidable. That is simply a way that we can cause a distraction, which enables us to sneak operatives and guests on and off Prime. The operative that spoke to you, Daniel—that was the reason for this attack. He was being sent down to speak to you. There are many people on Prime that wish to help our cause, but they are also scared of the Director and his controlling government. Even our planet's leader is a part of their greedy, treacherous leadership. We are known as rebels—rebels!

"With regards to the situation from the Director's side, well, imagine if a group of people said to your government where you came from that they were thinking about changing your entire way of life, that which they have spent centuries building up. That you plan to split the population in half, perhaps even more, to take them away and live somewhere completely different, back to where your ancestors lived, away from their rules and their taxes. I understand their reluctance, but why shouldn't the people have any choice? In the beginning, wherever we do resettle—likely in the dust of our ancient home, if you can help us—we would have new governments, our own rules and infrastructure. We would rise from the dust a better system, one built for the people, by the people."

"I guess I understand. If it leads to a better quality of life for the people, it sounds like it might be worth a try," Amber said.

"They don't want you to succeed, do they?" Daniel added.

"No. They are so controlling; the central government of the Dark Space Union does not want to relinquish their control over the people. Plus, there is a very small risk that this might not work. Without the spheres, this is only a mathematical model, but we are very confident in our work. I don't think that is their main reason, though.

"We have been planning this project for a very long time. Generations of people on both planets have sacrificed their lives to help calculate, design, and engineer this project. All that is missing are the spheres to test it. I have waited years to get my hands on a sphere, and that one person that would arrive through it, to help us get it. They don't even use the damn spheres anymore. One sphere would have been life-changing, but now two have arrived! And from our ancient home system, no less. I do not think this was random, nor do I think this chance will ever come again. We cannot get our operatives over on Prime anywhere near them."

He headed back down the ramp toward the black doorway. He waved them toward him and as they followed, he strolled through the doorway, disappearing.

They were outside again. One minute they were on a ship, and the next they were on the ground on another world in the Dark Space. The soil they now stood on was red and dusty like a desert. Daniel looked up into the dark sky and could see a dark slither of another rock, which must be Prime. The other planet was only a very slim, dark crescent, the same way Secondary had looked from Prime.

There was the start of a city behind them beneath a vast protective dome that looked to be made of glass. The dome was illuminated from beneath by lights in the ground looking up into the sky. The three of them stood at the juncture point of two domes. As the domes overlapped, they joined higher up but remained open at the bases, allowing for seamless passage from one to the next.

This planet also used the mini-Sun balls they had seen on Prime that hovered in the sky to provide light and heat.

Out in front of them, beneath the next dome in front of the city, were miles and miles of red dusty hills and mountains for as far as the eye could see until the blackness of the Dark Space took the view from them again.

There was a road in the red soil leading off away from the city into the desert from where they stood. It disappeared down into a large hole in the ground up ahead.

The three of them started to walk along the road, following

it for a couple of hundred yards just before reaching the top of the hole. Now they gazed down into a vast crater.

The road was still visible. It led down a gentle incline, following the side of the crater and gradually winding down into a flat plateau at the base that appeared to house a facility of some sort.

Right in the center of the base stood what Daniel could only describe as a huge industrial steampunk version of the Arc de Triomphe from France.

Around the top of the arch's frame were twinkling lights, struts, hoses, and cables. There was more framework linking its sides to other machines and large boxes that looked like substations with their own working consoles and engineers on either side of the arch.

The road then leveled off along the bottom of the plateau, leading to a ramp that passed right through the archway, carrying on again for a short straight run before coming to a halt a little further out the other side.

They walked down the side of the crater and along the flat access road, approaching the huge structure and its ramp. Several people who looked like engineers or scientists were busy working around the gaping structure, checking screens and gauges at either side and using their hand computers.

Daniel and Amber were surprised at how big this thing was up close. It was an awesome sight indeed—they had to crane their necks to look up at it. *You could drive a cruise liner right underneath it*, Daniel thought in awe.

# CHAPTER 19
# THE PASSAGEWAY

Several floating globes of light burned brightly above them. They were bright enough for it to look like daytime where they were. Back on Prime, where they had left Volya in bed, it had still been nighttime.

One of the machine operators, looking over from his station at the side of the archway, saluted Vanir. "Oh, perfect! Watch this." Vanir returned a nod to the operator in reply, which set the engineer off operating a combination of different controls in front of him.

The loud clunk of switchgear deep inside the structure making contact echoed around the complex. A low thunderous hum followed.

Amber and Daniel watched with interest. It felt as though something was spinning very fast deep inside the arch, and lights began to speed around the frame of the arch following the whirring noise. They could feel the ground vibrating beneath their feet. Amber watched as the dust danced atop the crater floor. This thing was deep as well as huge.

Right in the center of the space inside the archway, a bright white dot of light appeared. It appeared no bigger than a ping-pong ball at first, then the light started to twinkle, and it began rotating in time with the patterns of light around the archway. The light inside the arch was growing larger by the second. As the growing ball of light rotated faster and faster, its form changed from a white spinning ball to a large white pattern like a swirling galaxy. Then it disappeared in a bright flash, leaving behind a misty white veil that covered the whole of the space inside the arch's mouth.

A group of four people suddenly appeared through the cloudy veil. As they walked away from the mouth and down the access ramp, the white mist started to clear, the other side of the crater becoming visible again through the mouth of the machine.

The new arrivals each carried a silver briefcase and chatted jovially to the operators working around the arch structure.

"What was that?" Daniel asked, his eyes wide and impressed.

Vanir looked amused. "Those are my people. They have been using the passageway to visit some of the other planets in the Dark Space system. There are people on quite a few of the other worlds here that have been helping us by trading parts and tech advice. As I said, the only missing piece is over there on Prime—or where you came from, which brings me to how I can help you to help me.

"What I need from you, if you agree to help us, is quite simple and of low risk. It is in our best interests to engineer a way for you to get home. Don't worry—I am aware that so far you have been told that you won't be going home, but with the people we have on the ground there, I am trying everything I can to influence them and get that decision reversed. If not, I am more than prepared to make it happen by force, in which case there may be some risk. But I need you to get home so that you can help me, so I will do everything in my power to make that happen."

Amber felt her spirits instantly lift, making her shiver with excitement, it was the thought that somebody out here was willing to take risks for them to get home. She looked at Daniel and he smiled at her. She closed her eyes and thanked God. *Please make this work, and please let nobody get hurt making it happen.*

"When you do get home, and if you can help me, all I need is for you to wear this somewhere on your person." From his pocket, he pulled out a small golden coin with some detailing on it. A very small white light the size of a pinprick sat glowing in its center.

"Carry this with you in your pockets. That will suffice. They will not be able to see it or detect it, but this device will allow us to pinpoint the precise locations of you and the spheres in space-time. When you get home, simply place it on the ground next to your sphere. You will not have to do anything else. We should be able to make contact with the spheres from here, and we are confident that we can take control of them. This link will allow us to bring them back here to us without the people of Prime even realizing that they've lost them. They will wonder where they are after a while, of course, when they don't return home, but by then we will have already adapted them into the circuits on the passageway and started to use them. We will already be on Ancient Mars, building our new cities."

Daniel was beginning to look around at his surroundings now; his attention span could be quite short sometimes. He looked from the passageway to Vanir, then at the crater around him, and then sharply back at Vanir, as though suddenly coming back to reality. Realizing what he had just heard in the background, he said, "Wait a minute . . . did you say Mars? Our Mars?"

"Yes!" Vanir beamed. Obviously Amber and Daniel had not yet been made aware of the full details of where they were. "Our planet was once Mars, and Prime was once Earth. Didn't they tell you that?"

"No, they bloody didn't. They made out that we were off in

some faraway galaxy, somewhere out in space, and nowhere near our home."

"Well, I suppose they are not lying to you, from a certain point of view. Maybe not giving you the whole truth, but not lying. The galaxy at the other side of the black hole in the Light Space is a completely different place than it was in your time. In your time, the Milky Way galaxy is currently on a collision course to merge with your neighboring galaxy, Andromeda. You still have around four and a half billion years from your time yet.

"Most of the planets that were still around from your time were scattered and lost when your Sun burned up all of its fuel. What planets remained either got pulled into the black hole to make their new home here or were pulled into a different part of the new galaxy, forming new systems. Some didn't make it at all. But you are standing on Mars, my friends. And in case you didn't realize it, you have been back on Earth all along, albeit almost eleven billion years into the future from your own time."

"Oh my god!" Amber gasped. "They did explain about the Sun, the galaxy, and all that black hole stuff. But not once did they mention that we have been spending all of this stupid time on Earth."

Vanir continued trying to clarify things for them, for it wasn't quite as straightforward as Amber or Daniel thought.

"It is your Earth, my friends, but to be fair to them, it is a very long way from the planet as you know it. The solar system you knew is long gone. Earth had long since been abandoned. It was completely uninhabitable for a very long time, nothing but a hot hostile wasteland. You wouldn't have lasted more than a second on its surface. It's a miracle it even survived at all, in truth. Mars was left barely habitable because, by sheer luck, the force of expansion pushed her out into safer, cooler orbit.

"A few of the smaller planets and moons didn't make it though and were consumed into the Sun. The Earth was a hair's breadth from the same fate. Life as you know it was gone; it had to evolve on Earth and Mars from the very beginning. It wasn't until millions of years later that people started to move back onto the Earth, the Motherland, and that is when it became known as Prime. It was meant to be the home of the new central government, a diplomatic center for the whole Dark Space Union. Mars became known as Secondary. The Director and his new central government that was supposed to represent the people's interests only ended up looking after themselves, and greed took over.

"Prime was the first planet to be rebuilt. This followed a hundred years of war. All planets were supposed to have an input as to what kind of government and infrastructure would be the new way going forward. They were supposed to bring order to the system, but a thirst for power and wealth got into their heads, and the governors of the system craved more and more lavish lifestyles. They sit on their fortunes in their palaces now, enjoying riches taken from their people. The depths of the palaces, meanwhile, filled with prisoners collected from all corners of the Light and Dark Universes, including political prisoners from my home, Secondary—those that support us."

Amber understood that she was billions of years from everything and everyone that she knew and loved, and yet she had been on her home planet all along. She couldn't help but focus on the fact that right now, in this time period, her mom was dead—long dead. Amber should be dead. And the people that they had thought were being nice—keeping them here, but being as polite as they could be about it—were nothing but judgmental kidnapping sociopaths. *Keeping visitors here as prisoners! For what? For fun, for amusement, for some sort of weird collection? Just because they can?*

The more she thought about it, the angrier she got.

Vanir walked toward her, seeing the hurt and the anger emanating from her like heat, and put an arm around her shoulder. "Please, do not worry, Amber. I will make sure that one way or another, you will be returned home soon, back to your own timeline. Earth is a very important part of our history. I need to make this happen, for your sake and mine, and I will. That is a promise. All we want to do is to give the choice to as much of the population that wishes to join us as we can, whether they live where they are or relocate onto Mars in the distant past and enjoy the Sun on their backs. We will build our new home on our ancestral home planet, and we will prosper. I only wish to give them the choice—this is the most important thing.

"Our wish is to resettle on Mars, not far from your own timeline. I think that we will go back a little further into the past from your time, so that we will have at least half a century of growing our civilization on Mars before mankind even thinks about exploring Mars. Hopefully, we will be better prepared this time for what we know is to come. If we know the exact time and scale of what is to come, then better decisions can be made to prepare us."

Amber started to feel the weight gradually lifting from her shoulders. She was reading only positives from this meeting. This man and his people needed their help, and he seemed honest. And for their help, he would help them hugely in return. He needed them as much as they needed him. What reason did he have to lie to them?

"Well, I'm happy to help you. If I can help you and you will help us get home to do it, then I'm all in."

"Thank you, Amber."

Daniel took a quiet look around, scanning the red dusty horizon and also inside himself, thinking, trying to come up with any reason at all not to help them. He thought about Volya and the people he had met so far. He thought about all of the people that would benefit from feeling the Sun on their skin, and how much happier, lighter, and more colorful things would be, and then came to his conclusion. "Yes, I'll help you. I can't see anything wrong with your reasoning, either, and if you're going to get us home, why not?"

"Thank you, my friends." Vanir handed them each a gold coin from his pocket. "Put this in your pockets. They will not think to search you, so you will not come to any harm. Follow their leads. For now, remain polite and remember, when you do see the spheres again, put the coins down on the ground right next to them. We will do the rest from here.

"Just to warn you, I intend to move instantly on this. Now that I know that you are happy to help me, that is all I needed to know. I will arrange everything, so do not worry. You have nothing more to think about, aside from planting those devices next to your spheres." He smiled. "There will be some resistance to allowing you home. Prepare yourselves. I will have help ready to guide you when you get back to Prime."

Vanir's look took a slightly more serious turn. "Okay, now we need to get you back before you are missed." He opened up his personal computer and made a series of movements with his fingers. A black doorway rose from the floor in front of him. "Follow me."

They appeared back in his ship's control room. He walked over to a panel on a console against the wall and swiped his finger across its screen. "Right. Go through that door over there, please," Vanir instructed, pointing to the original doorway at the bottom of the ramp. "Good luck, my friends!"

Daniel stepped through, followed by Amber, who looked back at him gratefully as she disappeared.

# CHAPTER 20
# THE RELUCTANT HELP

Amber and Daniel reappeared back in Volya's bedroom in an instant. Volya was fast asleep in his bed; the fire was still crackling away. They crept back into their beds, moving through the room like a couple of mimes, heads full of new revelations, thoughts, and excitement. They tried their best to get some sleep, though both knew that would be near impossible.

Both tossed and turned for hours. The tide had completely changed. They now found themselves stuck in the middle of a political planetary war, befriending one race and trying to gain their trust and conform, mainly to show that they deserved to be sent home. And now they were on a course to support their captor's enemy, to double-cross them in an effort to get home. What was that saying Amber had heard before? *The enemy of your enemy is your friend,* or something like that.

But if this went wrong, they could be killed. At the very least, they would rot in a cell here and never be allowed home.

Daniel considered Volya, how nice he had seemed. But he couldn't help wondering whether he was as nice as he had seemed. He had kept so much from them. *Maybe he had to. It's likely that he didn't have any choice in this. He said that he had been petitioning for us, on our behalf. Had he been, really?*

It felt like only a couple of hours had gone by when Daniel woke, remembering his phone in his pocket as it dug into his side. He was thinking about home so much that he took it out and stared at it. How taken for granted this little device usually was. Your family and the world were always at your fingertips. Without them, you were so alone. Might it possibly start working again if he really wanted it to?

The screen staring back was black. Nothing whatsoever was shown on the display now, not even the time where it had frozen. He held down the power button, then the volume and power buttons together, desperately hoping. Nothing. "Damn it!" he whispered. *Still dead.*

Even if he couldn't make any calls or texts, how he would have loved to be able to see some photos of his family, maybe even take some photos of the future, or to simply be able to read some old messages from his family. No messages or calls would be able to reach home, of course—he knew that. The signal would need to bend back in time and space. Right now, everyone he wanted to call was dead.

And if, in some pocket of reality, they were still there, frozen, if the call could somehow travel back in time, well . . . how would they know, anyway? They wouldn't be able to answer him, and they probably didn't even know that he was gone.

Amber's face peered over the stone slab that formed the headboard of his bed. She nodded at Daniel, motioning with her eyes and head over toward where Volya had been sleeping; he was gone. She then noticed Daniel's phone in his hands.

"Does it work?" she whispered, her face lighting up.

"No, I'm sorry. It's still dead." He was starting to feel down himself now, missing his family more with each day. He noticed her face drop and knew how much it would have meant to her if the phone worked; it didn't help his mood that he couldn't help her to feel better. Daniel noticed her watch and, changing the subject, he brightly asked her, "What day and time are we on now?"

"It's Thursday, and a quarter to five in the morning. God . . . Thursday. We've been here for three days now."

"I know. I've lost interest in all of this now. It wasn't too bad at first, but I'm ready for home, I must admit," Daniel said. "I hope this Vanir is true to his word."

Volya appeared through the doorway a second after Daniel had mentioned Vanir— *That was close*—carrying a large tray. On top were three mugs of a steaming hot drink and plates of pancakes and scrambled eggs.

*This is so strange*, Daniel thought. *We're here, knowing now that this was Earth—but a different Earth—in the far future. And yet they still have eggs, and pancakes.* How did they know what to cook for them? Daniel looked at Amber's face and he could tell she was thinking exactly the same thing.

As well as the steaming drinks, there were also three smaller stone tumblers holding a kind of fruit juice and some actual fruit on the side. Daniel didn't recognize the fruit, though. They were round, apple-shaped green fruits with red seeds within the skin and red leaves flowing down from the top where the stem protruded out between the leaves. Volya put the tray down on the end of the sofa and had a serious look on his face.

"Good morning," Volya said. "I trust you slept well? No adventures off anywhere?"

Amber and Daniel exchanged nervous glances with a mutual look that asked, *What does he know?*

"Adventures?" Daniel asked cautiously, his voice breaking halfway through his words.

"Your dreams? I would imagine with everything that has been going on, you would have been having some wild dreams, no?"

"Ahhhh, dreams! It's not often I remember mine, to be honest," Daniel replied.

He passed them each one of the warm mugs. "It's a

wonderful morning outside. We are orbiting closer to the black hole every day; three more weeks and our planet will lighten and warm again significantly."

He pointed up at the ceiling, then drew a circle in the air. Then he cupped his ears. "They're listening," he mouthed, then he motioned for them to come in closer.

He opened his computer. Daniel and Amber moved closer to him and he put his arm around each of their shoulders. Now he whispered, barely speaking louder than the passage of air brushing past his lips.

"Private mode again." He looked up and around. "Keep it low, though, just in case. I know where you were last night." He spoke so quietly, the *T* at the end of "night" came out in a quite loud tutting sound—that formed the loudest part of his sentence.

Amber and Daniel, feeling very uneasy, looked at each other and then back at Volya, not saying a word yet. They were trying to read any sign of emotion on his face, difficult as that could be. Was he upset with them, or would he raise the alarm?

If need be, Daniel was ready to fight his way out of here. He didn't know how far he would get before Karen arrived or what would happen afterward, but he would try. He was confident that he could knock out Volya if he needed to. He didn't have much to lose, depending on how far Vanir was willing to go, and how quickly he could get here, in bringing the fight to Prime to help get them home. If not, they would be alone, and their chances would not be good on their own.

Volya continued, "I am not a rebel like Vanir—I want to make that absolutely clear. My family has been loyal to the Directorship for generations. But I do want to help you. I believe in Vanir's wish to give choice to our people. I have served the Directorship under two Directors so far during my time. I hadn't planned on a mutiny but, if that is what it takes, so be it.

"The Director told me this morning—after I petitioned him

again—that he does not, in any way, plan to return you home. It would just take up too much energy. For now, he is happy for you to stay with me; if all else fails, I would be happy to take you into my home. I know that this would not be your first choice. You are young, and having spent time with you, I can see that you need to be with your families. It is not right to keep you here. Maybe the Director deserves the consequences of whatever happens next."

Amber felt her stomach sink again. Every time she heard the words spoken that she would not be allowed home, it felt like they were killing more parts of her off inside.

"So we will have to go with Vanir and his 'plan B,' " Amber concluded sternly. She felt inside her pocket and could feel the coin rolling between her fingertips. She wondered what would happen next and how they might be able to get word to Vanir that he would need to step in and help them.

"Vanir has already been informed, don't worry. Just continue to follow my lead."

Volya looked around, his eyes narrowed. He was thinking something over. He got up and walked to the far end of the room then bent down, disappearing behind the seating area. When he came back up, he was holding an old wooden chest. He balanced it on the back of the seats, the metal clasps holding it shut clonking as he flicked them open. He took out what looked like a metal piece of either jewelry—or armor.

He put the sleeve-shaped piece of dull gray metal around his wrist. It went all the way from his wrist to just below the crook of his elbow, and he clasped it shut around his forearm. It was clamped tightly around his arm that contained his personal computer, Daniel noticed.

*It's so they can't track him,* he theorized.

"Follow me now. I have an idea. There is no point waiting now."

Volya's face had changed from that of a calm, gentle old man to a determined man on a mission. He meant business now.

Amber and Daniel followed him through the doorway, and within seconds they were outside again. They were back on the mountainside, the familiar viewing balcony on Mount Shasta.

Looking over the quiet city, the sky didn't seem as dark a black today. The floating globes below shined their light and warmth down onto the streets and homes, making it appear as though it was a bright sunny morning at street level. It was all artificial, though—nothing at all like the real thing.

Volya stood between them as he looked up into the sky, then unclasped his new sleeve piece, placing it on the wall separating them from the drop below, and flicked open his computer. He used the computer for a few minutes, swiping and typing very quickly, almost appearing to be in a panic while Daniel and Amber stood nearby nervously, wondering what he was thinking or what his plan could be. He was fully consumed, not offering any explanation of what he was doing, but Amber and Daniel suspected that this might be him somehow getting word to Vanir.

"My friends," he started to explain now, refastening his sleeve armor. "Things are about to get ugly, I'm afraid. Follow my lead—whatever I say, no matter how bizarre it sounds, just do it. Do not stop to ask questions. Do exactly as I say, immediately."

"What's going to happen, Mr. Volya?" Amber asked. She was the most nervous that she had ever felt. it was really happening—what exactly, she wasn't sure, but she didn't want anyone to get hurt for their cause. She felt a strange mixture of terror and hope. *Could all of this lead to us getting home?* Something in his voice suggested that this was going to be a rocky road for a while. And not without risk; Vanir had also said something like that.

"Honestly, I do not know yet. I suspect that, as Vanir needs you to return home so that he can reach the next phase of his ambitions, he will do whatever it takes to help us make that happen. I also suspect that it is going to take some force. It is unfortunate that it has come to this, but I can see its necessity. So, keep your wits about you. Do not lose concentration for a second.

"Gaining access to the old sphere manufacturing plant and returns suite will be tricky. Their only access is going to be deep underground, as the black doorways will be switched off as soon as an attack is detected on the surface. The city will be heavily guarded once an attack begins. Also, they will know where we are instantly as soon as we access it, so we will need to move very quickly, and . . . we will be in danger."

Volya ushered them back along the walkway toward the doorway. As soon as they stepped through it, they were back in Volya's living room. They sat on the couches, watched the fire, and waited.

Amber turned to Daniel. "Daniel, do you mind me asking your last name? I only ask because if we do make it home, I want to be able to find you on social media. At least we could keep in touch in the future that way."

"Austin. And you mean in the past." He smiled. "What about yours?"

"Roberts." She smiled. She would like to keep in touch with him once they were safely home. He was a nice boy, the younger brother she'd never had. She would request his sister too. He had said that she was very much like his sister, so she felt that they would probably get along—if his sister didn't think Amber was a big weirdo, of course. This stranger from Canada who . . . well, she supposed that would depend on what Daniel told her. Could they really tell anybody about all of this without sounding insane?

Breaking their thoughts and the serenity of the fire, an air-raid siren started blaring out once again. This was it. Amber and Daniel looked straight at Volya, whose expression was one of nervous expectancy. He looked like he had been expecting this yet wasn't looking forward to doing what he had made the choice to do. There would be no going back from this—he knew it.

"What do we do now?" Daniel asked.

"Wait for a second," Volya calmly replied, looking up. He took a deep breath in, closing his eyes. Then the doorway in Volya's bedroom changed from its standard matte black appearance to a simple gap in the wall, now showing a busy corridor behind it. Panic-stricken people ran amok, scared— this felt a lot more serious than last time. People were carrying their young and bags of belongings, some were crying, and they seemed much more rushed than during the previous attack. The siren blaring across the city sounded louder now.

The flow of people ran past Volya's doorway from left to right, young and old, male and female, whole families. Volya stood up and calmly took a position at his side of the doorway, looking out into the corridor and waiting. He poked his head out to check something, looking left and right, then said, "Follow me," waving them through.

The three of them walked out into the stream of shorter, gray-skinned people, Amber and Daniel towering over them. The Prime natives parted for them like water would part for large pebbles in a stream, and the three of them followed the flow of people down the corridor.

There were many doorways off the corridor going left and right, offering a view into other people's houses. More and more people were filtering out of their homes into the corridor with them.

None of the doorways were black anymore; they had all turned from the black automatic transport portals, taking you wherever you wanted to go, to standard doorways, just as Volya had said would happen in the event of an actual attack.

In the distance, pounding noises echoed followed by loud booms and the unmistakable loud whistling sounds of weapons falling from the sky. More panic arose in the corridor. The speed of the crowd increased dramatically, people scooping up their young as they ran.

"Was that an explosion?" Daniel shouted over the noise.

"Yes, it sounded like it," Volya replied.

They reached the end of the corridor and people spilled out from the open doorways at the end into a huge outdoor walled complex. The area resembled a military airfield complex, a huge flat concrete area with concrete walls surrounding it, in the shadow of the huge black pyramid. Concrete towers in intervals around the walls rose high above into the sky with huge cannons sat on top of them. Over on the far side there was a group of grounded aircraft, sleek as arrows and made from a metal as shiny as chrome.

An automated voice filled the air, "Civilians, this is not a drill. Please make your way to the safety shelters as soon as possible. If you can, fight with your lives. Protect your Director." The message was repeated over and over in the Director's voice.

Gray people in military uniforms ran through the crowd toward the shiny craft. The craft were about the same size as fighter jets, only instead of a cockpit, the whole craft was a shiny seamless chrome. No wings jutted outward from the sides; there were only very slim fins running along each side of the craft. Like the cars earlier, they did not make any contact with the floor. They floated just off the ground, awaiting their pilots.

Pilots scrambled toward the craft, hopping into them with determined expressions. The crafts bounced slightly in the air as they loaded in. Interestingly, the entry point into the silver craft appeared automatically—a hole opened up on the side like liquid metal, ready to accept the pilots as they approached. The hole in the craft sealed up again behind them, not leaving a single line visible as the pilot got comfortable inside.

Quietly the machines started to rise into the air with only a dull magnetic hum, like the sound an electrical transformer might make as current ran through its core. They were able to perform maneuvers as freely as they liked, much smoother and more mobile than the jets back on Earth. They rose and simply stopped in the air, then rotated with ease to get their noses up toward the incoming enemy with fluid, purposeful movements.

Amber and Daniel watched from the sidelines with Volya. He was waiting for something. As the enemy approached Prime's domes, high in the dark sky, they unleashed another light show, this time louder than before. A dull *thud, thud, thud* filled the space beneath. Lights exploded like fireworks in the dark sky as the weapons hit the dome's protective layer. The enemy craft had a lot more intent this time. This was no practice.

Prime's craft, numbering in their dozens so far with even more pilots running toward idle craft, rose into the sky, forming several triangle formations above the compound, ready to meet their attackers head-on when the inevitable happened.

Gasps and cries of terrified civilians echoed throughout the compound around Amber, Daniel, and Volya as the clear protective domes above began to struggle under the pressure of the bombardment. Bright blasts of energy rained down through newly created holes being forced through the skin of the dome.

A second wave of enemy craft followed, firing their weapons with precision, aiming for the holes before the dome had a chance to heal itself. Light rained down through the gaps. Beams of plasma drove down through the air toward the city, sending entire buildings up into the air in pieces and causing panic and carnage everywhere. Rubble and glass were thrown all over the place.

People screamed and ran for the protection of the covers that were only now opening in the ground, as they had in the city center. Glass shards and rocks rained back down, splitting people in half. Flying rubble knocked people sideways, leaving bloody bodies by the shelter access panels as people pushed each other, frenzied by fear, to get inside.

Things had taken a desperately sad turn for the worse.

"Well, this doesn't look like a light show!" Daniel shouted over the chaos, still looking up. Amber cowered behind Daniel, using the tall young man as a shield, or a comfort blanket.

Volya looked around purposefully, trying to see over the crowd around him. He watched as several garrisons of guards, similar in appearance to Karen, ran from one side of the compound to the other in the direction of the palace. They ran through gates that surrounded the palace, which towered over the compound to the far right of where they stood. He wanted to go left—this was good.

Volya shouted, almost sounding angry, but he was solely focused on the task at hand: getting them home. "It is time! Follow me, quickly now! They will be after us next."

He sliced through the crowd, lowering his head as he did so, trying his best not to stand out as he ran against the flow of racing families, still running for shelter. Daniel and Amber copied his hunched pose, needing to hunch down even further than Volya, being taller than everyone else around them.

They fought their way through the stream of people, cutting this way then that way, steadily making a route for themselves over to the far-left side of the compound. All the while as they hurried, more and more buildings and walls of the compound were turned to rubble, flinging debris in all directions, some just barely missing them. The whole compound groaned under the assault. The ground quaked and the screams of people could not be ignored. Neither of them had wanted it to come to this.

More heavy industrial-looking flaps in the ground parted for the civilians as whole slabs of concrete lifted into the air, supported by sturdy looking steel pneumatic arms, swallowing the innocent and granting them sanctuary from the bombardment. The normally calm and quite emotionless people were pushing and shoving their way down the steps now. Parents carrying their young were shouting behind them for the shoving to stop. The heavy concrete flaps groaned again, falling and sealing up behind them.

As the three escapees approached a wall at the far edge of the compound, a locked steel door cut flush into the thick-set concrete wall greeted them. Volya stepped up to the gate, unclasping his recently acquired wrist armor, and flashed his wrist to a black glass plate set into the wall.

Beyond the gate as it slowly creaked open under the stress of aged hinges, they saw a long patchwork pathway through a rather dull, old, and mostly dead garden. This was clearly a part of the city that was no longer in use. The path led to a large building only a hundred yards ahead of them. It appeared to be an old, abandoned factory.

Unbeknownst to Volya, he had been spotted by none other than Karen, who had been told to keep a close eye on Volya from afar. Karen and another member of the Director's guard kept their distance, staying out of view as they watched the traitor and his guests go through the gate.

The steel door to the plant ahead opened automatically as Volya, Amber, and Daniel approached it. Old machinery and work benches lay unused and dusty on either side of them as they proceeded to walk along a pathway through the middle.

Volya led the way whilst also keeping an active eye out behind them. Thinking he had been careful enough, they hurried through the antiquated factory. It was dark, but slits of light from the spheres outside spilled in through narrow windows higher up the walls, giving just enough light to see where they were walking.

They came to another door at the far end. Volya slid the huge door open. It had to be twenty feet wide and just as high. It looked to be very heavy metal, but it rolled easily enough on its casters as Volya pulled on its handle with two hands.

Another empty ancient-looking hangar lay beyond that with strange foreign markings in the stone and metalwork walls. This was a huge warehouse with empty racks that seemed to go up for miles. The noise of the intruders caused a flock of some-thing quite large and dark to fly across the space high above them, making them jump as unsettled dust fell around them from high up.

The low rumble of the attack and explosions from outside still echoed throughout the warehouse, causing Amber and Daniel to look up and around them with fear—not only for themselves, but for the civilians that they had put right in the middle of their mess.

Volya said, "They'll know we're here and that I'm helping you now. We must hurry."

Volya stopped midway in the old warehouse, getting down on his knees and yanking up a round metal hatch in the floor. It was like a heavy manhole cover in the ground on hinges. "Hurry—climb down to the bottom and wait for me."

They each climbed in, Amber first, then Daniel, and Volya last, who pulled the cover closed above them with another loud *gong*.

*Thank God I had a chance to get changed!* Amber thought. What she had been wearing would have only slowed her down.

The shaft beneath them was pitch-black once Volya had sealed them inside, and it smelled old. The brickwork that made up the circular shaft was aged and damp, sporting decades of growth.

They climbed down the long rusting ladder as quickly as they could. Once at the bottom, they were standing in nothing but blackness. It smelled even more of old damp metal, leaving a coppery taste in their mouths, and there were cobwebs every-where they turned.

Volya unclasped his wrist armor again and opened his computer, bathing the dark corridor with white light. He tapped a combination of buttons in the air, then a green holo-graphic 3D map glowed, showing tunnels and ducts hovering above his shaking hand.

He looked up, then around to gather his bearings and

started to run down the long tunnel. They must have been running for a mile along this tunnel. Amber concentrated as she ran, trying to get the directions right in her head. If she was correct, they were heading away from the city. The only thing in this direction that she could think of was the mountain they had viewed the city from earlier. *Are we running all the way underneath the mountain to the other side?*

Volya stopped as the tunnel came to an end and they came to another ladder. This one went up from the tunnel into another long, round shaft. He started to climb up it, moving swiftly. Amber and Daniel followed. They came to a metal hatch, this one with nutted bolts at the four quarters of it. Volya struggled to undo them with his hands, gripping one nut at a time in both hands, almost toppling from the high ladder as he tried to lean against the wall of the shaft around him. Daniel tried to help by climbing up the ladder to sandwich Volya's legs tightly against the ladder. Volya was finally able to spin the nuts, grateful for Daniel's help.

Daniel helped him to push the hatch; it was thick and heavy.

Amber thought, *Thank God!* when they opened it. More stale air poured in as they climbed up into another room. The only light was the dregs shining down through a circular hole in the roof. She stepped away from the hole and Volya disappeared into the shadows. Then they heard a loud echoing *clunk* sound. Moments later, old orange lights came to life and then buzzed as they started illuminating the huge room. One after another they came on until the length of this new hangar was revealed.

Like the other areas that they had come through, this room was also very old-fashioned, smelled of damp metal, and had obviously long been abandoned in this part of Prime, wherever they were.

"Sorry about that," Volya finally spoke. "Because the instant doorways have been turned off, it makes things a bit trickier. Let's hurry—we are almost there now."

He led them along a metal grated walkway and beneath an

archway in the wall into another large open room. He switched the lights on in here and they could now see where he had brought them. It was like an old Cold War nuclear testing facility from the fifties. Amber and Daniel looked around, taking in the decrepit machines that lined the walls against the right-hand side.

There were desks with screens and lifeless controls decorating them next to the machines. Some modern-looking black glass keyboards sat on the desks. *More modern than our keyboards at home*, Daniel thought. Around fifty yards ahead of them, protected by more glass partition screens, was another similar control desk.

On the far left-hand side of this room, running the whole length of the wall, were tiered seats protected again by large thick screens of glass separating the seating area from the rest of the room. Right in the center of the bunker, protruding through the floor with another one suspended above it, was a white round pad. It was around five feet in diameter and rose about a foot off the ground.

The other was suspended from the ceiling by stanchions and girders, the pads around eight feet apart from each other.

"And that is where you are going to stand, my friends. I'm going to send you home," Volya said, smiling nervously.

Amber ran to him, throwing her arms around him. "Thank you, thank you!" she effused, kissing him on his pale gray cheek. She had hoped that this was the plan, but confirming it was like all her Christmases had come at once.

Daniel was still standing next to Volya and patted him on the back for a job well done, then shook his hand. "Thank you so much for everything you have done for us. I know it wasn't down to you, keeping us here. I guess that you've also sacrificed a lot to help us get home. They won't be happy with you, will they?"

"I felt bad for what my people have put you through. I'm sorry for any hurt that you have been through. It never used to be like this; in the old times when these facilities were regularly in use, this whole facility would have been packed full of people ready to see off our guests with our thanks. But it hasn't been that way for almost fifty years. I am hoping this facility still works. We must hurry, though—they will know that we are here, and they will come for us!"

# CHAPTER 21
# DEATH & DESTRUCTION

"Amber, you stand on the pad first, please. Quickly now." Volya said from his control station.

Amber hugged Daniel, then moved around the protective glass screen and walked just a few feet to the set of upper and lower pads. Volya waved his hands frantically, indicating for Daniel to join him on this side of the screen.

Amber stepped up onto the pad. "Do I just stand here?"

"Yes, stand there, and I'll do the rest from here—if I can get it working again."

He looked anxious now. Sweat dripped down his forehead, his smile long gone. He knew, but did not highlight the fact, that their limited time alone was running out.

Daniel watched with his own increasing anxiety as Volya did his best to remember which lever brought which operation online first. It had been so long since he had watched this being done.

Then, adding to the already anxious atmosphere came the sounds of the door at the end of the hangar being beaten. Someone was desperate to get inside. *Bong! Bong!* Dents were forming in the smooth heavyset door panels.

Volya sprang back to life again, looking as though things

were now starting to go his way. Hurriedly, he keyed in strings of coordinates onto a black glass keyboard at the base of one of the larger monitors. On his left hand, he hastily removed the wrist armor, which dropped to the floor with a clang, and flicked open his computer. He looked to be comparing details between the two displays.

The door burst open at the bottom of the hangar into shards of metal and clouds of dust, leaving the broken door in pieces, only parts of it still hanging onto the frame. When the dust cleared, Karen stood there, his powered lance extended toward Daniel and Volya as he wore a broad angry smile of insanity, nearly splitting his face in two.

"Oh no!" Volya shouted, struck with the realization that all of his sacrifices had been for nothing.

Daniel and Volya raised their hands. Karen stood there triumphantly and breathing heavily.

Another one of the Director's guards that had been accompanying Karen, had crept from behind him around the perimeter of the hangar from the doorway while Karen had them distracted. He had managed to creep up onto Amber's pad behind her and now held her around the waist, jabbing a daggerlike weapon into her side.

"It's over," Daniel said glumly, looking to Volya for signs of a plan. Volya clearly couldn't see any way out of this. He, too, had surrendered—there was no sign of any ideas left in his empty eyes. He looked defeated, heartbroken. Daniel looked to Amber, so sorry that he could not make this happen for her as he had so badly wanted to.

Rather than seeing her upset, he was surprised to see that her mouth was twisted, teeth biting down onto her lower lip, and she looked furious—not scared or upset as he had expected. He noticed her left fist clench tightly into a ball. *Oh, God, what is she thinking?*

The next minute happened almost entirely in slow motion for Daniel.

Without any signs of fear—taking the guards by complete surprise—Amber swung with everything that she had. All the anger from the last few days, being told they would not be sent home, all of the fear surrounding her mom, the whole nine yards, connected her fist with the underside of the stocky man's jaw with a loud powerful crack.

At the exact same time Amber yelled out, "Owwww!" and held her throbbing hand in her other hand, the guard let out a completely unintentional "Ooomph!" A noise not unlike dry twigs snapping accompanied the connection between fist and face and echoed out around the hangar, the sound of the man's vitamin-deficient jaw breaking into pieces was not a pleasant sound. The people without a star clearly were not built—or used to—hand-to-hand combat.

Volya then let rip a volley of shots from a small handgun that he'd had ready at his side before the guard had even hit the floor, aiming straight at Karen's forehead, who also had not been expecting any resistance. They had never been tested like this in real life, not in proper combat situations, not in this generation. Volya, however, had. He was a decorated military man.

The guard who had taken the punch from Amber fell lifelessly to the deck, falling off the pedestal like a sack of potatoes. Amber felt the crack replay over and over in her mind, and her hand stung. Their bones were so brittle—she could not believe that she had done that.

Karen had taken such a volley of shots that Volya's energy ammunition had ripped holes in him from forehead to gut. He fell to the ground, a surprised look forever staining his dying face.

Daniel yelled out, holding triumphant fists aloft, "GO ON, AMBER! WOOOOOH!"

Volya shouted so that both could hear him, "Right, we'd better get you home! I'm going to try to send you back to around the time that you touched the spheres, okay? It may not be exact, but that's my aim! I'll do the best I can from here with what I have."

They both nodded in agreement. There wasn't time for any debates. The sounds of more guards' feet stomping through the corridors and hatches behind them grew louder.

Finally, Volya, wiping sweat from his eyes, shouted, "I've got it!"

He punched one more combination of buttons and then threw a long golden lever, jutting up from the floor behind the screen. "Goodbye, Amber—safe travels!"

She waved her hand, noticing that as she raised it her hand was turning transparent, becoming one with the strong beam of white light passing from the upper pad to the lower one. The light enveloped her and grew in intensity, and the pain in her throbbing hand died away when she felt herself separating from this world.

Loud pulsing engine noises coming from beneath the floor accompanied the light, which was also pulsing in time with the noises, ever-increasing. Louder and louder the engine noises grew, and brighter and brighter went the light between the pads.

"I've punched in your coordinates ready, Daniel!" Volya was shouting and he looked terrified. "All I need to do is throw the lever. Go! Get on that pad, quickly!"

Daniel looked over at Amber. "But . . ." Amber had already vanished. "Will you be okay?"

"Yes, I'll be fine. I'm high up the chain here, you know." He threw Daniel an unconvincing smile. "Quickly now!"

Daniel had no choice; If Volya had sacrificed himself, which Daniel knew he had now, he had better make it count for something. He hurried around the glass partition and stood on the pad in the spot where Amber had just been standing.

As Daniel moved, Volya followed him around the glass, pulling out his gun again in readiness from underneath his robe. He started firing it off at the top of the doorway at the bottom of the hangar as the surprised faces of guards started to appear, causing the lintel to crumble into pieces. The few guards that had made it through looked right at them, and then down at Karen. One approached the corpse on the ground, checking him. The other two tentatively marched toward Daniel and Volya, who was still firing at them to slow their approach.

There was a flash of light from the tip of Volya's gun, then nothing—not until the closest guard to them had his chest burst open, spitting blood in a spot just above the protection of his breastplate. *Direct hit. Volya is good at this.* He took down one and fired again at the top of the doorway, desperately trying to give them more time. The guards looked like they were starting to get through, perhaps also with second thoughts. Some returned fire through the dust and rubble from their lances, but they were not very accurate, often hitting the walls and redundant control stations around Volya.

Daniel could only watch and hope from his pad now, helpless. There were now at least five guards, either dead or writhing and crying out in agony on the floor, each holding parts of their bodies that had been let open by Volya's small but very powerful weapon.

Volya managed to hurry back around the screen before more came in and quickly threw the lever, starting Daniel's return sequence. Once he had, he walked back around the partition toward Daniel. Daniel mouthed the words "Thank you" as the light and sound between the pads grew bright and loud.

Daniel felt the light wrapping itself around him, and his feet lifted off the lower pad.

It felt like electricity was grabbing at his feet and fingertips. It tapped energetically on his skin, from the tip of his toes to the tallest hair on his head. His body tingled; it was like having pins and needles everywhere at once.

Daniel, now half himself and half light, was only barely still in the room—not in top or bottom halves, but his whole body was now dividing its molecules between the light surrounding him and the air as the now transparent room started to fade out completely. The return inverter was now almost done converting Daniel's body into light, ready for travel back through the black hole as pure energy.

The last scene that Daniel could make out was of another guard, now at the front of the queue, extending out his lance and with a determined look, he fired. Volya was hit in the back; the blast threw Volya forward from standing in front of Daniel at the pads down to the edge of the glass partition near the console, where he could take temporary cover. It didn't look good, though. Volya landed facedown and a pool of blood grew beneath him, spreading quickly over the concrete floor. He was still clutching his gun.

He turned over, now belly up. He had to hold in his guts with his free hand from his now open stomach to buy him the valuable seconds that he needed to finish this. Warm blood quickly seeped through his fingers clenched over the front wound, and he could feel that the end was nigh as a quick numbness spread through his body.

The guard that had fired the shot on Volya had now turned and opened fire on Daniel, who was still partially visible within the beam of light. Volya looked up toward Daniel, terrified that he might have failed.

One, his dying wish was to get them both home, and two, Vanir needed both of the spheres, or else his passageway wouldn't work to its fullest.

An arrow of light left the tip of the guard's lance from further down the room, darting toward Daniel. Daniel saw it coming in slow motion as time started to skew around him. He felt something hot pass through his stomach—a warmth drilled through his torso and out the other side.

*Oh no! Not now,* Daniel thought, panicking. *I'm hit.* He reached down for his stomach, but his stomach was not there.

Before he could even look down, the room had completely disappeared. Everything that was going on in the hangar was gone; he could only see white. Volya, the Karen's, and their weapons—all gone. "Nooo . . ." Daniel tried to scream out to no avail, fearing that his friend had been killed. He wanted to check on him so badly, but he no longer had a mouth to yell out of.

Volya watched Daniel fade away into the light, open-mouthed. In the darker room now, with life dripping away from him out through his stomach, Volya barely managed to pull himself across the floor. He was dragging himself back around the edge of the safety glass that surrounded the facility's main control station. A trail of blood followed behind him.

Peering down the center of the hangar toward the increasing number of guards, he knew that he didn't have much time left. His legs completely ignored his instructions to help him up when he pulled on the edge of the console.

More plasma munition was released from lances in a volley from the bottom end of the hangar, zipping past his head in purple-colored shards of light. The blasts punched holes right through the metal and glass of the console, releasing sparks and leaving scorch marks everywhere.

It was all he could do to helplessly watch the guards approaching him. As he started to slowly lose control of his upper body and he was almost flat to the floor now, he watched as their weapons tore apart the console. *It doesn't matter if they destroy it now!*

The metal panels surrounding the control station began to look like objects of target practice as the Director's guards stomped forward, raining fire on him. He had barely enough life left to lie and wait now. His view of the room around him had started to grow darker. He couldn't feel his legs at all. His stomach had a hole right through it from his back, and consciousness was coming and going now. He felt so tired, all he wanted was to sleep. His body shook as he woke himself again and again. He knew what was coming.

Another agonizing pain ripped through Volya's left

shoulder while he tried in vain to look up, the force taking out his arm, the only thing that was supporting him.

A guard had flanked the others, overlapping them and taking him by surprise from the left-hand side of the room and fired the shot. More blood splattered up the console and the glass.

His right hand still somehow clutched his gun. He had forgotten that he even still had it, although his arm was now twitching, and he was barely able to feel its weight. He felt that his hand only gripped the weapon by the sheer fact that his nerves were stuck, and he was unable to release it.

A numbness started to move forward from the back of his head, taking over his eyes as if his head was at death's mercy now. The last few thoughts he was capable of processing, as his vision switched to bright golden light and then back to the hangar, was pointing his gun up at the control station from close range and trying to analyze it. There was light everywhere, then when his sight came back, a hole burned through the metal console came into focus at eye level. Golden light everywhere again. The pain stopped, then blinking lights flashed through a hole inside the metal and he felt pain again.

*That looks important.*

Using the floor to help balance the grip of the gun, he took his last ever short gasp of air that his damaged lungs would allow, and applied the only pressure his fingers could manage. He managed to pull off three blasts from his gun—luckily, the trigger on the Node 3 model was a very sensitive one. Volya died even before the explosion took the room.

*Mission accomplished* was his last ringing thought as he left his body. He knew that he had died but still felt the warmth from the blast, then that his body was traveling through the air in parts, watching them painlessly in the third person now as golden light flooded around him.

The globes of light suspended in the air above the city

streets sputtered light as the energy sent to them through the normal city system was strained, then interrupted.

The streets fell extremely cold and dark rapidly before emergency backup systems could take over, replacing the lost energy with a temporary feed. The palace lights also dimmed, just for a couple of seconds, and then came back on at a new lower emergency level.

Delegates from around the Dark Space Union being accommodated in various suites around the palace, living the high life at the expense of the people they were supposed to be representing, wondered what was happening as their suites were temporarily plunged into darkness. Their servants looked up, dropped whatever they were carrying, and walked out.

High above the city, deep in the black cloudless skies but beneath the damaged protective domes, the bombing began to wane. Word spread like wildfire over the radios that the two special Earthlings may have made it home.

The Director's guards had surrounded the returns complex, trying desperately and in vain to get inside and stop Volya from helping the Earthlings and disobeying the Director's orders. Queues of guards had formed at the doorways and hatches that were needed to access it manually, whilst the Director himself screamed from his chambers in raging anger at his monitors to "Re-energize the doors—now, by the Creator! NOW!!"

When more guards finally managed to gain access to the hangar after the explosion that rocked the entire city, working their way through the narrow, collapsed corridors, hatches, and ladders that had all suffered damage in one way or another, all that greeted them was a bay full of smoldering remains of both control gear and bodies. Glass and metal fragments were sticking out of the parts of guard's bodies that had remained after the explosion.

All that remained of Volya was a long dark stain scarring the floor behind the wreckage that had once been the returns consoles, which were now lumps of metal melted to the floors. Not much was left of the control suite at all.

A melted lump of metal that could have been a gun near the console also remained, and there was no sign of the Ancient Earthlings—evidence that he had succeeded in both returning them home and at the same time disabling the returns suite. For a good while, at least.

Vanir had been monitoring Volya's life signs from high above Prime through Volya's computer. As soon as Volya's life signs had extinguished, Vanir ordered the complete bombing of what was left of the return complex and the adjoined antiquated sphere manufacturing plant.

"Blow it to the kingdom of the Creator!" he instructed his fleet. "I'm sorry, my old friend. I wish there had been another way. I will right this if my plan works."

Ship after ship dipped and dove down toward the complex, dropping all they had left onto it. Afterwards, as the smoke cleared, the complex was only rubble, piled high and wide, covering the western side of the city. Thousands of the Director's guards and many civilians around the city lay mixed in with its remains.

*I'm so very sorry, but their sacrifice will benefit millions, perhaps billions.*

Vanir ordered what was left of his fleet to return to the safety of Secondary space.

This would, in all likelihood, cause another century of war. His people had also suffered huge losses.

*They will be remembered forever.*

# CHAPTER 22
# TRAVELING AMBER

A mber was presently conscious of complete silence and darkness surrounding her. No longer was she blinded by the light from the pads or aware of sounds and vibrations of machinery. Any whirring and clunking beneath her that was being used to hopefully transport them home was long gone, as were Daniel, Volya, and danger from the guards.

She felt . . . at peace now. Her hand had stopped throbbing.

She didn't feel herself, though. It was a very odd sensation. She didn't know what it was that she felt, other than knowing that she was traveling and not whole—she couldn't see her hands, feet, or any part of herself. She was keenly aware that she was simply a tiny speck of life fleeting through space as light. All that she could feel was . . . speed.

She tried to use what awareness she could muster while speeding through time and space to try to look around herself, and when she did focus all of her thoughts and energy into doing so, there was only a dark blur all around her. Were her eyes even working? Did she have eyes? This was how she imagined it must feel being born. She focused harder and white blobs, closer to her than the black space behind, started to come into view.

The white blobs came into focus, became brighter, and then stretched out into white lines, disappearing in a burst as they flew past. She realized that these must be stars. There was something else around her—all around her. A presence, that feeling that you get when there is somebody behind you in a dark street but when you turn to look, the street is empty. She couldn't look all around herself as such, but she could feel something with her.

She was moving, and so fast—so very, very fast.

Things changed suddenly in what would have normally been the blink of an eye, for she was suddenly aware of light first, then images filling out in her vision—again, it felt like being born. She could physically feel her eyes blinking. She was also using her legs again, feeling solid ground beneath her. Familiar sights surrounded her, giving her a warm feeling inside. She was now walking down Manitoba Avenue, toward work, just as she had been days ago.

*Oh my God, I'm home!* She lifted her hand up to cover her mouth, overcome with emotion.

She was back—back in her hometown! A shiver of excitement tickled her from head to toe. It seemed she was here exactly as she had been before all the unusual, stressful crap had started. She was heading toward a small car again, but she stopped, frowning. Something didn't feel right. Everything about her town felt very odd. *Not my town?* She wondered.

She couldn't put her finger on what it was, to start with. Something was just . . . strange.

Amber looked around, first at the car in front of her, then at the buildings either side of her. The buildings and the car, she noticed, were there but not there. There was an odd sheen and a sparkle to everything. She found that she could see right through everything. At first, she suspected that maybe this was some sort of aftereffect of having arrived from space. Surely it was—what other explanation was there? But surely this effect would fade soon, leaving her fine and dandy. Or so she hoped.

She looked down at her hands and worryingly found that she could see right through them to the street below. Turning her hands over made no difference.

"What have they done to me?"

*This is so weird . . . what is this? Am I dreaming? Am I in a coma?*

This effect that she desperately hoped would fade away and return to normal . . . didn't. The only other explanation that she could come up with dawned on her all at once. *If I'm not in a coma, then Volya had to have done something wrong. It didn't work. Jesus Christ . . . I'm back, but I'm dead!*

She spun around in a panic, wondering what to do, until she saw something that quieted her thoughts again for a second. Something oddly familiar about the situation . . . herself!

Walking toward her down the road, staring at her and looking as shocked as she felt, was another Amber. It clicked. *Of course.* Amber realized in an instant that she was now that same copy of herself that she had seen the day that she left the planet.

The first thing that she wanted to say to herself was not to worry, that everything would be okay in the end . . . hopefully. *Should I tell her not to touch the sphere?*

But before she could put any order to the words that were rushing to her head, her surroundings changed again.

Manitoba Avenue turned into a melting liquid, then started to spin around her. The buildings merged with the sky and the street, turning into dark and light patterns and a big blurry mess. She felt like she was going to puke.

The spinning then slowed, the street and the town settling into a readable picture again. She was now standing back at the shiny ball at the side of the diner, feeling giddy and almost tumbling over.

"Owwwww! Shit!" she shouted as her hand turned into a beacon of pain. She held it tightly in her other hand.

The shiny ball was still there, sitting in its crater in the grass right next to the diner.

It was evening, the Sun now barely visible. The sky was heavily red. She felt the warmth of the light from the day's end stroke her skin. There was still no wind. She saw the water glisten, its surface painted by the orange starlight. However, it remained perfectly still. The weather felt too mild to be real.

The town had an eerie feeling of being stuck in a vacuum. She could breathe, but the air was still and stale. She closed her eyes and swore never to take the Sun for granted again, thanking God that she was home and praying that things would just go back to normal soon.

The town and its residents were still stuck on pause all around her, and the diner was silent.

She put her hands into her pocket, remembering that she had something to do. She was supposed to do something very important with this—she pulled out the coin.

Her head felt fuzzy, as though she had not long woken from a really long sleep, and she was finding it difficult to kick her brain up into second gear.

She strained to remember what this was for. There was a feeling inside her, more than a memory, that she was supposed to give the coin to the sphere. Then maybe her town's people would be saved?

Amber stared at the coin, turning it over and over. It was small but so golden and eloquently detailed. It would be nice to keep it; after all, it had come with her from space, and the future. *It's just beautiful.*

She didn't know if she could keep it or if it would simply disappear with the sphere when she placed it down on the ground.

She stared at the sphere. "You have caused so much trouble, my small silver friend," she said as she knelt on the grass next to the ditch.

# CHAPTER 23
# TRAVELING DANIEL

Daniel—after speeding through space, when he could finally open his eyes—found himself standing back in his bedroom.

"I'm home!" he beamed, excited and thankful that he had made it back alive. However, he noticed that there was something strange about those words. He had felt as though he had spoken but was suddenly conscious that no sound had left his lips.

He looked around the room. Bright white moonlight swooned in through the still blind-less naked window, highlighting mainly the bed; the rest of the room was still quite dark.

*Shit! They shot me!* Remembering what had happened as he was being sent home, he snapped his neck to look down and patted his stomach. Bizarrely, his hand passed right through his waist.

Lost for words and scared to death, he waved his hand through his waist and back again several more times.

*Well, that shouldn't happen. What the hell have they done to me?* Again, the thoughts and the actual intent to say the words were there, but no sounds came out.

He stood at the window thinking about it, then noticed that his bedroom had a strangely creepy, misty feel to it. It was like standing in an eighties horror film—dark, but with moonlight darting through and mist creeping around the bed. Something felt . . . different about it. It was a feeling of being in someone else's house. It looked but didn't feel exactly like his own room. This room somehow felt distant, out of reach.

*Oh shit! I'm dead!*

Even the beams of moonlight passed right through his body and his hands as he stepped closer toward the window and held them up. He looked outside. It was comforting to be back home—even if he was dead. Real life felt distant; his own neighborhood felt miles away as he looked out at the school through the same window that he had looked out of a thousand times.

He turned to scan his room. Would this not be his place of sanctuary anymore? Was this his chance to say a final goodbye to his family or something? His thoughts were based purely on what he had seen in movies.

*Hang on.* Somebody else was there, a shadow, kneeling in the dark on the floor of his bedroom.

It was . . . himself.

Then he remembered, the same as Amber did before him, the clear version of himself that he had seen in a vision all those days ago in his room. That was now him.

He wanted to tell Daniel, down on his knees, to not worry, that he wasn't there to hurt him.

And maybe it would be wise to tell him not to touch the sphere.

But what would happen then? Thinking about his favorite sci-fi films, he wondered, *Would I cause a paradox? Break the space-time continuum?*

If he had never touched the sphere, then would his parents —and whatever portion of the UK that this thing affected— remain frozen forever? How long would the spheres have remained on the Earth if he had not been given the chance to put this right? Would it just have taken someone else, maybe his sister or a friend? And then he would have been the one frozen here. What if his sister or friend didn't end up making the deal with Vanir to get home?

As he stepped forward, toward himself, he felt ever so odd, unsteady on his feet and in his legs. It was as though he was piloting an old car that wouldn't move as straight or as smooth as a modern car.

*This is like being drunk again*, he thought. He still could not speak. He started to feel his feet and then his legs disappearing from beneath him; he was fading away into the air. He couldn't control his legs at all, and when he looked down, they were not there to be moved.

All he could think to do while part of him was still here was to try to recreate what the transparent copy of himself had done to him earlier—so he smiled and held up his hands to indicate that everything would be ok. And then the room collapsed and spun away from him.

Daniel felt sensations that he imagined were the same as floating around inside a washing machine. *Off to heaven, then, I suppose*. Everything around him was still changing, so he attempted to close his eyes to stop himself from being sick.

He then felt steady again, whole, somewhere. When he opened his eyes he was outside, crouching down on grass next to the sphere in the school playing field.

Things felt better this time, more real. The grass underneath his palms supporting him felt wet. The only thing was, everything around him still felt eerily quiet and still. It was late, but there was not a sound from anywhere around the school.

The light from the floodlights looked normal and didn't go through his hands when he held up his palm against the light to check. He quickly patted his stomach with his hands while looking down. He was solid again! He took his hands away and looked at them. *No blood.*

He was back—he wasn't dead after all. Daniel wasn't at all religious, but he looked to the sky and said, "Thank you, God!"

Daniel put his hand in his pocket and pulled out the gold coin. He turned it absentmindedly, flipping it between his thumb and through his fingers.

He held it up to the floodlights, examining its bright gold surface, admiring it. *This has come from the future!* There were some strange symbols on it as well as small and unrecognizable writing around the edge of the face.

He crouched down again next to his sphere, taking another look around the school grounds and glancing at the back of his house. Was he making the right choice? He couldn't back out now, though. Volya—it came back to him in a rush that Volya had given his life to get them home. Daniel's next decision would affect a billion people and more in a completely different time, on other planets—including Earth.

He just couldn't think of any reason not to do it. He hoped that what he and Amber—if, indeed, she still chose to help them—would do next would have a positive impact and not cause any trouble. That he had not been somehow scammed into doing something that was wrong.

Back in Canada, Amber, still kneeling next to her sphere, was thinking almost the same. She, whether fortunately or unfortunately, didn't know the outcome for poor Volya, but she questioned whether it was her place to meddle in other people's affairs. To have a say in whether an entire race of people did or did not deserve to ever feel sunlight in their lifetimes, and to move away from their homes into a different planet or time.

Daniel placed his coin down in the dirt next to his sphere, just as Amber did, comfortable enough in their decisions and also curious as to whether this would actually work. Would those in the future also be able to control something this far behind them in the past?

The coins had small lights on them that started to twinkle brightly in a blue circle around the face. Both spheres started to make a gentle hum, possibly indicating that contact had been made between the coin, the sphere, and their future controllers.

The spheres' hum grew louder, turning into a loud whirring, the sound of machinery rotating inside them as they came back to life, now spinning at incredible speeds.

Both spinning spheres lifted themselves out of their small craters, one in England and one in Canada, raising themselves off the ground by around twelve inches and then pausing in the air as if to wish their targets goodbye. Both spheres disappeared in a blinding white flash of light, giving off a blast of harmless energy. Warm air blasted outward, bringing down their protective fields and knocking Daniel and Amber backward onto their behinds.

# CHAPTER 24
# THE SUN

Vanir was lingering around by his passageway complex, almost eleven billion years from Amber and Daniel's time. It had been three days since he had leveled the returns complex when they had—hopefully—been sent home. He still clung on to his hope that they would indeed help them and send the spheres to him. If they didn't, then things would be hot in this system for a long time. Worse still, he would need to once again hope that somebody else would be picked up by another lost sphere somewhere out in the Light Space, and perhaps they might help. But of course, people coming to Prime via the spheres was becoming less and less frequent in recent times.

Security over on Prime would be so tight now that even if someone else did appear from the Light Space, it was almost a certainty that he would not be able to get operatives close to them. He was starting to doubt that his plan would ever come to fruition now as he stood there contemplating on the red dusty Secondarian soil.

He had felt at ease with himself following the sacrifices that had been made, by both Volya and his people. He had done what he could to help his people. If he failed trying, giving everything he had, then so be it.

His thoughts were broken by an excitement building around the complex. One by one, heads began to turn. As one head saw another look up, so did the next. Then applause started to break out. Everyone nearby was stopping what they were doing to look to the skies and join the others in the applause.

He turned to look as well, looking west in the direction of the city above the rim of the crater.

What started off looking like a new star in the dark sky grew in size before splitting into two. Two streaks of light now approached, shooting right past them high above the crater. The streaks flew right around Secondary. After only ten minutes they approached again, but this time they had slowed dramatically.

They came to a complete stop just above the crater complex, bathing the base and sides of the crater completely in white light. Vanir's crew working around the base was lost inside the light.

*Thank the Creator. They're here!*

Vanir thought about Volya, overjoyed that he hadn't died in vain. He also thought that if there was a Creator, Amber, Daniel, and Volya now shared just as much importance with it.

As the light dimmed from the arrivals, which had now turned back to being standard silver spheres, one of the engineers operating a control panel at the left-hand side of the passageway shouted over that he had a lock on them.

The whole crew, including Vanir, watched as the two silver spheres slowly descended from the air to a dead stop in front of the entrance ramp.

They were stationary, hovering in the air inches from each other at waist height right in front of the passageway arch. The spheres looked ready, awaiting their next instruction.

Vanir nodded at his engineers, who were ready, waiting for his signal at either side of the ramp. Each sprang into action as soon as he nodded, pushing a special hovering flatbed. Each flatbed had a magnetic base on its surface especially created for this moment. They had a handle for the operator to push them into position wherever they needed to go. The almost infinitely heavy spheres were giving off a gentle hum and vibrating, sensing their closeness to each other.

Vanir's face said it all. He was grinning from ear to ear, admiring his catch of the day. Finally, he could complete his project.

It was something that he had been working toward and sacrificing for his entire life; all he had been waiting for was this moment.

He finally looked away from the spheres, shaking his head back into life. It was now that the work would begin.

His two engineers, holding onto their flatbeds, were patiently looking at him, also looking very cheerful as they awaited their next instruction.

He shouted over, "Take them into position, please!" They obligingly bowed their heads and pushed the flatbeds up the ramp, carefully positioning them directly underneath each sphere. The spheres seemed happy to accept being carried by the flatbeds, each sinking in the air to sit on the magnetic pads on top of the flatbeds.

The engineers gently pulled their flatbeds back down the ramp and split at the bottom. One engineer took his flatbed left and the other turned right, heading toward the control stations at either side of the structure.

Each engineer readied himself in position. Their next job would be to install the sphere into a chamber that had been prebuilt into the machinery in the hope that, eventually, the spheres would be integrated into it.

As the spheres approached the control station, a panel slid open, revealing a cradle inside for the sphere to sit into. The engineers raised the trolley with the handle, pulling back on it as you would with a pump truck on Earth to carefully make sure the spheres were at the required height.

This then triggered a mechanism inside the chamber for the seat inside to slide out toward the sphere, gently collecting it from the flatbed. Each seat, now complete with a sphere, slowly slid back into its chamber. The vertical panel then closed, sealing the spheres inside.

The chambers accepted the spheres, different lights now illuminated on the control panels above each station to signify that the giant machine had accepted the new source of information. Now it was integrating them into its circuits.

As the new spherical power sources began to interact with their host's mechanisms, a new section of lights flashed to life around the top of the arch.

The archway started to emit a deafening whirring noise that went on for a few moments. It was running a new test routine— the whirring noise was the motors inside running at much higher speeds than had ever been reached before.

The framework and mechanism around the arch rattled as the structure was pushed to its upper limits. Moments later, the humming slowed and reduced to a gentle hum.

As Vanir understood it, they were now all good to go. The engineers at both side-mounted control stations signaled Vanir with a simple salute and then they backed away from their stations, pulling their flatbed vehicles away from the sides.

With a press of a button on the handle, the flatbeds folded up, the horizontal load-bearing part raising where it joined the pump handle riser and closed into a narrowing V shape. Taking up less space, they were now stowed out of the way beneath the access ramp in case they were required later.

Vanir, knowing all was ready and safe, walked toward the right-hand side control panel, the main dialing unit for the structure. "Are we ready for a test?" he asked, aiming the question at the approaching Vidar who took a position next to him at the controls.

"Yes, sir, I believe everything is now in place. The spheres have been accepted."

"Good! Please proceed."

Vidar, as Vanir's chief engineer, swiped the large screen above the station and a different control screen was displayed. He flicked a combination of switches at standing desk height, which shone in different colors when switched. Then he watched the screen above the chamber holding the sphere.

The structure started its sequence. This sequence was similar to the normal Dark space transportation sequence, only slightly different.

As the procedure began, it started sending a current through the structure's transmitters and semiconductors.

Huge magnetic fields were generated by conductors around the insides of the arch. A mechanical hum turned into another whirring sound as the conductors around the edge glowed and started rotating inside the circle. A white light circled the mouth as they passed, flashing through the semicircle display around the very top of the arch, running clockwise in exact parallel with the now deafening whirring noise, and then the light would disappear underground in the other half of the structure.

In the center of the gap inside the arch, a small white light appeared like before. It then turned into a circular swirling pattern of white light, opening out into a large white swirling vortex. A white hole had been created. White fog emanated from the edges of the arch, creeping down the ramp like low clouds.

Then all at once the surface smoothed out. A picture came into view behind the fog.

It was a deserted red sandy landscape, but it looked to be daytime, strange and as clear as anything, inside the arch's mouth.

The passageway had made contact, as designed and as promised.

It was allowing them access to a whole other time—a whole other Universe.

None of the people standing around the arch had ever seen a planet with natural daylight before. They were stunned. It was silent; nobody moved a muscle.

Then heads started to turn left and right as they looked at each other in disbelief. The loud whirring noises had dulled, leaving now only a comfortable hum.

Vanir, after a moment of staring open-mouthed at the arch, walked around from the side of the ramp, stepped up onto it, and slowly walked up to the mouth of the arch. The fog rolled around his ankles as it descended the ramp. He took a central stance, staring head-on at the strange landscape beyond. He smiled.

He turned to look at Volund, the operator at the left-hand station.

"May I?" he asked, nodding toward the mouth.

"Bear with me, sir."

Volund jogged back around to his station. He knew how much this meant to Vanir, to everyone. He came back around and jogged up the access ramp, past Vanir, and stopped dead at the rippling barrier.

He plucked something from his belt and held it out. It was an instrument with a controls part and a long test probe that he then prodded right into the surface of the barrier—and what was hopefully Ancient Mars. He held it for a moment, measuring the composition of the air on the other side.

This sent a signal to Vidar, who was reading the data on display panels at the right-hand station of the arch. He raised his hand to get Vanir's attention. "Sir, the atmosphere is very dense and very rich in carbon dioxide. We would need to set up at least one initial biodome before stepping through."

"Please do that for me," Vanir answered.

Volund reclipped his probe. He looked down at his hand, opening up his personal computer.

He tapped the bright screen, then swiped his finger up. Next, with his right hand, he took a small silver ball around the size of a golf ball from his belt. These domes were a wondrous technology, a technology they had perfected to be practically instant. All he needed to do was pilot the small rolling ball into the next desired direction, and as soon as it was in position, *blam!* A new dome goes up, joining and sealing onto the last. Miles of protective layers could be created in a single day.

Volund skimmed the small device into the white rippling barrier, not unlike skimming a flat stone across a lake, then looked down at his personal computer again, drawing a pattern on it with his finger.

He was guiding the small silver ball into the desired position on the other side. When he was happy with where it sat, around two to three hundred yards from the passageway, he pushed the button. This was to provide them as much coverage as possible from here, to enable a decent-sized exploration zone. They could plant more domes later.

They couldn't see the small ball anymore through the shimmering surface, but they could see the launching of the projected dome. light sprayed out of the small stationary ball and then disappeared as it settled into a clear dome above the exploration area.

They now had an initial exploration floor area the size of a large football stadium. This would provide them clean, breathable air and regulate the temperature to a comfortable level.

Vanir watched in admiration from the mouth of the arch. Without checking with his engineer or even looking at him for confirmation, he stepped right into the rippling puddle.

He was protected from the harsh prehistoric environment on the other side by his first dome. Knowing that he would be fine, there he stood on Ancient Mars, his people's ancestral home.

# CHAPTER 25
# THE MARS MIGRATION

The landscape beyond the puddle was rocky, desolate, and cold—but light. Red sand and rocks abounded, and in the distance the tall sidewalls of a sprawling crater surrounded him, just as it did in the Dark Space where he had come from.

It was the very crater that his passageway was built into the base of in the far-flung future. Such a strange feeling—home, but different. They had done it. The sky was a pale hazy blue. There was also something else—a distant warmth. The temperature of the air was freezing cold here; however, beneath the protection of the biodomes, the Sun was given a helping hand, its warmth gracefully radiating the air inside the dome.

It was a warmth that he did not recognize from anything that he had felt in his lifetime. A natural warmth, it was less . . . pinpointed. He closed his eyes, allowing the sensation stroking his skin to continue. His cold gray skin seemed to come alive. It felt glorious. He turned and opened his eyes to spy a bright bluish-white circle piercing the hazy sky.

He had never felt anything like this in his life. It was so soothing that he didn't want it to ever end, but there was still so much to do. He let the feeling soak in for a moment longer before moving on again. Looking down at his hand, he opened his fingers and thumb to reveal his computer.

"Volund, this is amazing. Unless you can see any problems that I cannot, we are good to proceed as planned. Please set up more domes around the perimeter of this one. I want to get moving with the road and transport plant straight away."

"Yes, sir!"

Volund came through the passageway toward him and walked right past Vanir, continuing on toward the far side of the crater and the edge of the initial dome. The reserved but dedicated engineer reached for his belt, again unclipping another silver ball, and he then climbed the wall of the crater and disappeared over the top. A bright flash of light sparkled from over the top. Another dome was now in place. Volund was professional to the core.

Vanir, watching him silently go about his work with admiration, turned and walked back toward the shimmering doorway, back toward the miserable Dark Space.

On the other side, Vidar was waiting for him.

"Vidar, please instruct the groundworks crews that we are good to proceed with moving onto phase two and bringing the infrastructure plant through the passage, as quickly as you can, please." He was eager, as he knew that the life waiting for them in the Dark Space would now get very uncomfortable in the aftermath of returning Amber and Daniel home.

The Director, quite rightly, was most angry about the treachery, upset that his own people had helped the rebels and infiltrated his own ranks. No-fly zones had been introduced straightaway; any craft on all planets was grounded. Curfews were in place while they investigated every person from the top down to the cells beneath.

"Yes, sir, right away."

The Secondarians in Vanir's charge were very well rehearsed in all phases of the plans in readiness for this moment. Now the plans had very quickly moved from the planning tables and simulations in the city to real life, and onto the ancient Martian soils in the physical world.

All the people of the Dark Space had dreamed that they would one day be able to leave this dark system, maybe even feel a star on their backs, and now they could—and in their own lifetimes, no less. This had been a plan generations in the making. Vanir was about to become a legend, along with the two Earthlings and Volya.

Vidar looked at Vanir with wide questioning eyes. He asked Vanir with more enthusiasm than he had ever shown, or at least more than Vanir could ever remember him showing, "So was there a yellow Sun, sir? Were we right?"

"Yes, and it feels wonderful, my friend," Vanir replied, smiling and patting him on the shoulder.

Not much more than an hour after Vanir had returned from Mars, several large vehicles hovering in convoy came into view. The first appearing at the top ridge of the crater, they rolled down in line, following the access road down, and around the perimeter of the crater. Vanir watched them drive down and Vidar met them when they reached the bottom, issuing instructions at the start of the ramp.

The convoy of industrial vehicles were of varying types, each with different tools and attachments on them. There were cutting tools on some, drills, circular blades, and what looked like large guns, while on others there were scooping and moving tools—Martian soil moving tools.

The machines silently moved onto and up the access ramp, edging closer toward the barrier. Inching up the ramp in a line, they then stopped, awaiting the go-ahead to proceed through the passage.

Vidar walked up the ramp and waved them through. They disappeared one by one through the watery clear wall in front of them as it shook like a wall of silver jelly.

There were around a dozen or so engineers and scientists now working all around the passageway plateau. Shift patterns had changed, and more people had arrived to assist. There were many different departments here now busily patrolling the area, completing their required tasks.

No time was wasted at all; each group of engineers planned to start their task even before the last one had been completed. They overlapped like teams of athletes deftly passing batons. Surface engineers looked at their plans, the road building teams had theirs, utility teams had theirs, and so on.

Volund came back through the passageway and headed toward Vanir and Vidar.

Volund smiled and said, "Looks like everything is going exactly as we thought, sir. I have domes set up for miles now already, heading north, south, east, and west from the initial dome. It's strange . . . I was just over there"—he pointed at the barrier—"just there, but billions of years in the past from you guys. I could see you. Unbelievable! Construction of the first roadbeds has already begun. Main north to south routes will be down by tomorrow morning."

Vanir smiled. "Excellent. I could not have wished for a better start. It is now a reality, and not simply an idea. Our people will no longer be denied the choice of whether they want to move to the Light Space or not. The people of Prime and the rest of the union will be most welcome to follow. Those that wish to stay in the dark, can. Oh, what time period do we estimate it to be on the other side of the passage, Vidar?"

Vidar checked the sensor readings being fed to his computer screen from the domes on the other side. "We estimate it to be the late 1940s in that system, sir, based on the readings that I have here."

"Good, yes, very good. The passageway is working perfectly."

Vanir was a keen historian. He knew Martian history very well in particular; he had spent years studying every scrap of information that had been left in the caves beneath both Primary and Secondary. He knew that in this time period, man's travel exploits away from the Earth had been very limited. They had not even set foot on Earth's moon yet. It would be a long time before they came close to walking on the Martian surface. Amber and Daniel had not even been born where they were setting up. He would travel to thank them soon.

The plan for Ancient Mars from here would be establishing basic infrastructure to allow for the uninhibited movement of the plant and equipment, then to start clearing and building on the rocky mountainous land. Then would come the colonization of Ancient Mars, which would begin as quickly as the infrastructure allowed. But they would still need to be careful to remain hidden from view for as long as was practical. They still did not wish to alter this period of history for the people of Earth, after all.

Their domes would obscure the views of the expanding cities from Earth's curious eyes, scrambling the pixels within layers of domes to disguise all that was beneath.

It would be a very long time indeed before the population of Earth would realize that they were sharing the solar system with another race. Only in the future, when both parties were ready, would that time come.

Long before the Ancient "Earth-Mars Migration and Peace Treaty" was signed, the people on Mars would spend time observing and surveying the Earth using light vehicles. They would keep an eye on the Earth's technological and political progress, making sure that the Earthlings did not destroy themselves first.

Vanir would need to pay a massive tribute to Amber, Daniel, and Volya for helping him and his people. This would take some thought. *They will never be forgotten.*

"Vidar, I am taking a break now. Please contact me if you need anything."

"Yes, sir."

Vanir stepped back from the passageway complex. He looked at the crater road, then at the black doorway over to his left. He chose the more direct route, heading for the black doorway and leaving his engineers and scientists to continue with their plans.

The plans were all laid out and now swiftly moving on. It was simply a case of executing the phases of the program in order now that they were able.

Vanir stepped directly into his bedroom. It was time for him to get some rest now; he needed it. His bed was much the same as Volya's, a stone slab raised off the floor in a round room, though here there was much more color. His sleeping wife had turned off the lights, so at the moment it wasn't any brighter. Small lights guided the way around the room from the base of the bed. References to the red planet adorned the room. Red drapes clung to the wall along with abstract paintings of Ancient Mars that he and his wife, as keen historians, had painted in the brief periods of spare time they were afforded.

Fur throws and red blankets made the bed seem warm and homely. Vanir had a beautiful wife, Vana, who was already in bed sleeping.

She was used to him working around the clock. She appreciated his hard work and admired him for it. Vana looked after their two children and was easily tired from keeping them amused while he was working. However, she didn't resent him at all the way some other Secondary wives seemed to hold it against their husbands that had dedicated their lives to Vanir's projects.

It would be worth all the sacrifices. Right now, her husband was the most important man on Secondary.

Vanir stepped out of his uniform, deposited it into the laundry chute in the wall, and slid gently into the bed, holding his wife around her smooth waist.

He had missed her—and a large portion of his marriage, in fact—by working so hard. But if he could get to where he wanted to get to, they would all enjoy a better quality of life.

He spooned his little spoon, kissing her back lightly, moving her long dark hair to reach the top of her neck. Then he stroked the tips of his fingers from here, down her side and continued to draw a line down her leg. He knew that she liked that. She stirred, letting out a pleased deep breath that extended into a murmur.

He snuggled his face into the skin between her shoulder blades, took a long breath in, and let it out, tasting her pleasant smells, which tickled his senses. Then he got comfortable and gripped her tightly until the morning.

Vanir woke to the sound of Vana setting down a warm tea drink on the table next to the bed. The room was now light. She leaned over him and kissed his forehead. "Good morning, sleepy."

He rolled to a sitting position on the edge of the bed. she had tried to walk away, but her speed suggested that she wasn't really trying to leave the room in a hurry. He reached out and playfully pulled her in close to him by the belt on her evening robe. She turned and straddled his lap, and they embraced tightly.

"Thank you," he said.

"For what?"

"For my drink, and for being my rock."

She smiled. "What else would I do?"

She kissed him once more, very lightly. Then she stopped and smiled teasingly at him, signaling that the small kiss was merely a taster—that if he were to offer her some more attention, he might get better kisses in return.

He smiled in grateful acknowledgment. She dismounted him and walked out of the room, glancing at him expectantly as she disappeared into the dark doorway.

Vanir sat there for a moment on the edge of the bed, sipping his mug of tea. His mind wasted no time in getting back to his work.

# CHAPTER 26
# THE MONUMENT

Vanir's mind was a very busy place. In this moment, he was wondering where his engineers would have gotten to by now, and what he would do to show his people's appreciation for Volya, Amber, and Daniel.

This wasn't just so that *he* would remember them—no, this was to make sure that everyone on Mars, for generations to come, would remember them. It had to be right. Could it be a city named after them, as they had allowed the people of the dark space the chance to relocate to the light space and build their new cities? Could it be schools or colleges named after them? A statue, a mountain? Maybe a planetwide holiday?

He got ready, deep in thought, in the bedroom illuminated from above by the entire ceiling. It gently increased in lux as the room identified that everyone beneath it was now active.

The room was much brighter and more homely than the dwellings on Prime. The walls and floors were white stone, the ceilings seemingly made of light panels, and mirrors lined the walls. All of this helped to reflect the light in all directions for a bright, clean clinical finish.

A large mirror faced him, built flush into the wall. His clean, freshly pressed red uniform slid out sideways automatically from a tall thin groove next to the mirror as he approached it, and then the uniform turned so that it was facing him square on. He unhooked it from the hanger, got dressed, and then went out through the black doorway at the room's edge and into the next room, heading upstairs to the living room.

There, Vana was sitting at a small table in a large white room with a glass roof. She was reading something being projected onto the table from a light source underneath.

His two children, a young boy and girl, were in the next room through an alcove, playing with their toys.

"Don't you have work to do, sleepyhead?" Vana prodded, smiling.

"Yes, but as I have been working for four days and nights straight, I thought I would take a morning off." His voice sounded cold, but his smile insisted that he was being playful.

He ducked through the alcove and picked up his giggling children around their waists, the boy facing front, the girl facing the opposite way. They were laughing their little heads off now.

"Who do these little engineers belong to? I see them constructing bridges in the next room, but I don't see them working for me. Maybe I could send them through my passageway and get them building my roads on Mars!"

Vana laughed as he brought them to the table and sat down in front of her. He put down his son and flipped over his daughter, still laughing. They hugged him, kissed him on the cheek, and ran back through the alcove to their toys.

"What troubles you, my love?" she asked him, reading his eyes.

"I am trying to think of something grand that would show my appreciation for what Amber and Daniel did for us. And Volya, of course, who gave his life willingly for our cause. We owe absolutely everything to them."

"You'll think of something. You always do."

He finished off his mug of tea and then put the cup in the

cleaner. "Okay, you have gotten rid of me, for now." He smiled, kissed her on the forehead, and left through a black doorway.

On the other side, he stepped out onto the busy industrial bridge of his ship. Walking across the steel grating, with Amber and Daniel at the front of his thoughts, he recollected that this was where he had first met them.

Red uniformed officers were busy walking around the deck, going about their duties. Some looked down at their hand computers as they walked, while some were sitting at consoles against the wall looking at plans and details. Officers that looked up greeted him as they walked past him, saying, "Morning, sir."

Vanir admired the hustle and bustle as he strode. He stopped short of hopping up onto his navigator's seat, instead making his way past the steps and over to a console, one that ran against the right-hand side wall adjacent to his chair.

Here a rookie female officer was performing her basic navigational duties at her station. She had unwittingly stopped him in his tracks, as although she was a rookie—only six months into active duty on his ship—everyone had raved about her being very sharp and excellent with computing procedures and problem-solving. She had come most highly recommended by the college, coming straight aboard her first ship after commencement of practical training, rather than spending her final half year on a simulated vessel.

He stood behind her and put his hand on the headrest of her seat.

"Valda, I would very much appreciate your help with something very important."

"Of course, sir. I would be honored."

"Would you display for me a photo of Amber and Daniel, please, from their initial visit here? I ideally want a headshot of them."

He glanced around the bridge while she worked, getting a feel for what was going on this morning and intending to give her a few moments to find some images. It only took a second, though, and she was already there.

"Sir," she prompted as she had finished swiping and tapping on the console with blistering speed. "This one good for you, sir?"

On the two screens in front of them she had brought up an enlarged profile shot of Amber and Daniel standing side by side —a perfectly cropped front-on, shoulders up shot of each of them from when they had first set foot on his bridge.

Vanir smiled to himself. Both ancient Earthlings wore frowns of confusion, clearly wondering what was they were in for now, as they had appeared somewhere that looked completely different from where they had arrived from.

"Perfect, hold it there a moment for me. I'm just thinking of something."

"Sir? Anything I can help you with?"

"Well, maybe, yes. I need ideas. I'm trying to find a way to pay a massive tribute to Amber, Daniel, and Volya. Something that I could show to Amber and Daniel. Something that our people will see for a long time to come on Mars and remember them. I want it on Ancient Mars so that we can all appreciate it, but at the same time, it cannot draw too much attention to us being there. I know this is an unusual ask."

The two of them remained there for a moment, thinking, silently staring at the two images. Valda was the first to say anything.

"How about statues, sir?" She tapped and swiped on her input devices and on a large screen. Stretching above Amber's and Daniel's photos was now a landscape shot of the recently acquired Martian mountainous surface.

"I like that," he responded. "I was thinking along those lines, but something much grander than a normal statue."

Little did they know it, but they were both racing toward an idea that would give rise to a vast monument to Amber and Daniel that would last forever, one that would be dismissed by the governments of the Earth in that timeline but discussed by the Martian settlers for a very long time.

Valda had images flashing through her mind. She first looked at Daniel, then at Amber, then at the mountains of Mars. *Of course! It's so obvious, as plain as the noses on their faces.*

She turned her head toward Vanir and sent a confident smirk his way. He stood there, gripping the back of her chair. *They were right about her.*

Her eyes and her smile, oozing such confidence, told him that she was really onto something, no further thought required. Her confidence was magnetizing. He was inclined to agree with his contacts from the college—his team was lucky to have her. In mere minutes, she had proven to him she would soon be an integral member of his crew.

He moved closer to the screens, trying to anticipate what idea she could be heading toward. He scanned left, right, and up but couldn't quite grasp it yet. Next, she highlighted Daniel's face, encircling it with a semitransparent line on the screen, and then moved his face over onto Amber's.

Then she dragged the combined faces onto the mountains on the screen above.

Vanir cocked his head. He stared at the resulting image of the combined faces and mountain. There was a moment of silence, then he caught up with her.

She allowed him the time to catch up, then he confirmed under his breath, "Something inconspicuous but at the same time very visible and lasting."

He took a step backward and gawped at the image over Valda's shoulder from further away.

"You, my dear, are an absolute marvel. Send that to me, please."

He patted her on the shoulder, turned, and quickly left the console.

"I know," she said, out of earshot, and shrugged.

Vanir headed quickly through the bridge, walking around

his raised chair in the center and straight through a black doorway on the far side.

He was now outside on the surface of Secondary. His chief engineers Vidar and Volund were around a hundred yards ahead of him, fiddling with something at one of the consoles on the arch structure. Deep in conversation, almost arguing, they quickly silenced when Vanir approached. He could only smile; they were both passionate about their work.

"Good morning, gentlemen. I have an idea, and I would like you to recommend, without arguing,"—he smiled—"somebody to engineer it for me."

"Of course, sir," Vidar said, forming a rigid straight line with his body. "What did you have in mind?"

Vanir flicked open his hand computer, swiping his finger upward in a quick flick motion. Both Vidar and Volund felt their wrists gently pulse and they opened their screens.

They could see the picture of Daniel and Amber's faces interlaced with the mountain behind them. Both engineers were squinting and turning their wrists this way, then that way, trying to interpret Vanir's intentions.

"As a monument for Daniel and Amber, I would like to form something resembling this image onto one of the mountainsides on Ancient Mars, near the point of entry. I have separate plans for Volya that will require a different type of team."

Vidar still looked confused, staring at the image. "What . . . am I looking at, sir? A photo of their faces, up a mountain?"

"You almost have it, my friend! Not a photo, though—and not *up* a mountain. It is a combination of both of their faces, carved into a mountain, so that it will be visible from high above."

The engineers studied the two faces on their screens. It was obvious that Vanir knew what he wanted. Volund suggested the obvious, "Sir, if we alter a mountain into human faces, wouldn't that be making it obvious to the people of Earth that we are now there, thus changing history?"

"Yes, indeed you are correct. But not if we make it look like it 'could' be an illusion, a trick of shading, natural weathering on the rocks—that kind of phenomenon. Our people, though, will know what it is, and so will Amber and Daniel. It is my intention to go back once it is completed and explain it to them."

"Ahhhhhh," the two engineers said together, finally understanding. Sometimes it could be tiresome having to explain every little detail in his head so that people understood.

Thank the Creator for Valda, the next generation of engineers. She was going to go so far—he had big plans for her.

Once they had wrapped their heads around exactly what he wanted, both agreed that this would be a great monument to the Earthlings that had paved the way for the new milestone in their civilization to begin.

"Yes, not a problem, sir. leave it with us. We will begin consulting on construction for you immediately. I have a spot where this would be ideal, sir. Also, I know of a great engineer that would love to take this on," Valdar said.

Vanir smiled. "Thank you, gentlemen, I knew I could count on you. I look forward to any updates."

He turned and walked back along the access road, away from the arch and toward the crater perimeter.

He was about to enter a black doorway to go back inside, but he turned and took another look around. This was indeed turning out to be everything that he had imagined.

A wave of excitement sent a shiver down his back. Every plan that he had foreseen so far was now moving forward as smoothly as time itself. Frankly, he thought to himself that he could not believe his good fortune recently.

# CHAPTER 27
# CONSTRUCTION

"Hello, Valdar. What can I do for you, sir?" the face made of white light said. The face belonged to Valgerd and was hovering above the hand of Vanir's right-hand engineer, Valdar.

"I have a mission for you," Valdar said. "This has come directly from Vanir himself—you will love this. Would you be able to meet me straightaway at Vanir's passageway please? He is eager to get this started as soon as possible."

"Of course. I'm on my way."

The screen went dark and closed.

Valgerd was a stonemason by trade. He had been interested in the composition of rocks and turning it into art since he was a young boy; it had always been his passion and intended career path. He had since been responsible for the design and commission of several beautiful statues around the main square and parks. He was very well respected and widely known for his work.

Around five minutes later the scholarly stonemason paid a visit to Valdar, who looked busy instructing people around the massive archway structure. Valgerd appeared through the doorway opposite the passage, the vast crater complex stretched out before him. He had not had a reason to visit here before. It was an impressive sight.

Valdar was in the process of organizing his ground crews and the land moving equipment, ready to send them through to continue the day's work of clearing more pathways and creating more roads on Ancient Mars. The crews were organized to work in shifts, taking over as soon as another finished for the day so that they were building on Mars around the clock. Speed was everything to Vanir.

Valgerd stuck out a hand and said, "Valdar, my friend, how are you?"

Valdar reached out his hand and gripped Valgerd's hand at the wrist in a twist on a standard handshake.

"Thank you for coming so quickly, old friend. Come with me; this is right up your alley." Valdar signaled to another passageway controller, who signaled back that it was fine to proceed through. Valdar took Valgerd up the access ramp into the middle of the archway and vanished into the rippling surface to emerge on the other side.

The two men were now standing on Ancient Martian soil. Both took a moment to admire the view; Valdar was still impressed by it. The domes were barely visible unless caught by a glint of sunlight at certain angles. Valgerd had heard the buzz about the progress so far, but seeing it in person, well, he felt very privileged. How could one not be tantalized by the thought of working on the ancestral home that none of them had ever seen?

Valgerd closed his eyes and raised his head as he felt the Sun caress his skin through the clear skin of the domes overhead for the first time in his life. "Wow," he simply, but eloquently, put it. "I never thought I would feel that in my lifetime."

"I know. Amazing, isn't it?"

They both lingered there, basking in the Sun for a few moments longer. It was so invigorating, every cell in their skin felt as though it was waking up, now so much more alive, fluttering with joyous warm energy gently kissing it.

Vanir had been promising that he would lead his people from the Dark Space for so long, and now they were here. Valgerd opened his eyes and looked around. It was daytime; you could tell even through the misty murky sky overhead. It was much colder than it was on Secondary with their artificial lighting and heat sources. Valgerd shivered.

Aside from a new main road heading off into the distance across the plateau from the passageway portal for as far as the eye could see, there wasn't much else to see besides vast dusty, rocky landscapes, and hills.

"Well, Valdar, what is it that you need from me?" Valgerd asked, unable to take his eyes from the strange landscape out in front of him. Valdar went on to explain what he had been told about the image of Amber and Daniel. being very subtle. There, but not there, visible only if people knew where to look, Vanir wanted it carved into a mountain range as a vast monument to their Earthling saviors.

Valgerd, the craftsman that he was, immediately began to process the task over and over in his mind. He loved a good problem, and he understood what was being requested without much trouble. In truth, he was happy to be given such a task, and he was stunned at the thought of creating something that would be around for an extraordinarily long time. He eagerly asked Valdar to leave it with him so that he could immediately begin to draft some designs in his study.

Valdar watched as Valgerd walked with haste back through the passageway. Valgerd's form turned into a wobbling blob of dark colors as he entered the portal from this side of the passage toward Secondary. He knew that he could trust Valgerd to carry out this task to the best of his abilities. With that, Valdar turned and took another look at the soon-to-be-changed landscape. He kicked a brown pebble into the dust away from the new pathway. Up ahead of him was the first freshly laid main road across the crater bed that stretched for miles into the distance already.

In one week they would have one main avenue, complete with side roads, utility services, and the first batch of frames on either side ready for housing and commercial units.

Another unit would come in right behind them and would start laying the grids for the next zone, and then they would overlap. The cladding and glazing machines would be next, and the frames would look like houses in a very short space of time.

Educational buildings would follow, and then families would almost certainly be ready to start moving into the new zones to begin the first communities. Within a year, they would have completely operational zones and be well on the way to becoming a fully-fledged independent city.

Valgerd got comfortable in his study, realizing that the finer details and main requirements of this task would require some thought and be more of a challenge than the actual task of carrying out the work.

A face, made of two combined faces, grafted onto rock that would be visible but not obviously placed there by another civilization.

Something that the people on Earth would see but not immediately believe was created intentionally. Something that *could* have been carved naturally by the elements.

He started to draft some plans. He would use a mountain range on the Cydonia Plateau as requested. First, he printed off a plan of the area to look at on his desk. He grabbed his pencils and began shading. He was a traditionalist in that respect— paper and pencil all the way. This would help him to render the shapes and shading that would be necessary to generate the design.

Then he sent the map file of the mountain range from his personal computer to his Geoprinter which generated the file into a 3D sculpt of the range in light that would alter as he sketched his designs.

Between the 2D and 3D models, he would be able to visualize the whole concept.

He continued etching more marks and shading on his drawing, and as he did, the 3D hologram started to change above the printer, following his designs in real time.

He carefully scribed the main standout features of their faces. Their nose and eye ridges—those were his main focus, and creating shadows on the edges of a mountain was secondary. There were several times that he ended up wiping it and starting again, and each time he did, the Geoprinter also wiped itself and started with a new fresh plateau. It was the subtleness that was confusing things. His natural urge to draw a face was taking over the need to keep it simple and within the realms of natural weathering.

Eventually, after scrapping a pile of drawings and taking several rest breaks, he came across a design that he was finally happy with and promptly celebrated with a cup of wine. He sat back and locked his hands behind his head, staring at the page on his desk with some satisfaction and then at the 3D version adjacent to his desk. *Yes, this is it.*

He had been at this for almost three days with only limited sleep breaks. He flicked open his wrist computer, aimed the rear of his screen above the 3D image so that the whole thing was in view from his desk, walked around it, and saved it onto his computer. He touched a part of the screen that enabled him to send the images off to Valdar.

Hopefully, he would see what he had in mind, and it would tick all their boxes. He would have to take it to Vanir, of course, before Valgerd would be given the go-ahead to commence physical construction.

Several hours later Valgerd was in bed, getting a good night's sleep as a reward for finalizing his designs, when his wrist started to pulse. It woke him with gentle vibrations and a bright white pulsing light beneath his skin.

It meant that somebody had sent him a video message. He

composed himself in bed, first rubbing his eyes with the balls of his hands and then combing his hands through his thick white hair before opening his personal computer. It was Valdar, as he had expected. It was only a recorded video message, so it didn't matter that he looked half asleep; it wasn't live.

Valdar looked happy, cheerfully explaining that Vanir had been extremely excited by the designs and that as soon as he was able to, they were to pick a crew and commence construction immediately.

Valgerd was elated. He had completed many smaller projects on Secondary, even on Tertiary and Quaternary where he had been recommended over space, but this was the first time that he felt he was contributing something of great importance to everyone's future.

A project that would be a part of both their history and their future. His name would be remembered forever.

Valgerd woke himself up, made himself a tea, and began to collect his thoughts. He, too, had his own team of trusted engineers, ones that he called upon whenever he had something larger than a one-man building project on his mind. These contractors were not the usual road-laying types; these were more craftsmen, like himself. They took pride in their work.

He arranged a meeting for the next morning with his team, for first light at his home, to run through initial designs.

There were four of them that turned up the next day, all wearing smart utility trousers and snugly fitted tops in red to match their national color.

They sat around his table staring at his plans from different angles. There were his paper plans spread across the desk and, in the center, a rotating 3D hologrammatic render. This was a very interesting project, to be sure, far different from anything that any of them had worked on before.

Valgerd had to go through the need and the reasons again, explaining why this project had to be subtle yet visible and that when they initially start to cut into the rocks, his designs might not make much sense, but to bear with him.

They understood.

It took Valgerd another day of preparatory meetings with his team to decide which kit it would be best to manage this project with. Based on readings that they had taken about the ancient Martian soil and rock composition of the region, it could be quite crumbly rock. They also had to be mindful of any possible pockets of historic interests buried deep within the rock and in caves.

They decided on a particular set of equipment that had recently been used to clear land already on Ancient Mars, just clearing the top layer prior to the construction of the new habitat units. They had already discovered some ancient caves on Mars that would need to be carefully explored in the near future, halting some of the progress along one of the routes that had been planned as a commercial zone and thus slightly altering some of the routes.

They were very careful of sites that could have historical importance. There was no life currently habiting Mars in this period, but there had been some time ago.

The plant consisted of a plasma cut-and-store flotilla, a platform around the size of a refuse truck from Earth, complete with various cutting tools around the front edges. The advantage of this kit was that although it was completely autonomous and much slower than a rotating diamond drill cutter, it could complete a preprogrammed set of cutting instructions very acutely to within a thousandth of an inch.

When care needed to be exercised over volume cutting, and in not wanting to disturb areas of possible scientific interest, this equipment was the prime candidate.

The plasma flotilla could be given the coordinates and instructions remotely from Valgerd's personal computer and then begin, on command, to carefully cut the rock face using a multitude of different-shaped laser cutting tools.

Waste rock from the site would then be scooped up and crushed into dust by the flotilla itself. A slide-out sucker underneath the tools would pull in waste materials as soon as it was cut, then the waste would be sent to the back of the platform to a crusher. The dust would then be ducted beneath the base of the flotilla and pushed into chambers to be pressed into cubes.

When full, the cubes would self-detach from the flotilla, roll down the mountainside, and be collected by another machine later. Waste cubes would then be transported to other regions to be used as foundations for other projects during the next phases. All Valgerd's team needed to do was to supervise and manage the project in the field and stop the process if anything was found or if something went off-plan.

Roads and lev-pads for the train system that would run across Mars were well under way and quickly increasing in number. It was already much easier to move equipment around now on Ancient Mars.

After almost a week of cutting and tidying work, his project neared completion. Valgerd and his team headed to the region for their practical completion visit, using the lev-train to get there. They took the train early on the sixth morning of the project to the chunk of rock that they had been working on. The lev-train came to a smart, silent halt at the currently temporary station platform.

The engineers disembarked the train, which bounced very gently in the air as they stepped off.

They stood together in a huddle right at the foot of the mountain, which was just a twenty-minute walk across the soil from the train platform. That would get quicker as more transport links evolved.

Valgerd flicked open his personal screen and held out his arm, pointing the rear side of his computer screen at the mountain. The computer took several snapshots and then displayed a 3D hologram above his hand showing him what the mountain looked like from above. He then used different finger motions and pinches on his screen to make the hologram rotate and zoom in and out until he was satisfied that they had covered every angle.

It was perfect. Granted, you couldn't yet tell that it was Amber and Daniel's face, not standing down here. You could barely tell that the mountain had been altered at all, aside from a few new cleaner-looking rock faces around the top edges.

However, that was a major part of the brief—it was perfect! It looked exactly like his 3D renders.

Remaining waste rock cubes were being piled onto a flatbed float and taken away as they watched, ready to be used in other parts of the developments. They might become foundations for housing, lev-train pads and station bases, or used as bricks for other projects, leaving the area looking completely untouched and clean.

*This is exactly what Vanir wanted*, Valgerd thought. If mankind knew that rocks on Mars had been cut and shaped in this time period, as early as the 1940s, then they would have seriously altered human history forever, and that was not their aim . . . for now, anyway. At some point in the near future, the people of Earth would soon be out exploring their Solar system, and it would surely be photographed.

# CHAPTER 28
# AMBER'S MESSAGE

E cstatic with what his engineers had created at the Cydonia mountain range, the monument stood exactly as Vanir had envisioned. *They have done me proud yet again*, he thought.

Now all that remained was to relay this gift of his people's appreciation back to Amber and Daniel, to explain exactly what had been created for them. He was excited to see them again. Then it would be onto Volya and sorting out that little problem.

Vanir was about to make his way back to the passageway complex to continue the day's work, choosing this time to take a stroll through the city rather than simply moving door-to-door as he could have. The open air and time to think would hopefully help to settle his busy mind for a while.

He strolled with his thoughts away from his high-rise home in the new quaint garden quarter of Red City east toward Bamberg, which was the home of his passageway complex. It had been called Bamberg after a marking that had been discovered deep in the soil below it while excavating for the structure foundations.

It was around an hour's walk at a brisk pace. He was trying to find some order to the questions and ideas chasing each other in his mind, mainly things that he would say to Amber and Daniel when face-to-face with them again. He looked forward to seeing them again and rather wished that he could spend more time with them. Maybe he would someday.

He meandered along the statue-lined park avenue until he came to the travelator that ran from the edge of the park to the junction of domes thirty-three and thirty-four.

Dome thirty-four was on the way out of town, where the number of buildings and parks started to dwindle. The edge of the city limits and the beginnings of the dark sandy desert lay ahead of him, but he barely noticed.

Once the sandy desert started, the only things out here were the second Secondary military base and some other military structures—training craters, monitoring stations, and suchlike.

Once clear of the base, the road to Bamberg was quite short, taking only ten minutes to cross. Then you would hit the rim of the crater and its descending access road into the plateau complex.

Engineer Valdar was already waiting for him at the arch.

"Valdar, could you program a passage for me, please? For a visit to Amber first, I think, and then when I am done, on to Daniel."

"Of course, sir. Which time period do you have in mind?"

Vanir thought about it for a second. It was a good point, but there was only really one option—one where he knew that they were guaranteed to be standing in a particular place without him having to go around looking for them.

"Take me back to one minute after they gave us access to the spheres, please."

"Yes, sir," he replied. "I just need to make a few adjustments to find the exact time stamp. Please give me a moment."

Vanir nodded and patiently waited at the access ramp leading to the passageway whilst the engineer made the necessary adjustments on his control station. After a moment, Valdar sent a salute in Vanir's direction.

"Ready, sir!" he shouted over.

Vanir sent him a thankful nod in return and Valdar started up the passage mechanism. The view from the top of the access ramp of the nighttime red Ancient Mars turned black, then the familiar bright white spot appeared right in the middle of the space within the arch. The hum of the machines started up again and grew louder. The spot grew larger, brighter, and began rotating faster and faster until it evened out into a white sheet of light.

Vanir stomped up the access ramp and stopped at the sheet of light, turned back, and shouted down to Valdar, "Give us some privacy, please, Valdar!" Then he stepped through to Ancient Earth.

Amber was still sitting on her ass on the grass next to the diner. She had watched the sphere lift into the sky and vanish. The street remained silent and paused like a movie behind her. Then things changed.

Amber simply closed her eyes and listened, warm gratitude and pleasure flowed through her as movement and noises of the world around her started up again. Her senses were fully opened all at once. She felt the movement of air, footsteps and voices, cars. Smells carried around her from the diner—bacon, coffee, doughnuts. There was suddenly panic in the air now. People that had been frozen in the vicinity of the diner toppled over as soon as they were reanimated; some were still crouched down with their hands locked over their heads, and some even screamed. Others began to run away from the diner, some in the direction of the river and some back toward town.

She remembered that they had been frozen at the time that the sphere had landed here and set off its protective field. People then seemed to slowly calm down as they realized that the threat had vanished—or perhaps it had never been there at all. They righted themselves, looked confused and stood up. Making their way over towards Amber and the ditch, asking if she was okay and what had created the mark.

She nursed her throbbing hand, allowing herself to be helped up and took the stance of denying any knowledge of what had caused the ditch, or what had flown toward them. It was better to pretend that she was as confused as they were, she decided.

She sniffed the diner-sweetened air, picking out the different smells and tastes. *Burgers and onions frying, pancakes with syrup, French toast, bacon, coffee.* "Mmmmmmm."

*Everything is going to be okay.*

She also realized why people were looking her up and down as they walked away, remembering that she was dressed rather oddly—for her, anyway. The bystanders looked at her and then back at the new ditch dug into the town's nice lawn.

She had forgotten all about the futuristic clothes that she was wearing. Not that they were anything too bizarre, they were just . . . different. Local people would of course be used to seeing her ready for work in the diner, in that sickly cliché uniform. Her work uniform that was still on Prime somewhere —in the future. *Hah!* she thought, amused. Al wouldn't be impressed, but what an excuse that would be! Not that she could use that one; no way that would wash with Al.

She would have to go in and explain why she didn't have her uniform on when reporting for duty, and that she would need a replacement. She'd likely have to wear the diner's spare, one that would inevitably be bigger than she was and make her look like a cake topper.

No sooner than she decided to enter the diner and face the music, a warm blast of air hit her from behind. Bright white light flooded everything around her. "Oh no, not again!" She was home, but things were certainly not normal yet!

When the light had dissipated, the people around her and the cars had once again been paused.

That initial excitement that she had felt quickly turned upside down, transforming back into fear and anxiety. *Have they come back for me — to lock me up?*

She turned to look where the sphere had sat not long ago and there was Vanir, standing there looking as smug as ever and smiling at her warmly.

"It's good to see you again, Amber."

*Thank God!*

He turned, looking directly at the remnants of the Sun. Even almost fully set and swollen red, he admired its warmer touch.

"Oh my, that feels good . . . I have felt the Sun on Mars in your time, but it is much warmer from here."

She could see that his eyes were closed and that he was enjoying the weakening rays. Then he walked up the bank to her and threw his arms around her.

"Wooah! Take it easy," she said jokingly, protecting her right hand from stray touches. She was relieved that it was him and not one of the guards or the Director coming back from Prime to arrest her and take her back. "I only saw you the other day."

"Ah, yes, from your point of view you are right." He looked around at his new surroundings and up at the sky. "You only just got home, didn't you? For me, it's been over a month since I last saw you. We have been working around the clock since you left.

"And that is why I am here, Amber. I asked to be sent back to you specifically right after you had completed your journey home and sent the spheres back to me. I wanted to thank you in person for what you did for us—now that I can, of course, thanks to what you and Daniel made possible. An unlimited number of generations of people will benefit from our passageway."

Amber looked slightly confused and said, "I'm sorry, we'll get back to what you wanted to say in a sec, but I've just realized something. I've no idea what day I'm on. Am I on Monday? When I was walking to work and touched the sphere? Or am I on . . ." She looked around and then down at her watch. "Am I on Thursday at twelve thirty p.m.? My watch is telling me that we're on early Thursday afternoon, but it's clearly sunset again, and oddly things feel exactly the same as when I left. Am I right in thinking I am right back to the time when I first saw the sphere?"

Vanir looked at her in an endeared, entertained kind of way. His lips curved down at each end, then burst into a smile. He opened his hand computer.

"Bear with me a second . . . this tells me that it is now . . . thirty-five minutes after seven in the evening, and yes, you are right, you are back to Monday. So, roughly right back to the time when you first touched the sphere. Can you remember exactly what time it was when you left Earth?"

"Mmmm, not really. It feels like a lifetime ago. My head feels so foggy. Let me think, I was on my way to work," she said, really concentrating. Her eyes looked skyward. It felt as though her memories were still off in a distant Universe somewhere.

"I remember that I was on the rota to start at six thirty. But I set off slightly early so that I could grab something to eat at work . . . then all that weird stuff started happening where everyone was frozen, and my watch froze too. So, it had to be around or just after six o'clock when the lightning first hit and the town froze, and then around . . . probably six thirtyish by the time I touched the sphere."

"Then your town has actually only been on pause for one hour—not days. Everyone here should be fine, as though nothing has happened. I know that Volya attempted to send you back to the time that you touched the sphere, but with the black hole causing a distortion, time zones, et cetera, it looks like he was one hour off. Not bad, considering where you came from.

"Amber, back to the reason I needed to come back to see you —there are a few things that I need to say."

"Oh no, what is it?" Her face looked pained. Starting to feel queasy from a thousand possibilities rushing to her head all at once, she thought, *This can't be anything good, can it?* What was it? That she couldn't stay here? That he needed her to go back with him? That her mom was dead, or that time would be forever stuck like this?

"Is Volya okay?" she finally asked. "And Daniel?"

"I'm afraid that as you left Prime, Volya was killed. He sacrificed himself so that he could get you and Daniel home. He was taken down by the Director's guards, and then I had to bombard the place to stop them from coming back in time for you or trying to stop you leaving."

"I'm so sorry." She was genuinely sad. "He was a good man. He looked after us well while we were there. He was gentle. Did Daniel make it home?"

"Yes, he was a good man. I had great respect for him. He was loyal to his superiors yet believed in our cause to help the people of the Union, and he made the honorable choice to help us. Do not worry about Volya, though; I do plan to right that wrong now that I can, thanks to you. And yes, Daniel got home fine. I will be going to see him next—which leads me onto the happier news."

"But what we did wasn't that great a sacrifice, not like poor Volya. And what you did, setting it all up, telling us what we needed to do, and then, no doubt, making it possible for us to get home . . . it's me that should be thanking you."

"No, it was an unbelievable thing that you did. You decided to take that risk for us. Even with the number of people that we had working with us on Prime, nobody could ever get close enough or was brave enough to risk getting caught near to the hangar without raising suspicion. They are under constant guard. You were put in that position and succeeded."

"So, what's next for your people?" she asked.

"Well, thanks to you, we have cities thriving up there on Ancient Mars right now, and people from all over the Dark Space have registered to migrate also. Well, I say 'ancient'—it's ancient for me, but it's up there right now in your time.

"For the moment I am still based on Secondary, but not for long. I have been overseeing the Mars migration from the DSU as well as dealing with the extra security needed following the fallout from the attack on Prime—but that is a story for a different day."

"That's great news! I'm so happy for you. It's such an amazing thing, that the people from the whole system are free to join you on Mars. That was why I decided to help you. I thought, how could I not help you, knowing that the people of Prime and the other planets in the system would benefit so much from your passageway? I really hope things work out for you, and everybody up there." She looked up at the sky.

Vanir smiled and said, "I have more! The other reason I am here, Amber, is that I wanted you and Daniel both to know how much you mean to me and my people. That I was so desperate to find a way to convey my thanks and make sure that you would both be remembered by our people forever that I commissioned the construction of a monument to you both on our new home. Something that would be obvious to you both—once I told you, of course, but not so obvious that it would draw attention to our people on Mars from your people back on Earth.

"After deliberating over it for a few days, one of my crewmen and I came up with the perfect idea. It was as simple as looking at a photo of you both and the Martian soil. I have had a huge monument created, carved into a mountain on Mars. This monument will be in the shape of a human face—yours and Daniel's faces, which we overlapped, and there it will stay on Mars forever for my people to remember you. This is my people's tribute to you, Amber."

Amber was stunned for a moment, not knowing what to say at all. She thought back to her years in school. She had not been the kind of person that was picked first for any sports; she had never had a huge group of friends. She had not collected any accolades that might have gotten her name printed on something long after she was gone.

But here she was now, with a monument dedicated to her on another planet!

Tears of joy welled in her eyes. she felt such a rush of love and appreciation that she could not remember ever feeling in her life before. Sure, she looked after her mom, who she was sure appreciated that, but she had never felt such a feeling of gratitude—not on any scale like this. These were whole new feelings.

Could she even tell anyone about this? Now that she thought about it, they would lock her up for sure if she did, up at the funny farm. Funnily enough, that wasn't far from her house. *Hey, Mom, if you can get out of the house, come visit me up the road. I'll be the one in the padded cell and straitjacket.*

But she knew. This was for her. And for Daniel, of course. They would be remembered and loved by an entire race of people forever. Would it matter if anyone down here knew about it? She would definitely tell her mom.

*I've been into space!* An afterthought that was only just hitting her now. And she did appreciate that, even if all she had wanted to do while she was in space was get home. Now that she was home, it was . . . well, kind of cool.

He walked up to her and gave her another hug. She held onto him tightly, knowing that she probably wasn't going to see him again. When he stepped back from her, he held out a light-gray handkerchief taken from the inside of his sleeve to wipe her eyes.

"Thank you, Amber. Don't forget that whenever you see it, hear about it on your news, or read about it in books, you will know that the face on Mars exists only for you. I will let you carry on about your business now." He smiled as he looked the diner up and down. "I need to go and give Daniel the same news. That food smells wonderful, by the way! Goodbye, Amber, and thank you again from myself and all people in the Dark Space Union. They will be in the dark no longer."

Amber gave him a respectful bow of her head. Her emotions

felt overwhelming. If she spoke, she didn't know if she would lose control and burst into tears. Tears made up of both joy at the thought of helping so many people and also the thought that she may never hear from those people again. She had become quite attached to some of them.

And poor Volya. That was so very sad. She hoped that Vanir would remember to help him, somehow.

Vanir took one step backward, flicked open his personal computer screen, and said, "Valgerd, to Daniel now, please."

A small white light appeared in the air next to him, growing to become person-sized and oval in shape, in the exact spot where the sphere had been sitting only moments before.

He bowed his head to Amber before stepping back through the portal. Amber protected her eyes with her arm against the harsh white light. She watched as his shadow disappeared as he stepped through the oval into the other side. Then the white light faded into a single dot before completely disappearing.

As soon as Vanir and all traces of the white light had gone, cars and people nearby instantly reanimated. Everything was moving along normally as if nothing had ever happened. It was as if somebody had pressed Play after pausing a film.

"Food smells wonderful," she muttered to herself, deep in thought. She was thinking of food, the sphere, Al's grilled cheese, the smell of pancakes. *The sphere.*

"Of course! That's how they knew what food to prepare for us—the sphere was telling them what smells it could sense. Amazing!"

# CHAPTER 29
# DANIEL'S MESSAGE

Daniel sat on his now damp backside on the lawn in the school grounds, shaking his head briskly to try and clear the cobwebs. It took a moment before he was inclined to try to stand up. At first, he was confused, wondering if here was really here, and then came the strong feelings of loneliness and emptiness. He studied the dark quiet playground and school buildings.

It was a surreal feeling; he could not put a label on the exact emotions that he felt. Was it really all over? He was happy to be home, of course, and anxious to check on his family, but still that feeling of emptiness poked around in his gut. He would be going back to his normal mundane life after all that adventure.

God only knew what the time was, or even which day it was, come to think of it.

How long had they been on Prime? Three, four, five days, even. He had completely lost count, his brain felt so fuzzy. He pulled out his phone, but it was still of no more use than a doorstop.

A hint of movement caught his eye over his left shoulder. He bent down to pick up his torch that was still sitting in the grass and spun around, switching on his torch—which now came on instantly—and aiming it in that direction, but it was only a ginger cat walking behind him to get to the houses. The cat stopped walking to look at Daniel. Light from the floodlights at the school made its eyes look like hollow whitish green fog lamps.

The cat decided that Daniel wasn't a threat, or particularly interesting for that matter, so it continued its journey to patrol the houses and gardens.

First things first, Daniel needed to check that his parents and sister were okay. He could now hear background noises from the road outside of the school—and he had seen the cat moving, so he assumed all was going to be fine now.

He was also conscious that it had suddenly grown colder, the temperature drop causing him to shudder. The wind had picked up and there was even rain in the air now. He would need to get home quickly before it tipped down on him.

Daniel pocketed the torch and started to walk away from the spot where the sphere had been before he'd sent it to its new home. He had taken no more than two or three paces when he noticed something felt different. The weather had seemingly just disappeared; the rain and breeze had completely stopped, the temperature seemed to rise, and the floodlights around the school flickered.

Then a bright flash of light and a blast of warm air blew from behind him, blowing his clothes and hair all over the place. Daniel spun around. The light faded, and standing there in the now dark field next to the crater was Vanir.

That emptiness that Daniel had started to feel faded away when he saw him. Vanir looked as happy and as confident as ever, and the sight of him gave Daniel hope that maybe his adventures might yet continue.

"Hello, Vanir. What are you doing here?"

He was so pleased to see his friend from across time and space but also a little confused, as he had only just left them behind, he thought, to return to normal life.

"It's good to see you again, Daniel. How have you been?"

"How have I been? I've only just this second got back! But it's great to see you! Is everything okay? Has something gone wrong?"

"Oh no, no, my friend, please don't worry. I am here with good news! I have already visited Amber with the same. Funny, it's still daylight where Amber is, but it's dark here," he mused, looking around as he spoke.

Daniel also looked around. He laughed, then said, "Okay, I'm glad it's good news. I thought something might be wrong. And yes, it's a different time zone here from where Amber is; she's on the other side of the world. What news have you got for me? Did Volya make it out?"

"Daniel, I'm sorry. Volya sacrificed himself to get you back home. But do not worry, I do have a plan. If everything goes according to said plan, everything will be corrected.

"Right, onto the main reason I am here. I wanted to show my and my people's sincerest gratitude to you both for what you have helped us achieve. So, I had the inclination to erect some sort of monument to you on Mars. I must admit that at first, I was at a complete loss as to what to do, but then a member of my crew assisted me and we came up with just the solution. I have built a huge monument, one that will stand proud forever—hopefully. It is a whole mountain carved into the shape of a face. Yours and Amber's faces, combined. You will see this 'face on Mars' in literature, on your visual media, and in books. By now, I know that it has been discovered by your people, so it should be easily found. When you do see it, remember that my people built this for you, so that you will both be remembered by our people forever."

"Sick! I don't even know what to say—thank you so much! I'm going to look it up as soon as I charge my phone. If the electricity is back on, that is."

Vanir laughed. "Yes, you do that, and do not worry. When I leave you, everything will be restored to normal."

"You say the face on Mars is there right now?" Daniel asked.

"Yes, it has been there since the early 1940s when we first arrived on Mars through the passageway. It has actually been photographed by now by an orbiting craft back in the mid-1970s—or so I am told," Vanir replied, smiling at Daniel. He was so proud of them both. Had it been blind luck or divine intervention that they had been sent to the Dark Space? It still didn't make a lot of sense how they had happened to come to him just when he needed them—and as a pair as well.

"In my timeline, when you sent the spheres back to me, we immediately started to move onto Ancient Mars. I chose the 1940s to start building there, as you Ancient Earthlings were busy, distracted by war and rebuilding your planet in the years that followed. The monument was one of the first things I had built.

"Right now, up there," he said, looking up longingly, "I have thriving cities already, filled with families from all over the Dark Space in their new homes. All this is thanks to you and Amber —and Volya, of course. Who knows? Maybe our people in the generations to come will come up with a plan to save our people from ending up in the Dark Space and winding up in the same political mess again. Having a second chance at it may prove interesting, let's say."

Daniel had so many questions racing through his mind that he was sure not all of them would make it out. He noticed that behind Vanir, the ginger cat that had been prowling toward the gardens was now frozen again.

"Vanir, how will you help Volya, and remember him?"

"Volya was a great man. Volya was a man who was loyal to his Directorship. However, he was also aware of our plans and turned a blind eye to some of my dealings with you. He knew of our plans, and that you had been to visit me the whole time. Fortunately, he was also of the opinion that the people of Prime, and the rest of the union, should have the right to choose their own fate, whether that might be a move to a new home and feel the Sun again or remain in the dark.

"Whilst I was having the project built to commemorate you and Amber, I also used some of the waste material to form several pyramids around the region. The shape of these pyramids will be in the letter V, for Volya. These will be sacred burial grounds for our people. The first city of Mars was also named Volya City. With regards to helping him, I plan to use my new passageway to go back and assist him in getting out of there, not interfering with the return of you two for obvious reasons."

"That's nice, I like that. At first, we weren't sure whether we could trust him. We could tell he was loyal to the people he served, but he was good to us. He tried to be as honest as he could without risking his position. In the end, he turned into a full-on action hero, getting us to that hangar and back home. Will our people find out that there is life up there on Mars soon, then?"

"Not imminently, unfortunately. But not far into the future, your explorers will discover that there is indeed life on Mars and, in-fact, all around your galaxy. But unfortunately, it will be kept quiet from the general public for quite a long time. Your people need a long time to adjust to facts that will affect your entire belief system. It may not happen in your lifetime, just be warned. But of course, you now know that we are there, don't you?"

"Thank you so much, Vanir, for the opportunity to help your people, the monument, and for helping us to get home. I . . . I'll be sad that I won't be part of any more adventures. I'm going to really miss you and Volya. I'd so love to be able to visit Mars!"

Daniel shook Vanir's hand. Despite starting life in space as a prisoner and being beyond scared, he had enjoyed his time seeing what else was out there in the Universe.

Not many people that he knew of could say that they had had that opportunity.

Vanir took a step away from Daniel, smiling, and said, "Never say never, young man."

It occurred to Daniel that there was another thing bugging him that he wanted to ask. "Oh! Before you go, I almost forgot —I knew there was something else. Before I touched the sphere, when I was still in my bedroom, I saw a copy of myself. Then, when I was being returned home, that copy was me—coming home. Is that related to the spheres too?"

"Yes, most likely." Vanir nodded, amused. He did like these two young people and would miss their inquisitive hungry minds. "What you saw sounds to me like the sphere realigning your future self with your present self. Settling you back into the correct timeline, that is all. As you arrive back through space and time through the sphere, being converted back from light to your whole self again, you would have to be realigned properly so that you are not mistakenly put back into an incorrect timeline."

Vanir noticed Daniel's frown as he tried to process what Vanir had said, so Vanir elaborated a little further.

"For example, say the sphere had returned you during a time when you had been standing with your family, and there were now two of you in the room. Or worse, say if you had unfortunately passed away in one timeline, and then magically you were now standing there again, alive with your family due to a slight calculation error. See what I mean? So, the spheres and the controllers, for example—my passageway, or the returns facility on Prime that sent you home—must gently phase you back into your timeline, checking that it has put you back exactly where you need to be. They are extremely intelligent pieces of machinery."

"Ah, yes, I understand, thank you. It's pretty much what I was expecting you to say, to be honest, but if I hadn't asked, I know I would have been gutted later."

Vanir then gave Daniel a friendly hug. "Quite. Thank you

again, my friend. I will leave you to get back to normality again."

Then speaking into his computer, he said, "Valgerd, back to you now, please." Vanir stepped into the bright oval of white light that appeared next to himself and vanished into it. The light quickly disappeared after him.

Daniel was again alone, and boy did he feel it. Standing in the dark on the school field, he looked at the back of his house.

The temperature was quite cold again suddenly. He noticed that the cat had now long gone, and the grass was once again wavering. He felt some drops of rain on his face. He thought about what Vanir had said—"I'll let you get back to normality again." It felt like he had been away from his normal life for so long.

A plane caught his attention, silently flying overhead quite high up in the dark sky, its wing lights twinkling as it passed. Then there was another, much higher than the first one he had seen. Then another came from behind him and over him. *Must be busy up there*, he thought.

He heard traffic sounds again coming from the road outside the school.

As Daniel left the school field, he walked alongside the familiar science block and jumped back over the gate. The traffic was moving along Darlaston Lane. It was late, so it wasn't that busy, but a car went past him, then a bus in the other direction.

There was no way he would be able to get up to go to school in the morning. He had completely lost track of what day it was, and he felt tired, hungry, and a little light-headed after all that had happened. He didn't feel that he would ever be able to concentrate again. How boring was normal life going to seem now?

He would throw a sick day tomorrow and have a lie-in. If people knew what he had been through, they would understand. Not that he could tell them—assuming everyone else had returned of normal, of course.

As soon as Daniel's keys touched the lock in the front door, he saw the light on the stairs come on through the dimpled glass. His dad came bounding down the stairs in his jeans and a T-shirt and opened the door.

"Where did you go? I thought we were going over the school and then you just vanished!"

Thinking on his feet, Daniel said, "Oh yeah, sorry, Dad . . . I couldn't wait, I was so excited. I thought you might join me over there when you were ready," with a shrug.

"Well, what did you see? Anything?"

"No, Dad, nothing. Saw a ditch in the grass—looks like something did hit the ground, but whatever it was is gone now. Must have burnt itself up or disappeared or something."

His dad looked disappointed. "Oh, okay. Might as well not bother going round there, then." Daniel watched as his dad trudged back up the stairs. He did feel bad for him. *Bless him. He's disappointed. But at least he's okay now.*

# CHAPTER 30
# AFTER - WILLENHALL

A fter making sure that his mom, dad, and sister were fine, Daniel disappeared into the sanctuary that was his bedroom. They didn't have any recollection that anything weird had even happened to them, aside from remembering the possible meteorite landing at the school and then the feeling of needing a very deep breath, as if they had just emerged from a long swim underwater.

As soon as the door closed, he flicked on his television and looked longingly at his bed.

He rocked his head back into his pillow as he fell onto it, letting out an instinctive "Ahhhhhh."

It felt so good to be back on his soft bed, in his own space, where he could get his head back together.

His phone was obviously still dead when he pulled it from his pocket, so he reached down and plugged in the charging cable, lying loose on the floor, and rested it on his bedside table.

The local news was quietly playing on the TV. As he usually fell asleep with it on, he kept the volume minimal so as not to disturb anybody.

The bar along the bottom of the screen displayed Tuesday 01:35.

*Just as I thought—I was barely away. I was gone, what, an hour?*

His phone vibrated, making him jump as it began to boot up again.

At the bottom of the television screen was a scrolling yellow banner with large black text. The banner read:

**WHOLE SECTION OF THE UK MISSING FOR ONE HOUR, NOW BACK! STAY INDOORS FOR YOUR OWN SAFETY!**

*Mmmm, maybe I don't have to worry about going to school tomorrow anyway. I could say that I was trapped inside that section and didn't feel like coming in today. Who wouldn't understand that?*

He smiled. It wasn't that he didn't like his school. He did, kind of, but his head just wouldn't be in it after what he had been through. Would things ever be the same again?

Would anything feel normal, ever? He didn't think so.

Bob Norman, the most well-known, loved, and longest serving of the central region news presenters was now onscreen with Worcester Cathedral as the backdrop. Daniel grabbed the remote and turned up the volume.

"Safely stationed tonight outside the beautiful Worcester Cathedral, outside of the 'bubble' area, I am here to bring you the latest on what we know so far about tonight's major 'event.' Assistant Chief Constable for the West Mercia Police Rachel Jervis joins me. What can you tell me about the 'event' and what its effect has been on the West Midlands region, Ms. Jervis?"

"Well, Bob, all I can safely say right now—as I'm sure you can understand, information at this stage is still being collated from partner forces all around the country—is that shortly after midnight, we started to receive calls from the public reporting that at various points around the Midlands, traffic had become stationary for no apparent reason. That the region had become completely inaccessible. Also, there is speculation out there— yet to be confirmed—that what had appeared to be an unex- pected thunderstorm could have been linked to the 'event.' I would not speculate on anything at this stage, because that is all we know at this moment in time."

"So, the thunderstorm happened, as you say, 'unexpectedly.' Could you tell us any more about the storm?"

"Not really, Bob. All we know right now is that according to Met Office data, it seems to be a naturally occurring, non-weather-related phenomenon."

"I see, and the traffic problems— could you expand on those, please?"

"As with any road traffic problems, once the cameras started to pick up on the volume of traffic along certain main routes, combined with the calls from concerned motorists, traffic police were dispatched to the areas where most of the calls were originating from. The officers, to protect public safety, began to mark the various points around the edges of the anomaly, which allowed us to quickly determine the size of anomaly that we were dealing with. We have to say 'anomaly,' as we just do not know what it was. The affected area was circular, covering most of the West Midlands region. The area within was completely inaccessible by any sort of contact or intrusion for a period of approximately one hour."

"Could you clarify any further on what you mean by the term 'inaccessible,' please? And is it true that a similar event has also been reported in Canada, at the same time as here in England?"

"Sorry, Bob—yes, by inaccessible, all I can say is that our officers and partner region officers could not gain any physical access to the region, which seemed to be enclosed inside what is currently being called the 'bubble.' No communications at all could get in or out of the bubble, nor could anybody physically get any further into the area without becoming affected by a paralyzing force from its boundaries, either by foot or motor vehicle. The area inside was still visible, but not accessible.

"With regards to Canada, at the moment I wouldn't want to speculate on behalf of our friends there. But as Canadian news outlets are now reporting on it, I can confirm that yes, a similar event has occurred in Winnipeg. The prime minister of Canada will release his own statement to update his country, so we will await his announcement before commenting any further."

"Thank you, Ms. Jervis. It is understood that all areas that were affected are now back open. What can you tell me about the effect that this has had on people that were contained inside of the . . . 'bubble'?"

"I don't have much information on hand yet, Bob, but the people that had been rendered 'frozen' are completely fine, and so far they do not seem to be showing any long-term symptoms that require medical attention. Witness reports that I have had so far suggest that they do not have any memory at all of being in that state. As far as they are aware, nothing happened."

"Thank you, Ms. Jervis." Bob addressed the camera, one finger pressed against his ear. "I have just been told that Parliament has been called in early for an emergency COBRA meeting, which is expected to go on throughout the early hours and the rest of Tuesday. A press conference will be arranged with the highest priority to update the nation first thing tomorrow. Hopefully, this address may shed further light to clarify whether this could have been a terrorist event or just one big accident, with some speculation that this is either related to the test of an experimental new weapon, or the responsibility of the Large Hadron Collider. The British people need to know whether we, as a nation, are safe. For now, back to you in the studio."

If Daniel didn't know any better, this would look very serious indeed.

He sat on his bed thinking that he had been gone for well over three days, yet time here had not moved on at all. He had only been away for an hour in this reality. He was a time and space traveler! He had been a major part of it all, in fact—the reason for everything that was happening on the news. The sphere had wanted to register a connection with him. He felt lucky that he had experienced what he had, but this unfortunately also played a part in the emptiness he was left with.

He couldn't talk to anyone about what he had been through. Either they would laugh and think him an idiot or he would be locked up and experimented on, and neither option sounded nice.

He would love to be back on Prime, Secondary, or Mars, joining the excitement there. Well, maybe not so much on Prime now, considering what they had done. But he missed the excitement of being involved in something bigger than going to school and then worrying about what job he wanted to do.

*God, I hope Volya is going to be okay. Vanir promised that he had a plan.*

And that's all he remembered. Daniel couldn't keep his eyes open any longer.

He had allowed himself the luxury of relaxing for a change, knowing that everything was going to be okay. His family was safe, he'd saved a bunch of people from living miserable dark lives, and he was home.

Sleep first, then maybe a strong coffee once he woke up. and then tomorrow he would try and track down Amber through Facebook to check if she and her mom were okay.

Amber had become his new little (but older) sister through this, and he felt that they had a connection. He couldn't talk to anyone else about this unbelievable experience, but he could speak to Amber about it.

It would be nice to keep in touch. He doubted that his friends and family would understand the things that he had gone through, and she probably felt the same.

He smiled to himself as he drifted away.

# CHAPTER 31
# AFTER - SELKIRK

Amber hesitated at the door to the diner, still looking between the diner and the crater. It was approaching eight in the evening now by the time Vanir had left her. If things were as normal here as any other day, she should have started work over an hour and a half ago. But she noticed through the doors that the wall-mounted clock near the counter read ten minutes to seven. It had stopped along with the town. She wanted to go in and speak to Al, and maybe even go back to normal and start work, but she couldn't take her eyes off the crater and the people of the town who just seemed puzzled now. Without a sphere, they couldn't see why they had been left with a crater.

The confused townsfolk likely would have seen the first flash of lightning, and then what turned out to be the sphere arriving from the sky into the town, but would most likely not be aware of what happened after that. When the second bout of lightning hit, that's when she recalled the town being frozen.

Frazzled people brushed past her into the diner, making her late entrance among all of the commotion outside less conspicuous. She didn't feel too tired; she had probably gone way past tiredness. She could eat, though. She felt locked in a sort of two-way struggle between going straight home to check on her mom and heading inside for the normality of the diner. If it had only been an hour that she was gone, and nobody even knew—yet—that they had been frozen, then common sense would say that her mom should still be fine, sitting comfortably in her chair and watching *Two and a Half Men*.

On the other hand, if she stayed down in the town, she could grab a bite to eat and do a shift for Al. She could work overtime and make up for being late, and not in uniform, and get straight back into normal life again. Things down here in town also had the potential to get quite interesting shortly when people all around the province realized that something big had happened right here.

People from all over the place would start heading here, especially once it got out that there was a strange crater. She should probably stay in town to see what went on from here.

She turned and strolled inside, right up to the counter where Al was sitting and serving a group of people all at once. Mr. Conway sat patiently in between them with his coffee. Al looked her up and down, puzzled.

*Ah, yes.* Her uniform was long gone, likely still sitting somewhere in a carrier bag on Prime billions of years from now. Now that was a funny thought.

"I'm sorry, Al, I had a little accident with my uniform, and our washer is busted again. Could I just go change into one of the spares, please?"

"Sure, you know where they are." He jerked his thumb out toward the back area, multitasking as he interacted with his customers. It was nice to see Al moving and speaking again, even if he did seem a little put out by her lack of uniform.

Amber enjoyed a grilled cheese and an Americano before starting; she was starving. Al's place did the best grilled cheese —his secret was to put the slightest lick of Tabasco sauce in the cheese. She quickly changed and jumped straight in, helping on the diner floor. It seemed to be getting busier and busier, the busiest she had ever seen it, in fact.

She studied every customer as she topped up their coffee, thinking how nice it was to see regular human faces again, not gray or scaly skin, and not having to worry about knowing who the hell she could trust.

The place was heaving with both regulars and strangers. It was like everyone from across Manitoba had decided to come out to the Selkirk Diner. As she suspected, people from out of town were starting to swarm to the place like moths to light bulbs toward the center of the mystery—Selkirk and its new mystery crater.

They had a few tables packed away for busy times, and Al had quickly taken them out of storage out the back and brought them out front. But people were even sitting on the ground now, ordering food and drinks to enjoy on the grass, knowing full well they had no chance of getting a table inside.

Several news vehicles had pulled up outside, spilling crew out all over the grass around by the river. There was a real buzz around the town. It was dark and the excitement created a carnival-like atmosphere that was rather nice. The news crews were interviewing any town residents that passed by them. She noticed that the television up on the wall near the register was on. It was showing the news and had been turned up, everyone staring at it like zombies. The headline on the television stated:

**"21:16 - Half of Winnipeg and Northern Territories Cut Off from world for One Hour, Selkirk at the Center of the Mystery"**

The clock on the wall next to the television stated 20:16, still one hour behind the rest of the province, and she noticed that the customers were looking up and down at their watches, then jibber-jabbering to each other again.

*I know why that is*, she thought and smiled to herself.

She decided to get one of the customer's spins on it. It had gotten so loud in here that she couldn't quite make out what they were all saying.

"Hey, Bob," she asked the lone regular customer occupying a stool near the window. He'd had his eyes fixed on the events going on outside while looking up and then back down at his watch again. "What's going on? I'm not really hearing what the problem is."

"Oh hey, Amber, you been under a rock or something? Check this out—my watch says 8:18, right? Well, according to the news and what's causing all the buzz is that now it's really 9:19. We are an hour behind. Why? What happened in that hour?

"Apparently an area all the way from mid-Winnipeg right up to Winnipeg Lake just went completely off the grid! Social media blew up quickly, speculating this and that. Then people started to post about that crater out there. The news folks were waiting to pounce on the cause of this thing, put two and two together, and now the whole damn country wants to come here.

"They're tryna figure out why we were cut off and have no memory of it. Something did fly through the sky, we know that much, maybe even landed out there before running off again. But what? Nobody knows! And they can't explain why we're still one hour behind the rest of the province."

"Oh, right, wow! Any theories yourself, Bob?"

Obviously knowing more than she was letting on, Amber was careful not to draw any unnecessary attention to herself.

"Only explanation I keep coming up with is aliens! Something did land, and it froze time! Then high-tailed it out of here. We couldn't do nothing like this! People of Earth, I mean. Even if we wanted to. Whole town's probably been taken up into the spaceship. They've taken our sperm, and your eggs—pardon me if I'm being too vulgar, I apologize—and we've all been put back like nothing happened and sent out on our merry ways.

Makes sense, that's why we're all one hour behind here. Has to be!"

"Well, if it means anything to ya, Bob, me and my eggs think you're right and are with ya one hundred percent." She smiled good-naturedly and walked off. She cleaned the table next to him, so that it was ready for the next customers and carried a pile of dirty plates back to the kitchen.

Amber was sweating buckets. It was really warm in there now with all the bodies and too many people to keep happy. Hands and coffee mugs were popping up into the air all over the place. She had never seen it this busy. *Damn, should've just gone home and called in sick!*

Al was still at the register, which was opening and closing constantly. His smile wide, stretching from ear to ear, he was yelling at people to "Hold your horses!" She was sure that his pupils had turned into dollar signs.

The news crews outside were having a field day. This was the jackpot, the big one. The whole town was buzzing with excitement. Speculation was that Selkirk had been the town that had made first contact with aliens. Camera flashes were going off inside the diner and outside at the crater's edge. Microphones were being shoved into locals' faces and locals were also swarming around the news crews, trying to get their faces and stories onto the television.

Through the madness from her current spot at the back of the diner, carrying a pile of dirty plates in each hand, she suddenly stopped dead. Two familiar-looking police uniforms came walking in through the front door. She saw their faces and immediately burst out laughing, along with most of the diner. Luckily, they didn't hear her over the rest of the laughing clientele and the Rock 'n' roll pumping out of the jukebox.

She headed up the diner floor toward Al and a very embarrassed pair of police officers. She overheard them politely asking Al, "Excuse me, Al, could we use your bathroom please?" Al must have looked up and seen them, because he

305

released a laugh that sounded like he was honestly trying to hold it in for the first half a second. First it burst out as a spray, then it became a belly laugh that nobody could have held in.

The policeman had a comically big bushy mustache drawn on his face in black ink, and the policewoman, looking toward the floor and doing her best to stay as inconspicuous as she could, took shade behind the policeman. She had cheeks the color of bullseyes, contrasting with her black mustache with designer curled-up edges on either side of her face.

Al, doing his best to regain his composure, pointed with his thumb and said, "Yeah, sure, it's in the back!"

They skulked past him toward the bathroom, deeply embarrassed and not looking up from the floor at all as they gently carved past people standing around waiting for tables. Amber had completely forgotten about those two, but it totally made her day amidst the madness.

# CHAPTER 32
# MICK GOES HOME

I t was just after one in the morning. Almost one hour after the first lightning strike that Mick happened to see from the station windows at just after midnight.

Mick was driving his Audi toward Shrewsbury after leaving the station on the wet dark A49. The wipers cleared rain as fast as they could across the windows.

Mick gripped the wheel tightly in a state of complete confusion and frustration.

He wasn't sure whether it was his age catching up with him, but he was suddenly feeling unsure about where he was headed, knowing full well that there was something that he should be doing. Something really important, and not just driving home.

*So annoying.* "Damn it!" He hadn't got the foggiest what it was, and he was damned if he could pull the memories out of thin air.

He ran over the things that he could definitely remember from tonight, retracing his steps as best as he could. Starting from right before midnight. After that, well, things just started to get weird, and foggy.

He remembered sitting at his desk. He had had a quick chat

with the cleaner. He was done for the night and thinking of going home. He remembered that there was lightning in the distance from the southeast. He packed away his paperwork into his desk, ready to carry on with the job tomorrow.

Then he had put on his hat and coat and came down in the lift to the basement level to his car to leave. When he reached the parking garage, he realized that he had forgotten his phone's charging cable. He had gone back up in the lift to get it. He could recall all that as clearly as if it was replaying in HD.

The gaffer had seen him and called him over—there was something wrong. The gaffer had mentioned a problem with the motorways, and that the traffic was backing up all around the network.

So far, so good.

Then he . . . he was going to have a look on his way home and ring the gaffer. He went back down to the car. He started up the car . . . and this was where Mick's memory started to cloud over.

"What the bloody hell is wrong with me?" he said out loud in the empty car. Maybe he was simply supposed to go home? It was just that it didn't feel right. There was something else.

He checked the time. The Audi dashboard told him that it was 1:17 in the morning. He switched on the radio and set course for home, still feeling as though he should be doing something else. He hoped that it would come back to him at some point if he stopped stressing about it.

The radio was tuned into local station BBC Radio WM, the station that would let you know of anything significant going on around the West Midlands. It was a call-in show.

They were discussing something—something big. The disc jockey mentions that a large section of the UK, the center of which was speculated to be somewhere near Walsall, had been completely cut off for around one hour but was now fully accessible again.

Residents from within the area had been calling in, reporting "missing time."

"Missing time?" he repeated, setting him off thinking again.

Apparently, all affected areas had suddenly opened back up and started moving again after around one hour of the initial reports of traffic problems around the motorways. This rang a bell with Mick.

The understanding, from the reports of callers into the radio station, was that the affected area and its inhabitants had been cut off entirely from the rest of the world. It was as if they had been wiped off the map. And apparently, people that had been trapped inside the area had no memory of what had happened to them, or even that anything had happened at all.

People from within the affected area's clocks were behind everyone else's in the UK by one hour.

It was also just now mentioned by the DJ that an event mirroring that of the "Midlands bubble" had, very strangely, also affected parts of Winnipeg in Canada.

The governments of the UK and Canada had been called into session and were in deep discussions with the other nations of the world, trying to find out if, and why, they had been seemingly targeted by the strange event.

At this stage, terrorism hadn't been ruled out. It had been mentioned, quite often by callers, although nobody had yet claimed responsibility for it.

No official statement had yet been released by either country. There were going to be meetings in London and Ottawa later this morning to discuss the events and to hopefully enable statements to be disclosed to the public as soon as all available evidence could be closely examined.

"What the bloody hell is going on?" Mick muttered as he sat in his car scratching his head. He thought he'd better get home, try and get some rest. It sounded like he would be needed in the morning.

He drove his Audi into Shrewsbury and joined the A5 heading eastbound toward Wolverhampton.

*Something very familiar about all of this!*

After around half a mile, he noticed two police cars pulled over on lane one. A civilian vehicle was stopped and in darkness in front of them. There were officers in the rear police car, and the lead car's officer was out of his vehicle and walking on the carriageway towards the car.

It was dark along this stretch, so Mick checked in his rearview mirror, slowed right down, and surveyed the scene through his passenger window as safely as he could whilst driving past, just to check whether assistance might be required.

The lone officer standing outside of his car on the tarmac carried a torch. As Mick drove by, staring at the officer through the passenger side window, the officer stared back at him. Mick could see that the officer in the road had a confused vacant stare about him—but then the other officer must have thought the same about Mick. Something so familiar but indiscernible connected them. Mick could not put his finger on what the feeling was.

Mick didn't recognize the officer in the road, so he drove by and away into the night, the officer or the cars no longer in view.

Mick carried on driving, the road changing without much detail as he approached Telford from the A5 into the M54 motorway. He still held that puzzled feeling inside that something was amiss and that he should be doing something.

He almost drove straight past his exit, he was still so deep in thought. He pulled off late and exited the motorway at Junction 2, driving across the chevrons. Luckily there was nobody around to shout at him, as he would normally do to them.

He pulled straight into his estate down Bell Lane off the carriageway. Coven was a tight-knit community between Wolverhampton and Staffordshire. Currently, the chummy neighbors were standing outside of their homes, dressed in pajamas, gowns, and slippers.

They were talking and pointing, quite animatedly. House alarms were going off everywhere.

He sighed, rolling his eyes. All of his neighbors knew what Mick did for a living; they had already noticed him pulling in and had started to swarm toward his car. He knew that he was in for a long night.

# CHAPTER 33
# TOMMY'S MOM

I n Selkirk, MB, Canada, Alice was sitting in her car. She had just jumped out of her skin for no apparent reason at all that she could think of.

Her car was positioned in a queue of traffic. There were cars in every direction around her, all stationary. Her memory felt like a blank piece of paper.

She felt completely and utterly lost. Automatically, her mind started to try to patch itself, retracing its last steps to a time when things made sense, mapping what it could to see why she was here and what might have happened to her.

She remembers locking up the office. It was around five minutes to six on the office wall clock as she turned off the branch lights. More images came back. It was Monday, she thought—no, she was quite certain. Everyone else in the office was straight out of the door at five thirty sharp, but she always hung on a little longer afterward to tidy up her desk and make reminder notes for tomorrow. Nobody else was as organized as Alice. It was then time to make her way home to her husband, Steve, and her son, Tommy.

She had locked up the office doors and shutters, walked

down the side of the office to her car in the rear staff car park, unplugged her car charging cable, as she always did, and stowed it in its compartment in the trunk. Then she pulled out of her parking bay and joined the long lines of traffic as per normal.

If it had been a hard day, she would generally turn the radio to some soothing music. Other days she would have the local radio station on. Then nothing—her mind went blank. It was as if she had reached the end of her mental journal. There was just . . . nothing.

She took a deep breath, let out a loud long sigh, and scratched her head. She had awoken with that jumping feeling, one of those moments after you start to fall asleep where you feel that your body is in free fall. Her whole body had shaken in the seat, as though suddenly realizing that she was alive again, and it felt as though she had been asleep for hours. But that's what didn't make any sense; why would she have been asleep after getting behind the wheel? Nothing made any sense.

*What the heck has happened to me?*

She looked around herself, trying to get a grip on reality. She was on Easton Drive, not even out of Selkirk yet. She checked the clock and it told her that it was 18:46.

Had she dropped off at the wheel? That would have been very unlike her.

She changed the station again to a current affairs type of show, hoping normal voices may help her. On the radio, the DJ said something about it being 7:46 in Winnipeg.

"What? No, it's not!" she shouted at the radio, looking back at the dashboard clock and expecting to see 18:46. But then the clock blinked and now read 19:47.

She stared at it blankly. *What is going on?*

The traffic was still going nowhere, so she sneaked a look at her cell phone that was still in her purse in the passenger footwell. Her cell also showed 18:47, but before her eyes it changed to 19:47 and instantly started to go bananas. *Buzzz, buzzzz, buzzzz.* It vibrated incessantly, almost falling out of her confused shaking hands.

The car audio system was also ringing around her. She took a quick glance up at the road to double-check that she was still ok. The traffic still hadn't moved; she was fine. When she glanced down at the phone, she noticed that she had six missed calls from her husband and three from her mom, who lived in Neepawa.

She pressed Voice Command on the car's steering wheel and said, "Call Steve," hoping that he could help her piece together why she felt so out of sorts.

Hardly even giving the dial tone a chance to start, Steve answered. He sounded out of breath and deeply anxious, as though she had been missing for a month. "Thank Christ, are you okay?"

"I'm okay, Steve, but what's going on?"

"Where are you?"

"Still in Selkirk. It seems I've only just left the office. . . . It's weird, in my head I feel like I'm lost . . . I can't explain it."

"Don't worry, everything's going to be alright. We'll be alright as long as you're okay. I have Tommy here with me—he's fine, Mom and Jean are fine, too, just . . . do your best to get home as soon as you can."

"Okay, I'm on my way. See you soon. Love you."

"I love you too!" he said and then hung up.

Tommy's dad gripped Tommy tightly on his lap, relieved, as they sat on the back porch steps. Grandma Two was fine and well now, too. She was resting on the comfy lounge chair in the garden with her feet up and a sweet chamomile tea, made for her by Steve to calm her nerves. Steve had also brought his mom out onto the porch in her wheelchair.

He felt safe here with his family close to him and his wife now on her way, where he could keep an eye on them and watch the skies carefully for any signs of further strange events.

He heard sirens blaring in the distance, and there were now more than a couple of helicopters buzzing around. Like so many others living through the aftermath of this interstellar interruption, Steve didn't know what had happened, but his family was all accounted for. That would do for now.

# CHAPTER 34
# AMBER'S MOM

Lydia Roberts woke with a start in her chair. She was comfortable but short of breath—even shorter than usual. Rather than damaged, her lungs felt as though they had been completely emptied and then stretched out. She took a few deep breaths—as deep as she could muster, anyway, falling short at the top end of her breath, stopped by coughing that wouldn't stop. She took a drink from the glass of water on her chairside table and turned on her oxygen cylinder, pulling the mask over her head, and began sucking.

The light fixtures and the lamps in the living room flickered. She looked around nervously, still sucking her oxygen, but things began to settle down and feel easier, the lights returned to normal.

It seemed to have suddenly dropped dark outside the window. *Two and a Half Men* had been replaced by the news. She leaned back her head, trying to get her normal rhythm back and steady her aching mind.

*I must have drifted off and woke myself up with that falling feeling.*

She grabbed the phone from her table and looked at the screen. 18:46.

"It can't be! That can't be right. Feels like I've been out for hours."

Then, as she stared, in a blink, the clock on the phone had changed to 19:46.

*Well, that was odd! It's still going to be ages before Amber gets home.*

She had the strangest feeling that she had been on her own for days, and she could feel a tight knot, caused by worry that she couldn't fully explain in her stomach. She closed her eyes and tried her best to relax, tried not to get worked up. She would be fine, she tried to convince herself. It must have been because she had fallen into a deep sleep—that's all.

Oddly enough, she started to feel tired again and decided that a nap whilst she waited for Amber to get home might not be a bad idea, and that would also kill some time. She removed her oxygen mask now that her breathing had settled down and closed her eyes.

When she settled back into a nice deep sleep, she started to see light, and then images, a twenty-nine-year-old version of herself laughing. A scene that she lovingly relives often in her dreams, a day from her younger, healthier years. She treasured this memory. It was a single day from 1990. She was outdoors, the Sun was blindingly bright and warm, the spotless golden-tinged sky streamed past her.

She could smell and taste the outdoors. It was a sweet taste —a cocktail of grass and wheat, then whisky and cigarettes. She coughed then, both inside and out of her dream. Amber hadn't been thought of yet; Lydia had conceived Amber a lot later than her other friends that had settled down and started their families.

On that day in the past, she was riding in the back of her close "friend" Tony's 83 pickup truck. Also in the truck were her best friends, Dawn—who Amber would have recognized as Mrs. Richards—Linda, and Chris. They were all smoking cigarettes—Lydia had smoked heavily since she was fourteen—and taking turns sipping from a bottle of rye, enjoying the fresh open air, the music, and each other's company.

Bryan Adams's "Hearts on Fire" was blasting out through the open rear window of the cab. They were all laughing to high heaven as the truck bounded over the mounds in the bumpy, dusty back roads. Clouds of dust were kicked up and whisky was being spilled all over the truck. They were on their way back to town from a day at the Birds Hill Lake.

Dawn, sitting opposite Lydia, suddenly stopped laughing. She dropped completely silent and the color drained from her face. She stared blankly at the sky beyond Lydia.

This was different to her memory of this day, though. Lydia in the real world felt conscious of this--she was scared now. Why would a memory that she had relived more often than any other change just like that? *Something is not right.*

Back in the rear of the truck, Dawn very slowly raised a finger and pointed to something in the sky. Something was following them. A silver object, smooth with a sloping front and back, like an upside-down bowl. Sunlight glinted off it when it caught the light.

"Do you see that?" she asked after a minute.

They all looked around, and the music stopped as the truck's occupants all stared open-mouthed at the sky. The laughing and joking in the truck had all ceased.

What they saw was exactly like the spaceships from early science fiction movies.

The truck was still moving, and so was the disc. It didn't seem to be getting any closer to them; it was just kind of watching them from its position alongside them. The fear abated a little. Lydia and her friends were now in awe at their first real UFO encounter.

There had been a spate of sightings right across the province recently, and Lydia had really wanted to see one for herself. Now, though, she wasn't sure whether she should have. It felt as though it was staring right at her. Were they at risk—maybe of being abducted and experimented on?

They seemed safe for now. The craft somehow didn't seem aggressive and now started to slowly break away. It tilted upwards in the sky before disappearing in a bright flash of light.

Hidden from view inside the sky-based vehicle, whilst it was still tracking the truck, were two pilots. They were young military men that appeared to be human, only their skin was a shade grayer than ours. They watched the young people in the truck—one person in particular was enlarged on the screen—with interest, enlarged and in crystal-clear clarity on large screens in front of them. The craft had already been on the Earth for a while—to the United Kingdom, in fact, to check over Daniel's mother. Now they were in Canada, one hour later.

They could have cloaked the ship, blending away into the sky, but chose to make themselves visible. Not so much for the benefit of those in the truck, but more to make themselves known to any other technically advanced beings that might also be nearby with intentions to interfere with the timelines.

One of the pilots spoke into a control panel on his lower display. "Sir, we have eyes on Amber's mother now. Everything looks to be on track. There are no signs of others in the vicinity. Local readings all check out; nothing unusual here. Did you want us to intercept at all?"

"Negative!" came the reply. "We are only to observe that she is unharmed and that no one from Prime is around that could be trying to interfere with the timelines. The circle must be completed! As soon as you have observed, leave the area before you raise suspicion with the local military. Volya's last orders are that we check on the Earthling's mothers from time to time so that nothing or nobody from Prime comes back and tries to interfere with the timelines."

"Understood, sir. Disengaging and returning to Mars now."

The pilot punched in the coordinates for Mars, pulled back

on his navigation stick, and accelerated forward at a speed unknown to any vehicles of the Earth. It quickly became barely visible to the naked eye, disappearing from the surface of the planet. In a flash, it was gone.

Lydia, back in her comfy chair, was puzzled. It was as though this new memory had been inserted for her, replacing the old one. She never did see them again—that she knew of, anyway. But she felt happy that she had seen her own Unidentified Flying Object. She had always wanted to, as there had been many reports in recent years in the papers and on the news right across Manitoba, as well as the rest of Canada and the US, of people seeing UFOs.

What she did not know, which would have made her feel even more special—or maybe even terrified—was that they were there keeping an extra close eye on her.

The new memory continued playing, the group of friends in the truck were enthusiastically confirming with each other that they had all indeed just seen the silver object in the sky.

Tony, in the driver's seat, was her crush. Right through school, in fact. He was a little bit of a bad boy, but the nice kind; fiercely, he would defend his friends, often getting into trouble for fighting. He glanced around from the driver's seat inside the cab, smiling at her through the rear glass. She blushed and sent a shy smile back to him. If she wanted him, she could have him.

This would always be her perfect day.

Amber woke Lydia from her updated perfect day as she came in from work and put her keys on the little shelf by the door. She had brought her and her mom a white cake box from the diner. Her mom always looked forward to this. Inside were three Danish pastries and two chocolate-covered oat cakes.

"Have you been okay, Mom?"

"Yeah, fine. Why do you ask?"

"All hell broke loose out there earlier. Just wondered if you had heard anything?"

"No. Really? What happened?"

Amber began explaining to her mom what she had seen on her way to work, and then that she had been away from Earth for a few days. Of course, it was difficult for her mom to understand that Amber had been missing for days; to her mom, she hadn't been missing at all. Amber had gone out to work as usual, and then came home to her again. But maybe that's why she had felt strange when she had woken up earlier. *That does start to explain things.*

While they both sat watching the news, she thought about it further. She didn't have any memories of actually being frozen —just that Amber had left for work, though she did have a bout of very short breath. Unfortunately, this happened often enough not to be considered strange.

They sat together watching the events unfolding on the TV. A large area from Winnipeg all the way up to Lake Winnipeg had been cut off from the rest of the world for one hour, with Selkirk at its center. The same thing had even happened at the same time in the UK. She was shocked that she had been oblivious to all of this, and yet at the same time had been a part of it.

There were news crews and people from all over Canada flocking to Selkirk down by the river. It got her thinking again of that perfect day and how the memory of the UFO had strangely been inserted into her head. *Could it all have been related?*

"You were really up in space, huh?" she asked Amber.

"Sure was, up in space and in the future! I wasn't even sure if I was gonna get home at all. At first, I wasn't going to be allowed."

Whilst mother and daughter got cozy and continued watching the news reports together, they decided, even without speaking, that they were going to enjoy each other's company through the night. Amber made fresh coffee and they enjoyed the diner's leftover cakes.

Her mom began to divulge to her, for the first time in her life, the story of her close encounter. She even explained the apparent update and the rest of her perfect day back in that summer of 1990. Tony had left them when Amber was born, but Lydia still looked on him as her crush. He was simply not suited to family life. Some guys weren't.

Their combined experiences that strange day brought them closer than ever. Amber sure was glad to be home with her mom.

# CHAPTER 35
# RIGHTING A WRONG

V anir left Daniel to get on with his life. He could feel a sadness in the air, a fleeting thought told him that maybe Daniel didn't want to return to his normal, boring life.

He could tell that Daniel had enjoyed all the excitement and action—a lot more than Amber had, anyway. He would think about what to do for Daniel later, if anything needed to be done. But for now, he needed to make something more pressing right. Then he could relax.

Vanir strode down the ramp from his passageway toward his engineers on Secondary.

"Volund, get me a troop of our best soldiers here immediately, please. I've one last important job to take care of."

"Of course, sir. Any threats that I should be aware of?"

"No, no threats, just keep your eye on things from here. I have something that I need to get sorted out now, whilst things are still . . . fresh in my mind."

"Give me five minutes, sir."

Five minutes later, a group of around thirty soldiers arrived, all standing in the rear of an open-back troop-carrying vehicle at the passageway crater complex. It rolled silently over the crest of the crater and slowly hovered down the access road cut into the rock of the steep banks. When it came to a stop just short of the access ramp, the troops stepped off the rear of the floating barge in pairs, assembling themselves into parade formation.

The soldiers were dressed in maroon uniforms and black shiny boots, and each carried a chrome rifle-length weapon. Small shiny handguns and knives adorned their waist belts and straps around the top of their boots.

These guys meant business.

Vanir addressed them. "Gentlemen, we are going back in time to a short time ago. The scenario you will be facing will be quite clear when we get there. We are there to complete an important extraction from Prime. I will handle the extraction part; all I need you to do is cover me. Make sure that there are no interruptions to the extremely important scenario that is playing out at the time of our arrival. Is that clear?"

"Yes, sir!" they all shouted in unison, stomping their boot heels in understanding.

The large heavyset metal door at the bottom end of the returns facility on Prime exploded into shards and smoke. Karen was back again and looked furious as he stomped toward Volya and Daniel at the return console. Volya was still hurriedly trying to key in Daniel's coordinates to get him home, as he had for Amber moments before. Then, to Daniel's and Volya's complete surprise, Karen was gunned down from behind them. They had thought they were alone.

Soldiers had appeared from out of nowhere, running past Daniel and Volya and spreading out to form a crescent-shaped defensive position midway between the door at the bottom and the console, facing toward the door, ready for more action.

Daniel and Volya were stunned, looking around to see where these new guys had appeared from. The door at the bottom end was the only point of entry into the facility.

Vanir stepped out of a white doorway that had appeared behind them and stood right behind Volya and Daniel at the console. His dashing smile was wide and confident as he placed an arm around them both. Guards dressed similarly to Karen tried in vain to enter the facility through the single doors at the bottom end but were quickly met with heavy fire that they had not been expecting.

The Director's guards were completely unprepared for this level of resistance, having only expected a pair of helpless Earthling teenagers and an old man. They were gunned down no sooner than they entered the hall.

The remainder of the guards at the rear, outside of the returns facility, were obviously having second thoughts, slowing down their attempt at entering after watching what had become of the guards in front of them. They now kept a safe distance back from the entrance and out of sight.

"Daniel, it would be best if you hurried onto your pad now," Vanir said calmly.

Amber was already gone.

"Good to see you again, Vanir," Volya said. "Glad you could join us."

"Thank you, old friend. I'm happy to see you too."

Daniel hurried around the glass partition and stood ready on the pad in the spot where Amber had been standing not long ago.

Volya and Vanir worked together at the antiquated console and punched in Daniel's coordinates.

Shots were still being fired by both sides further down the facility, but the incoming guards were no match for Vanir's soldiers and seemed to have lost interest in trying to take them on.

Volya and Vanir watched the light grow in brightness at the pads around Daniel, who then mouthed the words "Thank you" at them. The machinery noises grew louder, echoing around the dull metal-clad hall. They watched as Daniel's feet lifted off the lower pad. It looked as though he was in pain, but they knew that he would be alright. It was known to be a strange tingling sensation.

Daniel started to fade away. Volya watched him and then looked up toward the entrance doors. Vanir's soldiers confidently kept guard, and the Director's guards were no longer any sort of a threat to them.

*Thank the Creator!* They had done it.

The room filled with blinding white light one last time, and Daniel was gone.

The Prime guards that had tried to gain entry to the facility lay silent in piles around the doorway at the far end of the room.

Volya looked at Vanir and smiled with such relief. Volya couldn't help it; he threw his arms around Vanir—he had honestly believed that these breaths would be his last.

"Thank you, old friend. I thought for sure that I would not make it out of here alive. I had begun to beg the Creator to take my soul unto his."

Volya was comfortable in the choices he had made. He knew that he had done the right thing, yet at the same time he couldn't help but wonder what would become of him now. His ancestors had served the Directorship for generations, and now he knew that this line of long-standing loyalty had been broken by him. This saddened him, but at the same time, deep down, he knew that it had been time for a change.

"You will come with me to Secondary, my friend. We still have much work to do, and I could do with you being by my side to help me."

Daniel was gone. The pads he had been standing on had grown lifeless, silent. The whole room had returned to its old dark antiquated self. Vanir flicked open his personal computer and made a few gestures.

Seconds later in the background, increasing in both volume and vibrations, the sirens of the city could be heard wailing, then the dull pounding of weapons hitting metal and rock as the building from high above was bombarded.

"Level it!" Vanir said into his computer before putting it away again. "Come with me, my old friend. It's time to leave."

He looked up toward the roof and then put his arm around a quite confused and worried-looking Volya, clearly in shock. Vanir ushered him toward a doorway made of white light that had appeared right behind them.

Volya followed him into the light, leaving behind his people, and everything that he knew, to join his people's enemy.

His conscience, though, felt completely at ease. But deep inside, his intuition told him that this was not over yet.

*~The End~*

# The Monument on Mars
## *(Actual Photo)*

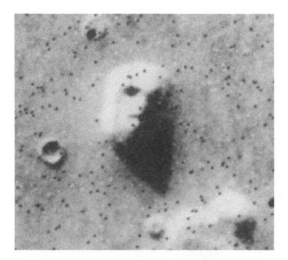

*Image Credit: NASA & The Viking Orbiter, 1976*

~Thank you for reading my story~

# ACKNOWLEDGMENTS

Right, I have a few of these to do, and hopefully I don't miss anyone! These people have helped me immensely throughout this journey, either by simply being there, reading early drafts, or just offering words of encouragement. I would like to thank my mom and mother-in-law, Sheena and Jeanette. My father-in-law, Mick. My friends Michael and Barbara Everitt, Richard Hyde, and Dean Wainwright. And my early beta readers who offered invaluable constructive advice, Tiasha Garcia and Electra Nanou.

I also need to thank my two bosses, Adrian and Stephen, for being patient with me and listening to my mad ramblings during work. Adrian has been forced to read it twice, too, so he is probably sick of it by now!

I thank my amazing daughter and son, Amber and Daniel, who didn't mind being the inspiration and namesakes for my protagonists. Both are amazing in their different ways. Amber has an amazingly creative mind, and in some ways, she inspired me to go out and pursue a creative idea myself. Daniel possesses incredible energy and an astuteness for business. I'm vastly proud of them both.

As I am writing these acknowledgements while *almost* being ready to put this whole thing together, I just want to give thanks to two people toward the end of my journey who have been invaluable: my cover artist, Shaun Stevens from Flintlock Covers, and my editor, Cleo Miele from Miele Proofreading.

And lastly, I must thank my amazing wife, Becki, for her incredible patience, love, and encouragement. There were lots of times where I would be in my own bubble while writing or, even when I wasn't writing, have my head up in the clouds or off in space. I was constantly thinking about my book; it does consume your thoughts for a long period of time! Becki did nothing but be there for me, listen to me, and encourage me. So thank you, baby—you mean the world to me. xxx

# AUTHOR'S NOTES

Hello! It's a pleasure to meet you! I hope you enjoyed reading my story, and I sure do appreciate you giving it your valuable time.

This story was born from a simple urge to explore the act of creating something, to produce something I could be proud of. Something I could hold in my hands and say, "I made that."

When I was younger, somewhere around ten to thirteen (which would place the year roughly around 89-93), I and my best friend at the time saw what we could only describe as a UFO. Now, I'm not saying it was definitely aliens we saw, but it was certainly an unidentified flying object. It had two rows of lights, kind of how a double-decker bus would look if it were high up in a dark sky. Chinese lanterns hadn't caught on over here yet—nor do they pause, tilt, and then fly off at incredible speeds.

Strangely, my dad also had a UFO story, and one that also took place in Walsall—on Alumwell Road, to be precise—a mere two streets away from my encounter. I didn't think much of it at the time. This was the street where my nan lived, which puts my dad's encounter around 1977.

He said that it was sitting just above the rooftops. It stretched right across the wide street; apparently it was huge. It had multicolored lights around the edge which seemed to come down from the ship, hit the road, and then bounce back up to the ship.

My dad sadly isn't with us anymore, but as kids we used to joke around with him and repeatedly ask if it was true. Now, my dad could spring the odd joke on you every once in a while, but the quality that stood out the most if you knew him was that he was unfailingly honest and genuine. My mom tells me that there were people talking about this sighting in the days afterwards in the local pub, The Belle Vue, so there had to have been other witnesses. I would love to hear about it if perhaps you or your parents also remember that UFO near Alumwell Road.

I like to think that my dad would have loved my story.

I'd wanted to write some of my ideas down for years, but I didn't really know what I wanted to write. Then one day, I read the words "Write what you would like to read." And so from all of the ideas floating around in my head—which I will happily admit came from the above UFO encounters, and also growing up in the eighties, loving science fiction films—came this. I might have even slipped in a few subtle references to some of my favorite films here and there. See if you can spot them!

Just before starting this book, I was looking out of my kitchen window at my back garden, thinking, *I'd love to see another UFO. I wonder what would happen if something from space did land*. Whether that "something" was a ship or a sphere, the ideas seemed to rush forward. My main two characters are loosely inspired by my son and daughter, along with parts of me and other family members. I also really wanted to base it around my local area, Walsall and the West Midlands. I'm a proud Midlander!

You may wonder, "Why Selkirk, then, for the other side of the Earth story?" Well, that was simply a case of looking at the globe and thinking that if two spheres did arrive from space and stop over Walsall, and then one of them sped off around the Earth in a more or less straight line, where would that one end up? So, I followed the path around the globe until I was drawn to somewhere. That somewhere ended up being Lake Winnipeg, and so my story expanded around that area. I have spent much time getting to know Selkirk from afar, and I even feel like I've been there. One day I might. I would quite like that.

If the current owners of that little Riverside Grill next to the river ever read this, I do hope that I haven't offended anybody with my writing. I've grown to love that little place.

I am supremely grateful that you have taken the time to join me on this journey, and if you would be so kind, I would really appreciate it, if you left my book a short review on the website of your choice. It's not easy—or cheap—writing a book; years of your life can go into it, and a short simple review really can help independent authors such as myself.

This journey has honestly opened my eyes to how much work goes into something like this. I will forever respect authors! Thank you again, and feel free to join me on social media to follow my journey and my future work.

www.facebook.com/authorwmbailey
www.instagram.com/marsmigration
www.twitter.com/wayneukwriting

# ABOUT THE AUTHOR

Wayne M. Bailey is an indie
author who has just published his
debut novel, *The Mars Migration*.
Born and raised in Walsall,
England, Wayne worked as an
apprentice electrician before
leaving the practical side of the
electrical field to move into sales.
During his youth, Wayne's fasci-
nation with the unknown was
sparked when he witnessed a
UFO and learned about his
father's own UFO experience.
This, coupled with being a right
sci-fi film geek growing up in the
eighties, provided the inspiration for creating a science fiction
work of his own.

Visit him online at: www.marsmigration.com

CPSIA information can be obtained
at www.ICGtesting.com
Printed in the USA
BVHW071233160922
647222BV00002B/107